Insatiable Kitten
The Insatiable Series (Book One)
Sarah JD

2024 Cover by Nat at DAZED Designs
Many thanks to my Beta Readers: Alana, Anoesjka, Melinda & Melissa, and my proofreader Jen.

For all the Kitten's out there grabbing life by the balls
and making the most of each moment
even when life tries to kick you down.
You are my inspiration!!

SARAH JD'S BOOKS

Sarah JD's Books

https://sarahjaneduncan.com/book-links/
https://sarahjaneduncan.com/my-books/

Kitten's Warning

I'm Rhys George. Welcome to my dark and depraved world.
Out of the goodness of my black heart, I thought I'd give you a heads up. A warning, if you will.

What you are about to read contains extreme smut. Like filthy, descriptive, no holding back sex scenes.

If you love what you read, then girl, we should be friends! You are my people!

Because I'm feeling generous, I'll warn you of some other things in my world that could be triggering to some readers:

- Non-consensual sex acts.

- Taboo – Age gap with a minor.

- Reverse Harem – meaning I'm worshipped by multiple partners in a sharing relationship that includes group sex.

- Humiliation.

- Fetishes such as food play, feet, blood play, and golden showers.

- Addiction.

- Blackmail.

The backstory includes references to grooming and assault as a child.

Do you still want to read my story?

I hope so! It's epic!

Will it make you cry? Maybe.

Will it make you laugh? Absolutely.

Will it make you all hot and bothered? Duh! Of course!

Will it make you feel like throwing your book or e-reader? Yes, but please don't do that! I promise the angst is worth it in the end!!

So, are you still with me?

Yes?

FAN-FUCKING-TASTIC! Let's do this!!

Chapter One

Kitten

S ex. It has a smell—sweat, smoke, and spice, infused with the intensity of arousal. As soon as I step through the door, it hits me like an invisible wave, igniting my veins with molten heat, and racing my heart with the thrum of anticipation. I've missed this. The gripping rush. The familiar comfort of letting myself be whoever I need to be. Whoever I want to be, without judgement.

It's been a while since I've graced these walls with my presence. I can't remember why I let myself endure the self-inflicted torture of staying away from here, of holding myself back from the one thing that truly makes me feel alive. That's in the past now, though. I'm back. Back where I belong. Back to the one place I can get what I need without fear of scrutiny.

"Kitten. I was surprised to see your name back on the list tonight." The gruff voice draws my attention, and I flash my teeth in a pleased smile as I take in Brock, the Vixen's Lodge head of security. Kitty purrs between my legs as I drag my gaze over him. I hadn't realised how much I missed this Vin Diesel wannabe, yet his dark eyes filled with lust, and the way his tongue flicks out to wet his bottom lip before he bites it, is a clear reminder of how I revel in attention. In being watched. In being worshipped. Maybe I can let him pet my Kitty before I enter the party?

"Brock. You look good enough to eat." I drag my tongue slowly across my upper lip before mimicking him and biting my lower lip.

My hungry eyes roam over his rippling body, and would you look at that? My Brocky Boy is straining in his pants.

"Don't look at me like that, Kitten. You know I'm working right now."

"Yeah. Working my Kitty into a weeping mess." Fluttering my thick dark lashes at him, I watch Brock re-arrange his hard length in his black pants.

Fuck me sideways. That thing is huge!

He hasn't let me touch it yet. Any time I've worked my Kitty magic on him, he has me ride his fingers or his face until he milks all the juice from my body. While the way he tweaks his fingers or swirls his tongue is mind-fucking-blowing, I *really* want to ride that cock.

"How about you go inside and party, and when the night is over, if you're still hungry, I'll feed you." Brock crosses his thick tattoo-covered arms over his broad chest, the black fabric of his t-shirt straining as his muscles bunch. His dark eyes stay locked on mine, not wavering from my face, so I start to slowly unbutton my jacket. It takes only two buttons popping free before his eyes betray him and follow the path as my fingers travel down to pry each button loose.

With satisfaction, I see the moment his breath hitches when I shrug off the jacket to reveal tonight's attire. His eyes morph into dark pools of lava as they roam over the black and purple lace barely covering my skin. It really leaves nothing to the imagination. The bra has no other purpose but to show the dark pink flesh of my nipples, and the G-string's front is narrow, barely covering my hungry little Kitty. I wonder if he can see how wet the thin scrap of lace is between my legs? Maybe I should just take it off now? The damn thing will only get in the way.

"The Master chose well for you tonight." Brock's words are like an ice bath.

"He did." My voice cracks a little as I reply.

Shit. Did he notice?

When Brock's brows furrow, I slam my façade back in place and seductively slide my hand down over my hip, where the lacy suspender belt sits. Like magic, his frown vanishes, and he's back to ogling me.

Good boy.

"Well, Kitten. You shouldn't keep him waiting. He asked me to remind you that you need to make time for him this evening." Reaching out his strong hand, Brock takes my jacket from me and turns to place it in the cloakroom. Yes, there is a fucking cloakroom inside Vixen's Lodge. Victoria and Terence Hill spared no expense when they built this Colonial styled mansion on the outskirts of Fox Pines. Settled securely behind a pine plantation and away from prying eyes, Vixen's Lodge looks big enough to house three families, yet only two people live here. If it weren't for what they call their 'Feast Nights', then this house would remain very empty.

"We'll see." I grin at Brock as I step in front of the mirror to confirm that I'm put together properly. My nearly black eyes stare back at me in the full-length mirror, but I don't see the *me* that my foster parents see or the *me* that my friends see. I see Kitten. The plaything for the Feasters. Not that I mind. I fucking love it. Kitten has power within these walls. She allows me to take everything I need, with the discretion of anonymity.

"I like how you've incorporated purple in tonight's mask." Brock comes to stand behind me, his towering height making my five foot eight look short.

I grin, shifting my eyes back to my reflection and the colours that adorn the skin of my face. A strict rule of Vixen's Lodge Feast Nights is that you *must* have on a painted or wrapped head mask. These parties are exclusive to select membership, and all members must remain anonymous. Master and Madam Hill are the only people who know *who* the members really are. But given Brock's security role, I wouldn't be all that surprised if he, too, knows each masked Feaster that walks through these doors.

3

As for me? I always paint my mask on. My style, and what all the Feasters recognised me for, is Sugar Skull Kitty.

Meow.

I love making *me*, not look like *me*. I'm good at it too. I've found a real passion for creating different looks with makeup. It's just a pity I can't share my little skill with anyone else. If I did, I'd risk someone recognising Kitten and potentially out myself and possibly expose the Feast nights. Since I'm only seventeen, a fact that Madam and Master are well aware of, I can't take the chance of ruining the one place I can be myself. Not only will that end badly for The Hill's, but every member of the Feast nights as well.

Even though I'm a more than willing participant, I'm still classed as a minor.

Booooo!

The thing is, no one my age has a sexual background like I do. Sure, my friends and even the irrelevant arseholes I go to school with know I act slutty, but they don't know the half of it.

"Kitten." Brock's warm breath floats over my ear, drawing my attention back to him. "It's time to go inside. I'll be waiting to escort you home later."

Oh yeah. I'm totally going to ride his gear stick tonight.

With one last glance at my near-naked reflection, I flick my long dark hair off my shoulder and kiss the air with my purple lips before turning to the door that leads into the cocktail lounge. My heels click with each step on the polished timber floors. It's actually something I love, just as much as turning up late. I like to make an entrance, you see.

Hey everyone! Pay attention! Kitten is in the house!

One of the reasons I prefer to arrive later than most guests at the Feast is because I hate the awkwardness that comes with the beginning of these nights. When everyone is nervous, and they make idle chit chat before Madam Vik announces that the Feast is ready. I'm not here to chit chat. I'm not here to talk about the weather or about who scored the best goal at the footy on the weekend. I'm here to fuck, and to be fucked. Plain and simple.

The cocktail lounge is empty, just as I knew it would be, and a shirtless waiter standing in the corner wearing a mask of his own stands taller the moment he sees me.

"Good evening, Kitten. Would you like a drink?"

I grin. They all know me here. They all love me here.

"Yes, please." My purple lips stretch wider.

"Scotch and coke or straight into the Fireball shots?" The topless waiter's eyes travel the length of my body as he speaks, and I let the satisfaction from that wash over me, boosting my confidence.

"You know me too well. Let's jump straight into the Fireball's tonight."

"Done. Head on in, and I'll get a tray ready for you."

I like this waiter. Not only does he have a tempting ready to lick chest, but he has one of those voices that instantly makes a girl melt. I wonder if he'd like to join Brock and me later?

My Kitty purrs again in excited satisfaction, and I take a steadying breath before turning from the waiter and making my way to where all the action is. Rounding the corner, I open the door and step into another hall, instantly engulfed with the steady beat of the music as it flows in from the mouth of the passage at the other end. With it, my ears perk up at the sounds that only come from a sex fest. Moaning, cries of pleasure, slapping skin, and grunting. My body ignites like an accelerant thrown onto a fire, and I have to stop myself from running to the end of the passage like a desperate whore. The smell is intoxicating. Some people would find this sort of thing vile or sickening. But I'm a dirty bitch. I love it all. I need it all. It's an all-consuming itch I need scratching. All. The. Fucking. Time.

In true Kitten style, I make sure my heels click loudly with each step, my heart pounding in my chest, desperate to find my high. As the soft amber hue of the room ahead gets closer, I stand taller and add extra sway to my hips, and just like I predict, when the room finally comes into view, all eyes land on me as I join the party.

What is usually the Hill's large living room now resembles a roman orgy. Every surface has naked bodies joined in some way. Some people have slowed their thrusts to take me in, while others have stopped altogether, their eyes heating with a new desire.

I have arrived!

"Kitten. Darling. Oh, I'm so happy to see you!"

The excited yet regal voice comes from Madam Victoria, or Vik as she prefers. I find her instantly, her lily-white legs spread wide as the dark hair of a male Feaster bobs as he eats her out. Fucking lucky bitch. I need that. Like right now. My Kitty hisses at me, this time with impatience. She's desperate.

With a confident grin and strut to match, I make my way deep into the room to approach Madam Vik. Her hand is clutched in the guy's hair, keeping him in place between her legs. I kind of feel sorry for him. I've been there, done that, on many occasions, and I'm not a fan of Madam Vik's flavour. Unlike the other females I've done the alphabet on, Madam Vik is kind of bitter in taste. Not sweet like most other girls. So yeah, I know that guy will need to wash his mouth out when he's done.

Madam Vik is going to want something from me tonight since I've been a no show for a while now. She won't care for excuses, only action, and that action will most likely involve me pleasuring her. I'll just have to convince her that she'd prefer my fingers rather than my tongue.

Even though the room has resumed fucking in full swing, many eyes remain on me, eager to see what their Kitten will get up to tonight.

"Madam Vik. You look delicious tonight." It's a straight-up lie. She doesn't look tempting in any way to me. Sure, she is fucking hot for a nearly fifty-year-old woman, but she isn't what I crave. She can't scratch *my* itch.

"I can say the same to you. Come here, my darling, Kitten" She beckons me with a long claw-like fingernail, and I fight hard to keep a cringe from popping free. She needs to think I like her and crave her, otherwise, my time here won't be as rewarding. Hell, the bitch can cut me off at any time. So please her, I must.

I step forward, ignoring the poor dark-haired soul who's munching on her snatch, and lean over Madam Vik to give her the kiss she's waiting for. As our lips touch, I remind myself *why* I'm here and *why* I have to play this role that I loathe in order to find my fix.

Her lips are soft but not smooth, and when her tongue pushes past my closed lips, anger bubbles up inside me. It's not because I don't expect madam to do this. Of course, I do. She's a hungry bitch, and she takes what she wants. No, I'm angry because, just like a traitor, my body ignites, wanting anything she has to give, even though my mind doesn't want this. I hate this part about myself. Why am I so desperately needy that I'd take just about anything?

I should be pissed off that the rules don't apply to Madam Vik or Master Hill. While everyone is here because they want to have sex, it is basic etiquette and a rule that you must ask permission to engage in or join any action. We are all free to refuse, and as a rule, it's asked once only. If you're refused, then you must move on. You're not guaranteed sex with someone else. But Madam Vik and Master Hill don't follow the same set of rules. After all, it's their good graces that allow us into their home and put them at risk for any illegal activity that may happen. That illegal activity is *me*.

I moan into Madam Vik's mouth, giving her and everyone else the show they ache for. Then, while in the character of the horny Kitten that loves Madam Vik, I pull back abruptly, as if I'm so turned on that I'm going to lose control if I don't stop. Another fucking lie. I deserve an award for my acting skills.

"Oh, Kitten. I can see how much you need to be touched. Let me do that for you."

Shit! Damn! Crap!

I *do* need to be touched, but not by her. Not by the old dragon herself.

I have to do this, though. Once I get this over and done with, then I can go off and fuck anyone and everyone I want for the next three hours. I need to be touched so fucking bad, preferably by someone who owns a dick. I need a good dicking.

Really! Fucking! Bad!

I'll just give Madam Vik what she wants and then block it out. It will be quick. My Kitty is desperately clawing at me now, so I gotta suck it up and dive in.

Preparing myself to let Madam Vik touch me, I watch as her face contorts into a frown, and her glare nearly drills a hole into the head that's practically suffocating between her legs. "I didn't tell you to stop, boy! Use your fingers too. Four of them. I want to come on your hand and tongue while I lick our Kitten's body."

Fucking hell, that poor guy. He's gonna need to be resuscitated. Madam Vik is hard to get off. It's a lot of fucking work making her come. She's been doing orgies for so long that she has de-sensitised herself, and getting her off takes a fucking village. In fact, by me joining in, I'll probably help the guy drowning in her bitter Micky juice. I can't even see his eyes behind that leather mask with the way Vik's legs are engulfing him.

He needs saving!

"Where would you like to lick me, Madam?" I purr, gaining her attention again.

She bites her bottom lip and pulls a face that I think is meant to be sexy, but it's fucking not. It's cringy. That's what it is.

"Bring me those perky titties. Let Madam Vik suckle them."

Ok, so I like dirty talk and all. Actually, I fucking love dirty talk, but *that* is not dirty talk. That is cringy as all fuck, yet my pussy purrs with eagerness, and I find myself straddling her waist, careful to not disrupt the four-finger Vik fucker behind me.

Looking down over Madam Vik, I arch my back and push my chest forward, hovering a nipple over her mouth.

"Suckle away, Madam." I hum, trying not to gag at my own words. After tonight, I'll need a lobotomy.

Vik doesn't waste another second. Using one hand, she hooks her finger into the black and purple lace and peels it down before her tongue darts out to flick over my pebbled nipple. That's all it takes. That one flick of her tongue, and I'm hers. Fuck it. I'm too easy. But I'm also starved for this. For anything. I need this like I need to breathe. I'm chasing this high in desperation.

Throwing my head back, I grind my hungry Kitty over the soft flesh of Vik's tummy, making contact with her navel piercing. My moan is audible in the room, floating up to dance with the other moans of ecstasy in the large space. Her lips latch onto me, suckling just like she said, and I feel her rotating her hips under me, seeking her own release as the guy between her legs keeps working like a slave.

Hang in there, buddy. I'm here to help!

As Vik sucks on one nipple, her other hand slides down my front, her fingers expertly finding my pulsing clit, and with gentle pressure, she rubs in circles.

"Yes." I purr, just the way she likes, and she moans over my nipple.

As I grind against her fingers, I notice her clamping tighter on my nipple. It stings a little, but I'm not going to stop her because she's about to come, and that poor guy between her legs needs a fucking break.

Gliding both my hands over Vik's shoulders, I drag them down to her nipples and start tweaking them. Then she releases my pink pebbled flesh and screams her ecstasy, gaining everyone's attention in the room. Not that they care, but they all know that if we don't give her attention, then she'll end the night early.

When she finally quietens down and notices I haven't come, she quickly catches her breath.

"Cass. Clean up your hands and grab a quick drink, then come back here and help me with Kitten."

I can feel someone shift behind me. Cass, the poor soul who nearly suffocated between Madam Vik's legs, deserves a fucking gold medal for what he just had to do.

"I can get myself off while you watch if you like, Madam?" I purr, and she smiles with satisfaction.

I really don't want her touching me again. I'm still straddling her, and all I want to do is swing my leg off and go to the back corner, where I think I spotted Moxie riding someone's dick. She'll be more than happy to let me join them.

Vik smiles, "Oh, I know. You have shown us many a time how you like to fondle yourself. But we have *missed* you, Kitten. I think you need a reminder of how much you like it here so you don't go AWOL again."

I didn't go AWOL, but I'm not about to have that conversation with her or even think about why I hadn't turned up here in a while. Those memories have no place in this house.

"I have missed coming here, Madam. I'm so happy to be back. My Kitty is *soooo* hungry." I turn my voice into a child's tone, and Vik's eyes flare. Sick bitch likes that.

Her hands wander up and down the front of me, pinching a nipple, teasing my clit, running a finger over my wet folds only to drag it away again. Fucking tease. I need to come. I need to get this shit with Vik over with already so I can go and party.

"Cass, help me, will you, darling?" Vik drawls to the guy standing behind me between her legs. I feel his warm hands settle on each hip before they start a journey over my skin as if committing it to memory. I close my eyes, loving the feel. *This* is what I want. A man. Strength. Dominance.

Warm lips press to my shoulder from behind as he snakes his hand around my front to cup my breast, while the fingers on his other hand seek out the wet heat between my legs. Instantly, I'm putty in his hands. My eyes stay shut in an attempt to remove myself from the part of this situation that involves Madam Vik underneath me, running her hands up and down my legs. Instead, I focus on the lips travelling up my neck. The fingers pushing the lace cup of the bra aside to glide over my nipple. The other fingers now slipping beneath the lace fabric of my G-string to delve between my Kitty's lips. Then two thick fingers slowly sink inside, giving me a little stretch, my moan loud as I reach back over my shoulder, tugging at the back of the guy's neck, needing him closer to me.

For a few minutes, he works at building my pleasure, his fingers sinking deep while the heel of his palm grinds against my clit. Fuck yes, this is what I need. I'm so close to coming. I can almost taste it.

"Cass. Do what you did to me. Eat her and fuck her with your fingers."

I'm in a lust daze. I hear Vik's words, but they don't register until the stretch of the fingers slip free, leaving me lonely and desperate. My eyes pop open right before I'm lifted off Vik and placed on the sofa next to her.

My position now mimics Vik's, and I can see her rubbing her own pussy as she watches on. I drag my eyes away from that, because ew, and take in the naked guy standing before me. His cock is so fucking pretty. Like, oh my lord, he is an actual God sent down to impale me on that thing of beauty. Not a foreskin in sight, just straining veins and thick girth that matches the longer than average length. I'm practically drooling.

I can feel my long dark hair fanning out under me, some of which is draping over the front of my shoulder, covering one breast and falling past my belly button. It's long and annoying, but the Feasters here seem to like it. Master Hill especially likes it. A very strict rule he issued me: I am to always wear it down.

Suddenly, the cock of beauty disappears as the God-like guy kneels between my legs, and Vik's clawed hand grabs my chin, turning me towards her.

"Are you ready to come, my Kitten?"

I nod, my chin still clasped in her hand as she directs her eyes to the guy.

"Do what you do best, Casanova."

My eyes widen at the name, right as the delicious sensation of a warm tongue flicks over my clit. Vik is too busy watching the action between my legs to notice my expression, and I'm helpless to fight how fucking out of this world it feels. Even though I'm too scared to look at the guy's face to see if I recognise him, my pleasure builds so blindingly that I'm not sure I care who owns that tongue.

Then I dare to look at the leather masked face between my legs right as three fingers fill me, giving me an aching stretch. I moan and push forward, desperate to swallow his fingers, the noise gaining his attention. It's then that familiar steel-grey eyes collide with mine. I'd know those eyes anywhere. No one else has eyes the colour of Fox Pines Catholic's Spanish Casanova.

Those eyes widen, and time slows as he lifts his head, his lips glistening in my Kitty juice.

"Rhys?" It's a whisper, so only I can hear it.

"Shaun?" I mouth, not willing to let my voice be heard.

"Don't stop, Cass." Vik hisses. "Make her come. We look after our little Kitten here, and you will not stop until you make her purr."

With his fingers still buried deep inside me, he hooks them and starts to rub over my upper wall. Then, he fucking grins.

"Yes, Madam Vik. I would love to make *our* Kitten purr."

My eyes widen as his mouth returns to my needy Kitty, and he laps at me, working me from the inside so intensely that a moment later, I explode.

CHAPTER TWO

CASANOVA

R hys George has the sweetest pussy I have ever tasted, and fuck me; I want more. I know I shouldn't. I know I've just broken the Bro Code in the worst possible way, but what the fuck am I meant to do? There is only one reason why anyone attends Vixen's Lodge Feast Nights, and that is to fuck.

Besides, how was I meant to know it was her? I've never seen Rhys' hair down like that. She always wears it in some weird twisty things on the sides of her head. I had no idea her hair was so long that it brushes over the top of that pert fucking arse. And straight? How was I ever meant to know she has such straight hair? It looks so fucking silky. I just want to wrap the strands around my fist and tug her to me.

Not to mention that painted mask she has hiding her face. How the fuck does she do that? I couldn't even tell it was her under all that paint. It's done in such a way that I can't even see her natural face shape. But those eyes. Fuck, I'd know those dark eyes anywhere. They've haunted my dreams so many times over the last couple of months that I've considered trying hypnosis to get her out of my head.

There's no fucking chance of that now. No way am I ever going to forget how she feels like hot silk under my tongue. Or how her tight cunt sucks in my fingers, wanting more. She was a real fucking turn on before I knew it was her straddling Vik, but fuck me, when I realised it was her, realised that I was finally tasting what I'd been secretly craving for so long. I was a goner. I fucking came all over the front of Vik's couch when I milked that orgasm from Rhys, like a fucking twelve-year-old boy having a wet dream.

Shit. I hope Rhys didn't see.

Or should I say, Kitten?

She is the prized possession I've heard so much about from nearly every single member I've fucked over the last couple of weeks since Vik let me join. I can't believe it's her. Kitten. But then again, maybe I can. Rhys George is the only chick I know that owns her sexuality with pride. Her drive for sex matches my own, and I've thought on more than one occasion that she is made for me. But Marcus, one of my best mates, is fucking in love with her. Yeah, he won't admit it, but it's clear as day, which is why I'm totally fucked.

"I see you're just as taken by our Kitten as everyone else is that comes to Feast with us. She's special." Vik, who has been my neighbour across the paddocks since they built this mansion over ten years ago, loops her arm with mine, smiling at Rhys like she's a proud fucking mother.

"She seems like she'd be a lot of fun." I can't take my eyes off Rhys, who has avoided eye contact with me after she landed abruptly from her high. A high that I gave her, I might add. Fuck yeah, I did! Her creamy thighs were trembling on either side of my head.

Peering up to watch her face as she came was fucking beautiful. The only thing that would've made it better would be to see her natural face under that painted mask as she comes undone and to be alone with her where I can enjoy her, and only her.

She's standing by a table at the side of the room now, talking to one of the waiters who brought her a tray of shots. He wants to fuck her, just like everyone else in this room does. I can see it in his eyes as he drinks her in.

"You have no idea. Our Kitten is up for just about anything. She aims to please, all while taking what she needs. She's a crowd favourite." Pressing her fake tits into my side, Vik trails her fingers up my chest, circling my nipple. "I should let you run off and play now, but make sure you come and see me before the night is through. I want to go out with a bang, riding that magnificent cock of yours."

I fight back my shudder, reminding myself that I can have all the fun I want if I just give this old bitch a little attention. She's been grabbing at me since I was fourteen. Creeped me the fuck out every time I had to bring a case of wine across for my dad. But I'm a guy, and a few weeks back, she was lying in the sun completely naked when I walked past her pool with her Merlot order. Of course, I got hard. And, of course, the sick bitch noticed. Did that stop me from letting the old bat slip her hand down the front of my pants? Fuck no. Sex is sex. If she was offering, then who am I to say no?

It was after that encounter that Vik made me a deal I couldn't refuse. If I come to the Feast nights, then she will buy two cases of wine each time. The bitch knows my family is struggling to keep our little vineyard and winery afloat. But hey, my dad needs the money, and I need to fuck. It's a win, win.

I offer Vik a smile when she tries to saunter off. Something she needs to stop trying to do. She looks ridiculous.

The moment her attention is on someone else, I don't waste another moment and make my way to Rhys' side. She doesn't look at me when I come to stand next to her, the bare skin of my arm brushing hers. It's a tempting touch that has her body stiffening. She knows it's me standing next to her, but she keeps her attention trained on the waiter who is talking about something to do with Halloween, which is only a couple of weeks away.

Snatching up one of her shots, I tip the burning liquid down in time to catch her glare.

"That was mine." Her hip cocks as her hand comes to sit on its curve, right over that sexy as fuck black and purple lacy thing. I don't know what the fuck it's called, but it's hot as all hell.

"Didn't see your name on it," I smirk, and her glare deepens. Oh yeah, I'd forgotten how fun it is to stir Rhys George. It's been about a month since I've seen her. She didn't show up at school when term four started two weeks ago. Lexi was freaking the fuck out because she couldn't get a hold of her, and we followed Lexi to Principal Rogan's office to ask where Rhys was. Principal Rogan is Rhys' foster mum, and she advised us that Rhys would be gone for a few weeks as she was visiting an old friend. Lexi saw through the lie, just like I did. I wonder if she knows Rhys is back now?

"Ah… this tray is for Kitten." The waiter speaks up, and I glare at him, not giving a fuck about anything he has to say.

"Since Kitten and I have some fucking to do," I snarl possessively, "why don't you run along and serve someone else?"

"Someone's grumpy. What's wrong, Casanova? Still shaken after coming to the party prematurely?" Those fucking kissable lips quirk up in a cheeky grin, and fuck, I can't even pretend to be mad about her calling me out on spilling my load on the side of the couch earlier.

"I wouldn't call it prematurely. Not when the reason was because I was in fucking Kitten heaven." As I say the words, I stroke some of her silky black strands back and tuck them behind her ear, letting my fingers glide gently down the side of her neck. When her lips part and her eyes fill with lust, I lean in and bring my mouth to her ear. "You and I have only just begun… Kitten."

My words cause her to lean into me, pressing those perfect fucking tits against my chest, and as I draw back slowly from her ear, I graze my lips over her painted jaw, coming to hover over her purple lips I so badly want to claim.

"Ah. Um. Kitten, I forgot to remind you that Master Hill would like ten minutes of your time in the den. With your sponsor."

Fuck this waiter, arsehole. His words do nothing but douse the fire burning in Rhys' eyes, and she stiffens before taking a step back from me.

"Yes. Ok. Do you know where Skipper is?" Dragging her dark pools from me, she turns back to the waiter, who looks a little too fucking happy about cock-blocking me.

"Sponsor?" I ask because I have no idea what she's talking about, and for some reason, I want to know everything about her.

"Yeah, saw him in the spa railing Savannah." The arsehole waiter ignores me, answering Rhys.

Why the fuck is he still here?

"Ok, thanks. Can you please let Master Hill know that we'll be right in?" Rhys turns back to the tray sitting on the table as the waiter walks off, and she snatches up another shot, downing it.

"Rhys? What sponsor? What are you talking about?"

"Shhh!" She hisses, her eyes wide before slamming her hand over my mouth. I don't care, though, because now she's touching me again, and my ever-hard dick is pressed snug against the bare flesh of her belly. "Don't use my real name. It's Kitten here."

I grin at her panicked voice. No one heard me, and there's no one close by. Everyone in this room is engaged in orgy mode.

"Ok, *Kitten*. Tell me what you mean by sponsor?"

"Why are you even here?" Rhys hisses through clenched teeth. I don't think I've ever seen her look angry like this before. Not towards me, anyway. She's usually the life of the party—fun and always ready to have a good time.

"I'm here to fuck. Just like you. Now tell me what a sponsor means? Who is Skipper?" My arm is wrapped around her skinny waist, holding her to me. I don't think she's even noticed. Then again, maybe she has, and she likes it.

She frowns. "What do you mean? Don't you have a sponsor?"

It's my turn to frown now. I've got no fucking clue what she's talking about. She must read my expression somehow, which must be hard since my face is covered in a leather mask.

"Don't you have a sponsor because you're…" She glances around to see if anyone is nearby, then she presses that delectable body tighter against mine to whisper in my ear. "Under eighteen?"

I shake my head, and she draws back in confusion. Well, as confused as a painted skull face can look.

"Huh. That's… strange." Rhys slowly pulls away from me, her eyes falling to the floor for a moment in thought. And just like that, I've lost her.

"Hey." Tucking my finger under her chin, I lift her face back up until her dark chocolate eyes meet mine. "Are you ok?"

"You shouldn't be here. We shouldn't have done that." She shakes her head, practically whispering, and her dark silky hair floats around her creamy shoulders like a sexy fucking cape. "Marcus…" Her normally confident voice is anything but, and fuck me if I don't want to wrap her in my arms and … what? Cuddle her?

What the fuck is wrong with me?

"Marcus is a big boy." I'm an arsehole. Marcus will never forgive me for what I've done. Or what I'm going to do. I've had a taste now, and there's no turning back.

"He doesn't know about this place. He wouldn't understand. I-I." She shakes her head and turns to the tray, snatching up the last shot and downing it. "I have to go find Skipper."

She struts off like she's walking down a catwalk, and fuck me if she doesn't own every single step. As she weaves through the naked bodies tangled together, almost everyone's eyes land on her. Either she doesn't notice, or she doesn't care. Probably the latter, since this is Rhys George we are talking about. She fucking loves attention.

When she disappears through the door that leads to the jacuzzi retreat, I wrap my hand around my hard cock and give it a few strokes. Hang in there, Thor. I'll give you what you need soon enough.

Yes, I fucking talk to my cock. And yes, I named it Thor. So fucking what? He's a beast that never fails to make the chick's cream, so his name is fitting if you ask me.

I weave through the writhing bodies, following the path Rhys did a moment ago, and take in the scene before me as I step into the Jacuzzi retreat. It's an outdoor area that has been built in, most likely for privacy. There are large daybeds in each corner of the room, with the sizeable sunken spa in the centre of the space. Each daybed is occupied. Some have drawn the sheer drapes closed for a bit of privacy, and another is piled with Feasters with no such qualms about people watching.

That's not what has my attention, though. My attention is on the adored Kitten as she watches a big guy slamming into some chick's arse, making waves at the edge of the spa. He's fit as fuck. Ripped with muscles with his head wrapped in a red leather mask, he pays the chick or the arse no attention as Rhys stands before him, demanding his gaze. Like the little minx she is, she glides her hands over her creamy skin, touching herself everywhere but the places I want to see her touch. She's teasing this guy.

Taking a few steps closer, I lean against the post of one of the daybeds and watch as the guy in the spa glares at Rhys.

"Back off, Kitten." He growls, and her purple lips spread into a grin.

"But my Kitty needs a pat." This time she runs her hand over the thin scrap of lace that's covering her perfect pussy.

The guy hisses, pumping even harder into the chick who is holding onto the side of the spa for dear life as he pounds her from behind.

"What do you want?" He growls between thrusts, and Rhys slips a finger between her purple lips before drawing it back out to travel down the front of her near-naked body.

"I need you, daddy."

"Stop! I told you not to call me that." He pulls his cock from the chick's arse and drags her around to face him, not taking his eyes off Rhys. "Open!" He demands, and the chick drops down with her mouth open, barely able to take a breath before he shoves his cock down her throat.

I hope she doesn't care that he just had that in her arse.

Rhys slips her fingers under the lace and runs them through her folds.

"But daddy. I need you."

"Stop." He doesn't yell this time. It's almost as if he knows she's not going to stop. Almost as if he knows her too well. Does he know who Kitten really is?

"Daddy." She purrs, exposing her slick folds to him, and after a moment of staring at her offering, he throws his head back, growling as he comes down the chick's throat.

Grinning in satisfaction, Rhys covers her weeping flesh and proceeds to lick her fingers clean. My cock jerks, reminding me that Thor is fucking hungry.

The guy in the spa leans down and says something I can't hear to the chick still trying to swallow down his cum. She nods, and a moment later, his eyes land back on a smirking Rhys before he leaps out of the spa to wrap his hand around her upper arm in anger. I can't stay in the shadows now. Not when he's hurting her like that.

"Hey! Back the fuck off!" Pushing in between Rhys and this towering guy, I effectively break his hold on her, and he glares down at me. Shit, he's gotta be close to seven foot tall.

"Who the fuck is this?" He ignores me and glares at Rhys.

"This is Casanova. He likes it up the arse too. Maybe you can show him how it feels to have you buried inside him?" In true Rhys style, her words are playful and teasing, but whoever this guy is, he's not a fan.

"Hard pass, thanks all the same, Kitten," I say with lightness in my tone, still wedged between the hulk and the girl my cock is trying to point toward like a damn compass.

"How about you step away so I can have a quiet word with *my* Kitten?" The hulk in question hisses in my face, and my brows shoot up under my black leather mask.

"*Your* Kitten? I don't think so, arsehole." I hiss back, trying to make my nearly six-foot seem taller.

"Oooh, yes. A dick swinging contest. I do love me some of that. Swing away, fellas." Rhys grins, waving her hands between us as she steps back from me.

"Kitten." The guy hisses again, and all I can think about is how cold my back feels now that Rhys has moved away.

"Oh, daddy. You really do get your panties in a bunch, don't you?" Rhys tugs at my arm, pulling me away from the guy and blows him a kiss before turning to me.

"Cass. I need a moment with my sponsor." She flutters her dark lashes at me.

"*This* is your sponsor? I thought you said his name is Skipper?"

"It is." She nods.

"Then why were you calling him daddy?" I know why she was calling him daddy, which is the same reason I asked the question. To piss him off.

"Fucking hell." The guy, who I'm trying my best to ignore the fact that his massive dick is bobbing between us, clenches his hands by his sides in frustration.

Rhys laughs and leans into me, and fuck if that's not a win for me. She trusts me. She may have been shocked to see me here earlier, but she's comfortable with me around. Hopefully, that means Thor and Kitten will get to meet each other really fucking soon.

"What was so important that you need to interrupt me, Kitten?" Her sponsor asks, not caring that I'm still standing here. He's an impatient fucker.

"Master Hill would like to see us in the Den." There's no playfulness in Rhys' tone this time, and I glance between her and Big Daddy as they seem to have a silent conversation. A very serious, silent conversation.

I stand there looking between them like I'm watching a tennis match, and eventually, the guy's face softens, all menace gone.

"Right, well, let's get it over and done with, then." He offers Rhys his elbow, and she gives him an almost apologetic smile before she links her arm with his. Before they walk off, she turns back to me and winks.

"See you later, Casanova."

Chapter Three

Kitten

I should be freaking out more about Shaun Bossier being here at the Feast. I definitely should be freaking out that he had his fingers deliciously deep inside me not that long ago while I rode his tongue to happy town—Scratch that. Happy isn't a big enough word to describe where he took me. Epic is close. Ultimate is closer. Wherever it was, I want to go back.

Like now!

But I can't because right now, I'm sitting in the quiet Den of Vixen's Lodge, pretending that Master Hill doesn't creep me out.

His eyes, framed by black-rimmed glasses, travel over me like I'm his next meal while Skipper, my sponsor, sits in the plush chair next to mine with a frilly pillow in his lap, hiding his thick cock. He's obviously not comfortable having it poke its head up for this conversation. I have to say. I can't blame him.

"It's nice to see you again, Kitten. Your presence was noticeably missed. Would you mind telling me where you have been over the last couple of months?" Terence Hill, the Master of the Feast nights and Vik's husband, always wears suits to these events. He looks like a high-class businessman, and given that he's a successful lawyer here in Timber Valley, I guess he is. He looks out of place in the throes of the Feast nights, though. Always fully clothed while everyone is clad in lingerie or nothing but the skin they were born in.

"Like I told Madam Vik, I've had some personal stuff happening with a very close friend. Things are better now, though, and I have time to Feast again." I'm surprised my voice sounds as confident as it does. With the Master's eyes on me, as well as Casanova's from the mouth of the room, I'm secretly squirming in my lacy G-string. And not in a good way.

Master Hill studies me, his glasses making his eyes appear brighter than I'm sure they are. He has a kind face. There's nothing menacing about the way he looks. But I know better. His words are spoken with gentle calmness, yet they hold a controlling power.

"I'm sorry to hear that your friend has had a hard time. I'm glad things have improved, but you see, Kitten, what happens outside the Feasts is none of my concern. People pay a very high membership for exclusivity and anonymity. They expect a high level of service here. They expect to see *you* when they come here." Terence links his fingers in his lap and keeps his green eyes focused on me. "Have you forgotten our arrangement?"

"No, Master." I jut my chin up, hoping to look more confident than I am.

"Hmmm," he tuts, "I'm a little worried you might have. Let me remind you, Kitten, so you and your sponsor remember your obligations."

I want to roll my eyes. I don't, though. For one reason, it would show my age, and the other is because Master Hill wields all the power here. I am here by his good graces, after all.

"To enter the Feast nights, one must pay a membership and adhere to rules. Since you cannot pay the membership fee, the agreement is that you adhere to a different set of rules. You cannot attend unless your sponsor is in attendance. You must attend at least once a week but must have an overall attendance of 90 percent. So really, coming to both Feast nights each week is in your best interest. You must wear what I choose for you. You must interact with more than ten members each night, and you must not have favourites. You must not refuse a request from myself, Madam Vik, or your sponsor. And you must always be the last to leave. It goes without saying that your age must never be discussed, nor are you to share any of this information with anyone outside Vixen's Lodge." Master Hill tilts his head towards me. "It is worrying that you don't take your responsibilities more seriously."

"I can vouch for the personal issues Kitten was having that kept her from attending. It was quite a serious situation." Skipper jumps in to save me, but I know it won't do any good. Master Hill doesn't care that my friend was being hunted by her brother and dad. That they did unthinkable things to her and her mum. To her little neighbour and also Jared, one of Lexi's closest friends. Come to think of it, I dare say that Master Hill and Lexi's dad, Maxwell West, would probably be good friends if they had ever met. Fuck, they probably had for all I know.

"Should I remind you of *your* agreement, Skipper?" Master Hill snaps, sending a glare in my sponsor's direction. "You were the one that brought Kitten to me, asking on her behalf for an arrangement so she could attend. *You* are the one responsible for her. Maybe I should rescind your membership?"

"Wait. No!" I sit forward on the soft, cushioned seat, gaining Master Hill's attention. "Please. This isn't Skipper's fault. It was me. I was disobedient."

Those words, *I was disobedient*, send a flare of excitement to Master Hill's eyes. One that is familiar and makes me want to run in the other direction. The sick fucker likes it. Disobedience means punishment, which is exactly where his mind went to. I just know it.

"You were disobedient, yes. Who will inflict your punishment, Kitten? Me? Or your sponsor?"

Fucking hell. In my absence, I forgot how bad this guy can be. The punishment will be something he knows I'm not comfortable with. Something he knows I will never forget so I don't make the same mistake again. The thing is, he knows I'm terrified of him. He likes it that way, so he knows I don't want to choose him. But he also knows that I don't want to choose my sponsor, and he knows the reason behind it as well. He doesn't care that it won't just affect me, that it will be worse for Skipper.

"Is there another option? How about Madam Vik?" I offer, knowing too well he won't let me get off so lightly.

"Not this time, Kitten." Master Hill chuckles and grins with satisfaction. "Choose. Who will it be?"

My chest feels tight all of a sudden, and I find it a little hard to breathe. My eyes dart to the doorway where I know Shaun is still hovering. I don't know why I look at him, but he must see the panic in my eyes because his eyes widen, and he takes a step forward. I look away quickly, hoping he gets the hint to stay back, and I direct my eyes to Skipper. Fuck. I can't do that. Not to him. But the alternative is just as bad. For me anyway, not him. I can't put Skipper in that position.

Taking a shuddering breath, I know what I have to do.

Turning back to the Feast Master, I try to relax my throat so I can speak.

"You, Master. I choose you."

"No!" Skipper growls, sitting forward on this chair, the frilly cushion tumbling to the floor. "She is my responsibility. I will do it."

Master Hill's grey speckled brow rises. "Really? Are you sure about that, Skipper? You know what could happen if it got out. Your career would be over, and you would have to move away. Your reputation will be ruined. Is that what you want?"

Motherfucker!

He fucking wants Skipper to hand me over to him. His words aren't just a reminder. They are a clear threat that he holds all the power here. He can expose Skipper at any time and destroy his life.

I shouldn't have come back here. I should have fought my primal urges. Should have fought harder to somehow find a way to live like a normal person. But I'm not normal. Nothing about my life has been normal, which is exactly why I'm here.

"I am well aware of the risk, Master Hill. But she is my responsibility, and therefore I will punish her as I see fit."

A chill runs up my spine from the menace in Skipper's tone, and part of me wants to smile and punch my chest and get in Master Hill's face screaming, *yeah, arsehole, I'm his, not yours.* I don't, though, because that would just land me in more trouble than I've already put Skipper and me in.

"If you're the one punishing her, I will be the one to choose the punishment. Don't forget whose house you are in right now, Skipper!"

My sponsor's chest rises and falls as he works to control his anger, and I wish now more than ever that I never blackmailed him into getting me into this sex club.

"Very well. What will the punishment be?" Skipper grits his teeth, his blue eyes glaring at Master Hill, who doesn't seem at all fazed as he eyes Skipper back.

"Since you like arse play, let's do that." Master Hill suggests, and my heart basically stops.

"No! You know Kitten is still a virgin to that. I will not take that during a punishment." Skipper snarls, his top lip curling back.

I risk a quick glance at Shaun, who is now inside the doorway, his arms crossed over his chest and his magnificent cock now lax between his legs. I look away just as quick, hoping like hell that he can't hear our conversation in this quiet part of the Lodge.

"Fine. Maybe just a simple fuck will do. Since you both have kept away from each other all this time, I'm sure it will be punishment enough for this first offence."

"Fine." Skipper stands from his chair. "I'll tell you when it's done."

Master Hill chuckles. "It doesn't work like that. Punishments must be public and happen immediately. Let's take this to the podium."

Shit. Fuck.

The podium. The sick fuckers have this stage thing they bring out for Feast Nights, and I'm often on the podium, doing something to myself or someone else while under the spotlight, so it draws everyone's attention.

But to do this. To have sex with Skipper is just... wrong. Well, let me rephrase that. It should be wrong, and probably from Skipper's point of view, it is, but I've been dripping over my sponsor for a long time and have tried on so many occasions to make him cave and give in to me. He's held strong, though, because he has morals. He doesn't want to take advantage of me, not like I did of him when I practically forced his hand to get me on the list to attend the Feast nights.

No one but us knows why it's wrong, though, so, to everyone else, it will just be a show of fornication. One they will most likely get excited about because Skipper and I are never seen together.

"Wait. No." I turn to Skipper. I can't let him do this for me. Give up everything for me. He knows I would truly hate Master Hill inflicting my punishment, so he is sacrificing himself. His morals. His livelihood. I can't let him do that. "I will go with Master Hill."

I nearly choke on the words. If Master Hill delivers my punishment, it won't be public. It will be in private. Just me and him, down under the lodge, past the wine cellar where his fucking sex dungeon is. He could do anything to me in there, and no one would know. No one would hear me if I screamed for him to stop. Not even if I used the universal Feast safe word. He wouldn't care. He wouldn't stop. I know his type.

"No." Skipper and Master Hill say in unison.

"The decision has been made." Master Hill stands from his chair and buttons up his suit jacket. "Boring vanilla sex on the podium. You must both come. In fact, I expect our Kitten to come twice. I will be able to tell if she fakes it, so make sure you get the job done, Skipper. And when you are through, I expect to see a cream pie, so no condom."

With that, Master Hill turns before calling over his shoulder. "You have five minutes to prepare." Then he leaves the room, not even caring that Shaun is still standing inside the doorway.

I shake my head, my panic rising.

"Tyler, no." I hiss in a loud whisper, "I can't let you do this. You know he'll have his cameras on recording it."

"Kitten, have you forgotten we have company?" Skipper asks after I use his real name.

"It doesn't matter. It's just Shaun." I shake my head, "Please. Let me convince Master to take me downstairs. I'll be fine. He'll punish me, and then we can move on. It's a safer option."

"Rhys?" Shaun comes to my side, his voice filled with concern.

"Shaun who?" Tyler asks, glaring at Shaun, who glares right back at him.

"It doesn't matter. Focus, will you!" I snap, but still, Tyler ignores me.

"Oh, fuck me. Is this Shaun Bossier? The fuck boy?" Tyler growls, and I tip my head back in frustration.

"Who the fuck wants to know?" Shaun puffs his chest out, shooting daggers toward my sponsor.

"You know what? Fuck you both. I'll convince Master myself." Spinning on my heel, I storm towards the door, only to have strong arms wrap around me from behind, lifting me off the ground.

"For fuck's sake, Rhys." Tyler hisses in my ear as he carries me back to the corner we were in a moment ago. "We don't know what he'll do to you down there. I'm not letting you risk that. It could be ten times worse than me having my reputation ruined."

I slump in defeat in his arms. "It might not be that bad."

"Remember what Moxie told you? She didn't make that shit up. We come here to play because it's private and because of the level of class that's offered. We can't get that anywhere else around here. We either play by his rules, or we lose it all. It's the price we pay."

"What the fuck is going on?" Shaun pipes up then. "I heard that whole fucking conversation with Terence. Wanna tell me why it's such a big deal for you two to fuck? This is a sex club, isn't it?"

Tyler releases his hold on me, and I turn to face him and Shaun. I can't be the one to out my sponsor and tell Shaun the real reason why Tyler and me having sex is wrong. That's not my place. I'm already regretting dragging Tyler into this mess just so I can come to a sex party every week.

"Rhys. He's probably been recording us since we started. He'll have enough to ruin me just for being in the same room as you like this." Tyler gestures to his exposed junk. "May as well make it worth it."

"I didn't want it to happen like this," I whisper, feeling unusually self-conscious, which is weird as fuck because that's not me. Not in public, anyway.

"I know." The care in Tyler's tone is something I've only heard a couple of times. I've fucked up this man's life, and he still has kindness in his heart for me. I'll have to find a way to repay him. To make this right. Somehow.

"Rhys, fucking hell. Who is this guy?" Shaun snatches my hand, gaining my attention from Skipper, and I step towards him, wrapping my arms around his neck, pulling him in for the hug I need. I'm just as surprised by my actions as he is, but it only takes him a moment to relax and hug me back. He buries his head in my neck and squeezes me tight.

"You're scaring me," Shaun whispers.

"It's ok. I'm sorry that you found out what I'm really like. I'm sorry that I've made you feel like you've betrayed Marcus."

Who am I right now? Clingy and cuddly isn't Rhys George!

"I'm not sorry." He whispers in response, and I pull back, smiling up at him with sympathetic eyes.

"You will be."

I step back from Shaun and turn my back on him as I leave the room. Shame is gnawing at me from the inside at the situation I've put Tyler in. I should leave now. Walk out and never come back. It's pointless, though. Master Hill probably already has enough to use against Tyler to punish him. To ruin him. He will use it to ruin us both if I quit now.

Slight trembles travel up my legs as I make my way through the lodge, back to the main room. The music seems loud after being in the quiet Den and does nothing to calm my nerves when eyes fall on me and my clicking heels as I weave through the crowd.

"Try to relax, beautiful." Warm breath fans my hair, covering my ear, and I stop and face Tyler, quirking my brow at his endearment.

He smirks, knowing what has caused my reaction. "We may be stepping over the line now, but be assured, I will treat you right, Kitten."

Shit. What the fuck did my heart just do? Did it... flutter?

"I'm not sure that Savannah would agree with how you treated her in the spa before." I counter, and his white teeth show through the opening in the red leather mask.

"You will find she was quite happy with my service. I gave her exactly what she asked for, Kitten."

I am so screwed. Giving Tyler access to my body is going to ruin me. In a good way.

"Is that so?" I can't hold back my grin. Not when he's looking at me like that. Wow! This is a side of my sponsor I haven't experienced.

"It is. And I will make sure you are satisfied as well. I'll try to keep it simple, but I don't do vanilla Kitten, so you need to tell me now what you're *not* willing to do."

The lights dim in the room, and an excited buzz starts to stir as I turn and walk the rest of the way to the podium that now has a spotlight shining down on it.

"Kitten?" Tyler asks again, and I turn back to him as I swipe up a glass of bubbles from a waiter's tray as he passes by.

"My arse needs to stay a virgin, please. And no role-playing."

Tyler squints at me as Shaun steps up to the both of us, and I eye them as I take a sip of the sweet champagne.

"What? Like naughty schoolgirl or something?" Shaun butts in, and I spit the champagne out in shock before trying to play off my reaction with a laugh. The sweet drink sprays Tyler's chest and Shaun's arm, and I quickly spin to place the glass down, happy that my painted face hides my flush.

"Yeah, something like that," I mutter just before a warm hand finds mine, and I glance up to see concerned steel-grey eyes peering back at me.

"Kitten. I'm not sure what's going on. And it might be none of my business. But if you need me to step in and join you, or just be close by so you know I'm here, then I'll do that for you."

Warmth fills me from head to toe from Shaun's words. He said them with a level of care I'm only used to hearing from Marcus.

Shit. Marcus.

If he only knew who I really am. He would be so disgusted.

"Kitten?" Shaun urges, and I smile at him.

"Can you please stay where I can see you?"

"Of course." His smile is broad, and I almost wish I could see his entire face.

"Feel free to stroke that massive cock of yours. I wanna see you come." I grin cheekily, and his growl is the only warning I get before he slams his mouth to mine. I'm helpless to refuse what my body wants. Him. His hands tangle in my hair, and he pulls me flush against him so I can feel his arousal straining between us.

A large, firm body presses to my back, and I feel lips brush over my shoulder as I kiss Shaun, and I moan as my Kitty purrs with satisfaction at being pressed between them.

"It's time, Kitten." Skipper's voice is close to my ear, right before his teeth nip at my lobe. Shaun breaks our kiss and reaches for my hand. I'm not sure what he's doing until I feel the smooth, straining skin of his magnificent cock under my fingers. Instinctively, I wrap my hand around it, and my Kitty throbs with need. Fuck, I want him buried deep inside me.

"This is all for you," Shaun whispers in my other ear as he pumps my hand up and down his shaft a couple of times. Then, he peels my fingers free, and I whimper, feeling the loss deep inside.

"It's my turn, Kitten." Tyler rasps. "Let's make Master Fuckface know that this is no punishment. This is all pleasure."

I melt back against Tyler's chest as Shaun moves away to take a seat right next to the podium. Tyler's hands travel down my front, giving our growing audience a good show before his fingers brush over my lace-covered nipples, and I instinctively push my chest out, wanting more.

"Tell me this is ok, Kitten? Tell me my touch doesn't repulse you."

Tyler's words surprise me. Is he feeling self-conscious? Does he think I don't want this? Even as I think it, I know that's exactly what he thinks. We are doing this under coercion, after all.

I turn in his arms and look him dead in the eyes. I need him to know I speak the truth.

"You could never repulse me. *This* is ok, I promise."

A small grin tugs at his lips as he runs a finger across my bottom lip, "Good because here we go, Kitten. It's time to fuck."

Chapter Four

Kitten

The glare of the spotlight is almost blinding as Tyler lifts me onto the podium, my arse at the edge as he tugs me toward him. His large hand fists in my hair, and with a sharp tug, my head is pulled back, so the only thing I can do is look up into his bright blue eyes. Then he claims my lips.

I never imagined I'd ever get to kiss Tyler. Sure, I insinuated I wanted to so many times over the last year, but I never thought it would happen. Never thought this secret dream of mine would come true. It's a deep and claiming kiss that has me weeping with need, and it's a welcome show of dominance on my sponsor's part.

What a pity I'm a little brat.

I bite his lip hard, and he grunts, pulling back.

"Did you just bite me?" He hisses, his blue eyes flaring with excitement.

"Yeah. What are you going to do about it?" I hiss back, baring my teeth like the animal I am.

Lightning fast, his big hand wraps around my throat, applying pressure at the sides as he bares his teeth back at me. My Kitty gushes, and my moan comes from deep in my chest, stirring his primal side even more when he returns my bite with his own, right over my lace covered nipple.

Oh yeah, this is going to be good.

I shouldn't want this. Not with *him*. But here we are, under the spotlight, surrounded by horny Feasters, going through with this act under duress. Yet I fucking love every second of it. I love the attention. I love hearing the moans of those around us pleasuring themselves or someone else as they watch on, getting carried away with us. But most of all, I love the way Tyler reacts to me. He wants this just as bad, even if he knows it's wrong. Hell, maybe that's the turn on. Who fucking cares because it's happening, and I'm here for the ride. Fuck the consequences.

With a nip of his teeth, Tyler tears the lace covering my nipple, and a moment later, his moist hot mouth closes over my straining bud. My back arches even more, and he flicks his tongue over the pebbled nipple, his free hand pressing into the arch of my back, forcing my chest closer. The bright spotlight disappears as my eyes fall shut, and I let myself feel every sensation. That's what the Feasters like about me. I let myself go completely. I don't hold back, and they revel in it.

The pressure on my neck loosens as Tyler releases my breast, and he slowly lays me back on the podium while his lips sear a path down my bare tummy. I'm needy as fuck, my Kitty twirling in excited circles in anticipation as his hands glide down my thighs before gripping my knees and tugging them wide. My lids fly open, and my eyes are met with the intense, heated stare of Shaun Bossier sitting to my side. His hand is fisted tight around his cock as he slowly strokes it up and down, a light sheen of sweat peppered over his chest, making him look like the Casanova he is. A second later, my Kitty purrs when the hot silk of Tyler's tongue glides up the middle of my slit.

I'd been so focused on Shaun that I hadn't even noticed Tyler move the G-string aside. My hungry eyes search for his as he peers up at me from between my legs. Fuck, that's hot, seeing him there, words silenced as he takes his time to worship my aching Kitty. Just knowing it's him there between my thighs, my sponsor Skipper, ignites my senses even more.

Kitten is here now. She is in the room, owning the room as all eyes take her in. Kitten holds nothing back, and I let her take the reins, giving into the part of me that fights hard to get free nearly every second of the day. I grind Kitty hard against Tyler's mouth, and I feel the rumble of his growl as his control starts to slip.

I love this part. When I push my subjects over the edge, and they can't hold back anymore. It's an ultimate high, wielding that sort of power. So naturally, I clasp the red leather wrapping Tyler's head and hold him tight to my core as I start to thrust and fuck his face.

My grip is firm as I fight him for power. Not because I want it, but because I like pushing him to see how far he will go. He doesn't disappoint, trying to shake me off, but I hold firm, and it's only when I feel three fingers push inside do I lose my grip.

He pulls away then, standing to tower over me, and I instantly miss his tongue, but his fingers are still there, pumping and curling and dragging, pushing me close to the edge.

"Casanova! Get over here!" Tyler's growl takes me by surprise, and a moment later, Shaun comes into sight.

"Skipper?" He asks Tyler, not taking his eyes off me. They eat me up. Every inch of my skin feels his heated gaze.

"Sit up near her head and hold her arms up there. Don't let her go."

I didn't expect Tyler's demand. Didn't expect him to ask someone to help or join us. I thought this was just meant to be between the both of us. A punishment of sorts that we have secretly craved for so long now. But if Master Hill has an issue with my sponsor calling Shaun up to help hold me down, he doesn't make it known.

Shaun nods before leaping up on the podium just above my head, taking my hands when I reach up to him.

"Move back a bit. Drag Kitten back with you." Skipper demands, and Shaun obeys, my body sliding over the smooth surface of the podium until my legs no longer hang over the edge.

Tyler's fingers remain inside me, working a slow rhythm. "Knees up, Kitten. Keep them wide, and do *not* move your feet off the podium."

I nod, excitement pumping through my veins in anticipation of what he will do next. I secretly love it when he orders me around.

"Good girl." Those two words alone nearly send my Kitty into a frenzy, and I see his satisfied grin peek through the mouth hole in the red leather.

Then, his fingers start working faster. I gyrate my hips in response, loving the pleasure building, and Tyler places his free hand over the top of my pubic bone and applies pressure that meets the motion of his three fingers buried inside me.

It only takes a couple of strokes for me to lose control. Any power I have to repress my orgasm is ripped away as Tyler takes over, leaving me helpless to fight it. With the pressure over my lower belly and the magic his fingers are conjuring, a scream rips from my lungs as Tyler mashes his fingers, milking a gush of wetness as the pleasure sends white light behind my eyes.

Wave after wave surges through me until Tyler backs off the pressure and slows his fingers. As I come down from a cloud I've never floated on, I feel the ache of my arms as they remain restrained above my head by Shaun.

My hearing, which I didn't know had vanished, slowly returns, and the pleasured moans in the room far outdo the volume of the music. I don't even bother looking at my audience. Instead, I work to focus my gaze on Tyler as I pant, trying to catch my breath.

"That has to be the hottest thing I've ever seen." Shaun's hot breath flutters against my ear, and I flick my gaze up to find his steel-grey eyes. They're darker than usual, consumed with lust and excitement. A look I'm beginning to love on Shaun's face.

The moment Tyler slips his fingers free of Kitty, I whimper, instantly missing the fulness.

"Open," Tyler's command grabs my attention from Shaun's, and I drop my jaw, my lips falling open as he slides his three fingers into my mouth.

"Wider." He demands, and I force my jaw to obey.

"How deep can you take my fingers, Kitten?"

Does he want me to answer that? It's kinda impossible with his fingers filling my mouth, so I raise a brow, showing him the challenge, and he grins, sinking them deep until I gag. A satisfied growl rumbles through his chest. And just like that, I'm ready for round two.

Leaping up to join Shaun and me on the podium, Tyler leans down so only I can hear his words.

"I'm going to enjoy choking you with my cock, Kitten. But not now. Not tonight. Now I need to make you come one more time and give Master Fuckwit the cream pie he's dreaming of." Tyler is a dirty fuck. I knew he was, but he's never directed it at me. I've always had to sit on the sidelines and watch him give that side of himself to other Feasters, but tonight, his words are all for me.

I nod eagerly and lick over my lips. "Give me your cream, Skipper."

"Fuck." Shaun curses, releasing my arms before making to move off the podium.

"Stay there, Cass. Since our Kitten likes cream so much, why don't you give her yours as well? She looks thirsty."

Fuck me. Tyler is going to kill me with pleasure. My Kitty perks her little ears up and nearly hisses with glee. Kitten wants it, and she wants it all. I want it all. My eyes lock onto the straining cock bobbing above my head, where Shaun has frozen in place at Tyler's words. A moment later, his steel-greys come into view, a silent question in his gaze. I nod without hesitation, showing him how bad I want to taste him, and he grins behind his black leather mask.

Slowly, with his eyes still locked on mine, he wraps his fingers around his wide girth and starts to pump. I want him in my mouth. I lick my lips, desperate to taste him. He doesn't give me his flesh, though; he just sits back a little as Tyler perches over me.

"Kitten?" Tyler gains my attention again, and I take in the seriousness of his eyes. "He wants me bare. I'm clean. Just so you know, but if you're not comfortable with this, I'll tarp up."

"Such a gentleman, aren't you, Skipper?" I grin. "You wanna know if I'm clean?"

"Are you?" He smirks.

"I've never had naked dick before. You'll be my first."

His eyes flare with something more than desire, and I realise he fucking likes that he's my first flesh on flesh fuck.

"Dirty me up, Skipper." I purr, and he growls, bracing himself on one hand as his other fists his engorged cock. Fuck, he's a thing of beauty. If he grew his hair long, he could be a Viking with his tanned skin, blue eyes, blonde hair and the sharp manly features of his face.

"Rub your Kitty. I need you nice and juiced up. This is going to be hard and fast, Kitten."

I should probably tell him that his words juice me up enough, but like a good little Kitten, I press my fingers to my clit and start circling. I watch him as his eyes travel over my body, lingering on the torn lace of my bra before he lines himself up at my entrance.

True to his words, his first thrust is hard. He slams into me, and I understand why he wanted me juiced up. He didn't want any resistance. And he didn't get it. My Kitty has been starved for this man, and now she is finally getting fed.

I cry out, arching my back as his size stretches me deliciously, slicking me up even more. My lids flutter open, and my eyes dart between the skin of Shaun's dick and his firm grip as he strokes it over and over, then to the red leather-clad face of my sponsor as his eyes pierce mine in an intensity I've never seen.

Each thrust sends me to a height I know I'll never want to come down from. Over and over, Tyler thrusts while I continue to circle over my bud, adding to the consuming sensations building deep inside me.

"She's close, Cass. You ready to give her a drink?" Tyler grunts through clenched teeth, still pumping into me.

"Fuck yes." Shaun hisses, and my eyes go to his celestial dick. I need that dick so bad. I think I'll die if I don't have it.

"Open your mouth, Kitten," Tyler demands and fuck yes, I obey. The brat in me has disappeared.

The sound of moaning is like the roar of a concert audience in the room around us as Shaun leans down, directing his cock closer to my open mouth, making his demand.

"Come for me, Kitten."

I've read books where the heroine came on demand but never has that happened to me until now. I come in a dizzying rush that I can't stop, right as the first warm spurt of Shaun's cum hits my cheek and lip. The sensation of my orgasm ignites my entire body in a searing explosion, and I climb to euphoric heights.

My scream turns into gurgles as my mouth fills with Shaun's seed, and as I come down, I feel Tyler still above me as he roars out his own release.

Needing to breathe, I swallow Shaun's offering and flick my tongue out over the tip of the engorged head of his cock. He hisses before pushing forward more, letting the tip slip between my lips. I swirl my tongue over the silky skin, and I know what the three of us just did will be hard for me to top. It should be a good thing. But for me, it isn't. It means that I'll seek this out again. Either with the two of them or with others who may be able to take me higher.

Where will it end, Rhys?

"Are you ok, Kitten?" Tyler's voice snaps me out of my brief moment of self-loathing, right as Shaun's dick slips free from my lips with a pop.

I nod and grin at Tyler, hoping to cover up my moment of weakness.

"I feel thoroughly dirty. Thanks, Skipper." I kiss the air, and he grins, shaking his head before looking up at Shaun.

"Thanks for joining the show. Pleasing Kitten is our top priority here at the Feast nights."

Shaun dips his head in acknowledgement and shoots me a wink before backing off the podium and going to stand to the side. I miss him instantly, which I need to get control of. He's one of Marcus' best mates. And Marcus is my kinda, not ex. Kind of not, in the way that we weren't officially a thing, and ex in the way that I ended whatever it was we were doing about a month ago. The fact that I'm attracted to Shaun or any of Marcus' friends is nothing new to me. Everyone is a possible fuck. The only problem is that somewhere during my brief, casual fling with Marcus, he caught feelings, and so did I. So, I ended it. Naturally. A chick like me can't maintain a relationship. Not one that involves monogamy, anyway.

"Kitten. We have to do this one last thing. I'm sorry." Tyler pulls back from me and climbs off the podium. Turning his back on me, he searches the crowd that now has a front-row view to my exposed Kitty, and when he spots Master Hill up the back, he steps aside, using both hands to spread my bent knees further apart.

Pushing myself up on my elbows, I watch Master Hill's face, which is hard to see in the shadows, and the fact that the spotlight still illuminates me spread wide on the podium. Then Tyler uses his fingers to part my sensitive folds and turns back to look at me.

"Sorry, Kitten. We have to show him the cream pie. Can you squeeze tight for me?"

There's regret in Tyler's tone and gaze as he studies my sugar skull painted face. I've done a lot of stuff within the walls of Vixen's Lodge, and I've done a lot of things outside them too. Some, or should I say a lot of people, judge how far I'm willing to go in the throes of sex. What I do isn't for everyone, mostly because people are too scared to take what they really need. Not me. Not Rhys George. And not Kitten.

I often feel some shame after some of my sexcapades. My therapist tells me it's natural. But never have I, during or immediately after a session, felt humiliated. So, the feeling surprises me when I realise what I have to do to finish my punishment that Master Hill demanded. I hadn't thought it would be humiliating earlier when he issued the punishment. Yet now, dread fills my gut. I know that all the eyes on me have seen me in extremely intimate positions. But I have never had to do *this* before.

A memory slams into my mind, so graphic that I know it's real. It's not something my brain simply conjured up for the hell of it. I stiffen as it engulfs me, and my breathing quickens as I get the feeling I've done this before. I get the feeling I've had bare sex before. That I've had eyes on me like this before as they take in the evidence left behind.

"Kitten?" Tyler's concerned tone slaps me back to the present, and I suck in a shuddering breath and do as he asks. I squeeze the walls of my Kitty tight, and a moment later, I feel the warm oozing evidence of Tyler's orgasm seep out of me. My face is burning hot as the humiliation washes over me, and I clench my teeth tight, wishing for the first time since I started coming to the Feast nights that this night was over.

The tall frame of Master Hill steps out of the shadows, and he comes to stand before me, his eyes locked between my legs before nodding.

"Thank you. I got what I needed." Master Hill mutters, looking from me to Tyler, before turning and walking out of the room.

He got what he needed. He's not talking about coming in his pants from the show we just gave. No. Master Hill means he just got all the evidence he needs to ruin both Tyler and me. We were already screwed when we made the deal with Master Hill and Madam Vik last year. Now, we've just set our downfall in stone.

CHAPTER FIVE

RHYS

Going back to school today is a bad idea. I feel it in my bones, and I feel it in my Kitty. She should have been well sated after last night. But she's not. She's controlling my thoughts, and I know nothing good will come from what she is conjuring up.

I hate this about myself, which is fucking annoying because Rhys George doesn't dwell on shit. She lives each day as it comes. Lives in the moment and makes the most out of each day. But my purring Kitty rules my world. She owns me, and even after last night and the humiliation I felt, even after the guilt and shame that kept me awake most of the night, my Kitty knows only one way to make me feel better. She needs a hit. And she needs it soon.

"See ya, Rhysie!" Connor yells in my ear, making me jump in the front seat of the car. I'm about to yell at him for scaring the fuck out of me when he pops his head through the seats from the back and slaps a sloppy, wet kiss on my cheek. I turn to see his cute little face barely an inch from mine, sporting a cheesy grin. As if I can be angry at the little shit.

"See ya, dork. Have a good day." I ruffle his dark hair, and he pulls back, trying to make it neat again, the action nearly causing his black-rimmed glasses to fall off his face.

Giggles come from the back seat as Connor climbs out, and Archie pops his head through the seats this time.

"See you after school, Rhysie." Archie only offers me a hug. He's the spitting image of his identical twin brother Connor—you know…

because they are identical. He's never been one to hand out kisses, unlike Connor. I accept his open arms in a quick squeeze and flick the edge of his red-rimmed glasses when he pulls back.

"Don't chase all the girls at school today."

"Ew! Gross Rhys!" I laugh at his reaction, which is the same as every other time I tell him not to chase the girls around. He follows his brother and gets out of the car, slamming the door shut before joining the crowd of kids walking into the primary school.

The car slowly pulls away from the curb, and I watch the backs of my two little Asian foster brothers as they walk hand in hand without a care in the world.

I wonder if I would have been different if Cin and Will had found me when I was Connor and Archie's age? Surely, I wouldn't be what I am today.

Connor and Archie are eight years old. They came into our home when they were five. If I'd had the stability and love that Cin and Will give us now, back when I was five, or even a bit older, I just know I wouldn't be as fucked up as I am now.

Instead, I was thirteen when Cynthia and William Rogan walked into the group home I was staying in. For some reason, they wanted the messed-up girl I was, and they took me in, changing my life. There are some things they can't change, though. They can't change what happened to me before they found me. And, even though they've tried, they can't change the person I became because of my past.

"You're extra quiet this morning, Rhys. Are you sure everything is ok between you and Tillie?" Cynthia, my foster mum and the current acting Principal of Fox Pines Catholic, has asked me this question three times since I dragged myself out of my bedroom this morning. I was meant to stay at Tillie's house last night. It's what I do every Sunday night when the Sunday Feast is on. When the Wednesday Feast is on, I usually stay at Bell's. It's my cover story, and my friends are well aware of the situation and are more than happy to help me out. They're good to me. They know a little about my past. They know what I live with daily. So, they help, by being my alibi, and offering me a warm bed to fall into whatever time I stumble in from Vixen's Lodge.

As much as I was dying to leave the lodge early last night, I didn't think pushing my luck with the Master was a good idea, so I stuck around and purred at the Feaster's as they left. Master Hill stood next to me as we farewelled the guests. His eyes were like red hot lasers zeroing in on my tits so often that the fucking things betrayed me and pebbled under his gaze. I was worried he would ask me to stay longer or offer to drive me home afterwards, but thankfully, Madam Vik insisted Brock drive me like he normally does at the end of the night.

I cleaned myself up before I left the barn at the edge of the Hill's property, which is where I get ready for each Feast. Since I'm underage, I walk onto the property once the other guests have already arrived and go to the barn to paint my face and put on the outfit that Master Hill leaves me. At the end of the night, it's where I change myself back from Kitten to Rhys. Usually, I can't help but grin at my reflection in the old mirror that Master Hill left in the barn for me. But last night, with each wipe as I cleaned the paint off my face, the flaming red evidence of my humiliation shone through, and it made me sick to my stomach. Literally.

That was my excuse when I wandered into my house after eleven last night. I felt sick. I should have continued the charade today and taken a sick day. Going to school today really is a bad idea, but since I've already missed the first couple of weeks of term four, I know I need to suck it up and go.

"I'm ok. Still feeling a bit queasy, I guess." It's not a lie. The thought of seeing Marcus has my stomach in knots. As does the thought of seeing Shaun. Fuck, how am I meant to act when both Marcus and Shaun are together?

"Maybe you came back from the retreat too soon," Cynthia says as she turns the corner that leads to school.

"Maybe the reason I feel so shit is because you sent me there in the first place!" I hiss and glare at the side of Cynthia's head as she drives.

"You know as well as I do that you needed to go there. You needed to take some time to…" She can't finish the sentence, so I scoff.

"To what? Get better? You know it doesn't fucking work like that."

"Watch your mouth, Rhys. I know you've been through a lot lately, but you will not speak to me like that." Cynthia's stern voice holds authority, which is why she's a good principal. She's also a fair person, which makes it hard for me to be angry at her. I know she's just trying to help me.

I sigh. "Sorry."

She glances at me quickly before returning her eyes to the road.

"I wish you would tell me what really happened to make you run off like you did when we were away on our trip. I want to help you, Rhys."

Clamping my mouth shut, I pretend to look out the window as we drive, but I don't see anything. My mind is back at our little family holiday up the Great Ocean Road and the phone call I received from a number I didn't recognise, leaving a chilling voicemail that sparked my disappearing act and all the crap since.

"It's been a while since we've talked. Your message recording sounds cheery. It seems like life is good for you. It's a pity you've grown up to be so fucking ungrateful, though. In all these years, you haven't once visited Brian. How can you do that to him after everything he did for you? Have you so easily forgotten that he was the only person to ever care about you? That's pretty disappointing. It really is. But it's not too late to make it up to Brian. He wants to see you, and since you have been on his approved visitor's list since the day you let him take the fall, you should have no

problem getting in to see him. So make it happen, or
our next conversation will not be so fucking nice."

Even though I didn't know the number, I knew the voice: Julie Bates, my old foster mum.

"Can you just drop me off here? I'm meeting Tillie on the corner."

Cynthia huffs, probably hating that I ignored her, but she flips the indicator on and pulls over at the corner, which is only a short walk for me to get to the back of the school hall.

"Think about popping in to have a chat with Mr Matthews today. I'm sure he'd love to see you."

Turning to Cynthia with my hand on the door, ready to flee, I raise a dark brow.

"Sure, Cin. I'll go see Mr M, and he can tell me to write my thoughts in a journal, and then someone will get their hands on that journal and read my thoughts, and guess what? I'll bring shame to the family *again* because my thoughts are a little too fucked up for the average person, and you might even lose your job for being associated with me. That sounds like a brilliant idea."

"Rhys." Cynthia's stern voice doesn't sway me.

"See you tonight." I snap and get out of the car, dragging my school bag behind me before slamming the door shut.

Cynthia's hard eyes stay on me as I heft my bag over my shoulder and start down the path towards the back school gate while trying to straighten out my uppity catholic uniform. A moment later, I hear Cynthia pull away from the curb, and I glance up to see her car joining the busy school traffic.

I feel like shit. More so than before. Now I've just gone all bitch on Cin when she didn't deserve it because she just doesn't understand. No one ever does. Sure they say they do, but they don't *really* get it. It's always the same. They eventually try to fix me when all I really need from them is to accept the way I am, even if it makes them uncomfortable.

When I round the corner of the school stadium, I spot Tillie waiting on the steps, exactly where I asked her to meet me when I sent her a message earlier this morning. Hearing my steps crunch on the twigs and gravel, she pops her head up from studying her phone, her blue eyes finding mine just as a smile tugs at her lips.

"Am I hallucinating? Is it really you?" She teases, standing from the steps as I approach.

"You missed me that much while I was gone?" I smile wide, and she shrugs.

"Maybe just a little." She throws her arms around me when I step up to her, and I breathe in the sweet scent of berries, which is Tillie's unique scent. She's a fruity smell kind of girl, which matches her cutesy personality and auburn pixie haircut.

"Hug me too tight, and I'm gonna start rubbing myself on your leg." I tease, and she giggles, pulling back to look at me.

"You didn't get enough last night?"

"Yes. No. I don't know. It's a complicated story." I shrug, and she grins.

"Girl, you'd better fill me in with all the filthy details later. I want to know everything, as usual." Tillie shoots me a knowing wink.

"You know I will." I smile back, knowing too well I may not tell her everything, even though I usually do. It's part of our deal. She lets me stay at her house every Sunday night, effectively using her so I can fuck like it's my last day on earth, and in return, I tell her all the juicy details. Normally I do that as soon as I get back to her place, but I didn't go back there last night.

"You got my shit?" I ask, and she rolls her eyes.

Pulling her hand out of her navy blazer pocket, she opens her fingers to reveal two rolled joints in her palm.

"You know I owe Travis a blow job for those, right? He's calling me tonight to arrange a time."

"You're such a good friend." I beam, and she shakes her head.

"You're lucky I love you." Tillie's small finger jabs into my chest, and I fake a giggle.

"Don't pretend like you're doing me a favour, Tills. I know your pussy throbs when you see Travis. You should be thanking me for introducing you."

"Technically, it was *Lexi* who brought Travis into our lives, so I think I'll thank her. Besides, I'm still not sold that my vagina is excited to see him." Tillie shrugs and starts walking off. "I have to go to the library before homeroom. Don't smoke too much before class. You don't want to get busted for being stoned on your first day back."

Shaking my head, I laugh and sit on the steps, watching Tillie retreat. I pop one joint into my blazer pocket and the other between my lips, taking out a lighter and lighting it up.

The moment the burn of the smoke travels past my throat, I close my eyes and tip my head back, chasing the calm I'm going to need to face the hordes of students for the rest of the day. I take a drag for Marcus, knowing I'll need self-control to not fall into his arms and confuse the poor guy even more. I take a drag for Shaun, knowing that when we see each other, our minds will go back to last night and the acts we committed together. I take a drag for Skipper, AKA Tyler, knowing that our situation has just gotten seriously illegal and complicated.

"Rhys!" The sound of Lexi's voice pulls me out of my head, and I glance up to see her running up the gravel path toward me. Her boyfriend, Ayden, stays put at the corner of the building, his eyes lingering on his prize. Lexi West.

The last time I saw Lexi, we were out of sorts. I'd been an idiot and taken her concern for Marcus and me the wrong way. It's not her fault she doesn't fully understand. I haven't told her about my dysfunction. I know I should. But part of me is scared that it will send her packing in the other direction. For good.

When she nears, I stand from the steps, coming to meet her at the bottom, and without warning, she throws her arms around me, the force nearly sending us to the ground.

"Whoa. I guess you missed me, hey?" I stir, and she pulls back.

"Fuck yes, I did." She slaps my shoulder. "Don't leave me again. Even if you're pissed at me."

My smile falters, and I take in my blonde-haired, blue-eyed beach babe look-alike friend. Her beauty has a level of innocence to it. But this chick isn't innocent. She's as strong as a warrior queen. To look at, we couldn't be more opposite with my dark hair, dark eyes and goth girl appearance. I don't know why I dress myself like this. I can't say I love it. But it just feels like a big fuck you to society's norms. I want to be different because, let's be honest, I am different.

"I'm sorry about that, Lex. I was a brat. I can't believe I wasn't here for you when you needed me. I'm so sorry about Muz. And that your brother hurt you again. And your dad…"

"Hey. Just forget it. I'd rather not think about that shit ever again. It's finished, and now I'm starting over." She grins at me.

"You do seem different now. I think normal people refer to it as happiness." I tease, and she beams. "Wouldn't have anything to do with your bodyguard over there, would it?"

Lexi beams again. "Maybe a little."

"The sex good?" I ask because, of course, I do. I'm Rhys George, after all.

"It's fucking epic." Lexi pretends to melt to the ground dramatically, and a laugh leaps from my chest.

"Girl, you're not vanilla anymore, are you?"

"What do you think?"

The sparkle in Lexi's eyes tells me exactly what to think. She's been a naughty girl. Man, it sucks I couldn't snag her before Ayden did. I could have blown her mind. My Kitty pops her head up at that thought, so I take another deep drag of the joint, needing it to lull me so I don't act like a horn dog and start humping people's legs in the halls.

"I think Ayden's cock is a lucky bastard."

Lexi throws her head back, laughing, gaining Ayden's attention from the corner.

"It's ok, Ayden." I call out, "She's just telling me all about that pretty cock of yours and what it's been doing!"

Lexi giggles, and I see Ayden chuckle from where he stands, shaking his head. He probably thinks I'm crazy, and he'd be right.

"Rhys. Where have you been? When you didn't show up at the start of term and I couldn't reach you on your phone, I went to Cynthia to see where you were." Lexi's blue eyes fill with concern as she studies me.

"What did she tell you?" I ask, meeting Lexi's seriousness with my own.

"It doesn't matter what she told me. I need you to tell me because I know she was lying."

I smile. Of course, Lexi would see through Cynthia's lie.

"Let me guess. I was visiting an old friend?"

Lexi's brows lift. "Yeah. Something like that."

Taking one last drag, I butt out the joint, blowing the smoke up into the sunny spring sky just as the warning bell goes to remind students to stop socialising and head to homeroom.

"Yeah., she lied. Can we talk at lunch? I'll need a bit of time to fill you in."

Lexi smiles and hugs me again. "Of course."

We start walking toward Ayden, and I link my fingers with Lexi's. She grins at me, probably thinking I've just missed her, and that's why I'm being all touchy-feely, but really, it's because I need her to keep me grounded. My heart is racing despite my attempt to trick it into submission with the joint.

"How's Marcus?" My words don't seem to surprise Lexi. A slight grin tugging at her lips as if she were expecting me to ask.

"He's ok. He's been keeping busy. Started cricket training, even though he hates the game."

"Fuck. I have screwed him up, haven't I?" My words are playful, making Lexi grin, but underneath my playfulness is my awareness that Marcus is struggling because he hates cricket. There's no way he'd play that game unless he was going through something.

When we started screwing around together, I'd told Marcus Grady that I didn't do relationships. I told him we were just fuck buddies and that we weren't exclusive. I told him to see other people. But he didn't. He devoted his time to me, and despite all my own rules, I let him get closer than I should have. I even stopped going to the Feast nights.

Marcus Grady wanted more. He wanted me to be his girl. He didn't listen to me when I said I couldn't be in a relationship. He begged me to explain why. But I couldn't do it. I couldn't tell him that I will never be able to have a normal relationship because I'm a sex addict.

Chapter Six

MARCUS

She hasn't noticed me yet, hasn't even looked this way down the corridor. It's probably deliberate since she knows my locker is in this direction, but she can't avoid me for much longer. She has to walk past my locker to get outside, where I'll probably follow her around during recess. It's inevitable.

Fuck, she looks hot. My dick is hard just seeing her in the flesh again. This last month has been hell. I didn't think she'd be heartless enough to completely ghost me. I lost my fucking shit when I thought she must have blocked my number or something. But then Ayden told me that Lexi couldn't get a hold of her either, and when I reached out to Tillie, one of Rhys's closest friends, she said she was worried because she also couldn't reach Rhys on her phone.

Principal Rogan, Rhys' foster mum, lied to our faces, telling us Rhys was visiting an old friend when she didn't show up at the start of term. My fucking brain naturally assumed she was fucking someone else. That she was staying with some guy somewhere, moving on from me. Lexi reminded me that Mrs Rogan wouldn't allow something like that, and I had to slap myself out of the bullshit I was letting my brain conjure up. I've always known I'm not good enough for someone like Rhys George, yet I still want her.

In the beginning, it was nothing but a bit of fun. At least that's what I told myself. Rhys told me the same thing, but I thought I could somehow win her over. Somehow be enough for her that she'd want to commit to me or some shit. I'm a fucking dickhead for thinking it. Rhys George is a force of nature. She commands attention without even trying. She's the life of the party and the free spirit we all wish we could be. I should have known her interest in me would be brief. Someone like her, with so much experience in the bedroom, will never be satisfied by a fucking seventeen-year-old amateur delusional dick like me. She has never been known to date or even fuck guys my age. The fact that she chose me gave me the false sense that I was different.

I was wrong.

"I think her skirt is shorter than it was last term." Garrett comes to stand by my side, and I glance up at his towering height. His blue eyes are on Rhys, and a fucking jealous pang tightens my chest. I've seen the way my mates look at her. Hell, I look at her the same way. But that used to be ok because I was the one fucking her. Now, she's free game.

"Yep. She's probably already got detention after school for wearing it so short." I sigh, turning my gaze back to where Rhys is doing some weird handshake thing with her friend Dale.

"What are we looking at?" Simon's blonde head pops between Garrett and me, and when his eyes land on Rhys, he barges through us and bounds up to her like a fucking excited puppy.

"George! Where you been, girl?" Simon's voice bounces off the walls, gaining the attention of the students milling around their lockers. When Rhys turns, hearing Simon's voice, I finally get to see that gorgeous face with skin that looks like it glows, dark eyes that are almost black, and lips to match. I nearly lose all self-control and walk up to her.

No! She doesn't like you anymore, douchebag!

"You doing alright, man?" Garrett asks, but I don't look at him. I can't take my eyes off her, so I shrug.

"Fucked if I know."

He chuckles. "In other words, no."

I shrug again.

I watch her interact with Simon. They have always had easy banter, both similar in a lot of ways. Their playfulness. Their need to always find the fun in a situation. Fuck, maybe he'd be a better match for her than me. I don't care, though. I'd cut off his dick before I'd ever let him stick it in my girl.

But she's not my girl, is she?

Laughing at something I can't hear, Simon turns with Rhys, and they start to make their way in my direction. I hold my breath. I have no fucking idea why I keep the air trapped in my lungs because I start to feel dizzy, but I hold it anyway, watching and waiting to see if she will acknowledge me.

A few feet before Gaz and me, Rhys, still laughing, looks up, and those dark chocolate eyes lock onto mine. I'm sure she didn't mean it. She probably forgot about the invisible pull we have on each other, but now she's remembering. I can see it in the way her breath hitches. The way her eyes flare, even though it's brief. And I can tell by the way her cheeks turn pink before my eyes.

Oh yeah. She may have said we weren't a thing. She may have said we weren't exclusive. She may have said that she felt nothing for me, but her body doesn't lie. I affect her, even though she doesn't want me to.

Garrett, being the fucking epic mate he is, steps to the side a little, blocking Rhys from passing. Ha! This fucker is making sure Rhys has no choice but to interact with me. The question is, will she?

"Good to see you, George. Have a good break?" Garrett asks, and with cocky confidence that only Rhys George has, she grins and shrugs one shoulder, turning her beautiful dark gaze to him.

Don't look at him. Look at me!

"Hey there, Cole." She smiles using Garrett's surname just like he used hers, her straight white teeth making an appearance from behind those black lips.

Fuck, I miss those lips. They are so soft and so fucking naughty.

"I had a great break, thanks. You fuckers miss me?" She raises a dark brow in question to Garrett, and he chuckles right before she turns those dark eyes back to me.

There she is.

"I'm not sure that *miss* is the right term to use. Perhaps more like it was quiet while you were gone." Garrett grins, and she rolls her eyes dramatically, looking back at him.

"That's because you fuckers are boring. You need someone like me to light up your life."

Garrett grins down at Rhys, and she kisses the air before shooting him a wink. When she goes to step past us, Garrett side steps, forcing her closer to me, and her arm has no choice but to brush mine. Without a second thought, my hand finds hers, and as if it's totally natural, our fingers link.

Her steps falter as she stops beside me, her body facing in the opposite direction to mine when her head tilts up to glance at me. Those deep dark eyes of hers find mine as her delicate fingers squeeze tighter, our shoulders pressing together.

"Miss me?" I don't know when the fuck I grew elephant-sized gonads, but fuck if they didn't grow bigger at the flare in her eyes.

"Maybe." Trying to hide her smirk, Rhys bites her bottom lip. She should know better. I know all her tells.

"Yeah. You did." I smirk, my eyes flicking longingly at her black lips. Fuck, those lips look so good wrapped around my dick. I wonder if she'll ever kneel before me like that again?

"I don't know, Grady. The way you are eye-fucking me right now tells me you most *certainly* missed me more."

Fuuuck. My dick twitches at her words. I love the way she speaks. The way she doesn't hold back. Any other girl would have giggled shyly at my words and skipped off. Not Rhys George. No fucking way. She tells it how she sees it. It's fucking refreshing, even when I don't like what she has to say.

"Maybe." I throw her words back at her, and she grins sexily. "Are you ok?" I ask the question I've wanted to ask her since she went radio silent four weeks ago.

There's a brief second where Rhys lets her barrier fall, and I see the uncertainty in her eyes. In fact, if I'm not mistaken, there's a slight tremble in her hand. She was definitely hoping I would keep our banter light. Not too serious. But her reaction isn't because I asked a serious question. No. Something else is going on.

"I'm peachy. Thanks for the concern, Grady." Her façade slams back in place, and I no longer see the vulnerability in her eyes. Her fingers loosen in mine, and just like that, I've lost her.

Rhys quickly steps away from me and skips ahead to catch up with Dale. My eyes follow her as she links arms with him, and he joins her, skipping together like a pair of eight-year-olds. It's only when Rhys glances back over her shoulder at me before she bursts through the doors at the end of the hall that I realise my concerns are right. Something is wrong.

The worry in her dark gaze is unlike anything I have seen her express before, which tells me all I need to know. Rhys George may not want to be involved with me anymore, but she sure as shit is getting me, even if it's just as a friend. Because if something can make Rhys George look so scared, it means something in her life has gone wrong. Terribly wrong.

Chapter Seven

RHYS

There's this strange feeling deep in my chest. My heart feels like it's twisting in agonizing knots, squeezing tighter and tighter as the day goes, and it makes me feel like I'm going to... cry.

What the actual fuck?

Rhys George doesn't cry. Ever!

Fucking Marcus Grady. Why does *he* have to be *him* I don't even know what that means, but a girl only has so much self-control when he's around. I didn't know if I was going to fall into his arms and beg him to love me—whatever that means—or leap on him like a bitch in heat and grind Kitty against him. And that was just my reaction when I locked eyes with him in the passage.

Then the fucker had the nerve to grab my hand as I passed by. Why does he affect me so much? Why has Marcus gotten under my skin? Is it those deep brown eyes or that messy brown hair that falls in such a way over his forehead sometimes that it's hard not to reach out and brush it back? And fuck me sideways. Did his lips get plumper over the last month? Shit, what if they look like that because he was kissing someone before I ran into him? Maybe he has a girlfriend now. Does he have a girlfriend now?

Fucking bitch is going down!

Ugh! I can't stand these feelings he stirs in me. They make me think I have the possibility of a future with him. Which is fucking ridiculous. Rhys George doesn't commit. To anyone!

When Dale and I enter the courtyard at recess, like a slap across my face, I get the reminder that me and monogamy don't mix.

Shaun Bossier, AKA The Spanish Casanova, comes into view, and my stupid knotted up heart does a flip in my chest. As if he feels my presence, Shaun's head turns my way, and those fucking sexy steel-grey eyes connect with mine. Kitty, the traitor, pops her head up, purring as our eyes lock, reminding me that last night didn't sate me. All it did was make me hungrier.

"Girl, everyone has missed your cute arse. Look at all the guys eye-fucking you right now. What's a guy gotta do to get a little attention like that?"

Dale, my flamboyant and overly dramatic but loyal friend, grins towards the tables where Lexi's pack is gathering. Lexi West and I became friends a few months back when her world fell apart and our paths crossed. By crossed paths, I mean I was in the toilet stall and heard one of Fox Pines Catholic's top bitches having a go at Lexi. They used to be friends, but after Lexi's violent home life was broadcast on the local news, her old friends turned on her. It's ok, though, because good old Rhys George was there to step in and be Lexi's new bestie.

Lexi's pack, as I call them, are the group of boys that didn't turn their backs on her. Instead, they showed her more loyalty than anything I've ever seen before. Marcus, yes, *my* Marcus, who is Lexi's childhood friend, Garrett, Shaun, Simon, and Jared, Lexi's other childhood friend, all stepped up to protect Lexi. They stayed by her side as much as possible, and I was sure the lucky bitch had snagged herself a reverse harem. I was wrong, though. Sure, Marcus and Jared cared about Lexi a little more than just friends at the time, but her heart belonged to one guy. Ayden Mitchell. Marcus' cousin.

Even though Marcus was still drooling over Lexi when I first invaded their pack, he quickly turned his eyes to me. I shouldn't have liked it so much. I should have run the moment I felt that way, yet I didn't. I stayed and let him get under my skin.

"Firstly, *Dale*. If you want some eye fucking from those delicious guys, then you need to have a vagina. You know they prefer fish over sausage." I grin at Dale when he cringes, "And secondly, I can't help it if everyone wants to taste my Kitty."

"Stop! I think I just threw up in my mouth." Dale gags and I laugh, throwing my head back as we walk arm in arm up to the table engulfed by the very guys who have their eyes on me.

Marcus steps around me and takes a seat on the tabletop. He must have been mere feet behind us as we walked. I'm surprised I didn't notice.

"Good to see you, George," Shaun smirks as he speaks to me, his sly grin knowing. Yeah, that arsehole knows a hell of a lot that he shouldn't.

Like what Kitty tastes like.

"Bossi. I see you're rebelling." I gesture my head towards him. "Have you been given a detention for that earring yet?"

It's a fucking hot earring, too. It's a dagger hanging from a loop in his right ear. I couldn't see his ears last night. The black leather mask covered most of his head. Fuck, he's a thing of beauty, though. His sharp jawline makes him look older than his seventeen years, and the uptight FP Catholic navy uniform he wears actually looks good. He makes it look good.

"Not yet. I've talked my way out of it so far today." He's a cocky bastard. Sitting up on the table next to Ayden, his expression holds nothing but full of himself attitude. "Where were you in English, George?"

"You weren't in Maths either, Ree. You only just get to school now?" Marcus really is trying to kill me. He just used the pet name he started calling me last term. Usually, he used it when he whispered his intentions in my ear. He has never used the name in front of other people. Now, as my eyes find his, I see the challenge in them. Marcus is bringing out the big guns. He hasn't gotten over me. He hasn't moved on. No. Marcus Grady has set his sights on breaking me down until I give in to him. And fuck me. If I'm not careful, he's going to succeed.

"I've been here since the start of the day. Just didn't feel like coming to class." I raise a dark brow at Marcus and return my eyes to Shaun. Bad decision. His eyes have a challenge of their own.

Fuck. This isn't good. Not for my sanity, but it is for Kitty, who is practically salivating with the attention. And that's the big problem right there. I need to put a lid on the heat building between my legs before I do something stupid, like ask Marcus to come to the bathroom with me. Or worse. Ask Shaun.

"Oh, you're a naughty girl, aren't you, Rhys? What were you doing instead of going to class? Or should I ask *who* you were doing?" Simon's playful tone draws my attention away from Casanova, but with looking at Simon comes a whole new problem. He's a clown. Fun. Outgoing. Likes to take the piss out of himself, and although he's not quite as built as the other guys, he's definitely athletic and loves to get his clothes off any chance he can get. Simon's favourite party game is strip poker, even though he's crap at it. He doesn't care because he loves getting naked. So, I've seen what he's packing under his uniform. I've even seen that pretty cock of his which is fucking mean to show me because I'm practically helpless to walk away from a dick that's foreskin free.

Hey, don't judge! We all have our vices! And mine is pretty cocks with lickable heads and no extra skin.

But there's just something about the blonde-haired, hazel-eyed, funny bugger that has my Kitty lifting her tail and swaying her arse in the air. I'm so screwed. Everyone is a possible fuck. I don't know what other people do when they look at people around them, but me? I zero in on their lips, their tongues when they make an appearance, their body language, or how their eyes connect with me. When I look at someone, I wonder what it would be like to make them lose control. Lose all of their restraints and let loose on their darkest desires. I wonder what it would be like to lose ourselves together.

It's always there. Always present. While people talk about what they want to wear to a party, I'm thinking about what I can wear that will be easiest to peel off my skin. When people talk about watching a movie, I'm wondering if there will be sex scenes and how heated they will get. I wonder if those scenes turn others on and if they wish they could just turn to the person next to them and fuck them until they can't walk. When we are in Maths class, and people are trying to calculate something. I'm adding up how many orgasms I think I could milk out of someone sitting close to me. It doesn't matter who they are. Girl or guy. Student or teacher. Sex is sex, and it's all I can fucking think about.

Trying to focus back on Simon instead of the orgy going on in my head, I feign indifference and shrug. "Wouldn't you like to know Hastings? I mean, I could tell you, but I don't *fuck* and tell."

Simon's hazel eyes widen and flare, and the poor guy can't help but rearrange his junk at my crass comment. Yes, I like that I've affected him. I could so easily walk up to him and slide my hand down his pants and wrap my hand around...

"Stop teasing the poor fellas, Rhys." Dale huffs dramatically next to me. "She was in the photo lab catching up on her portfolio." Dale offers to Simon, and I huff back.

"Dude, you're killing my vibe." I don't miss the anger contorting Marcus' face as I turn my sights to Dale.

"What vibe is that? Everyone's welcome?"

My head jerks in Marcus' direction at his comment, and I can't hide my reaction to the invisible slap he just dealt me. Did he really just say that? I've seen Marcus angry before, but he's never been nasty.

"Dude!" Garrett and Shaun hiss in unison at Marcus while Ayden butts his shoulder with Marcus, and Lexi's mouth drops open.

Marcus ignores them all, though, his dark pissed off eyes trained on me. This is what I want, isn't it? For Marcus to lose interest in me? For him to *not* want me. To move on. Right?

Fuck if his remark doesn't cut like a blade to my heart. It shouldn't, though. I'm used to people telling me how I'm a freak. Reminding me that I'm a slut. It's never really bothered me. I am who I am, and if people don't like it, well, they can fuck off. Yet here I am, letting Marcus' snide remark slice my chest open.

"That's right, Grady. Everyone *is* welcome. The more, the fucking merrier." I smile, flashing my teeth, preening like I have no cares in the world. I didn't realise I was such a good fucking actress.

The guy's snicker, but Marcus just glares at me, not finding my comment the least bit funny.

Touché, motherfucker!

Lexi moves away from Ayden and links arms with me, dragging me away to sit on the grass to soak up the spring sun. She's in her element with her golden blonde waves and blue eyes, looking like she is the very sun that beams down on us. She's all light and beauty, so natural and unblemished.

Me, I belong in the shadows with my dark as night hair and eyes brushed with black liner, thick and bold, with lips to match. My skin isn't bad. I have a slight tan, but I rarely show it the sun, instead opting to cover myself up in dark fabrics that hold edgy personality in themselves. The only time my skin comes out is at Vixen's Lodge Feast nights. Or the nights I spent with Marcus, just the two of us getting lost in each other.

"Want me to knee him in the balls for you?" Lexi's voice drags me out of my head, and my lips twitch at the seriousness on her face.

"You'd do that? For me?"

"Ahhh, probably not." Lexi cringes. "Firstly, I don't want to get that close to his dick. And secondly, even though he was being a bit of an arse, it's gotta be hard for him. He clearly still has a thing for you, Rhys."

My shoulders slump at her words, and it's hard to swallow the lump of guilt sitting firmly in my throat. "I know. I don't know how to help him move on."

"You really want him to?" Lexi frowns, and I nod slowly.

"Well... yeah. That's why I put distance between us."

"I don't know, Rhys. I see the way you look at him sometimes. I think you care more than you're letting on."

Sighing, I lean back on my hands, closing my eyes as I tip my head back, soaking in the sun. "Maybe what you're seeing is my lust look. He's a fine-looking specimen. It's hard not to admire his physique." I pop one eye open to peer at Lexi, and she grins, shaking her head at me before falling silent to enjoy the sun.

We don't get much more time in the warm rays before the bell goes, and we groan our way with reluctance to our next classes. I debate ditching and going to the photo lab again, but I know I can't avoid *this* class and the fact that I'm already two weeks behind has me feeling anxious.

Health class is basically a lazy person's PE class. We learn about the body and health stuff but don't have to use our bodies in the physical activity that the PE students do. Unless there's an orgy Olympics I don't know about, then I don't need to kick a ball around or try to jump a further distance than the other students.

My gang of misfits are all in this class with me. Let's face it. Tillie, Bell, Allister, and Dale will only run if someone is chasing them. Even then, I don't think Bell would run. She'd turn her dark Wednesday Addams glare onto her aggressors, and they would probably drop dead on the spot from fright. Fuck, I love that chick. She's wonderfully cold and brutally straight to the point.

We take our usual seats up the back of the room while Mr Foster stands tall at the front, marking the roll as each of us enter. His eyes linger on me a little too long, and Kitty starts purring again. Attention, attention, attention. Such a needy little Kitty.

Today we are learning about nutrition. While the class discusses sources of protein, I fight to hold back my thoughts. Surely someone will say it soon. Surely, I'm not the only one thinking it?

Of course, I probably am. No one else at FP Catholic is like me. In fact, I doubt there are many seventeen-year-olds like me anywhere.

My hand shoots up before I can stop it, and Mr Foster's attention immediately turns to me.

"Miss George. Do you have a source of protein to add to the list?" Mr Foster's deep blue gaze locks onto mine, almost begging me to behave. Like a lot of the teachers here, he knows me too well.

"Semen has protein in it."

The class erupts in laughter. Boys hoot, and some of the girls giggle while others roll their eyes and shoot daggers at me. They are just jealous they didn't think of it first.

Up the front of the room, Mr Foster shakes his head in disappointment, releasing a big sigh. I can't hear it over the laughter, but I can see it, and I flash him a cheesy smile.

"Quieten down!" Mr Foster uses his outside voice to scare everyone into submission. Unfortunately, it brings out the brat in me. I stand, pushing my chair back, allowing it to scrape loudly over the linoleum floor, gaining everyone's attention again. "Sit down, please, Rhys." Mr Foster uses my first name this time, showing how annoyed he is at my comment.

Seriously though. Surely someone brings this fact up each year that he teaches this irrelevant bullshit.

"But Mr Foster." I let sweetness roll off my tongue, not fooling anyone. "This is a class about nutrition, right? Surely this is important for the girls to learn about. And maybe some boys too." I wag my brows. "I mean, a girl has to watch her figure these days. Did you know a guy's load can have up to 25 calories in it? If a girl is on a strict diet, she should know about that so she can include it in her calorie counting."

Again, the class erupts in laughter. Some of the girls who shot me daggers before are struggling to hide their smirks now. Uptight bitches.

"Is that so, Miss George?" Mr Foster crosses his thick arms over his broad chest, not looking at all impressed with me.

Oh well.

"It is, Mr F. And did you know that studies have shown that a good dose of sprog can give you up to three percent of your daily zinc requirement? That's pretty good if you think about it. We need zinc to help our immune system." I drag my eyes from Mr Foster's reddening face and glance around the room to all the girls, "Who needs multivitamins when you can have some salty jiz?"

"Rhys! That's enough!" The boom of Mr Foster's voice kills the laughter around the room, and everyone turns to the front again.

Whoops. Looks like my teaching stint is over.

I glance at Mr Foster, biting the inside of my cheek, fighting to hold back my grin. Fuck, it's hard to do while looking at those blazing blue eyes and the furious expression contorting his face. "Rhys, you will stay behind after class, please." And with that, Mr Foster sucks in a deep breath and returns to the lessons, teaching boring nutrition.

Sitting back down, I sneak a peek at my friends. Tillie has her lips sucked into her mouth as she tries not to laugh, while Bell wears a shit-eating grin, which isn't something she brings out very often. Meanwhile, Dale is on his phone googling nutritional information about sperm while Allister looks over his shoulder.

My work here is done.

I zone out for the rest of class. Not that I do it on purpose, but because I'm thinking about jiz and remembering how Shaun fed me his last night at the Feast. Kitty flutters between my legs, and I rub my thighs together, desperate for the friction. This is fucked. It's not even lunchtime, and I'm drooling for a bit of D. In my mouth, then deep inside Kitty. It takes everything I have not to slip my hand between my legs and mash my bundle of nerves.

The vibration of my phone gains my attention, and I slip it out from my blazer, holding it low on my lap to see a Snap notification, so I open it.

Shaun Bossier
You ok?

Hmmm. My Casanova is concerned. Isn't he adorable?

Rhys George
Sure. Why wouldn't I be?

Shaun Bossier
Because Marcus was a dick to you.

Rhys George
I like dick!

Shaun Bossier
Are you ever serious?

Rhys George
Serious is boring.

Shaun Bossier
Serious is real!

Rhys George
You want me to be real?

Shaun Bossier
It wouldn't hurt every now and then.

Rhys George
I feel like it would. Hurt, I mean.

Shaun Bossier
Not if you're serious with the right person.

Rhys George
Are you the right person, Casanova?

Shaun Bossier
In this situation, I think I am.

Rhys George
And what situation is that?

Shaun Bossier
The one where my friend is being an arsehole to my Kitten.

Oh damn. He went there. And now my Kitty is ready to prowl. She heard his silent call.

Rhys George
Kitten isn't here right now.

Shaun Bossier
Damn it, Rhys! Are you ok?

Rhys George
I'll be fine, Casanova.
No need to worry about me. I'm a big girl.
A few harsh words won't kill me.

Shaun Bossier
They were unnecessary words.
Want me to rough him up for you?

Rhys George
Get in line. Lexi wants to knee his gonads.
Wait! No!
She decided she didn't want to go near his dick.

Shaun Bossier
Well, he deserves it.

Rhys George
Why?

Shaun Bossier
Why does he deserve it?

Rhys George
Yes.

Shaun Bossier
I thought we'd been over this already.

Rhys George
Well, yes. But why do you care, Bossi?

Shaun Bossier
Because you're my friend Rhys.

Rhys George

Marcus is your friend, too. He was your friend first.
Shouldn't you be sticking up for him or something?

Shaun Bossier

I've already checked in with him. But just because he's
got his dick out of joint because you don't want to
be with him doesn't give him the right to act like a
fuckhead.

"Miss George. Put your phone away, please." Mr Foster's voice comes quiet, close to my ear. I jump a little, startled that I didn't hear him approach or even the fact that the class is now chattering away as they work.

Glancing up through my dark lashes, I flutter them and smile innocently.

"Sure thing, Mr Foster."

Slipping my phone back into my blazer, I'm thankful that it was Mr Foster who caught me on my phone and not one of my other teachers who would have confiscated it on the spot.

As Mr Foster gives me his back, walking off, I turn to Tillie, who is grinning ear to ear, and let her catch me up on what I meant to be doing in class. It's all boring stuff that I couldn't give two shits about, and by the time the bell goes for lunch, I'm sure that a double period of health class is a form of torture.

Knowing that I have to stay behind after my 101 lesson on sperm and nutrition, my friends scoop up their books and laptops and file out behind the other students, leaving me to face Mr Foster's wrath.

"Really, Rhys? A lesson in semen?"

I snicker at Mr Foster's amused voice and glance up from my desk.

"Come on. You have to admit that was a good one. It's all true, by the way." I smile, and he shakes his head, staring down at me from his skyscraper height.

"I guess if it's on the internet, then it must be true." He teases, and I poke my tongue out. Leaning back, he props his fine arse on the table in front of mine. "Are you ok?" His voice is quiet but sure.

"Why does everyone keep asking me that today?" I huff and pout like a little brat.

"I don't know why everyone else is asking you," he glances around as if checking to make sure we are still alone, "but after last night, I need to ask."

Uncomfortable with the serious talk, I start to squirm in my seat.

"I'm fine." I keep my voice quiet, too, wishing the door was closed so we can't be overheard.

"I don't believe you." He shakes his head, his short blonde hair not moving a millimetre.

"I can't control what you believe." I shrug, and he frowns.

"How about you help ease my mind?"

My dark brows shoot up. "You want me to tell you that…" I drop the volume in my voice to a loud whisper, "everything that went down last night *is* ok?"

"Are you fucking kidding me!"

Gasping, my eyes dart to the door to see Shaun standing there glaring at us, most certainly having heard my conversation with Mr Foster.

"It's you?" Shaun hisses, and Mr Foster stands from the table, hissing back, his face turning red in fury.

"Shut the door!"

I flinch at his menacing tone, but Shaun doesn't miss a beat as he turns back and closes the door behind him, shutting us in the space together.

"*You're* Skipper? Her Sponsor?" Shaun spits with venom, and the anger behind his eyes takes me aback. I don't think I've ever seen him wear this look before. I should be scared. Concerned. But I'm not. Because right now, heat floods between my legs as last night rushes back to the forefront of my mind.

Now I know I'm truly fucked up. I should be worried about other students or teachers overhearing. I should be concerned about the situation I was forced into last night. But all I can do is remember how good it felt to have Tyler inside me, bringing me undone, while Shaun held onto me and fed me his seed.

Chapter Eight

Shaun

Mr Foster is Rhys' Sponsor?

WHAT THE ACTUAL FUCK!

"You're a fucking teacher, you sicko!"

"Keep your voice down!" Tyler, FP Catholic's Head of Sports, hisses back at me.

I can see it now. Skipper and Mr Foster are the same height and built like a brick wall. With the mask he had on last night, it was hard to tell, but now that I see his eyes and see his lips which kissed Kitten's pussy with lustrous nips, I can tell it definitely was him.

"This is like… against the law!" I hiss again through clenched teeth, and Rhys laughs, gaining my attention.

"Bossi, come on now. Everything about what happened last night was against the law, even for you. We both go there knowing we are underage. That adults are using our bodies for pleasure. Don't pretend like this is news to you."

My brows shoot up as I let her words sink in. I know she's right. The truth of it is we don't know who we are fucking at the Feast nights. The people there are probably from all walks of life. They pretend like they don't know we aren't of legal age, and they enjoy us as much as we enjoy them. Still, I can't get past the fact that Mr Foster, my fucking PE teacher, is involved.

"No, fuck that, Rhys. He is totally taking advantage of you." I point an accusing finger at the man in question, but he just lifts a brow, looking bored.

Dropping her chin to her chest, Rhys sighs. She looks utterly fuckable as usual, wearing her hair in those twisty things on each side of her head. So different to last night when her hair was down in a cascade of dark silk. It's like Rhys and Kitten are two different people. To look at anyway. Not personality. They are both just as sex-crazed as each other.

"Shaun, calm down. You have it all backwards. Tyler isn't taking advantage of *me*. I've been taking advantage of *him*."

"What?" My brows furrow. "I don't understand."

"We can explain it to you, but not here and not now." Mr Foster walks to the front of the room and takes out a sheet of paper, scribbling something on it.

I can't take my eyes off Rhys for long. Fuck, she's in my head bad. I hardly slept last night, my brain replaying everything again and again. I even had to rub one out before I left for school this morning, I was so worked up. This chick is a siren, and fuck if I'm not under her spell.

"Here." Mr Foster snaps me out of my thoughts, and I see him holding out a slip of paper. "Detention slips. Go there after school. I'll swing by and select you both to help me with some community service work. We can talk then."

I take the slip he hands me and then watch as Rhys takes hers, scrunching it up and sliding it in her pocket.

"I'll put it with the other two I've already gotten for uniform violations today." She grins like a brat, so proud of her accomplishments.

Mr Foster smirks, shaking his head and returning to the front of the room while I stand feeling like a lost puppy, not sure what to do. This whole situation isn't sitting well with me, yet Rhys doesn't seem that bothered by it.

I follow Rhys out of the room a minute later, and we slowly walk side by side down the empty corridor, my head swimming with what the fuck is going on.

"Don't overthink it, Bossi. You'll find out later who the real predator is." At my confused glance, Rhys adds, "Here's a hint. It's not Skipper."

We walk silently down the long passage that runs along the stadium, passing by the entry alcoves along the way. I can hear the sounds of lunchtime well on its way outside, and I'm compelled not to fucking join in. Sneaking a glance at Rhys, I notice that she's unusually quiet, and as I take in her face, I can see the worry hidden just under the surface.

I don't think. I act. Snatching her hand, I drag her into the next alcove to hide us from, well, anyone who starts walking down the passage.

"What are you doing?" Rhys whispers as I push her up against the wall.

Caging her in with my hands on either side of her head, I press my forehead against hers. It takes a beat, but I feel the moment she finally relaxes against my invasion.

"I'm just trying to wrap my head around last night," I admit, and her dark eyes meet mine as she glances at me through her dark lashes.

"You need *me* to help you do that?" She asks, and I smirk.

"Maybe." I let one of my hands fall as I lean in closer, pressing my body against hers, revelling in the way our bodies come together. "Last night was something else."

"Yeah. You can say that again."

Her pink tongue darts out, wetting her lips, and fuck if my cock doesn't get ten times harder at the sight. Fuuuck. Now I'm thinking about her tongue and the way she licked the cum from my dick last night.

"I want to kiss you," I admit. "Can I?" I rarely need to ask for permission. I can tell by the way chicks lean into me, almost frothing at the mouth to taste my lips, that they would welcome my lips on theirs. But with Rhys, I don't know where I stand. We both know we are attracted to each other. That's not the problem. The problem is, last night, at the Feast, was a different situation. A situation set up purely for sex. For pleasure.

Here, now, we are at school. Not in a situation where it's a given that our lips will connect. I tasted those lips last night, something I've dreamed of doing for a while now, and no, I'm not talking about the lips in between her legs. I'm talking about that bratty mouth and those black lips that beckon me.

"I don't know if it's a good idea," Rhys whispers, her warm, minty breath fluttering over my lips.

"Why?" I whisper back and lean in a fraction closer, my dick jerking with eagerness.

Hang on, Thor, buddy. I'm working on it!

"Because I'm horny. I'm likely to attack at any moment." Her admission sends all the blood to my dick, making me lightheaded.

"I don't see the problem." I lean in a little closer, our lips hovering so close I can feel the heat of hers. Her chest is rising and falling rapidly, and I love how much I'm affecting her. Fuck, I'd nearly do anything to have some time alone to get lost with her.

When Rhys doesn't respond, I throw the last curveball I have, hoping like fuck I get over the line.

"I want you, Kitten."

Before I even get a chance to see her response, her lips slam into mine. I press my weight against her as she fists my blazer, dragging me tighter against her body. Her lips part for me hungrily, and I slip my tongue in, desperate to find hers. She doesn't disappoint. Our tongues dance as our kiss deepens, and our moans get swallowed down.

I'm a horny fucker. I know that. All the chicks know it. I've been with too many to count, yet none have me going as crazy as Rhys George does. Maybe it's because she has the same drive as me. The same desires or the same need to let go and fall completely into the moment. I can't put my finger on what it is, but shit, I want it bad. I want her bad. I want to own her.

The thought has me pulling back suddenly. I've never been possessive or viewed a chick as an object to own. What the fuck sort of thought was that?

"What's wrong?" Rhys asks, her black lips looking fuller than a minute ago. Shit, are my lips black too now?

"Nothing. I shake my head. I thought I heard something." I lie. A lie that turns into truth when we hear footsteps nearing the alcove we're hiding in.

I take a few steps back from Rhys, watching as her eyes go wide and she glances to the passage beyond, waiting for someone to spring us. I drag my thumb over my lips, pulling it back to see if any of Rhys' black lipstick is on me. Nothing.

"Are my lips black?" I whisper, gaining her attention again.

When she turns her gaze back to me, her grin spreads from ear to ear, her eyes locking on my lips.

"I could tell you no and let you walk out like that, but that would be mean."

Her words have me moving quickly for my phone, and I quickly unlock it to open the camera app, turning the screen to selfie mode. Frowning, I try to find the black that Rhys hinted at, but there's nothing except for Rhys' teasing laughter.

"Smart arse, aren't you?" I smirk at her, and she just keeps laughing. There's no black lipstick on me.

"What's so funny?"

Garrett's voice has my head swinging to the alcove opening to see him glancing between Rhys and me.

"Oh, nothing." Rhys giggles, looking between us.

I shake my head and look at Garrett.

"Are you looking for me?"

He nods. "Yeah, man. Wondered where you'd gotten to."

That's when I notice how Garrett's eyes are almost accusing as they take us in, hidden in the darkish alcove. Shit. I'm the worst friend ever. Garrett's gaze reminds me that Rhys isn't my girl. She's Marcus', even if they aren't a thing anymore.

"I'm on my way out. Ran into this brat on the way." I lie, and Garrett's eyes sharpen, accessing me.

"Let's go then. I'm hungry." Rhys skips out of the alcove, brushing by Garrett while I try not to think about how she used the word hungry. It sounded more like she was saying she was horny.

Out in the courtyard, the sun is warm, and most students have ditched their blazers on a growing pile as they soak up the sun. Lexi quickly snatches Rhys away when she sees her, and they share some food, talking quietly. I don't miss the way Marcus' eyes stay glued to Rhys' every move. He's done his nuts over this chick for sure. I've never seen him like this. Well, except for the bursts of jealousy he threw Ayden, his cousin, when Ayden first got together with Lexi. When Marcus and Rhys first started hooking up, we were all relieved. It turned his sights on someone other than Lexi and eased the tension within the group. Except for Jared. That poor bastard is still pining over Lexi.

What I did with Rhys last night crosses so many lines in the Bro Code it's not funny. And yet, I sought out more just minutes ago. Fuck, this could get really messy if I'm not careful.

"You wanna tell me what you were *really* doing with George?"

Garrett's voice is low as he dips his head towards me so the others don't hear. We are sitting side by side on top of the picnic table in the courtyard. It's our usual hang out, although we've also been spending some time behind the stadium of late. It's usually where Rhys goes to smoke her joints with her weird friends, but today she's here in the courtyard, so that's where we are.

"What are you talking about, man?" I keep my voice quiet, avoiding Garrett's gaze and keeping my eyes trained on my phone screen while I mindlessly scroll through Instagram.

"I've seen the way you two look at each other. Don't even think about lying to me." Garrett hisses, and I turn my glare to him. He's a big fucker. Built like a brick house and forever sporting a fucking brooding glare on his face. He doesn't smile much, but when he does, his whole face changes into something different. A teddy bear comes to mind.

"Is it the same way *you* eye fuck her?" When his brows reach his hairline at my question, I huff, shaking my head. "Don't come at me with your bullshit, Gaz. I've seen your lingering looks, too. Don't act like I'm the one doing something wrong."

I'm a piece of shit. I *am* the one doing something wrong. All Gaz is guilty of is drooling over a hot chick.

"So what if I get hard every time she's around? The point is, I don't act on it."

I dart my eyes around to see if anyone heard his slightly raised voice. We don't need a fucking audience for this conversation.

"And I have?" I sneer, and his eyes search mine for the truth. It's fucking unnerving the way his blue eyes study mine. It's also unnerving the moment I know he can tell I'm lying.

"Yeah, man. I think you *have* acted on it. I don't know how far you've taken it. But you *have* taken it somewhere."

I want to argue with him, but what's the point? I made out with that juicy cunt of hers until she gushed over my mouth. I kissed her purple lips right before another masked man fucked her in front of a naked audience. I shredded the skin off my cock, jerking my cum into her mouth. And mere minutes ago, I reclaimed those lips, desperate for another taste.

When my face falls, so does his. Garrett looks fucking disappointed in me. Fuck if that doesn't sting.

"How far?" He growls, and I shake my head.

"Too far," I admit, flicking my gaze to the girl in question, who is animatedly chatting away to Lexi.

"Fuck." Garrett hisses and turns his eyes to my siren.

"You gonna tell Grady?" I whisper like the fucking coward I am.

Garrett's hard eyes return to mine, and his nostrils flare a few times before he responds.

"I won't. But only if it ends. Now."

Well, fuck me. He may as well put a gun to my head. I can try to avoid her at school, but if we are at another Feast night together, I don't think I'll have the self-control to stay away. No one knows I go to Vixen's Lodge for sex parties. I've kept that little detail to myself since it first eventuated. I haven't told the guys because I don't think they'd understand. I've been with so many FP Catholic chicks already, and none of them give me what I need. I have a reputation as the school's Casanova, but my promiscuity is from trying to find what I'm looking for. I wasn't sure what that was until the opportunity to attend the Feast Night presented itself. There, I can be who I want to be. Who I need to be. No one knows who I am there. No one judges me there. If I want to do some freaky shit, I can find someone at those Feasts to share it with.

Then, Kitten turned up last night and showed me that while I have been searching for something that the Feast Nights offer, my real desires rest in the palm of Kittens' hands. Rhys' hands.

"I can't," I admit, and Garrett's head jerks back in shock. "I can't tell you the reason here. Can we catch up later tonight?"

Swinging his eyes back in the direction of Rhys, mine follow, and we sit quietly for a moment, taking her in. She makes the school uniform look utterly sinful. It's hard to believe that her foster mum is the Principal here. Rhys George is so rebellious. Gets detention nearly every day for uniform violations or attitude issues. This place would be boring as bat shit if she weren't here.

"Tonight then." Garrett turns back to me. "And you tell me everything." He jabs a finger into my chest, and I nod because his glare is fucking scary, and he makes me feel like I'm a six-year-old getting scolded by my old man.

Chapter Nine

Rhys

K itten is out of control. From the moment Shaun dragged me into that alcove, she's been clawing at me like a feral beast, desperate to rub herself against something. Anything. I've been in this place before. The most recent was only a couple of weeks ago when I received the voice message from my old foster mum, Julie. I went straight into flight mode and ran off on my family somewhere along the Great Ocean Road to go on a sex bender. The problem with a bender of any kind is the comedown and the withdrawal.

Can someone who's addicted to fucking go through withdrawal, you ask? Hell yes. The spiralling. The panic. The sweating. The shaking. The willingness to do anything to make it go away. Even things that fill you with nothing but shame afterwards. Yes. Yes. Yes. It's very real and fucking scary.

When Cin and Will finally found me amidst the beginnings of a gang bang, I was so far gone I didn't even recognise them. Everything in my head was about sex. I couldn't get enough, even though my body was already used and abused, wracked with exhaustion.

A shudder crawls up my spine just thinking about what Cin and Will witnessed when they finally found me. How can they even stand to look at me after springing me in that provocative position? It's enough to make my stomach roll with loathing disgust for myself. Any other foster parents would have run back out of that room, shut the door and walked away so I wouldn't be their problem anymore. Not Cynthia and William Rogan, though. Nope, they bundled me up in a blanket and took me back to the hotel they left Charlotte and the twins in, putting me in the shower and washed me even while I screamed and clawed at them, desperate to escape and return to my bender.

The only thing that calmed me down was a strong sedative. Cynthia has them in her bag everywhere she goes, just in case I need them. How fucked up is that? Imagine needing to carry around potent sedatives to knock out your teenage foster daughter in case she turns into a sex-crazed animal who is willing to screw anyone like she's at a fuck festival.

Standing with my head hanging in my locker, trying to take a moment to hide my pained expression, I debate if I should just go home. I should remove myself from the presence of anyone I can manipulate into sex. It's not fair to them, and I know it's not fair to Cin and Will after the shit I've brought into their life. I should just go home and fuck my own hand while watching porn. Doing that won't completely fix my rapidly growing need, but it will ease it temporarily until I can figure out what the fuck to do to get myself under control.

"Ready for Food Tech, Rhys?" Simon's voice startles me, and I jump a little, spinning to find him standing behind me.

"What?" My head is scattered, and my heart is racing as I look around the bustling corridor. There are numerous eyes on me—guys and girls who I rarely interact with flick their gazes to me.

Shit.

Can they tell how fucked up I am right now? Do they know that I'm ready to grind Kitty against any one of them?

"You ok, George?" Simon's voice gains my attention again, and I glance up to his hazel eyes, finding comfort in the warmth they hold.

"I… um."

Get a hold of yourself, girl!

"Are you coming to Food Tech or ditching that class, too?" Simon asks, and my eyes follow the way his lip quirks up at one side. I wonder what it would be like to kiss those lips?

Marcus takes that moment to walk past us with Lexi and Jared, his dark eyes flicking to me briefly, this time not holding the anger they did earlier. I know it shouldn't matter since I'm the one who pulled the brakes on whatever Marcus and I were, but it makes me feel a little better to see the anger gone. My heart begins to slow, giving me a glimpse of calm, but not enough to kill the chaos inside me.

"I-uh… don't know if I can stomach Food Tech today." Turning my gaze back to Simon, I don't miss the curious glances from Shaun and Garrett where they stand by their lockers down the hall.

"So, you gonna ditch?" At Simon's question, I nod, not really knowing what I plan to do. "You want some company? I can't be fucked dealing with Mrs Brennan today."

My brows shoot up, and he grins his signature playful grin. It's full of mischief and hell if it doesn't appeal to me.

"You wanna ditch with me, Hastings? You'll likely get caught."

"How do you get away with it?" He asks, and I smirk.

"I don't. I just don't care if I get caught."

He chuckles, "Then I don't care either."

Grinning, I turn to my locker and make quick work of re-applying my lipstick, *Blackest Parts of Hell*, before swinging it shut and locking it. "Photo lab, theatre, or behind the stadium?"

Doing a whooping jump, Simon rubs his hands together. "Photo lab. You can take photos of me. I'll be your model."

I throw my head back laughing before I start walking, and Simon hustles up beside me, wearing a proud grin. Garrett and Shaun keep their eyes on us as we pass by, paranoia slithering its way inside my head. Can they tell what I'm thinking? What I'm planning? Their gaze makes me feel uneasy, so I try to pay them little attention while I pretend to listen to Simon chat about some party he went to last week. It's no use, though. Whatever Simon is talking about goes in one ear and out the other because all I can focus on is Shaun's heated eyes piercing the back of my head.

The photo lab doesn't get used as much as it used to with the digital era sweeping in. The once empty classroom off one end is now filled with computers and equipment for photo editing and manipulation. The only room that gets used as much as ever is the studio, while the aging darkroom sits at the back of the building, out of the way, gathering dust. Unlike most students, I love traditional photos, so I spend a lot of time snapping pictures and printing them the old-fashioned way. I also love to capture video recordings and edit them to create something worth watching. It's my thing.

"This is sick. How have I not been in here before?" Simon's eyes dart around the lab as I lead him into the darkroom, closing the door behind us. I quickly flick the switch to indicate that processing is underway, which will warn anyone outside not to open the door. It also dims the lights in the small room, and Simon looks around in appreciation.

"Oooh. Mood lighting. You trying to sweep me off my feet, George?" Simon jokes.

If only he knew how close to the truth he is.

"Sure am Hastings. Wanna get those clothes off?" I sound like I'm joking, which is on purpose. If he thinks I'm kidding and he has no intentions of getting naked with me, it won't leave anyone embarrassed or feeling awkward. But, if he's keen, he'll keep the joke going until it steps over a line that tells us both that we are serious. It's a tactic I learned a long time ago. A time I try hard not to think about.

"Ladies first." Simon grins, doing a bow as if I'm some royal lady or some shit.

My dark lips head north at the corners while I circle the island bench in the centre of the room, watching Simon as he circles opposite me.

"How about a game? An article of clothing, for an article of clothing." I suggest.

Simon stops abruptly, his expression serious as he studies me. This is where he either goes along with it to push the boundaries or changes the conversation, which will tell me he thinks I'm joking around or he isn't keen.

"Don't tease me, Rhys. You know how much the Hastinator loves to play party games."

I can't hold back my giggle at the nickname he calls himself sometimes. He's such a dork. A cute, sexy dork, all tall and lean with silky blonde hair that's getting long enough to tie back. Certainly is long enough to grab a fist full of.

"Rhys George doesn't tease about party games, Simon. You should know that."

He grins, "True. But my party games are always about getting naked, so there's no turning back once we start playing. We play to the birthday suit."

I shrug. "Why not? There's nothing else to do."

For the longest moment, Simon's eyes stay locked on mine from where he stands on the other side of the bench. He's studying me to see if I really am joking, so I let him see my honesty. I let him see that I'm committed to this game with the way I hold his stare and quirk a brow. Then, his hazel gaze darkens, and a level of confidence I haven't seen on him changes his whole persona.

"Simon says, take off your blazer."

I freeze.

Holy fucking shit!

I've never heard Simon's voice so serious and demanding. Gone is the goofy, playful tone he uses all day, every day. It's almost as if he stepped out of the room, and someone new stepped in to take his place. And fuuuck! Kitty is turning in excited circles, almost drooling.

My breath quickens with excited anticipation as I shake myself out of my daze and ease my blazer slowly off my shoulders. I don't break eye contact with him as I work it off, watching him watch me. I make a point of holding my blazer up at my side and dropping it to the floor after I tug it free, and once the heavy fabric hits the floor, Simon quickly shucks off his own blazer, tossing it carelessly on the floor next to him.

"Simon says, take off your shoes."

Wow. That voice. It's so rich and deep—nothing like his normal voice.

I toe off one shoe and then the other, bending down to pick them up and show him they are off before dropping them on top of my blazer. Then, he moves quickly to do the same.

"Simon says, take off your shirt."

His eyes widen a little, waiting to see how I'll respond when he speaks this demand. Will I do what he asks, or will I chicken out? I can tell he's unsure, so I free my grin as I start unbuttoning my shirt, watching his eyes as they travel down with each button that pops free. Impatience gnaws at me, so I pull the remainder of my shirt out of my skirt and draw it open before peeling the sleeves down my arms, letting it fall to the floor behind me.

"I think you're the only girl at this school that would wear a sexy bra underneath your uniform." He hisses between clenched teeth, and I shrug.

"You never know when a situation will present itself." As if to send him a reminder that this is one of those situations, I push my chest out a little, letting the red silk and lace of my bra strain across my needy tits.

"Simon says, take off your skirt."

"Hey, hold on a minute. You're still wearing your shirt." I remind him, gesturing with my hand before he frowns, looking down at his shirt, realising I'm right.

Quick as a flash, he undoes his shirt and pulls it off, returning his heated gaze to me.

"Simon says, skirt. Off now!"

Ooooh yes. He's an impatient fella. So naturally, I don't hurry. I take my time, slowly popping the button free. The zip is next, smoothly sliding down at the side of the navy tartan kilt while my eyes remain trained on him. The fire in his hazel pools is intoxicating, adding to Kitty's wetness and need. A heated ache building deep in my belly.

Once my skirt is undone, I let it slip off my hips to pool around my feet, all while keeping my eyes trained on Simon. He licks his lips and stands on his toes to get a better view past the bench that separates us, and when his eyes finally lift to mine, I raise a brow. He understands my silent challenge immediately and makes quick work of getting his pants off.

I now stand before Simon in my red matching bra and knickers and the navy knee-high school socks, while Simon only has on black boxer briefs.

"You're beautiful, Rhys George."

The compliment makes me squirm. I'm not good with compliments. Especially when they sound so genuine. Tell me my mouth is like heaven, or my pussy feels amazing, and I'm all for it, but tell me I look pretty, or I'm a nice person, or I'm good at something that isn't sex, then I can't handle the compliment.

Weird, I know.

"Simon says, come here." His voice is quiet, as if he's afraid of saying the words.

Stepping over my discarded uniform, I make my way around the island bench to stand before Simon. I've already seen what he's packing from the games he's played at parties, but I've never seen him like this. His eyes are dark with desire, his expression doesn't have a hint of playfulness in it, and I certainly haven't seen the swell straining underneath the thin fabric of his boxers. The dark red hue of the room picks up the shadows, showing his defined muscles, sculpted from regular workouts, no doubt. This version of Simon Hastings is quite magnificent.

"Fuck, you scare me."

I frown at his words.

"I scare you?"

"Hell yes." His eyes travel the length of my body, taking me in, committing my curves to memory.

"Why?"

He doesn't answer straight away, taking a moment to flick his gaze to my lips, his tongue darting out to wet his lips. Then his eyes find mine again.

"Because you're Rhys George, and I'm… just me."

"That doesn't make sense."

"Let me put it this way, I'm a virgin, and I'm likely to make a fool of myself and come in my jocks the moment you touch me." Even though Simon's face is red already from the light in the room, I can tell the colour has deepened with a blush at his admission.

"Simon," I giggle, "If you come in your jocks, then I'll just lick it up."

"Fuuuck. I think I nearly came just then." Simon rakes his hand through his blonde hair, and I can tell he really is struggling to hold himself together.

"You wanna know the good thing about taking the virginity of a guy?" At his brow raise, I add, "After they come, they're ready to go again in a matter of minutes. So, I'll tell you what. Let me fix your current situation, and then you can service me while you recover."

"What do you mean?" His brows knit together in confusion, and I smile. This is going to be fun.

"Simon needs to tell me to get on my knees."

"Wha— Oh." He stands taller, rolling his shoulders back and bringing that deep voice back to the party. "Simon says, get on your knees."

Like a good girl, I drop to my knees while keeping eye contact with Simon. Thank fuck Simon's clothes are there on the floor to provide some cushioning. I know from experience how hard this old floor is on the knees.

"Hastings, I'm a little confused." I brush my hands over the backs of his calves, feeling the dusting of hair.

"Abo—" He clears his throat, and I watch his Adam's apple bob as he swallows, "confused about what?"

I grin. "I'm confused because I could have sworn you've fucked chicks before. Didn't you bang that cougar nurse in Melbourne when you visited Lexi in the hospital?"

Simon had bragged about fucking one of the older nurses while we were all held up at Lexi's bedside after one of her brother's attacks. At the time, I remember thinking Simon might have a thing for older women. That, and feet. He was constantly massaging Lexi's feet or painting her toenails. I wonder if he likes my feet?

Simon peers down at my hands as they glide up his thighs while I drag my eyes away from his face and glance forward to take a better look at his junk, which is now eye level. "I'm all talk, George. I didn't bang that nurse, but I did eat her out, and she gave me a pretty decent hand job."

And now I'm picturing Simon eating *me* out. Kitty is purring, ready to pounce, but Simon was right before. He is very worked up, and if I don't give him a quick release, our fuck won't last long at all.

"So, you're not *that* inexperienced, then?" I smile and flick my eyes back up to him. "You want to lose your virginity today, or do you just want to fool around?" I flutter my dark lashes for added dramatics, waiting for his response.

Please say lose your virginity.

He goes to speak, but he hesitates a moment, his face falling serious.

"Marcus." He whispers, and my heart sinks.

"Marcus isn't here. It's just you and me." I'm a fucking bitch. I should have picked someone else to be my prey instead of going for one of Marcus' best mates… again. Fucking hell. A decent girl would back away. Convince him to leave and never speak of this again. Me though? I'm being ruled by Kitty. She has no interest in emotions, only pleasure.

"I… He…" Simon is clearly conflicted, which makes it even harder because he's a good guy. He doesn't want to hurt his mate. The problem is, I know all too well that a lot of guys are weak when it comes to refusing a naked chick.

"Marcus and I were never a thing. I'm only interested in sex, Simon. I don't want to marry you, so you need to decide. Are we doing this?"

His face shows how torn he is. He thinks over my words for a few long moments before he comes to a decision, standing taller and puffing his bare chest out.

"Make me a man, George." His words are confident, and I waste no more time. He's given his consent. There's no need to hold back any longer.

Reaching for the waistband of his boxers, I ease them down, his hard length popping free right before my face. My oh my, the Hastinator's cock is deliciously pretty in all its stone-hard glory. By the time I've tugged his boxers all the way down, pre-cum is balling at his tip, so I glide my hands up the coarse hair on his thighs before taking his straining dick in my hand and guiding it to my lips. Simon sucks in a sharp breath when my tongue flicks out to lick the salty goodness from his tip, and then I ease him past my black lips and into the heat of my mouth.

Not even fifteen minutes ago, I was trembling, trying to hide how anxious and worked up I was. Now, there is no tremble in my hands. No anxiety in my chest. No worry building to panic. Now, I'm in my happy place.

Simon bucks when I slowly draw him from my mouth, only to glide him back in. He's right. This won't take long, which is good because Kitty is practically begging to be touched.

I work my hand up and down his length as I slide him in and out of my mouth, my tongue gliding over the bulging veins and ridge of his head. Some people think that falling to your knees for someone is weak. They are wrong. It's powerful. And right now, I have the power over Simon. I have the power to make him feel good and push him over the edge to lose some of his control. I also have the power to end his pleasure if I wish. I don't wish that, though. No fucking way. Simon's pleasure is my pleasure, and when I feel his legs start to quake, I know he's about to soar.

"Fuck, I'm going to come." He hisses, his eyes latched onto mine as he watches himself disappear between my lips.

I pick up the pace a little, dragging my tongue over his shaft with each draw back, and the moment my hands find his swelling balls, he shouts out, his hands gripping either side of my head. Hot cum pulses into my mouth over and over as he loses any restraint he had, and like a good girl, I drink him down until there's not a single drop left.

The deep, breathless pants coming from Simon fill the darkroom's small space, and after a moment, he gazes lazily down at me. I drag his cock out of my mouth and lick it clean, not leaving a drop of his come behind, and he gently strokes a stray dark hair back off my face that's escaped my buns.

"Do you have any idea how long I've dreamed of doing that with you?" His words take me by surprise, and I sit back a little to peer up at his face better.

"Uh. No." I mean, sure, I've noticed Simon eye-fucking me numerous times over the last couple of months, but I didn't think he actually thought much about me.

"Before you and Lexi became friends. That's how long. Those black lips are so fuckable, Rhys."

Now that's a compliment I can get behind.

"What else have you dreamed of doing with me?" I'm still on my knees, but the moment I finish that question, Simon bends and lifts me to stand.

"Simon says, get on the bench."

Kitty purrs.

I grin as my heart rate picks up. There's that anticipation I love. With his hands on my hips, Simon steers me toward the bench and lifts me onto the cool surface, which is a drastic contrast to how hot my skin feels right now. The moment I'm there, he steps between my parted knees, spreading them wider with his hands.

"Simon says, kiss me."

I grin before making a point of licking my black lips. Simon watches the move like he's under my spell, and then I slowly move in to press my lips to his. At first, his kiss is stiff and unsure, reminding me of his inexperience. I need him willing and relaxed, so I slip my tongue past his lips, into his mouth, and just like that, he melts. As our tongues get to know each other, I feel the muscles in his back loosen as he relaxes into the kiss, his hand moving to cup the back of my neck, holding me in place.

We get lost in the kiss, which starts out sweet and morphs into desperation. Simon's hands roam over my curves like he's not sure where he's allowed to touch me, and because I'm impatient, I break the kiss and grab his hands, guiding one to cup my aching tit and the other to palm over my throbbing clit.

That's all the invitation he needs.

"Simon says, lay down."

Oh, there's that voice again. It has power, that voice, working like magic to make Kitty cream. Grinning, I shuffle back and ease myself down on the bench-top before Simon hooks his fingers in my red panties, tearing them down with desperate need.

I'm not shy. I have no problem spreading my legs wide, giving him an all-access view of Kitty. I love eyes on me. I love knowing that I turn someone on. And right now, I love the way Simon looks at Kitty, licking his lips, his nostrils flaring, his eyes dark. Nearly lost.

"I'm probably going to come again while I do this." He admits, and my mind instantly flashes to Shaun the night before, doing the same thing as his mouth tore an orgasm from me. Kitty weeps even more.

"I don't care. Just do it. I need your mouth on me now."

With one last lust-filled look, Simon dives between my legs and glides his hot tongue right up the middle of my folds to my aching bud. There's just something so fucking erotic about the feel of a soft, moist tongue sweeping over the sensitive skin between my legs. This is something I love and something I'll never get sick of. My back arches as I revel in the feeling of the freedom Simon is allowing me right now. I've been walking the fine line of needing to come all day and to finally be in my place of happiness after feeling the ache so bad, I know that this won't take long.

I lift my hips to meet Simon's mouth through each movement, each swipe, each dip into my slit. My hand's fist into his blonde hair, and I glance down my mostly naked body to see his eyes on mine. He's watching me while he works Kitty into a frenzy. He's studying me to see if he's doing it right. To make sure he's making me feel good.

Hell yes, he is making me feel good.

"I'm close. You feel fucking amazing, Simon." I say the words before my panting increases, and his tongue dives into my entrance. "Yes."

Knowing what I need, I feel two fingers ease inside me as Simon makes out with my clit.

"More," I beg, and he adds a third finger, giving me the fullness I'm seeking. "Yes."

My voice is louder than it should be, and if there were a photography class outside the photo lab right now, I'd definitely be heard. But there isn't a period five photography class today, and right now, I wouldn't care if the entire school heard me. This feels too fucking good.

A few more thrusts of Simon's fingers and another flick of his tongue, and I soar to the clouds in an exploding orgasm. With my hands fisted tight in his hair, I ride his face, grinding for extra friction to drag out my release. Then I collapse into a floppy bundle.

Standing from between my legs, Simon shoots me a shit-eating grin before using his tongue to lick up my juices from around his mouth.

"That was... I can't even put it into words."

I grin. "Did you come again?" I prop myself up on my elbows, and he nods.

"All over the side of this bench." He drags his finger over something and then holds it up to show me his come. I throw my head back, laughing. Simon is fun.

"You still want to fuck me? Lose your virginity?" I give him another chance to bow out. Losing your virginity should be special, and the photo lab darkroom at Fox Pines Catholic is definitely not special. Not that I'd know about that. There was nothing special about when I lost my virginity. I didn't even know what virginity was when it happened.

"Simon says, take my virginity. Right here. Right now." He bites his bottom lip in the cutest way after speaking the words. Jesus, this guy does something weird to my heart. It flutters and flips and aches and races, and I'm pretty sure I might need to see a doctor soon. Maybe I have an underlying heart condition?

"Does Simon want me to take the lead, or does he want to do that?" I ask, and his brows knit together.

"I want to fuck you." That's all he says before snagging my legs in each hand and dragging me to the edge of the bench-top. Kitty peeks her head up again, and just like that, she's moist and ready to go.

"I have a condom in my blazer if you don't have one." I remind Simon because it looks like he's about ready to drive himself into me bareback.

"Oh yeah." He steps back, dragging his hand through his blonde hair. "Nah, all g. I have a dinger in my pocket." He moves quickly to his pile of clothes, ruffling through them to find the pocket. I can't hold back my grin. If he didn't look like a sex god with his ripped muscles and straining cock, I'd almost call him adorable.

He's back in a flash, tearing open the wrapper with his teeth before rolling on the protection. Then he looks up to meet my gaze.

"Fuck me, Simon. As hard as you want. Don't hold back. Do whatever makes you feel good."

"And that will feel good for you?" He's so unsure, but I like that he considers me in this scenario. He doesn't realise that a lot of my pleasure comes from people letting go completely to their animalistic needs. That fucking sends me wild.

"Yes. If it doesn't, I'll let you know."

With that, he nods and trains his eyes to Kitty as he lines himself up. The tip of his dick presses gently against my entrance, and with one last glance up at me to make sure this is ok, he slowly eases himself in.

"Fuuuck." He hisses, throwing his head back as Kitty squeezes him, but he quickly rights himself and looks back down to see his cock disappearing inside me.

"What does it feel like?" I pant, loving the fullness and the burning stretch.

"Tight. Hot. Heaven." He mutters as he drags himself out again before easing back in. Then, as if he's comfortable with how it feels, he starts to thrust. At first, it's a steady motion, not too hard or fast. I can tell he's feeling his way through this, learning what feels the best. While he's busy doing that, I use one hand to pull down the cup of my bra and start pinching my nipple between my fingers, raising my hips to meet each of his thrusts. His eyes dart up to see my exposed skin, and he tugs me forward, dropping his warm mouth to my nipple.

I arch back, moaning and loving the combined stimulation. It's all Simon needs to pick up his pace and add a little more force. As he lets go of his restraints, I do too, letting him know that I'm riding this high with him, completely and utterly crazed with need.

The sounds of our skin slapping together is an added turn on, and Simon's grunting pants are fucking sexy as hell as he lets his inner animal loose. I can tell he's close, and I want to fall over the edge with him, so while he holds me up with one arm wrapped around my back and the other digging fingers into the flesh of my arse, I slide my hand between our bodies and start working on my clit.

The moment I reach my peak and the intense pleasure crashes over me, Simon's dick pulses inside me as he joins me, filling the latex wrapped around his cock with his seed. Our thrusts ease off as my hearing returns, and our panting fills my ears. His heavy body crushes me to the bench-top as he loses the use of his limbs, and I can't hold back my satisfied smile at what we just shared.

If you had asked me this morning if I thought I'd be fucking Simon Hastings today, I would have laughed. But then again, if you had asked me yesterday morning if I would be coming in Shaun's mouth last night, then I'd have the same reaction.

"Rhys?" Simon mumbles into the crook of my neck, his breathing still heavy.

"Yeah?" I mumble just as breathless.

"If Marcus finds out what I just did, he's going to kill me."

Chapter Ten

Shaun

Hastings looks like he's walking on cloud nine, with the confident smirk he's wearing that screams *I'm invincible*, and his shaggy blonde hair more ruffled than usual. If I had to analyse it, I'd say he looks well fucked.

"Fucking hell. This shit is getting out of hand." Garrett grumbles next to me as he watches Simon swagger down the corridor with Rhys at his side.

Then I get this weird fucking feeling, right in the centre of my chest. I don't know what the fuck it is, but I don't fucking like it because surely it's not... jealousy?

"First you, and now Hastings. Fucking hell. Marcus is going to flip." Garrett adds before turning to his locker and slamming it shut.

"What? You think they..." I leave the sentence hanging when Garrett nods before I've even finished.

"Yep. He's wearing the glow of someone that's just lost his virginity. They went off together to ditch class. What else could his shit-eating grin be from?"

"What? Virginity? Simon's not a virgin." I scoff. Garrett has lost his mind.

"He's not a virgin *now*." Garrett turns to me with a 'duh' look on his expression, "but, before period five today, he was."

"Nah, man. He fucked that cougar nurse in Melbourne. And what about those other chicks? He nailed them."

Shaking his head, Garrett shoots me a look of pity. "Everyone assumed he nailed them. But he told me he didn't. He's had a couple of hand jobs, one blow job, and spent the rest of his time exploring chick's bodies with his mouth and hands. That's it."

My brows knit together, and I glance back at Simon, watching the way he looks down at Rhys with affection. Then, he leans down and whispers something in her ear, and when he pulls back, she grins and shoots him a sexy fucking wink.

Motherfucker!

Turning back to my locker, I grab my bag out and slam it shut in time for Simon to approach us.

"Fellas. What's cooking?" His cheesy grin is from ear to ear, highlighting the playfulness in his eyes. He almost looks drunk. Fucking hell. Gaz is right. Simon totally fucked Rhys.

"What did you and George get up to?" Garrett completely disregards Simon's question, asking his own.

"Just ditched." Simon shrugs like it's nothing.

"Where?" Garrett grills him, and Simon doesn't even pick up on the hostility in Cole's voice. He's too busy watching Rhys saunter past with Tillie.

"Photo lab," Simon answers, returning his gaze to us.

"So, you lost your virginity in the photo lab?" Garrett deadpans, and Simon's brows shoot up.

"Shhh, man." He darts his head around to see if anyone heard. "You'll ruin my rep if people realise I..." He leans in conspiratorially, "was a virgin this morning."

"Fuck." I can't hold back the growl in my tone, like some possessive arse hole that I'm not.

Right?

"Fuck, man. What about Marcus?" Garrett hisses, and Simon flinches, his post-sex glow vanishing in an instant.

It's kind of painful to stand here and witness the class clown as deep regret contorts his face. I know that regret. I also know how easy it was to forget about that regret once I was around Rhys again.

If Hastings really did just have his first lay, then he shouldn't feel like shit about it. Fuck Garrett Cole for making him feel that way.

"Hastings, man. I want all the deets later tonight. But before I go to detention, tell me one thing?" At my words, Simon's playful façade slowly eases back into place, his hazel eyes brightening in that typical Simon Hastings way. "Was it good?"

His grin turns into a blinding smile. Fuck, I don't think I've ever seen him smile like that before, and the fucker smiles all the damn time.

"If anyone ever says that something is better than sex, then they are either lying or haven't boned Rhys George." He tips his head back in a dramatic moan before dropping his eyes back to mine. "It was fucking epic."

Throwing my head back, I laugh, happy to know he enjoyed his first time. Meanwhile, Gaz groans in frustration, shaking his head at the both of us. Simon doesn't know what went down with Rhys and me, but Garrett does. I understand his reaction, but I struggle to remember why I should be reacting the same way. I'm pretty sure that makes me a fucked-up friend to Marcus. No. I know it makes me a fucked-up friend to Marcus. So why am I still eager as fuck to go to detention and see Rhys?

I leave Garrett and Simon by the lockers and head to the detention room, my eyes immediately seeking out those dark chocolate eyes and black lips that call to me like nothing else ever has. There are no seats left near Rhys, so I sit across the room from her so I can see her beautiful face while I take my phone out, opening up our messages.

Shaun Bossier
What did you and Simon get up to in the photo lab?

I glance up and bite back my grin as I watch her glance at her phone screen and then up to me when she sees I've sent her a message. Rhys doesn't hold back her smile, though. She flashes her white teeth at me before returning her eyes to her screen.

Rhys George
Oh, you know… Photo lab stuff.

Shaun Bossier
Sex is classed as photo lab stuff?

Rhys George
I don't know what you mean.

I glance up to see her shooting me a sweet innocent look, fluttering her black lashes.

Shaun Bossier
Sure you do.
You and Shaun did the deed last period.

Rhys George
Casanova, you should know me better than that!
I don't fuck and tell!

Shaun Bossier
You don't need to tell me. I already know.

Rhys George

If we did, and I'm not saying we did, does it make you jealous?

I can't hold back my chuckle, but the detention teacher, who I've seen before but don't remember his name, shoots me a glare that is meant to be threatening. It's really not. Someone needs to tell him to work on that.

Before I can respond to Rhys' message, Mr Foster, AKA fucking Skipper, walks into the room and speaks quietly with the teacher. A moment later, he glances up at the handful of students in the classroom serving their punishment.

"I need two volunteers to help me clean off some graffiti at the back of the stadium."

Hands shoot up around me, and I glance at Rhys to see that, like me, she hasn't got her hand up.

"Right, let me torture the two who couldn't be bothered volunteering. Mr Bossier. Miss George. Come with me."

Rhys rolls her eyes dramatically and groans, moving sluggishly like he really is torturing her. Fuck, she's a good little actress. I'll have to remember that.

Mr Foster holds the door open as I follow Rhys out, and we walk in silence as Mr F leads us to the stadium, through the empty courts, and onto the upper level into his office. Closing the door after we enter, he flicks the lock and draws the blind, leaving me to wonder how many times he's done this. Does he bring all his prey to his office and lock the doors to take advantage of them?

Anger swirls in my gut, reminding me of the fucked-up situation I'm in. Last night, I watched a man, an adult, fuck Rhys, who is only seventeen, in front of an audience. Sure, I didn't know it was my fucking PE teacher at the time, and I let myself think the situation was ok. But now that I know Skipper, Kitten's sponsor for Vixen's

Lodge, is Mr Foster, I'm struggling big time to see how she is ok with this.

"Calm down and take a seat, *Casanova*, before you blow a gasket." Mr Foster growls, taking in the anger reddening my face.

Rhys flicks a glance at me and rolls her eyes, plopping down lazily in one of the chairs in front of Mr Foster's desk.

"Chill Bossi. You're directing your hostility at the wrong person." Rhys sits back in the chair like she doesn't have a care in the world, and I watch as she directs her eyes to Mr Foster. They stare at each other for a few moments like a silent conversation passes between them.

With reluctance, I sit my arse in the chair next to Rhys and turn my eyes to Mr Foster as he eases into his chair behind the desk. He doesn't look at me. His eyes remain on Rhys, so I glance back at her. I don't know why I thought she didn't have a care in the world, though, because right now, the typically well composed, fun-loving girl I know has her eyes trained on her fidgeting fingers in her lap, looking like she has the weight of the world on her shoulders.

Shit. It reminds me of last night and the way she looked while she was forced into a conversation with Master Hill in the corner of his den. It was hard to tell exactly what her expressions were with the pretty skull that painted her face, but her eyes couldn't lie. She was worried last night, and she carries that same worry now.

"You want me to tell him?" Mr Foster asks Rhys, his deep voice cutting through the silence of his office.

She shakes her head, not looking up, taking a few deep breaths while her mind mulls over something I'm not yet privy to. It seems like she is struggling to say what needs to be said, so instead, I ask a question.

"Why am I directing my hostility at the wrong person?"

Finally, those chocolate eyes glance up through the thick fan of her lashes to look at me. It's even clearer now how anxious she is about telling me. This is very un-Rhys-like.

"Tyler isn't the predator in this room, Shaun. I am."

My frown is so intense it almost hurts as I take in her words. She's the predator? What?

Rhys can clearly see the confusion written across my expression, and she bites the inside of her cheek, fighting off a smirk.

"I'm gonna tell you a little story, Bossi. After you hear it, your opinion of me will change. Most likely, you'll keep your distance, which is understandable. But you will understand the situation, and you will understand that Tyler is not taking advantage of *me* and that what happened last night was a huge sacrifice on his part."

I'm still confused, but I don't say anything as I think over what she just said. I doubt that my opinion of Rhys could change so much that I'd want to keep my distance from her.

"Before I came to this school a couple of years ago, I went to Redfield High, where my foster mum was the principal at the time. She knew about my past when she fostered me, which, by the way, will *not* be involved in this conversation. She also knew I was already promiscuous, even at that young age. What she didn't know is that I preferred older conquests. Mainly because guys my age at the time knew nothing about giving me pleasure, only taking it. It was all about getting themselves off, which was usually very bloody fast." She smirks smugly, and I can't help but feel my own lips quirk. "I set my sights on two of my Redfield teachers. I figured out how to manipulate them before they realised it was happening, and I got what I wanted. What I was looking for. Each of them didn't know about the other. One a male, one a female. My experiences with them went on for a number of months before Cin caught on."

Rhys returns her eyes to her lap momentarily, like she is falling back into a memory.

"Knowing my past, Cin went against all her morals and covered it up. She asked the teachers to leave quietly and look for employment elsewhere, and she withdrew me from Redfield and sent me here. The terms she laid out to me for not getting punished were simple. Don't mess with any more teachers, and she will allow me more social freedoms to explore new friendships. That's what she calls the people I fuck. Friendships. As long as I'm safe and not getting into trouble, then she's happy."

My mouth is hanging open a little, but I snap it shut when she looks back up at me. I don't know what she just told me has to do with what's going on here, but that's a pretty damning revelation. She had sexual relationships with two of her teachers at her old school. Her foster mum found out and sent her here. And she's also cool with Rhys fucking people. It sounds weird as fuck, but for some reason, I know there is more to the story as to why her foster mum would allow that. It probably has everything to do with her past and what she said she *won't* talk about.

Fucking hell. What happened to her?

"Anyway, let's fast forward to what's relevant to this situation." Her tone perks up a little, "As you know, I like sex parties. The ones I used to go to were nothing more than orgies arranged by immature guys who wanted to use women and even humiliate them instead of sharing the pleasure and experience. I quickly learned that older guys were better, hence my sights on my Redfield teachers, so I started looking for sex parties that were more mature. I managed to talk one married couple into taking me to one of their swinger's nights, which was pretty fucking amazing, I might add, and after that, I just knew there had to be more parties that would be classier like that. More my style, just without all the married couples.

I found some in the city, but it was hard trying to explain to Cin why I wanted to go to the city all the time. Even though she gave me some freedoms, I wasn't about to admit that I go to sex parties with adults. The ones in the city also cost a lot to join, so it got tricky. Then one night, when I was in Redfield at The Railway Bar, a drunk guy was whining about being kicked out of some exclusive sex club. The hundred bucks I spent filling his veins with alcohol was worth it because he spilled all the juicy details."

Her grin is broad as she looks between Mr Foster and me. "Vixen's Lodge Feast Nights. Exclusive. Expensive. And anonymous. Exactly what I was looking for. I found out where it was and who Master

Hill and his wife were. The only thing I couldn't figure out was how to get into the club. I didn't have the membership fee, and the fact that I was fifteen at the time should have been another reason, but it wasn't. You see, this guy told me that they are known to have minors there. They get in by sponsorship, and even though everyone knows they are underage, no one addresses it. They all pretend like it doesn't happen. The guy told me that their old princess had come of age a couple of years ago, and they hadn't replaced her because of him. He had threatened to expose them unless they let him do some freaky thing, which he never told me about, and I have a feeling It's something I wouldn't want to know. Anyway, apparently, Master Hill got some dirt on him and used it to buy his silence and kick him out. Not that the idiot was silent that night.

So, I was left with needing to find a sponsor to introduce me to them. Then, one day after class, I came up to Mr Foster's desk to hand in my work, and I noticed a message pop up on his phone. He didn't know that I saw it at the time since he was busy with one of the other kids, but I saw the message from 'The Lodge', and it read, *here is confirmation of your booking at tonight's Feast.*"

Rhys glances up at Mr Foster now, but he has his eyes cast down, staring at his lap.

"Changed my message settings after that day so no little fuckers can read my messages when they pop up." His voice is a low grumble, and he looks nothing like the authority figure of my PE teacher.

"You see, Bossi. This is how I got in." She points to Mr Foster. "I cornered him in *this* very office. I told him I knew about the Feast Nights. I told him I wanted in and that he was going to be my sponsor. When he said no, I told him about my past at Redfield and that if he doesn't be my sponsor, I will tell Cynthia that I am having sex with him."

That's when I see it. Regret. Disgust. She hates herself for doing it. The remorse is only there for a moment on her face, but I see it plain as day before she masks it again.

"I am the predator here, Shaun. I blackmailed him until he said yes. I even doctored some provocative photos that look like him and me together. That's why he finally caved. He didn't want to say yes. He didn't want me to go to the place he openly fucks people. And until last night, he hasn't even touched me, even when I begged him to."

"You begged him to touch you?" I can't hide the surprise in my tone.

"I begged him to fuck me. You saw him rail that chick in the spa last night. Why the hell wouldn't I want some of that?" Rhys rolls her eyes at me like I should know better. The whole thing sounds a little too fucked up for what I'm used to. Does it make me want to run from her, though? No. No, it doesn't.

"Jesus Christ." Mr Foster rakes a frustrated hand over his face before tipping his head back to stare at the ceiling.

"But you were so conflicted last night, before you two…" I can't even say the words now that I'm face to face with Skipper, with no mask to hide his identity.

"I was conflicted because I know he never wanted to go there with me. Tyler has morals, even though it probably doesn't seem like it, given the situation. He agreed to be my sponsor on the condition I stay away from him sexually."

I scoff, "I saw you last night by the spa, Kitten. You were teasing the fuck out of him. I'm pretty sure the only reason he blew his load with that chick was because he was watching you."

Mr Foster growls, but Rhys shrugs and grins. "I never agreed not to be a brat. It's his fault for not being more specific when we made the agreement."

I glance back at Mr Foster, waiting for him to add his opinion, but he doesn't speak, his blue eyes dark as they remain fixed on Rhys. He can claim that he has morals all he likes, but that fucker likes her. He enjoyed fucking her last night, and I bet he's thinking about that right now, too. It should creep me out, but it doesn't. They may have stepped over a line last night, but he didn't do that without her best interests at heart, no matter how fucked up it sounds.

"I eavesdropped on some of the conversation you guys had with Master Hill last night, but at the time, I didn't understand what he was blackmailing you with. Now I get it." I feel both their eyes turn to me, and I see a little of the tension drop from Mr Foster's shoulders. I don't understand everything, but Master Hill must know Skipper is Kitten's school teacher. He forced them to do something they had been avoiding, and now he can hold that over their heads. But why?

"So now you know. Tyler isn't the predator here. I blackmailed and manipulated him into doing something he didn't want to do. He was tougher to crack than most people, which is why I had to resort to the threat of releasing photoshopped images. All he's guilty of is trying to save his own arse."

Rhys stands then, brushing her hand over her skirt before bending to pick up her school bag. She avoids my eyes as she walks past, beelining for the door, but stops with her hand on the knob to glance back at me.

"It's what I do, Bossi. I manipulate people into thinking they want to have sex with me. Just ask Simon. He'll think it was his idea, but we both know it wasn't. When he went into the photo lab with me, he honestly thought we were going to hang out and hide. He had no intention of doing anything sexual with me, let alone lose his virginity to me."

"Christ, I don't want to hear this." Mr Foster hisses, but Rhys ignores him, her eyes sad but her voice strong.

"It was easy, really. He made a joke about intimate lighting, and I agreed like it was a joke, asking him if he wanted to take his clothes off. Just like that, I insert an idea in his head. Naturally, because guys have a one-tracked mind, and the blood was probably already rushing to his dick at the mention of removing clothes, he pushed to see if I was serious. He acted gentlemanly, saying ladies first, hoping we were both on the same page."

Her tone is steady and serious, and while I don't need details on what happened between her and Simon, I know there's a reason she's telling me.

"It was perfect because I knew how much he likes playing games, so I used that to my advantage and suggested a game of removing an article of clothing for an article of clothing. That's the hook. He took it willingly, even though he was still unsure if I was being serious. Simon reminded me of how he likes party games that involve getting naked, and that's the point where he thinks he's the one who suggested it. He thought it was his idea, and when I went along with it, and the game began, he took over. That's when I knew my manipulation worked."

"Isn't that just normal flirting, though?" I ask because it sounds like it to me.

She shrugs, "It has that element, but the thing you need to remember is that he didn't go to that room wanting to fuck me. I, on the other hand, only took him to that room because I was horny and needed a fuck. He was never going to leave that room without getting me off. He thinks he wanted it, and I'm sure he did because what guy doesn't want to dip their dick in a chick? But if he had a choice of who his first root would be, I can assure you, Rhys George wouldn't have made the cut."

With that, she unlocks the door and exits the room so fast that I barely have time to register it. I dart my eyes back to Mr Foster, who looks concerned, a frown creasing his brow.

"Of course, she would have been on Simon's list. She didn't manipulate him." I spit, anger fuelling my words.

"Kid. I know that, and you know that, but Rhys George doesn't know that. Her currency is sex. She struggles to believe anyone actually likes her if something sexual hasn't been exchanged." Mr Foster stands from his chair and gestures to the door. An unspoken fuck off out of his office.

"But... Why?"

"Everyone has their demons. My guess is it has something to do with her past. But that's not our business." Mr Foster adds as I approach the door.

"What is our business, then?" Because fuck, this is a lot, and I know she thinks I'm going to think differently of her after her revelation, but I don't. If I am feeling any differently, it's more like I want to run to her, not away from her. Something I don't fucking understand for the simple fact that I'm a one fuck and then move on type of guy.

"Well, If she's someone you want In your life, then you gotta protect her." Mr Foster shoots me a pointed look. "Be there for when she falls because it will happen one day. And honestly, with her erratic behaviour lately, I have a feeling that day isn't too far away."

Chapter Eleven

RHYS

You know you've had a good night when you wake up cuddling your vibrator. Big Jim was sitting snug between the twins, AKA my tits, while Little Jim was under my thigh tangled in my sheets, and Pink Peter Rabbit was digging into my lower back. Did I watch three hours of non-stop porn while fucking my battery-operated love gods?

Duh! Yes!

Am I sated? No, I'm fucking famished!

My appetite is growing by the hour, and I'll be honest, it's freaking me out a little. Nothing good ever comes from having this insatiable randiness pulsing through my Kitty. In fact, I may have to rename her. She's becoming more of a vicious tiger than a fucking cute kitten.

To try and take the edge off before I leave for school, I rub myself up against any surface I can find in my bedroom and bathroom until I have extracted another four o's. It's a futile attempt. The only thing that will get me through longer than a class period is flesh on flesh. What I need is withering body against body. Lips clashing. Tongues dancing. Breath's mingling. I need a willing participant, and I haven't even been awake for more than two hours yet.

Fuck my life!

Arriving at school after ignoring Cin's grilling questions about my current state of mind, Garrett Cole, the mouth-watering tortured soul that broods quietly and rarely smiles, chooses today to get all up in my business. He bails me up before I can enter the building that houses my locker, towering over me like the hulk he is.

"George. Meet me in the gym at recess." He has no idea what his demand does to my insides, liquifying my Kitty to drip molten lava.

"Oooh. You're the dominating one, aren't you?" I let him see the mischief on my face as his icy blue eyes study me. It's cute that he tries to hide the grin tugging at the corner of his mouth. "If I say no, will you spank me?"

For a few moments, he doesn't speak. Those icy eyes pierce me, and my heart starts to race in anticipation. What is going through that head of his?

"If I say yes, I'll spank you. Will you show up?"

I can't help it; I throw my head back, laughing as I clutch my chest. "Touché, Mr Cole. But I need to know if I say yes, and I show up, will you *actually* spank me, or are you all talk?"

This time, he doesn't hold back his grin, and man, oh man, what a fucking piece of art it is to see that smile on his face. It's rare, like an exotic museum piece that only gets displayed once every ten years because no one wants anything to ruin its beauty.

"There's only one way to find out. You'd better turn up Rhys." With that final word, Garrett gives me his broad back, walking off into the sea of students that are hustling to get to their lockers before homeroom.

If I wasn't already burning up with a needy pussy before, then holy hell, it's on fire now. An inferno. Kitty is ravenous. I have a right mind to hunt Garrett Cole down and make him pay up on his threat. Or promise. I can't tell which way he was leaning with our brief conversation.

After homeroom, I throw myself into my photography classwork. It's one of the few things that keep my mind from falling too deep in the gutter, and since it's a double lesson and Lexi is in my class, I'm able to survive without dry humping any passers by.

We are working on our final portfolio piece, which I have basically finished, but Lexi came into the class late last term, and because of all the shit that went down with her family, she is behind. Naturally, Super Rhys comes to the rescue!

My portfolio is called 'Beauty in Darkness', and my pieces are black and white and so dark that the focal feature is the point of highlight on bare skin. No one knows the images are of me. My long dark hair and the use of the dark contrast hide my features. When I look at these photographs of myself, I see the beauty in them. In me. It's rare for me to see myself like that, but the way I captured myself really tells my story. It's a story only I know, but the intrigue in each image is what draws others in.

Since we are pressed for time, Lexi has chosen the simplicity of a single object. It's her butterfly knife. She told me that Muz, her gang thug enemy turned friend who died a few weeks back, had left it to her. She keeps it with her all the time now, even though the threat to her life is over. What happened to her haunts her. I can still see the dark circles under her eyes, probably from nightmares. I want to ask her, but with ears always ready to spread tea around the school, I decide to keep my questions for another time when we can talk properly.

When the bell for recess pings over the loudspeaker, my heart does an excited little flutter, knowing it's time to meet Garrett Cole in the gym. I know he's not going to spank me. That would be too easy, and there is nothing *easy* about Garrett Cole. But a girl can dream, and a Kitty can purr.

The school gym is new. Something my foster mum delegated to Mr Foster at the end of last term to get set up. With everything that happened to Lexi and the way she couldn't contain her rage, it was suggested that the school provide boxing bags so students can get their anger out in a safer way. So, Mr Foster, being Mr Foster, went all out with the budget he was given. He created a gym that not only has bags to beat up but weights and bikes to exhaust yourself on. I've considered coming here to exercise my pent-up horniness out by exhausting myself, but shit, I'd probably end up dry humping a fucking boxing bag with the way I'm feeling.

After entering the new gym that's been set up in an old storage area in the stadium, I glance around the practically empty space until my eyes land on taut, defined muscle. Hallelujah! Garrett Cole has his shirt off! Kitty practically leaps towards him like he's her prey, and fuck, I think she might be right.

"I wasn't sure if you were gonna show," Garrett speaks between the forceful punches he's delivering to the hanging bag.

Shit, that's hot.

"You dangled a spanking before me. As if I'd shy away from that."

Garrett stops hitting the bag and lowers his head while shaking it. His shoulders visibly shake with the quiet chuckle that floats across the room to me. Then he tips his head back and takes a deep breath before turning to me. There's a trail of sweat beading down his chest, and hell if my tongue doesn't crave to lick it up.

"I'm not going to spank you." His deep voice has a hint of humour in it as he pins me in place with those dominating eyes.

I pout. "I can be brattier if it helps?"

Again, he shakes his head at me like he can't believe my words. He can, though. He knows what I'm like. Everyone knows what I'm like.

"Come here." His tone is demanding, and I fight Kitty by keeping my feet firmly planted in place.

"Make me."

"Is everything sexual to you?" The rasp in his tone tells me I have affected him. Good!

"You know it," I say lightly, popping my hip and placing my hand on it, flashing him my teeth in a ridiculous smile.

His nostrils flare as he quietly studies me before he turns back to the bag and starts throwing punches again.

"I'm not going to make you, George. Come here or don't. I don't care either way."

Ouch. Kitty didn't like his words. Or his tone. So, of course, I go to him, not ready to end whatever this is.

"I think you do care." My words are quiet, but because I'm closer to him, he hears them and whirls on me with fury on his face.

"You're right! I do care! What game are you playing by fucking Marcus' mates?"

I take a few steps back, a little thrown by Garrett's sudden mood change. He follows me, though, looming over me with a fierce glare. "Don't try to deny it, George. First Bossi, and then Hastings. Are you trying to fucking rip Grady's heart out?"

The truth of Garrett's words is like a slap to my face, reminding me of who and what I am. Someone not worthy of Marcus. Not worthy of Shaun or Simon. My chest aches right in the centre, but in true Rhys George fashion, I use the only thing I've got.

"Why do *you* care, Cole? You want a piece too?"

Lightning fast, Garrett has my chin gripped painfully in his large hand as he tips my head back, drawing close to hover his lips just over mine.

"Even if I do, I will *never* do that to Marcus."

We remain there in a stand-off, eyes boring into each other's, lips a breath apart, desperate to meet but held back by honour.

"Are you going to tell Marcus about Shaun and Simon?" There's a quiver in my voice that I've never heard before. It's not fear. I'm not scared of Garrett. So, it can only be shame.

With force, Garrett pushes my face away and steps back from me, causing me to stumble.

"No. Not if you stop." He hisses between clenched teeth. "Even at that Lodge place you and Bossi go to. You can't hook up there either."

My brows practically shoot through the roof. "You know about Vixen's Lodge?"

"I don't know much, but I know enough," Garrett admits, and I spin away from him as anger heats my face.

I can't believe Bossi has divulged that confidential information. Not because I go there, but because the Feast nights are only successful because it's top secret. How dare he spill details about that place. Then again, can I talk? Tillie and Bell know about it. They don't know everything, but they know enough.

"I get it, you know." Garrett's voice is quieter this time, and he starts punching the bag again, so I turn back.

"Get what?"

"You, and why you go to that place. Why you act the way you do." He stops punching again to look at me. All the anger that was there moments ago, now gone.

"If you're about to call me a slut, Cole, save your breath. I know what I am, and I make no apologies for it."

His brows shoot up this time, surprised at my words.

"I wasn't going to say that, and *I* don't think that." His brows furrow like he's disappointed that I'd even suggest he'd think that way.

"Enlighten me then. I can't wait to hear your theory about me." I cross my arms over my chest and push out my black lips in a bratty pout while I wait for him to speak.

He shrugs. "I think you have an addiction to sex. I've seen the tells, Rhys. I had a cousin stay with me a few years back, and he was a heroin addict. You have similar tells, maybe just not as bad."

My pout is gone, my face neutral as I look at this all-knowing giant in front of me. When I don't respond, he continues.

"You're more erratic and agitated since you came back to school yesterday. Your hands tremble sometimes. I bet you haven't been able to concentrate on much, especially when your appetite gets bad. Yesterday you were agitated as fuck until you went off with Hastings. Afterwards, you were calmer. More refreshed. More focused. Tell me I'm wrong."

I don't tell him he's wrong or right because I can't fucking speak. No one has called me out on my addiction before besides the rents and my therapist, and even then, they don't class it as an addiction because there isn't enough research to prove that you can actually be addicted to sex. I guess researchers haven't met me.

"When you start feeling that way, I want you to come to me," Garrett says quietly, stepping closer to me, tilting my head up with a single finger pressed under my chin.

"To fuck?" It's a legitimate question.

Garrett's lips spread into a warm grin. "No. To punch stuff."

"To punch stuff?" I frown. "Is that a new kink I don't know about?"

Garrett shakes his head, stepping back and picks up a set of gloves before tossing them at me. On reflex, I catch them.

"Put them on, and start punching the bag, George."

"I'd rather fuck." I pout.

"No fucking. You're agitated now. You need to fuck now, so instead, punch the bag." Garrett points a stern finger towards the bag closest to me.

"Fucking sounds like more fun," I whine like a little bitch. "I'm pretty sure punching something isn't going to give me the dopamine neurochemical brain high I need, Garrett."

"Give it a try. You never know." He insists and turns back to his bag.

I could be a bigger brat and throw the gloves down, stomp my foot and demand he spank me, but honestly, there's a part of me that hates how he looked at me before with such disappointment at screwing his two friends. I kind of feel like I want to please him, and the only way I can do that isn't by falling to my knees. At least not right now.

Right now, I need to punch the bag like a good girl.

Tugging on the gloves, I unhygienically use my teeth to pull the second one on properly. Let's be honest. It's not like I haven't put worse in my mouth before. Once the gloves are in place, I approach the bag nearest to me and widen my stance before throwing my first punch. I land a good hit, but I get no relief from it. Kitty is still circling, waiting to pounce. So, I throw another punch, and another, and another. I hit the bag over and over, yet I get no relief.

I let out a frustrated growl and turn a murderous glare toward Garrett.

"Hey, big guy. It's not working. It's making me worse."

Garrett stops mid-punch, turning to glare back at me.

"What's that glare for? I can't help it if I find punching things incredibly hot. This has had the opposite effect on me." I'm about five seconds away from leaping on him and climbing the big guy like a tree. Fuck, why does that sound so hot?

"You're not trying hard enough." He hisses, so I throw my gloved hands up in the air.

"Dude, if I try any harder, I'm going to end up grinding myself against the bag until I come. Is that what you want?"

"Fucking hell." Garrett hisses under his breath, turning away from me right as the bell goes, indicating the end of recess.

I try to tug my gloves off without success, which just makes me more frustrated, but a moment later, Garrett's large feet come into view, and I forget what I was frustrated about. Reaching down, he helps me out of the gloves with a jerking tug, his icy blue eyes flicking to mine.

"I don't suppose you could lend me your fingers for a couple of minutes?" I sound like I'm joking. Garrett knows better, though, shaking his head at me once again.

"I'm not touching you, George. You'll have to find another way to get yourself off."

I spin on my heel and head towards the exit, with Garrett only a few steps behind me.

"Fine. I will."

Once I pass through the exit, I storm towards the toilets on a mission to calm the raging inferno bubbling under my skin. I hear Garrett call out to me. Something about being late for class, but I couldn't care less about being tardy for Pastoral Care. I barge through the heavy door of the girl's bathroom, happy to see that the small space is empty, with all stalls open and unoccupied.

Taking the first stall, I slam it shut, flicking the lock before slamming my hand between my legs. I can't hold back my moan as I rub friction over the barrier of my clothing, igniting a delicious ache that needs more and more. When the squeak of the heavy bathroom entry door swings open, I ignore it and whoever may be entering. I don't give a fuck if they hear me find my release. If they don't like it, then they can go pee somewhere else.

"You're going to be late, George." Garrett's deep voice comes from the direction of the bathroom doorway, and it sends a shiver up my spine from just hearing his deep rumble.

Applying a faster pace to my rubbing, I grind my Kitty over and over. "Unless you're going to join me in here, Cole, you should probably leave." My voice is breathy as I speak, feeling a knowing heat creep slowly over my skin.

"I'm not going anywhere," Garrett grumbles, and I tip my head back against the stall wall, loving the aggressive tone of his voice.

"Why?"

"Because you have a class with Hastings now, and I need to know you won't try to coerce him away again."

Well, damn. He really does know me. And much better than I thought because I already sussed out if the photo lab is free for period three in case I needed to use it. Alternatively, I could take Simon to the toilets. It's a bit more restrictive, but I'm resourceful.

"If you don't leave, you're going to hear me come. Is that what you want?"

"What I want is to know you've done the deed, so we can hurry up and get to class." Garrett hisses, but it lacks the frustration his voice held before. I could be wrong, but it almost sounds as if he's excited to hear me come.

"Help me then, or I'm going to need more time. It's not the same when I do it to myself."

When Garrett doesn't respond, I worry he's bailed, but then his voice comes from just on the other side of the stall door. He's right there.

"What are you doing to yourself right now?"

Kitty purrs.

"I'm rubbing myself."

"Over your clothes?" He asks, and I moan at the gravel laced in his tone.

"Yes." I pant.

"Slide your hand into your panties." He orders with that dominating tone, and fuck me, I feel myself gush.

"Ok." With eager movements, I tug out my school shirt and slide my hand down the front of my skirt and into my soaking knickers. When my fingers brush over my aching bundle of nerves, I release another moan, and I hear Garrett's sharp intake of air on the other side of the door. "I'm so wet."

"Shit." I hear Garrett whisper, and I grin. Fucking A, I grin. He may not want to touch me, but he's involved in this with me right now, and that's close enough to what I need. Garrett clears his throat. "Does it feel good?"

"Oh, yeah. It feels fucking amazing." I moan again, not needing to fake it because it does feel amazing.

"Are you rubbing your clit?" He asks, and I nod, even though he can't see me.

"Yes."

"Slide three fingers into your pussy." He demands, and my Kitty pulses, nearly ready to explode.

Doing as I'm told, I widen my stance, ease my fingers through my folds, and push them inside myself, loving the stretch. I'm moaning like a wanton whore now, and I hear Garrett quietly curse again.

"Use your thumb on your clit."

Fuck, his voice is sexy as hell. I do as he says, and it's all I need. With my fingers curling and my thumb flicking, my pleasure builds quickly with ecstasy, slamming into me in a crash of waves. I take a few seconds to revel in the feeling before returning to reality.

I'm desperate to share this moment with Garrett, but I'm scared he's about to flee, so I use my free hand to quickly unlock the stall door, pushing it open abruptly. With my right hand still down the front of my skirt, delved into my heat, I stare at Garrett, expecting him to shy away or bolt. He doesn't. His hands are braced on either side of the door, and those icy blue eyes of his burn with desire as he takes in my state, glancing past the brown curls that partially block his view. Then, as he watches, I slowly drag my hand out, lifting it between us to show my glistening fingers.

"You wanna taste?" I quirk my brow, hoping like hell that he'll say yes, but he keeps his mouth shut, only giving his head a slight shake. I shrug. "More for me then." His eyes widen as I part my black lips and sink my three wet fingers deep into my mouth, closing over them and sucking them clean.

Garrett's nostrils flare as he watches my every move, and once I've thoroughly licked each finger clean, he pushes back from the stall.

"Tuck yourself In, and let's go. We're late for class."

Chapter Twelve

RHYS

P astoral Care class is bullshit. I don't even understand why we have this class, but I use it to my advantage, zoning out with my mellow mood, all thanks to my narrated masturbation session with Garrett. Unfortunately, my calmness reminds me of the real issue, which is Marcus, and what I've done that I know will hurt him.

It's rare for me to hit lows like this, to dwell on things and let them bother me. I keep myself serviced enough sexually that it's usually hard for me to feel the ache of my shame and guilt. Today, however, it's really digging its claws in. It's so bad that I feel like everyone will see it written across my face.

Rhys George. Slut. Whore. Friendship destroyer.

Shame! Shame! Shame!

Laying my head on my hands on top of my desk, I pretend I'm too tired to do any work, and I peek at Simon sitting next to Allister on the next table over. He blushed when I walked into class earlier. Not shyly, though. No, Simon Hastings is anything but shy. He likes attention. He enjoys being the centre of it. So, his spine was straight with confidence, and his grin was mischievous, causing those hazel eyes to almost seem green. Even though he was blushing, he still shot me a wink that held promises I so desperately want to explore, yet I can't. Not just because Garrett asked me not to, but because I know in my heart that what I'm doing to Marcus is cruel.

I care about Marcus. I know I do. I know I still want him, but it's not enough. I hate that I'm like this. I really wish I could fall in deep with one guy and be happy. He might not realise it now, but putting distance between us is what's best for him in the long run.

When my phone vibrates with a message, I move like a sloth to pull my phone from my blazer. My mood is too flat to find the energy to sit up, so I rest my chin on the tabletop and reach my arms out in front of me, holding my phone up.

Simon Hastings
What's wrong with my girl?

Guilt slams into me as I read his words. Not because I don't like him thinking that way, but because I *do* like him thinking that way. I love the thought of being his girl. I also love the idea of being Marcus' girl and Shaun's girl, and dare I say it? Garrett's girl.

I am so screwed.

Rhys George
I'm all g! Just a little tired today.

Simon Hastings
Did I wear you out yesterday?

Rhys George
I think you did!

Simon Hastings

Simon says, smile!

I can't hold back the grin that morphs my face, and I turn my head on the cool surface of the table to see Simon watching me, his lips turning up at seeing my smile. Then he mouths, "That's better."

Damn. I like this feeling. It's kind of strange and reminds me of the term 'having butterflies in your stomach'. Marcus made me feel like this a few times, too. I tried to ignore it because Rhys George doesn't do rainbows and butterflies. Rhys George does spreader bars and strap-ons!

When my phone vibrates with a message again, I assume it's Simon and smile as I check the message. Oh, how wrong I am.

Fuck You Julie

Why haven't you been to see Brian yet?
How can you treat him this way after he loved and cared for you so much?
Visit him by the time this weekend is through, or there will be consequences.

The blood in my veins freezes as I read the message from my old foster mum, Julie Bates.

Rhys George

I have no way of getting there!

Fuck You Julie

Not my problem, Patrice.
Just make it fucking happen!

Heat explodes through my body as my head spins, and the walls of this stuffy classroom feel like they are closing in on me. No one has called me Patrice since the night the cops grilled me for five hours when I was thirteen years old. I'd been so scared, and all I wanted was to go back home, but then Child Services took me and placed me in a group home. And once again, I was back in the system.

After I was dragged away from Brian, I defiantly refused to acknowledge the name on my birth certificate. I either ignored people who called me Patrice or corrected them. From that day, I referred to myself as Rhys. It's one of the few good memories I have of my birth mum. She shortened Patrice to Rhys when I was little, and I found out later from a therapist that it was my way of taking back my control when others had decided who I could and couldn't live with.

Seeing my real name isn't the most significant issue here, though. For some reason, Julie is demanding that I visit Brian in prison. I haven't seen him since that night four years ago. I'd thought he would've forgotten about me by now. And the sick, twisted part is, I don't know if I'm happy or sad about it.

My therapists have spent so many hours trying to drum into my head that what Brian did was wrong. And a part of me knows they are right, but there's a part of me that doesn't see my time in Brian and Julie's care as wrong. How could it be wrong when it felt so right?

When the bell goes, I fly out of my seat, ignoring Bell and Allister when they call out to me, and I stalk through the busy corridors, slamming my shoulders into anyone that doesn't get out of my fucking way. I debate if I should go to English class or just bail on school altogether. I should probably leave. I feel like a loose cannon right now. The calm I had after recess has vanished, and in its place is pure need. It's so fucked. Why does my body respond like this?

Standing in the doorway of my English class, I take one look inside and decide to go with plan B. It's time to leave. I'm about to turn and haul arse out of there when a firm hand lands on my shoulder.

"Keep moving, George. You're blocking the doorway."

The warmth of Shaun's hand seeps through my blazer and slightly eases my spiralling, causing my feet to move forward into the room, even though I want to leave. I should turn and run like a bat out of hell, yet I can't. It's like he has some sort of power over me, controlling me like a puppet, bending me to his will. And fuck, Kitty shakes her horny little arse, eager to please Casanova.

Traitor!

With his hand still on my shoulder, Shaun leads me to a row of joined tables up the back of the classroom and pulls out a seat. Like a fucking lust drunk zombie, I sit my arse in the chair, wishing like hell that everyone in this class would disappear so I could have some alone time with Bossi.

Dropping his books onto the table next to me, Shaun pulls out the chair, ready to sit, but before he can, Garrett pushes Shaun out of the way and slides his books over to the other table adjoining it, stealing his seat.

"What the fuck, man!" Shaun protests, glaring at the back of Garrett's head, but Garrett ignores him, keeping his eyes trained on me with a raised brow.

I don't give him anything, keeping my face neutral and hoping he can't see my inner turmoil. Garrett Cole must be a fucking mind reader, though, because he sees straight through my façade.

"What's happened?" He whispers, leaning closer to me, ignoring Shaun as he huffs and throws himself down in the seat on the other side of Garrett.

My lips part to answer Garrett, but then I snap them shut.

What the fuck, Rhys?

Was I really about to tell him about Brian and Julie? Hardly anyone knows about them. Not even Tillie or Bell know much about my past. Cynthia and Will know. They knew before deciding to foster me. My therapist knows, obviously. But Garrett Cole is someone I hardly know. Why the fuck was I about to tell him about the messages I've been getting?

Shaking my head, I drag my eyes from Garrett's piercing blue gaze, turning my focus on my book and laptop, getting things set up before Miss Fletcher starts the class.

"Rhys?" Garrett whispers in my ear, and my lids flutter shut as I take a moment to let his scent wrap around me. It's clean and fresh with a hint of spice. It's calming.

Without looking at him, I whisper my response.

"I'm fine."

"Liar." He hisses quietly, and I can't stop my head from snapping in his direction, my eyes glaring.

"Excuse me?" My dark brows are high on my head as I take in his scrutinizing expression. Then he leans in close.

"Rhys, when I left you at the start of last period, you were calm. Sated. Now, you're agitated."

"I am not!" I snap back, gaining Shaun's attention, his steel-grey eyes peeking at me as he leans back in his chair.

"Then why are you trembling?" To prove his point, Garrett takes my shaking hand in his under the table.

Shit!

I try to snatch my hand back, but Garrett holds tight.

"What's happened?" He asks again, and I suddenly find it hard to breathe. I shake my head, eyeing Shaun, who is still watching me, and I turn back to my laptop.

The scrape of a chair draws my attention, and I watch as Shaun stands with his books and whispers something in Garrett's ear. Garrett glares up at Bossi and shakes his head, but Shaun clenches his teeth, turning a deadly glare at his friend.

"Move, or I'll fucking make you."

Uh… ok. Angry Shaun is kinda hotter than regular Shaun. Didn't know it was possible, yet here we are.

Grumbling under his breath, Garrett drops my hand and shifts over to the seat that Shaun had occupied. I have no idea what's going on, but a moment later, Shaun drags the chair out that Garrett had been sitting on and pushes it behind him before leaning down and shifting my chair, with me still on it, into the spot that Garrett had been sitting. My mouth drops open because what the fuck is he doing? But then he slides my laptop and books over in front of me before dragging the spare chair into the now vacant spot. The next moment, Shaun drops his stuff on the table and sits down, leaving me with Shaun on one side and Garrett on the other. The cheeky smirk Shaun shoots me as he gets comfy is fucking panty-melting, and a slither of peace eases past my pent up anxiety.

"For fuck's sake," Garrett grumbles, and I reluctantly drag my eyes from Shaun, looking to my left to take in Garrett's expression. He's pissed, and it's a reminder of what I'm doing to Marcus.

I kinda hate Garrett right now. How dare he call me out! I mean, I knew what I was doing wasn't good, but I was quite happy pretending to be in denial about it all. I wish I could be different. I wish I could get what I need from someone else. Someone Marcus doesn't know. And I did try, but I hadn't counted on running into Bossi at the Feast night. It's what changed things for me. Finally, getting a taste of Fox Pines Spanish Casanova opened the door I had tried really hard to keep shut. Add to that some alone time with Simon, and any control I've had has gone right out the window. I was controlled by my need, and nothing else mattered.

Miss Fletcher starts the class, drawing our attention, yet I hear nothing she says. I stare absently towards the front of the room, not taking anything in. All I can think about is how close Shaun is. How close Garrett is. Garrett told me to stay away from Shaun and Simon, yet he joined in with my finger bash in the bathroom earlier. He may not have touched me, and he may not have seen me, but that doesn't mean he is innocent. Garrett was there in that room with me. I didn't ask him to do that, yet he did. In the end, it was his demands, telling me what to do to myself, that took me to where I needed to go. He stood on the other side of that cubicle door, listening to my panting, my moaning, to whatever sound I made when I came on my own fingers.

A warm hand lands on my left leg, and I turn my gaze to Garrett with a quirked brow.

"Your leg is jigging around like a jumping jack." His deep voice is quiet but loud enough that Shaun hears, and I feel him shift in his seat next to me before he rests his hand on my other leg.

I moan.

"Fuck." Shaun and Garrett both whisper, and I relax back in my chair, loving their warmth seeping into my bare skin.

I fight really fucking hard not to spread my legs apart in an invitation to the both of them. I hold strong because their hands, their touch, is keeping me grounded. Yes, I'm still horny, but I feel less like I'm about to spiral out of control with the way the heat from their palms warms my skin.

When Garrett moves to lift his hand off my leg, I slap my hand over the top of his, keeping it pressed to my thigh as our eyes meet. I give the slightest shake of my head, hoping like hell that he understands my silent plea, and a moment later, his palm relaxes again, so I move my hand back to rest on the tabletop.

This is how I spend my English class, with Garrett's warm palm on one leg and Shaun's on the other. I still don't hear a word Miss Fletcher says, but at least I find some sort of calm which temporarily eases my trembling.

Towards the end of the class, my phone vibrates with a message. I'm not sure if it's worth checking or not. It could be from Julie again. I don't think I can handle another message from her right now. Not while I'm so highly strung, but curiosity gets the better of me. So I flip my phone over on the table and, with relief, see that it isn't a message from Julie.

Marcus Grady
I owe you an apology.
I'm so fucking sorry for what I said yesterday.

Marcus' comment yesterday has been playing on repeat in my head.

"What vibe is that? Everyone's welcome?"

He said it because he's hurt, and he knows I don't want to commit to a relationship with him. He knows I just want to sleep around and have no-strings fun. Unfortunately, he wants the opposite. His words shouldn't have affected me the way they did. There's just something that kills my light at the thought of Marcus thinking I'm the slut I actually am.

Rhys George
All g, Grady. You didn't say anything that isn't true.

Marcus Grady
Don't say that. It's not true.

Rhys George
Marcus, I know you feel bad.
Of course, you do. You're a great guy.
Kind and sweet.
But please don't forget who I am.
It was pretty accurate, actually.
Everyone's welcome… You know I'd be into that. It's no lie.

It takes a few minutes for Marcus to reply. He's probably struggling with a response. I never came out and said to him that I like group sex, but I did throw hints a time or two. I had been hoping he'd be into it. It could have meant our time together could have been extended. But he only has eyes for me, and I'm pretty sure he'd kill any other guy or girl that tries to touch me.

Marcus Grady
Still, it was an arsehole thing to say.

Rhys George
Stop. It's fine, Marcus.

Marcus Grady
I was wondering… Could we maybe catch up tonight or after school?
To chat.

While Marcus says the word chat, what he's really hoping is that we will hook up and fuck. I'd really like that, even though I know I shouldn't. It would only confuse him. Make him think he has a chance. Make him think I'm committing myself to him when all I want is some Marcus sexy time. Because it *really* is sexy time. He is an all-consuming lover. It's like he worships me with each encounter we have together. What girl doesn't love that? I do, but shit, it confuses me. The feelings that guy draws out of me isn't something I'm used to, which is exactly why I need to steer clear of him.

Rhys George
Sorry. Busy tonight.

Marcus Grady
How about tomorrow night?

He's not going to give up. I don't know what to do. How can I make him understand that what we had is over?

Rhys George
I'm busy tomorrow night too.
Sorry, gtg.

Like a coward, I jump out of the conversation and slip my phone back into my blazer just as the bell goes. The slight bit of calmness I felt before is slipping again. The combination of Marcus' messages and the fact that Garrett and Shaun have removed their hands from my thighs to pack up their books has brought back my jitters.

"You ok, George?" Shaun asks, shooting me one of his sexy Spanish grins.

I don't respond because if I say I'm ok, they will see straight through the lie, so I focus on gathering up my things before turning to see them both waiting for me.

I'm rooted on the spot as I take them both in. They could almost be brothers. Garrett is taller than Bossi, but they have similar brown curls, and their eyes are a shade of blue. Shaun's are greyer than Garrett's icy blues, though, but they both have similar sharp jawlines. Shaun's face is shorter and a little rounder than Garrett's longer heart shape. Their skin is notably different. Shaun's skin glows with his Spanish heritage, whereas Garrett's is paler, with a faint tan.

"I need you guys to do me a favour." Damn, my voice lacks my usual confidence. I'm so fucking rattled today.

"Anything," Shaun replies, still grinning at me.

Garrett doesn't reply. He just waits quietly for me to continue.

"If I message Marcus and tell him to meet me somewhere, I need you guys to run interference."

Shaun's grin drops as he takes in my request, but Garrett speaks.

"You want us to stop him from coming to meet you?"

I nod. "Yep. No matter what I tell him to get his attention, don't let him come to me. Do whatever it takes."

Shaun frowns. "If you don't want to do that, then why would you message him?"

"We can do that for you." Garrett ignores Shaun, already understanding why I'm asking them to do this for me.

"Thanks." I offer a black-lipped smile, but Shaun is still frowning.

"I'm confused."

I sigh, wishing I didn't have to make this admission. "I'm weak, Bossi. I'm trying to do right by Marcus and keep my distance because I can't give him what he wants. But when he's nice to me, I find it hard not to want to jump his bones, and I'm a horny bitch." I raise a brow. "Ok?"

Shaun grins again. "Got it. We'll make sure he doesn't come to you. Whatever it takes."

Chapter Thirteen

Shaun

Something isn't right with Rhys. She's even more edgy than usual, which I didn't know was possible because that chick is a ball of energy most of the time. Yesterday, it felt like she was a little more on edge at times, but today it's off the charts. I'm not even sure if she's aware of it, but she was trembling when we were in English class. Garrett noticed it before I did, which pissed me off. He's been acting like my dad, telling me to stay away from her, yet here he is, fucking putting his hands on her.

Rhys fled to the back of the school to hang with her other friends for lunch. Garrett grumbled something about her needing to go to the gym instead of hanging out with those potheads. I don't know what that was about, but I *do* know Rhys smokes her fill of Mary Jane on a daily basis, which usually mellows her. Maybe she skipped it this morning before school?

I've been hovering around Marcus all lunch, taking my promise to Rhys seriously. If she messages him, I need to run interference. So, when I notice his phone light up on the table next to me with a message, I glance over to where he's wrestling Hastings on the grass before snatching up his phone.

Marcus is one of those people who uses their birth date as their phone password, so I quickly type in 290402 and open up the phone. Sure enough, Rhys has sent him a message.

Rhys George
I've changed my mind about catching up.
I can't wait, though. Wanna ditch Maths and meet me
in the photo lab?

I feel like a prick for what I'm about to do, but she practically begged Garrett and me to stop this from happening, and she had a point. If she keeps hooking up with Grady, then he'll never get over her. The only thing is, I can't leave her hanging. At least that's what I tell myself. So, I respond on Marcus' phone.

Marcus Grady
Sure! I'll meet you there!

After I hit send, I glance up to see Marcus and Simon still wrestling, so I slip Marcus' phone into my pocket, alongside my own, and bail, heading to the dunny just as the bell rings. I take my time in the bathroom, taking a piss and washing my hands a little longer than I usually would, trying to drag it out so Rhys has time to go to the photo lab before I surprise her.

My plan could backfire. She wants Grady, but she's getting Casa-fucking-nova. I'm sure I can make her forget about him for a little while. Hopefully, if she's mad, she'll just angry fuck me. I'll be happy either way.

Once the halls are quieter and most students have made their way to their period five classes, I hustle across the quad to the arts centre and make my way to the photography unit. I've been here before. I kissed Marcy Gilmore in the darkroom back in year 9. Even got a handful of her tits before the teacher sprung us. I had to hold my textbook in front of my junk to hide Thor until he went back to sleep. The guys pissed themselves laughing for days about that. Fuckers!

I wrap my knuckles on the darkroom door, noticing the occupied light is on. I really fucking hope it's Rhys in there and not a teacher. I'll have to make up some bullshit for being here if Rhys isn't the one inside.

When the door swings open, Rhys' black smile comes into view, but it immediately drops as her confusion takes over and a frown draws in her dark brows.

"Ah… Hey Bossi."

"Hey, George." I grin, leaning my arm on the door frame while I wait for her to step aside and let me in.

"What are you doing here?" She looks over my shoulder nervously, as if she's worried Marcus will approach and wonder why I'm here. I could tease her a little, make her sweat in her boots, but her unusual mood has me re-thinking it.

"You said, do whatever it takes. So, I did. I stole Grady's phone. He never got your message."

Her dark eyes dart between each of mine as she considers my words.

"It was you who replied?" Her voice is soft and unsure, so I nod, feeling like I may have made a mistake. But then she nods and pushes the door open, stepping aside.

I watch her face as insecurity sweeps over her expression, and I join her in the room. It's very un-Rhys-like, and I don't like seeing it there. It's out of place on her beautiful face. When the door clicks shut, and the sound of the lock bounces around the small space, I turn to look at her nervously.

I think I've fucked up.

"Look, if I've overstepped, I'm sorry. I was trying to do what you asked me to do." I place my finger under her chin, lifting it so her eyes find mine. I hate seeing Rhys like this.

"It's fine." She shakes her head.

"It's not really. You're disappointed that I showed up, and not Marcus."

"I am disappointed, but only because I'm weak and I've been sprung." She rolls her tongue in her mouth, obviously struggling with her feelings. I can't help it. I step closer, tugging her flush against me, and I love how she automatically melts into my hold.

"Kitten." My voice is low as I stroke a thumb over her cheek, "I'm here to help. If you have an itch, let Casanova scratch it."

Her black lips spread wide, and her teeth make an appearance in a more confident grin that is more Rhys worthy.

"Shouldn't you wait until tomorrow night's Feast?" She asks, all while running her hand up to rest over my chest. I can feel the heat of her hand through my school shirt, and fuck, it takes everything in me not to rip this uptight fucking uniform off.

"But Kitten is hungry now. Isn't she?"

"She is." Her voice is breathy as she presses herself tighter against me, and there's no way I can hide Thor. He's practically tearing his way out of my jocks.

I haven't fucked Rhys yet. Even Hastings beat me to that, the cheeky fucker! She did come apart on my mouth and fingers, though. And she has swallowed my cum down like it was a tasty treat, so I shouldn't complain, but having Rhys George under me, coming around my cock is a fucking wet dream that plagues me. I need this with her. Bad.

"Let me feed Kitten then," I whisper as I lean forward, hovering my lips over hers. I wait patiently, needing her to make the final call to do this. To decide to step over this line that I know has consequences, yet I can't seem to stop.

A moment later, Rhys closes the distance. Her soft lips meet mine in a kiss that starts slow and sensual but quickly becomes a frenzy of need. Our hands tear at each other's clothing as we rip piece by piece off until we are nothing but flesh on flesh.

Grazing my hand down her side, savouring her soft skin searing with heat, I wrap my hand around her thigh and lift it, hooking her leg around my hip. My cock nudges against her wet heat with a mind of its own.

Calm down, boy. Not yet.

Her moan is loud as the head of my cock grazes over her sensitive clit, so I push the big fella out of the way and replace the motion with my fingers. Rhys moans again. Louder this time.

"You're so fucking wet, Kitten. Is that all for me, or is some of that for Marcus?"

She bites my lip. Hard. The metallic taste of blood trickles into my mouth, and I'm about to pull back, not wanting to freak her out, but the little minx follows me, licking at the small wound she inflicted. Pulling back, she grins at me, and I see a crimson smear just below her black lips. Fuuuck, that's hot as hell!

"It's all for you, *Casanova*." She purrs my nickname, and fuck if I don't love the way it rolls off her tongue.

I drag my fingers slowly through her folds, revelling in the slickness, and my mouth waters, desperate for another taste. Dropping her leg, I let her watch as I bring my fingers to my mouth, and I lick them clean, moaning around my digits before pulling them free.

"You're the sweetest thing I've ever tasted."

Her smile grows wide right before I walk her backwards until her back collides with the island bench in the centre of the small darkroom.

"The moment I realised it was you at the Feast, I nearly came there and then Kitten. That's what you do to me." Using my foot, I nudge each of her feet, silently telling her to spread her legs apart. She widens her stance while bracing her hands on the counter behind her. "The moment you came on my tongue, I knew I'd never get enough of tasting you." I press my mouth against hers again, loving the way her tongue wraps around mine in untamed hunger. Then I pull back and drop to my knees, my eyes level with her dripping folds. Glancing up to lock eyes with her, I lean forward, using my hands to push her legs further apart and watch as her nostrils flare. My fingers part her slick flesh, and I dart my tongue out to flick over her needy bud.

Her moan is loud, and maybe I should be concerned about someone hearing us, but fuck, my cock jerks at the sound, pre-cum leaking out.

"You wanna know what else I fucking loved about Sunday night, Kitten?"

Her black lips part in a needy pant as I flick my tongue over her clit again, loving how impatient she's becoming with my slow perusal.

"I loved holding you down while Skipper fucked you."

Her moan comes before I even get my tongue back on her searing pussy, and I settle between her legs, knowing how desperate she is to find release.

The moment I bury my face in her cunt, her hands latch into my hair, holding me in place. There's no way I could escape her grip if I wanted to, so, luckily, I'd happily die suffocating in the sweet scent of her pussy.

"Cass!" Her voice is husky, but I ignore her as I lose myself in the act of eating her out. "Cass!" She tugs on my hair, effectively pulling me out of her heat, and I look up at her flushed cheeks.

"What's wrong?" I frown before I glide my tongue over my lips, not doing a very good job at cleaning her slickness off me.

"I want to come on your cock."

Well fuck! She doesn't need to tell me twice. A grin tugs my lips up, and I flash my teeth.

"Your wish is my command, Kitten." I stand before her, and she surprises me by pulling me forward and darting her tongue out to lick her juices off my chin.

"Fuck. You're gonna make me come before I even get inside you."

Her laugh is like music to my ears. It's also loud, and if anyone is nearby, they are sure to hear. I should care since I'm not only ditching class but committing sin on catholic school grounds. Not that I haven't done that before, many times. But this time, it's with the principal's foster daughter, so I could end up getting expelled.

My dad would be pleased. Then I'd have no choice but to work on the farm and say goodbye to any other future I may want for myself.

I should care more, but right now, all I want is to bury myself deep inside Rhys.

I move back reluctantly, tossing our mingled clothes around until I find my pants, pulling out the latex protection that sucks to wear, but I know is necessary.

"Let me do that." Rhys offers, and I grin, stepping back to her and handing over the foil packet. I don't think she means to, but even the way she tears the packet open with her teeth is fucking sexy, and then when she drops to her knees before me, Thor jerks again, eager to get beaver. I wait for her to roll the protection on, but she decides to have her own taste, and the next thing I know, Thor's head is disappearing past her black lips.

"Fuuuck Kitten." I clasp each side of her head as she slowly sinks my engorged cock into the heat of her mouth. The feel of her tongue nearly undoes me as she glides my cock back out, and when I think she's about to take me in again, she replaces her mouth with the dinger, slowly rolling it on.

"One day, I'm going to let you choke me on your cock, Bossi." Her words hold promise, and fuck, I'd be happy to comply. "But today, I want you to rail me."

A growl escapes my lips as I meet her heated eyes, and I grab her upper arms, lifting her quickly off the floor.

"You want me to rail you?" I growl, and she nods. "My Kitten wants it hard?"

"Yes." She pants, and fuck, I love how open she is about this. Most chicks don't say what they really want. This is why Rhys George was made for me.

"How hard?"

"Rail me, Shaun. Hard and punishing." The way my name sounds in her husky tone makes my heart fucking flip. I don't know what the fuck that's about, but if she wants to be punished, then she'd better fucking hang on.

In a quick move, I wrap my arm around her back, pulling her to me for a hard and heavy kiss while my free hand finds those dark rose-coloured nipples, pinching them. The way she pushes her chest out instead of pulling away tells me everything I need to know. When she says she wants it hard, she really means it.

Ripping my lips from hers, I look down between our bodies, lifting her leg to hook over my arm, opening her wide as I push her back against the edge of the counter. Then I grip my dick and line up.

"You ready, Kitten?"

"Fuck yes."

I slam into her. She throws her head back as a part moan, part scream escapes her, and I slap my hand over her mouth, not wanting anyone to hear and interrupt us. Taking a panting second, I wait for my thick length to become accustomed to her tight walls. Then, I lean forward, biting one of her nipples before I start my punishing strokes, revelling in the way her needy cunt grips me.

Thrust after thrust, I slam into her so hard that I feel my tip punch her womb. Rhys doesn't protest. Instead, she meets each of my thrusts with her own, and fuck me, I have died and gone to heaven because this chick is the ultimate.

"Harder." Rhys pants, and I know what I have to do to make her feel me deep in her bones.

Pulling out abruptly, I don't give her a moment to realise what's happening before I spin her small frame and push her head forcefully forward, bending her over the counter. Her needy little arse sways in the air as she willingly widens her stance, desperate for my dick. Lining up again, I push back into her heat, gripping her hip with one hand and keeping her pushed down with my other hand at her nape. Then I do as she asks and fuck her harder. The slap of our skin is loud in the small space, and my nuts slap against her clit with each forward thrust.

"You feel so fucking good." I hiss, and she moans.

Needing more momentum, I release her nape and grip the other side of her hip as I continue driving into her. My eyes travel down the creamy skin of her back to the round globes or her perk arse, and using my hands, I spread her cheeks wider so I can see how her arse puckers with each of my thrusts. It's fucking hot as hell to watch, and it calls to my fucking dirty mind as I slam harder into her.

"Kitten." I grit out. "You ever been fucked here?" I drag one of my fingers over the puckered flesh, and she moans louder before replying.

"No. Not yet."

Fuck, I nearly come.

Not yet. It means she's not opposed to it. The thought of her taking a dick up that tight passage is hotter than hot. I drive harder as I sweep my fingers down to where we're joined, gathering up her slickness on my finger. Then I press it against her back passage and sink the digit in.

That's all it takes before a scream rips from her chest as her walls clamp down tight, squeezing me until I explode inside her. Strings of my cum shoot into the latex covering, and I fucking wish I was filling her with my seed right now, instead of this fucking condom. Our mingled moans are too loud in the small space as we puff and pant, falling back down to earth.

"Oh. My. God." Rhys puffs out, her face plastered to the bench-top. Her hands are still gripping the edge of the counter as I slowly ease my finger from her arse, then, reluctantly, I slip my cock from her heavenly pussy.

"Did I rail you hard enough, Kitten?" I can't keep my hands off her skin, which is damp with sweat. I love the way my darker skin contrasts with her creamy arse cheeks.

"Uh-ha." She puffs out, her breathing still heavy.

I can't help but smile as I look at her splayed before me with not an ounce of shame. She's fucking beautiful.

Leaning over her creamy flesh, I trail kisses up her spine until I come to her neck. Tasting the salt on her skin, I drag my tongue up the side of her neck before nibbling on her ear.

"You're fucking beautiful, Rhys George."

She stiffens.

Interesting. I've noticed how she gets uncomfortable with compliments. Not all compliments, just some. Like if I told her that her pussy was beautiful, I'm pretty sure she'd preen. But I just told her *she* was beautiful, and now she's gone cold on me. I wonder if I'd said Kitten instead of Rhys if it would have made a difference? One thing is for sure, there is more to Rhys George than a good fuck, and even though I know I shouldn't want to, I really do want to know more about her. Especially the parts she shows no one else.

That thought alone should make me want to run in the opposite direction because Shaun-Casanova-Bossier hasn't ever wanted to know more about who he sinks his dick in. Until now. I'm not running this time. No, I'm fucking staying, and I never want to leave.

Leaning back, I give her room to pull herself up off the bench, watching her closely as she avoids my eyes, coming to stand before me.

"Not a fan of compliments, I see."

Her dark eyes dart to mine, and would you look at that, she fucking blushes. Fuck, that's an even more beautiful sight.

"Why don't you leave the compliments to me? I'm sure Casanova revels in them." Her grin is shit-eating, and fuck, I love that part about her. She loves taking the piss.

"He sure does. He's waiting." I quirk a brow at her, and her eyes light up with mischief.

"Well, Mr Casanova," standing taller, Rhys presses her naked tits against my bare chest, "That cock of yours is worthy of a gold medal."

This time it's me who is throwing my head back as a laugh rips free. I feel her giggle more than I hear it, but then as my eyes lock onto hers again, I turn serious.

"What's going on with you?"

Like I knew she would, she tries to move away. God forbid Rhys George has a serious fucking conversation. I'm not letting her go anywhere, though, so I wrap my arms around her, drawing her against me. It feels fucking amazing to have our bare bodies pressed against each other like this.

"I'm fine, Bossi." She lies.

"Is it because of what happened at the Lodge on Sunday night… you know, with you and Skipper?" I still can't believe that our PE teacher, Mr Foster, is her sponsor at Vixen's Lodge. I also can't believe that I watched them fuck. That I interacted with them while they did that. It should creep me out, but it doesn't, mostly because I believe what Rhys said. Tyler Foster isn't a predator. The way he cared so much about what happened to her, cared so much about making sure she was ok, has kind of won me over with the whole situation.

"No." She answers simply, but then her eyes fall distant. "Yes." She shakes her head. "I don't know. Maybe. There's just so much…"

"So much what?"

She tries to pull away, but I hold firm.

"I'm not letting you go until you talk to me, George."

After a moment of struggling against my hold, she realises that I'm not talking shit, and I'm not letting her go, so she sags against me.

"I don't talk, Bossi. I fuck."

That statement alone is sad. Heartbreaking. I shouldn't care, yet I do. A whole fucking lot.

"Maybe this time fucking isn't enough. Maybe you should try talking."

Her brows lift. "I have a therapist to talk to. That's all I need."

Again, what a fucking sad statement.

"We need to get dressed. School's almost over." This time, Rhys manages to escape my hold, and she dashes to our pile of clothes, rifling through them for the articles that belong to her.

As she does that, I peel the rubber off my half limp cock and tie a knot at the top, looking around for where the hell I'm meant to stash it.

"Just chuck it in the trash can." Rhys points to the corner of the room. Once I've thrown it in, she unravels some paper towel from the wall dispenser and throws it on top.

I've gotta be honest. It makes me wonder how many times she's done this.

Chapter Fourteen

Rhys

A drop of sweat rolls down my spine as I scoop mashed potato into my mouth, trying hard to avoid everyone's eyes at the dinner table. I keep my gaze trained on my plate, my mind going over the last few days. Especially today. The incident with Garrett in the bathroom. English class with Shaun and Garrett. The darkroom with Shaun. Then, of course, that fucking message from my old foster mum, Julie. It keeps plaguing me, knowing that she somehow got my number. I can't even imagine how she got her hands on it. I'm not listed. My number is private, so how did she find me? Her demand for me to go and see Brian in prison is confusing. I haven't heard from her or Brian since the day I was taken from their care, so what the fuck do they want with me now? One thing I know about Julie is she doesn't fuck around. Back when I lived with her, if I did something that wasn't to her liking, she always followed through on her punishments. She was brutal at times, which was why I found comfort with Brian. He cared for me when Julie dealt her punishments. He made me feel loved and safe. I quickly learned not to upset Julie if I could help it, and I'd be an idiot to ignore her now. That's why I need to figure out how to get to Allansdale Prison this weekend. I don't know how she can possibly punish me from wherever she is, but I know she'll try.

"How was your second day back at school, Rhys?" The deep voice of my foster dad, Will, snaps me out of my thoughts, and I look up to see all eyes on me.

Great!

"It was ok." I shrug before returning my gaze to my plate.

"Rhysie, is that Lexi girl still your friend?" Archie asks, and I glance up to find his curious eyes as he chomps into his corn. The steam rises and fogs his glasses, blocking his dark gaze from mine. I grin.

"Yeah, Arch. Lexi is still my friend."

He nods, dropping his corn and removing his glasses to look at me. It's cute that he thinks he'd be able to see me properly without his glasses. He and Connor can't see shit without the assistance of them. Identical in every way. When he squints, trying to focus on me, I can't hold back my laugh—such a cute dork.

"I like her. She seems like a good friend." He smiles before Charlotte butts in.

"You like her pretty blonde hair, don't you Arch?" She teases, and his adorable face goes bright red.

"Shut up, Char! He does not!" Connor jumps in, sticking up for his twin.

"That's enough!" William snaps, silencing everyone before the squabbling turns into an all-out argument.

An awkward lull falls over the table, so I focus on my plate again before glancing up at Cynthia to change the conversation.

"Can I ask you something, Cin?"

Her brows lift in surprise as she looks up from her meal, taking a moment to study me before nodding and laying her fork on the table.

"Of course, Rhys." Her smile is warm, reminding me of the decent human she is. I don't know why I got so lucky to win her as my foster mum. I can be such a fucking handful, yet she puts up with me. I never deliberately set out to cause her distress, though. Somehow, she tolerates my flaws.

"Have you ever heard anything from Brian or Julie Bates?" My words cause Will to freeze with a piece of steak hovering before his mouth, and Cynthia's face pales.

"Ah, maybe we can have this conversation after dinner?" Her question sounds more like a statement.

I'm hoping that by asking here at the dinner table with the twins and Charlotte present, I can avoid the hard questions they will want to ask me about why I'm even mentioning my old foster parents. If we have an audience, I know they won't say too much.

"No need," I say, feigning boredom. I need them to think this is not a big deal. Just me being curious. "I was just wondering. No biggy."

"Ah…" Cynthia glances at Will, unsure, before looking back at me. "To answer your question, Rhys, no, we haven't heard anything from *them*."

The way she says *them* tells me she may not have heard from them, but she's heard something about *them*… maybe?

"Cool." I nod, chasing peas around on my plate and stabbing them onto my fork. "Do you know if Brian is still in prison?"

"Yes." She answers quickly. "Still there. You are safe, Rhys."

If only that were true.

"What about Julie? Whatever happened to her?" I ask, and Cin shares another look with Will.

"Why are you asking?" Will speaks this time.

I shrug again. "Just curious." I shove the peas in my mouth, hardly noticing the taste as I pretend that my heart isn't racing like I've just run a marathon. Why do they have to question this? It's my life. Surely I deserve some answers without being scrutinised for it.

"It's just a little out of the blue. Has something happened?" Cynthia asks, and I glance around the table to see the twins and Charlotte sitting quietly, taking everything in.

I could tell Cynthia that Julie has called and messaged me. I could tell her that's what sent me over the edge and straight into a sex bender while we were away, but what good would it do? If they don't know where Julie is, then they can't stop her from following through on her threat. I'm almost tempted to see if it's empty, to see if Julie still has consequences to dish out to me. It's a risk I'm not willing to take, though. I've managed to keep that part of my life a secret, and I'd like to keep it that way.

I sigh, dropping my fork and shooting Cynthia a glare I know she doesn't deserve.

"Nothing has happened. I'm just curious about where those people are. I know Julie never went to prison, so she's out there somewhere, right? Don't you think I should have a right to know if there's a chance I might walk past her one day?"

"She doesn't live in this area, Rhys." Cin declares quickly.

So, she *does* know something.

"How do you know?"

Cynthia darts her concerned eyes to Will, who gets the silent hint she's throwing and takes over the conversation.

"Rhys. You are safe here. There's no need for you to be concerned."

I roll my eyes. "Why can't you give me a straight answer? I have a right to know where they are. How do you know Julie isn't living locally? Shouldn't I know if she's at least in the state? What if I had run into her while we were on holiday or on a school excursion? Shouldn't you prepare me for that possibility?"

"Is that what happened when we were away? Did you run into Julie?" Cynthia's eyes widen in fear as she darts her gaze between Will and me.

"No."

I'm not lying. Julie only left me a voice message while we were away. I didn't see her, but her call was out of the blue. It did cross my mind that maybe Julie saw me. That maybe I walked past her on the street, and that's what sparked her to reach out to me.

"I'll be eighteen next year, probably moving out sometime in the next few years. I should know these things, don't you think?"

An unsettling sadness wells in Cynthia's eyes when I mention moving out, but I ignore it because it's irrelevant to my current need for information.

Will nods in understanding, though, offering his wife a sympathetic look before turning back to me.

"The truth is, Rhys, we don't know where Julie is. We check with the authorities every month to see if her name has popped up anywhere. But she's a ghost. It's likely she's using a different name now. We haven't let it affect things here because we were of the belief that Julie isn't a threat. Is that wrong? Is she a threat?"

I shake my head, even though I'm not sure how to answer that. Julie was mean to me when I lived with them. She loved to stand over me, letting me think she would hurt me if I didn't behave. Sure, she smacked me around a couple of times, but I'd had worse before I even went into their care. She didn't hurt me too much, but she made me think she would hurt me worse.

The cops believed Julie was never involved in my activities with Brian, so she was never charged with anything. I'm not sure if she's a threat in a violent way like Will is insinuating. Still, I can't bring myself to voice that information to them.

"Do you know what prison Brian is in?" My question throws them both, and their eyes practically pop out of their sockets.

"Rhys, you don't need to know where he is," Cin states, keeping her brown gaze locked on me.

"Did you not hear anything I just said?" I hiss, standing abruptly, my chair scraping the tiles behind me. "Jesus Cin! Don't you know information is power? Shouldn't I be the one to have the information on this stuff? What if you both die tomorrow? Then how am I meant to know any of this?"

"You're going to die?" Conner whimpers, shooting puppy dog eyes at Cynthia at the same time that Archie starts to cry.

"Good one, Rhys!" Charlotte snaps, jumping up from her seat to hug Archie.

"For fuck's sake! Just forget it!" My yell is loud as I bolt up from my chair, letting it clatter to the white tiled floor before I storm off. I ignore Will's scold for swearing and retreat quickly.

When I reach my bedroom, I slam the door hard, rattling the windows and walls before I flip the lock and throw myself face first onto my bed. Then I suck in as much air as I can and scream into my pillow until I can't breathe.

My questions were useless. I learnt nothing but the fact that Cin and Will know jack shit. What the fuck am I meant to do with that information? If I ask them to drive me to the prison, they will freak, and I'll never get there to see Brian before Julie makes good on her threat.

A knock sounds on my door, but I ignore it. I don't want to talk to anyone right now. The only thing I want to do is impossible because I have no one to do it with. I could sneak out and get my fix, but with the way my body is trembling, I'm scared of what I might do. What lines I might be willing to cross to ease the ache.

I don't want to end up in another sex bender. I don't want to put myself in a position where I'm in danger, where I'm being used and humiliated just so I can get the high that always seems so unreachable when I'm like this.

Not for the first time this week; I feel like crying. Hell no! I'm not shedding a fucking tear over this crap. I just have to figure out a way to get to the city without making the rents suspicious. Then somehow get to Allansdale Prison, which is an hour on the other side of the city.

Needing a distraction, I pick up my phone to scroll Instagram but instead find some messages from Lexi, Marcus, Shaun, Simon, and Garrett. My stupid heart flutters again at seeing the four guys' names on my screen. I know it shouldn't make me happy, yet it does. It brings a sense of calm to the chaos that was there only moments ago.

Since I need to pull my head out of the gutter, I decide to open Lexi's message first.

Lexi West

I miss you! We haven't had a chance to catch up properly yet.
Can we have a girl's night this weekend?

Rhys George

Absa-fucking-lutely!
What do you have in mind?

Lexi West

Wanna stay over at my new pad?
Mum scored us this adorable little house around the corner from Ayden and Marcus.
I have the attic bedroom upstairs. It's sick!

Being that close to Marcus is probably not smart, but I do need some girl time.

Rhys George

Sounds perfect! I'll bring the chips and porn!!

Lexi West

OMG! NO porn Rhys!

Rhys George
But why? Porn is so fun!

Lexi West
Yeah, sure!
If you're watching it with the person, you're going to fuck!

My laughter fills my bedroom as I picture Lexi's face, flushed with a blush and a look of horror on it.

Rhys George
So, you watch porn with Ayden, do you?
He really has turned you into a dirty bitch, hasn't he?

Lexi West
Stop it!
And yes!
Hehe.

Rhys George
Girl, you need to spill the deets!

Lexi West
I will when you come to stay!

Rhys George
I'm holding you to that!

My grin is genuine, and I'm thankful for the much-needed distraction, so I move on to my other messages.

Marcus Grady
I know you said you were busy tonight, but I'll be up late if you want to chat.

My stomach dips as I read over Marcus' words. I so badly want to talk to him. It's tearing me apart, having to stay away from him when everything in me is screaming to go to him. I should probably ignore his message, but I'm weak.

Rhys George
Hey Grady. Wanna FaceTime later?

His reply comes quick.

Marcus Grady
Yeah! What time?

Rhys George
Give me an hour?

Marcus Grady
You got it! Talk soon xx

Ugh! Those two kisses at the end of his message do stupid things to me. I'm so screwed. I should message him back now and cancel our call. He should be focusing on moving on from me, not spending his free time calling me.

Do I send him a message to cancel, though? No.

Pathetic Rhys!

I click out of Marcus' messages and look at the ones remaining. Simon, Shaun and Garrett. I choose Simon because he's fun and I need a pick me up.

Simon Hastings
Simon says, let's chat.

Rhys George
I'd better not be a naughty girl and ignore you then :)

Simon Hastings
Ahhh. There she is. How's my girl?

Shit. He called me his girl again. Even though I secretly love hearing him say that, I should probably nip this in the bud.

Rhys George
Since I don't belong to any one guy, but all the guys belong to me, I think I should be asking, how's my guy?

Simon Hastings

Hahaha! Good point! I'd happily be your guy, Rhys!
So, to answer your question, I'm good.
I've been thinking about photo labs and darkrooms a lot lately, though.

Rhys George

I've heard they can be a bit sketchy. You should never enter those rooms alone!

Simon Hastings

You're right. I'm only going to enter them if you're with me.

Rhys George

Haven't you heard?
That's where I take my prey.

Simon Hastings

I'll happily sacrifice myself!

Fuck me dead! How do I get myself into these conversations?

Rhys George
You've already done that!
I should go. Got homework to do.

Simon Hastings
Wait!
Before you go, can you answer something?

Rhys George
Sure.

Simon Hastings
What was wrong with you in class today?
I've never seen you look so flat.

Damn. He wants to talk about real stuff. And damn, I want to answer him. But I can't. Not with the truth, anyway.

Rhys George
Dude, are you saying my tits are small?

Simon Hastings
What? NO!!!!
Fuck no!
Your tits are perfect!

Rhys George

Hahahaha, Gotchya!
And yes, I know my tits are perfect.
The twins are a thing of beauty.

Simon Hastings

You call your tits the twins?

Rhys George

Of course. It's not a very interesting name for them, but they know who I'm talking about.
How about you, Hastings? What do you call that magnificent cock of yours?

Simon Hastings

You think my cock is magnificent?

Rhys George

Hell yes! What's his name?

Simon Hastings

Conan

Rhys George
Conan? Why Conan?

Simon Hastings
You know, like Conan the Barbarian?

Rhys George
Oh! Hahaha
I'm crying!!

Simon Hastings
It's rude to laugh at a man's cock, George!

Rhys George
I'm sorry. I'm not laughing at it. I swear!

Simon Hastings
You're still laughing, aren't you?

Rhys George
Yes!!!!

Simon Hastings
You'd better keep looking over your shoulder tomorrow at school.
Conan is pissed! He's going to come after you!

Rhys George
Promise?

Simon Hastings
You know it!

Fuck me! Now I've promised a FaceTime call to one guy and basically agreed to a showdown with fucking Conan the Barbarian! I should quit while I'm ahead, but these convos are helping me to forget the shit show going on behind the scenes. So naturally, I open Shaun's message next.

Shaun Bossier
I have a theory.

Rhys George
Oh! I can't wait to hear this!

Shaun Bossier
You need a reverse harem.

Rhys George
What?

Shaun Bossier
You know—a reverse harem. With multiple guys.

Rhys George
I know what a reverse harem is, Bossi! I was the one who told you about it when I thought you guys were Lexi's RH!!!

Shaun Bossier
Right! Well. That's what you need.

I mean, it would be fun, but what Shaun doesn't know is that I can't do relationships.

Rhys George
Why do I need it?
Because I love dick so much?
What? A girl can't just fuck around and love sex as much as a guy?
We have to be a slut or into something weird. Is that it?

Shaun Bossier
What? No!

Rhys George
GTG

I know I shouldn't let his comments get to me, and yes, I know I'm taking it out of context, but that's where my fucking head is at right now! I'm all sorts of messed up.

I'm about to open Garrett's messages, which I'm sure are going to be nothing but shaming me for my inability to *not* fuck his mates, but then my phone starts ringing, with Shaun's name flashing across the screen. I decline it, and then he sends another message through.

Shaun Bossier
Don't dodge my call, George.
Pick it up!

My phone rings again, and my heart stops for a moment. Do I pick it up? My finger hovers over the red icon, hesitating. Then I hit accept.

"What?" I snap as I sit up on my bed, dragging myself off it to start pacing.

"You've taken my words the wrong way, Kitten."

Oh, sweet Jesus, he's Casanova right now, and fuck, there's my Kitty, purring like a horny bitch. I stop still as I feel the heat build between my legs.

"Just because you've met Kitten doesn't give you the right to speak to her all the damn time. She's not here right now. And she doesn't appreciate you using her love for dick, and pussy for that matter, to slut-shame her."

"Stop! I'm not slut-shaming you! You love sex, Rhys. I fucking love that part of you!"

Shaun's words are fierce and strong as they come through the phone, and my heart stops again as I replay what he said. He *loves* that part about me?

"Why?"

"Why what?" His voice *really* is sexy. He could be one of those guys that get paid for phone sex. He'd be rich as hell.

"Why do you love that part about me?" I start pacing again, nervous to hear his answer.

"Honestly?" He hesitates for a moment. "Because it matches my own need, I guess."

OMG, Shaun Bossier sounds fucking nervous. Huh!

"So, you're basically a slut, too?"

He chuckles at my comment.

"No, I'm not a slut, because you're not a slut. You and me. We're different from most people. Sure, everyone loves sex, but most of them are too scared to have sex the way they really want. That's why we are the same. It's also why I started going to the Feast nights, and I'm pretty sure it's why you go there too." He's quiet for a moment before he adds, "Am I right?"

I sigh. "If I say you are, is your head going to swell?"

He laughs, and it's a beautiful fucking sound.

"Probably."

Since I'm in the privacy of my bedroom, I let my smile burst free.

"You'd better rein it in, or you won't get through the school doors tomorrow."

He chuckles again before falling quiet.

"Before, you said that Kitten loves dick and pussy. Is that true? Does Rhys George munch carpet?"

"I dabble in seafood. I prefer meat, though."

Again, Shaun's laughter is loud over the phone, and I'm helpless to hold in my smile. I glance at my reflection in my dresser mirror, seeing my white teeth framed by my black lips. When Shaun's laughter falls abruptly silent, I frown.

"Hang on a sec." He mutters into the phone, sounding annoyed, before I hear scraping come through the speaker. He's trying to cover his phone, so I can't hear. Even though it's muffled, I can hear him talking with someone, and it doesn't sound like a happy conversation.

"You there?" Shaun asks, obviously finished talking to whoever was there.

"I'm here. Everything ok?"

"Yeah. I've gotta go help the old man with something. See you at school tomorrow?" He sounds like he doesn't want to hang up. I kinda don't want him to either, which is weird. I don't typically enjoy talking on the phone.

"Yeah. I guess I'll be there." I sigh, and he chuckles.

"Later, Kitten."

"Later, Cass."

I flop back on my bed with my phone clutched in my hand. Tonight has been strange. Yet weirdly fun. A little anyway. I still have to read Garrett's message before Marcus FaceTime's me, so I decide to get his scolding over and done with.

Garrett Cole
We need to talk.

Rhys George

Nothing good ever comes from those four words!!

Garrett Cole

Don't be so sure.

Rhys George

Really? So, you're not going to remind me to stay away from Simon and Shaun?
You're not going to remind me to stop messing with Marcus?

Garrett Cole

Listen, I'm only looking out for my mates. All three of them, but I also know it takes two to tango, and I know they aren't making it easy for you to walk away.

Rhys George

I'll be honest with you. I haven't tried all that hard to walk away from them.

Although I really am trying not to interact with Marcus. He sure as shit isn't making it easy.

But that's not on him. I should be stronger, and guess what?

I'm not!

Garrett Cole

Yeah. I know. Marcus hasn't stopped talking about you. He's still got it in his head that he's going to win you over.

Shit. This shouldn't surprise me, but it does. The fact that he's openly talking about it means he's on a mission. He's even more determined than I thought.

Rhys George

He's not going to give up.

Garrett Cole

You really want him to?

Rhys George

Yes!

Garrett Cole
Now answer me truthfully!!

Rhys George
middle finger emoji

Garrett Cole
Come on, George. Be honest with me.

Rhys George
Fine! I don't want him to give up, but I NEED him to!!

Garrett Cole
Why?

Rhys George
Come on, Cole. You're a smart guy.

Garrett Cole
Your addiction?

My heart sinks seeing those words. I know I'm an addict. I'm not in denial about it, but I hate other people knowing about it or calling me out on it. I have no idea why.

Rhys George
Bingo!

Garrett Cole
I've been doing some research, and just because you have a sex addiction doesn't mean you can't have a relationship with someone.

I roll my eyes. This is what happens. People find out and think they're helping by doing their own research and come up with their own theories on how *I* can get better. Guess what? It doesn't help!

Rhys George
I'm gonna stop you right there.
I appreciate that you're trying to make an effort to understand the inner workings of the fuckery in my head, and for the life of me, I don't know why you'd even bother, but you have to know. I already know all there is to know about sex addiction. I fucking LIVE it!
I was serious when I told Marcus I didn't want a relationship because I knew I would eventually go looking for more.
It doesn't matter how much I care about him. He's not enough.
It's fucked up to say, and I'm sorry for that, but it's the truth.

No single person will EVER be enough for me!

That's not Marcus' fault! He's fucking amazing! Perfect.

Me though? I'm not perfect.

I'm tainted and screwed up, and I'll only bring him a life of pain.

Some bitch is going to be lucky to snatch Marcus up one day.

But my needs are fucked, Garrett. Some would even say sick or twisted.

If he really knew what I was like. What I'm into, he'd spit on me and call me trash. Jesus, you heard him yesterday. He already knows I'm a slut.

Garrett Cole

What if you're wrong? Have you even tried?

Rhys George

I tried really fucking hard not to hit on you, Bossi, and Hastings while I was with Marcus. That's not right, Garrett.

Garrett Cole

But you didn't hit on us. Did you?

Rhys George
No. I ran because I nearly did, though. Then I went and found a random dick, and for a short time, I felt like me again.
What does that tell you?

Garrett Cole
You found a random dick while you were with Marcus?

Rhys George
No. It was right after I finally ended things with him.

Garrett Cole
Was it at that sex place you and Bossi go to?
Do you get what you need there?

Rhys George
Kind of. It's enough for now.

Garrett Cole
What happens when it's no longer enough?

It's something that plagues me. Eventually, things get boring, and I need to amp it up. How far will I push my boundaries? When will it be enough? Am I going to be alone forever?

Rhys George
I don't know.

Garrett Cole
How does that make you feel?

Rhys George
You sound like my therapist.
Is that what you want to do when you finish school? Be a therapist?

Garrett Cole
Don't change the convo, George!

Rhys George
Too late. I already did.

Garrett Cole
One last question.

Rhys George
Fine! What?

Garrett Cole
Have you considered that maybe you will find someone that is happy to have an open relationship with you? That way, you will get what you need sexually while having what your heart wants?

I don't respond to Garrett. I can't because I'm crying. I don't know why, but his words have reached into my chest and pulled out my heart. It's the only way I can explain it. More than anything, I want to feel loved. I want to love someone back and share sacred moments with them. The thing is, people like me don't get the happy ending. We just get orgasms, empty beds, and nothing but a wet patch to remind you that you're nothing.

Chapter Fifteen

Rhys

M y body is fuelled by nothing but anticipation. I barely slept last night after another full-on day of spiralling out-of-control yesterday, and after my chat with Garrett last night, I couldn't even sum up the energy to accept Marcus' FaceTime call when he rang.

I can't believe I actually cried. Not that I think crying is weak. It isn't. I've just never let myself get to that point before. So, sleep evaded me, and now I'm going through the motions of another school day with the only thing to look forward to is tonight's Feast night.

I skipped breakfast, ignored Cynthia on the way to school, and then met Tillie and Bell behind the stadium, where I smoked too much weed. With squinting red eyes, I tried to convince Ms Holland, my Viscom teacher, that I was fine. But she took one look at me and sent me to the principal. AKA my foster mum. Ugh. So annoying. So then, I kind of slept for a bit on the couch in Cin's office, and when I woke up, she had a slice of vanilla mud cake and a hot chocolate for me.

Then, she tried to talk to me.

> *What's going on, Rhys?*
> *Why won't you talk to me, Rhys?*
> *This is unacceptable behaviour in school, Rhys.*
> *Do I have to send you back to the retreat, Rhys?*

That one pulled my head out of my arse, and I apologised. I still didn't divulge the chaos in my head, though.

When I finally promise my foster mum that I'll behave, she sends me back out into the bustling school, where I reluctantly drag my feet to my Health class, which I'm about thirty minutes late for.

Mr Foster ignores my tardiness as I stroll to the back of the room and pull up a chair at the end of the table next to Dale. After a few minutes of listening to Dale catch me up on the classwork, I feel eyes on me.

Glancing up, I shift my gaze to the front of the room where Mr Foster's eyes meet mine. There's a glimmer of concern in his expression as he studies me, and heat rushes to my cheeks. I turn back to Dale because I'm a coward. Normally I'd have a standoff with Mr Foster or any teacher who is eyeballing me. Not today, though. Today I just can't.

"Do I look like shit or something?"

Dale glances up from his laptop at my question, raking his big blue eyes over my face.

"Girl, you look hot."

I grin and shimmy my shoulders. "Why, thank you."

He rolls his eyes. "Not that sort of hot. More like you're running a fever type of hot. You're all flushed." He leans back a little, raking his gaze from my face down my body and back again, his expression a mix of worry and disgust. "Please tell me you weren't just bumping uglies with some herpes infested high schooler? Ew girl! That's gross!" To emphasise his disgust, Dale shoots his hand out, turning his head in the other direction before bringing his hand back to his chest.

I giggle.

"What if I did? What if my Kitty just got some action?"

He gags. "Stop. You're making me ill. Don't speak about your..." He gags again.

"My? VAGINA?" I tease, and he gags again. "What's wrong, Dale? You don't like seafood?"

"Ew!" Dale leaps up from his seat, gaining everyone's attention.

"Sit back down, Mr Martin." Mr Foster grumbles from the front of the room; meanwhile, me and Tillie are in fits, while Bell just raises a brow at us lowly creatures, and Allister cringes.

"Can I switch seats, Mr Foster?" Dale asks, all whiney, making me laugh harder. Dale does this all the time. It's like he forgets that I'm a chick, and when I remind him, usually through some sort of torment, of course, he freaks out. It's the funniest thing ever.

"No, Dale, you can stay right there. Miss George is going to come and sit at the front." Mr Foster approaches our row of tables and gives me a stern look as he rests his hands on his hips.

Oh, he's all authority-like right now, which just wakes Kitty up more. I know I should pretend like I'm annoyed, but I'm feeling extra bratty after waking up from my Mary Jane nap, and I want someone to play with. It looks like Mr Foster will have to do.

"I'd rather stay here, Mr F." I flutter my lashes, and he rolls his eyes this time.

"I don't care if that's what you'd rather, Miss George. Pick up your things and move to the front of the class." He points towards the front, and I deliberately let my eyes travel the length of his arm, loving the sight of the way his muscles strain from the action. When I return my eyes to his, he doesn't look impressed, so I smirk, peering up at him through my lashes like I'm nothing but innocent. He raises a brow.

"I tell you what, Mr F. If you give me one of those lollipops you keep for the year seven students in your desk, I'll move, and I'll stay quiet for the rest of the lesson."

"This isn't a negotiation Rhys." He grumbles low, so I smile and lean back in my chair, crossing my arms over my chest in defiance.

"Isn't it?"

His nostrils flare, and his face reddens, and I can tell he wants to yell at me. Hell, if I were any other student, he would. So why isn't he?

"Fine." He grits out between his teeth, and this time my brow shoots up.

Wow. That was easy.

I flash my friends a victorious smile before gathering up my things and walking to the front of the room to the only free table, which just happens to be directly in front of Mr Foster's desk. I can feel him walking a few steps behind me, so I add a little extra sway to my hips as I walk. There's no way he's not watching. I'm going to be in so much trouble after this.

Hopefully, he punishes me.

In the best way.

I lay my things out on the table as I sense him pass by. I'm hyperaware of him now, more than ever. It must be my pretty dick radar kicking in. Or it could be Kitty able to smell the pheromones he's excreting. Either way, I feel him all around me, consuming and addictive.

In my peripheral, I see Mr Foster sit down at his desk. A quick glance around the room shows me that everyone is busy working. No one is paying me any attention, so before I take my new seat, I, oh so accidentally, nudge my pencil case off the front of the table.

"Whoops," I say quietly, quickly flicking my gaze to see Mr Foster's eyes on me, just as I hoped.

Moving around the table, I face the class, giving Mr Foster my back, and bend at the waist to slowly pick up my pencil case. My face heats, probably turning red as I hold in my laugh because right now, Mr Foster, my Skipper, is getting a very intimate view. My shorter than regulation skirt is doing anything *but* hiding my red cotton panties with the words, 'Fuck Me' painted over the arse.

Oh damn, this pencil case is hard to pick up. I try once, twice, three times before I get a good grip on it, each time moving my arse a little. Then, ever so slowly, I stand upright and make my way around the table to my seat. I take a few moments to continue my charade of innocence before looking back up.

Holy shit, Mr Foster looks mad. Furious.

I grin and mouth, *'punish me.'*

His face turns redder.

Fucking hell, I think I just got pregnant!

With his eyes still glaring at me, I flutter my lashes and slowly raise my hand to ask a question. He doesn't say anything for a moment, and I think he's going to leave me hanging, but then he glances back down at his laptop and mutters.

"What is it, Miss George?"

"Oh, um, I was just wondering when you are going to give me the lollipo*p*?"

I pop the p on the end of lollipop, and his eyes dart up to mine again, his frustration evident. Then he huffs, moving back in his chair to open his drawer before standing and walking to my table with a lollipop. I smile up at him, playing the role of innocent schoolgirl, and watch as he places the lollipop on the table, his deep blue eyes darting to mine in the briefest of glances.

I don't know why, but Mr Foster looks hotter than usual. Probably because I know how good he fucks. Actually, good is an understatement. I can't even find a good enough word to describe how truly epic it was to have him pleasure me. To have him pumping inside me. Fuck, even knowing I walked around with his cum dripping from me has me squirming in my seat.

Hot. As. Fuck.

As I unwrap the lollipop, I watch the way his strong muscles ripple under his shirt as he moves, and by the time he takes his seat again, my panties are wet. I don't even bother with doing any work. I just sit there, dragging the lollipop in and out of my mouth, imagining that it's the head of his big, hard cock.

He must feel my eyes on him because a few minutes later, he looks up from his laptop and lounges back in his corporate style office chair, pressing the end of his pen to his bottom lip. His eyes travel the classroom for a moment before they land on me, and then I let him watch how I work the lollipop in and out of my mouth. When

I spread my legs further apart under my table, he notices, his eyes darting lower.

I don't know if he can see right under the table, but he knows enough to use his imagination, and I can see his eyes darken, even from where I'm sitting. It takes everything in me not to slide my hand under the table and touch myself. My Kitty is wide awake and practically hissing at me for some action. I haven't had any today. In fact, I haven't come since my time with Shaun in the darkroom yesterday afternoon. That's… odd.

Before I know it, the bell rings for lunch, and Mr Foster is dishing out homework instructions before everyone flees. I take my time because I already know what's coming, so I'm not surprised when he asks me to stay behind.

I smile and wave to my friends as they file out of the room while I stay seated and finish off the last bit of the lollipop.

"Miss George, will you have your overdue work in by tonight?" Mr Foster's question is code for *"Are you coming to the Feast night tonight?"* It's how he has asked every Wednesday since I started going. On Sunday nights, he simply sends me a text message with a question mark, and I send a thumbs up or thumbs down. The fact that he's asking like this means there must be people still loitering around.

"Yes, Mr Foster. I'll have it in tonight." I smirk knowingly at him, but his eyes don't linger. Instead, he walks to the classroom door and closes it before turning back to me.

"You are walking a fine fucking line, Kitten." The deep rasp in his voice has my Kitty pulsing with need. I keep my smirk in place and start fiddling with the white plastic stick left behind from the lollipop.

"I don't know what you mean." I purr innocently, and he shoots me a dagger as he moves to his desk, placing one perfectly taut arse cheek on the edge.

"Who are you wearing those panties for?"

Oh, so he did see them. Nice.

My grin spreads wide, and I'm sure I look smug as fuck.

"For whoever wants to play." I shrug like it's nothing.

He grunts, almost possessively, and OMG, why does that turn me on so much?

"Your foster mum is worried about you."

His words wipe the smuggery right off my face.

"What?"

"I know why you were late to class, Rhys. What's going on?"

I frown. What the fuck?

"What do you mean? Why was I late?" I stand from my chair, apprehension creeping its way in.

"I believe you were pretty baked when you arrived to first period this morning." He smirks a little, like he's trying not to laugh, but I'm not smiling.

"Did she tell you that?" I hiss, clenching my fists by my side. I can't believe Cynthia would blab about that.

Mr Foster stands from his desk and takes a step closer but stops, knowing someone could be watching through the window in the door.

"No, but she gave Emily a serving when she overheard her snitching about it in the staff room at recess."

"Who the fuck is Emily?" I grit through my teeth as I watch him continue to try and suppress his smile.

"Emily Holland. Your Viscom teacher."

"Oh." I drop my head, staring at Tyler's sneakers. They are black Nike's. Expensive looking. My eyes travel up his bare legs to the hem of his shorts. Nike as well. He even has a Nike t-shirt on. Nike really should pay him to model their clothes. He'd make them millions.

"Earth to Rhys." A hand waves past my vision, and I look up to see Tyler trying to get my attention. "Where did you go?"

I shake my head, looking down again. "Somewhere that's not here."

"Hey." It's the care in his tone that has me looking back up. "Talk to me."

"I don't talk." I want to say I just fuck, but I can't even bring myself to say that right now.

"Maybe you should try. If not to me, then someone else."

"You really wanna know what goes on inside this head?" I poke my finger to my temple and widen my eyes in challenge.

"Would it surprise you if I said yes?"

I can't speak because hell yes, that surprises me.

"I should go." I turn back to the table and scoop up my things, stepping around Tyler when he doesn't move out of my way. Just as I'm about to reach the door, Tyler grabs my free arm and pulls me to the side, pushing me up against the wall, a little way from the door where we are out of view.

"Prepare for that punishment, Kitten. Because I am delivering it tonight."

And… I'm gushing.

The husky rasp in his voice is primal and possessive, and fuck me; I want to drop to my knees right here, right now. I don't, of course, because we are at school, and I also don't want him to go to jail. Also, for some reason, since we did the deed on Sunday night, our relationship has changed. Tyler has never acknowledged me much at the Feast nights and typically pays me little attention here at school. Sure, I know he keeps an eye on me at the Lodge, and there are times he has watched me fuck others when he didn't think I noticed. Yet now, since we were blackmailed into stepping over that line we both drew, he's not backing off or bolting in the other direction. If anything, he's showing more interest. He's showing more concern.

"Are you going to spank me, daddy?"

His strong hand wraps around my throat as he pushes up against me, sending searing heat to every part that counts.

"Don't call me that!" His growl is nearly a whisper. His lips are close, and I can feel the heat of his breath dance across my skin.

"But I know how much you *really* love it. *Daddy*."

I'm playing with fire, and I don't care if I get burned. He says he doesn't like me calling him daddy, yet his hard cock doesn't lie.

His breathing quickens as he presses against my body, and I feel every inch of his hardness against my front.

"Kitten. You need to leave now. Before I take this too far."

Fuck! I want him to take it too far. Desperately so. What I don't want is to ruin his career or his life. Which is big for a sex-tracked mind like me. I deserve a fucking medal.

"Promise you'll punish me tonight?" I practically beg.

"Yes." He grits out through clenched teeth. "You can be sure of it."

My black lips spread wide.

"Thank you, Daddy."

Chapter Sixteen

Skipper

The old barn at the back of Vixen's Lodge is the oldest structure on the property, yet it holds a rustic charm that the colonial-style home can't compete with. I've only been out in this barn once. It was the night that Rhys, *my* Kitten, came to her first Feast night. Terence Hill, otherwise known as Master Hill—which is a crock of shit. He's a master of nothing—set up a small area in the barn for Rhys to discretely get ready in. Since she's underage and needs to keep her attendance a secret, she enters the back of the property on an old dirt track and slips unnoticed into the barn. Then she works her magic and applies her mask makeup. I've never told Rhys this, but she's extremely talented. Her masks always look exotic. Beautiful in a dark way. And most importantly, she disguises her face well. After she morphs her face into someone unrecognisable, she dresses in whatever scandalous outfit Master Hill leaves for her.

It's sickening the way he looks at her. The way he sizes her up as if she's his prey. Everyone at the Feast's set their sights on her, tempted and salivating for a taste. Master Hill, on the other hand, is a true predator. If I'd known before that first night, I would never have let Rhys join.

So now it's on me to make sure she is ok. What Master Hill did on Sunday night was fucked up and definitely *not* ok. He knows me and Kitten had drawn a line that we agreed not to cross. Yes, she has pushed the boundary many times, but it was a dance we played regularly, adding to the excitement of our time here. So, when he gave her two impossible choices, I'm sure he thought she'd pick going with him into his fucking creepy dungeon under the house. I bet the prick was salty as fuck when he had to sit back and watch us finally cross that line.

There's no doubt in my mind that he filmed it. He has hidden cameras everywhere. It's how he manipulates people to either stay or go. Or, in our case, cross a line. He's probably watched the footage a thousand times, and fuck, I hope the motherfucker saw how much Kitten and I loved every moment. I hope he fucking felt every bit of the passion we have for each other.

Passion she doesn't have for him.

Even though we had to follow Master Hills' commands and perform the act following a specific criteria to get the evidence he wanted, I made sure Kitten didn't have time to think about that creepy fucker. I made sure she could only feel how I set fire to her from the inside out. It was fucking beautiful. I haven't been able to think of much else but the taste of her, the feel of her, the way she ached just as badly for me as I did for her.

And that's the problem, isn't it?

I'm her fucking teacher!

I'm thirty-two years old, for fuck's sake. Rhys is only seventeen! What the actual fuck am I thinking? Obviously, I'm not because right now, I'm slipping through the slightly ajar barn door in search of my Kitten when I should be waiting inside the Lodge, keeping my distance. Yet here we fucking are.

The soft glow of light filters through a cracked door off to the side and some sort of god awful music is playing, which tells me all I need to know. My bratty Kitten is in there. Peering into the room, I spot Rhys kneeling on the dirt floor in front of a mirror as she brushes out her hair. She never wears it out like this unless she is here. It's usually in some weird twisty things on each side of her head, but Master Hill likes her hair down, and fuck, I have to agree. Her hair is beautiful. Nearly black with a hint of chocolate through it, it falls like silk down her back to rest on the top of her arse. I'm glad she doesn't wear her hair like this normally. I kind of like knowing I'm the only one that gets to see her like this.

Now, unfortunately, so does Fuck Boy! Shaun Bossier.

Pretty boy prick!

Quietly nudging the door open so I can slip inside the room, I step to the side to get a better view of my Kitten. She still has her school uniform on, and I bet underneath, she's still wearing those fucking naughty panties.

Fuck me.

That's what's written across the arse of them in white lettering. It's hard to miss, standing out against the red cotton background. If there's one thing you need to know about Rhys George, it's that she's a dirty, naughty little brat. And fuck, she makes my dick hard.

All. The. Time.

As I get closer, stepping slowly towards her, I notice for the first time that Rhys isn't wearing any makeup. I'm not talking about the painted skull mask she crafts over her delicate skin for the Feast nights. I'm talking about the black lips, the dark liner stuff and other dark powdery shit that covers her eyelids. Right now, Rhys George doesn't have a speck of makeup on her face, and she's fucking beautiful.

Stunning.

Her gasp is loud in the small space when she notices my reflection in the mirror. Darting up to quickly to face me, she slaps her hand over her heart. I'm speechless as I approach her, taking in her creamy skin and the natural pink flush to her cheeks. She isn't even wearing those god-awful piercings she wears to school in her nose.

"Tyler." She whispers, and hell fucking yes, I love hearing her say my name. Not Mr Foster, not Skipper, and not *Daddy*. Although, when she calls me daddy, it does weird things to my insides which I know I should probably seek counselling for.

"Kitten." It's all I can say as I close the distance, reaching out to brush my thumb over her flushed cheek.

"What are you doing here?" She looks a little panicked and glances over my shoulder as if she's expecting someone else to be there. Probably looking for that fucking Master of nothing.

"Well, Kitten." I lift my other hand to brush her silky hair back off her face, so I can see every inch in its current virgin state. "I've come to deliver your punishment."

The smile that lights up her face is breathtaking. Why she plasters that dark shit on her face is beyond me, but once again, I like that I'm the only one getting to see her this way.

"You can't wait until the Feast starts?" Her delicate hand comes to rest against my chest, and I can feel the heat through the hoodie I'm wearing. Her dark eyes are like caramel crystals, bright with excitement and anticipation, and her dark lashes flutter a little as she peers up at me.

"The punishment is just between me and you, Kitten. I'm not sharing it with anyone else."

"Oh." Her lips drop open as she takes in my words, and a brief moment of uneasiness flits across her face. "Are you sure? Doesn't this go against your morals?"

My lips quirk up at one corner. "Kitten, I threw my morals out the door on Sunday night. But, if you would like me to keep things to the Feast, then I will leave you to finish getting ready."

Fuck I hope she wants me to stay. I know I shouldn't want that. I know it's not right, but the thing is, it *doesn't* feel wrong. My pull to this little brat has never felt wrong, and it scares the shit out of me. I don't want to pretend that I don't care anymore, though. I actually don't think I can even if I tried.

Rhys takes a few very long-drawn-out moments to consider my words, and then her face contorts with the sassy attitude I know so well.

"Punish me, daddy."

A growl rips from my chest right before I lean in and claim her lips. I had my first taste of these lips on Sunday night, and fuck if I haven't dreamed of doing this again, just without the audience. So, to feel her pressing up against me, standing on her toes as those lush lips kiss me back with carnal desire, is fucking perfect.

As we kiss, I glide my fingers through her silky strands, and when I reach the ends, I twist her hair around my fist. Gripping tight, I tug, her head falling back as our lips separate, and she pants with wanton need.

"Do you know how hard you made me in class today with that little stunt? You purposely bent over to show me this fine arse." I slide my free hand up her thigh, clutching a fistful of her panty clad arse under her school skirt.

"But Daddy. I was just picking up my pencil case." The innocence in her tone just adds to her brattiness, and she shoots me a cheeky fucking wink.

"I should spank you," I growl, and she moans softly. Oh yes. My Kitten *wants* to be spanked.

Releasing my grip on her hair, I point to a chair in the corner. "Bring that over here."

Like a good girl, she does as I ask, but she takes her fucking time about it, dragging out the anticipation, which just makes me harder. When she gets close enough, I take the chair from her grip and position it a little way back from the mirror, taking a seat.

"Stand here and face the mirror," I command, pointing to the dirt ground in front of me. My little heathen smirks as she does as I ask, her eyes on my reflection in the mirror. "Take off your shirt and skirt."

Again, she obeys without protest, and I watch as she slowly peels her school shirt off, tossing it in the corner with her bag. Goosebumps spread across her skin, disappearing under the strap of the red bra she's wearing, and my fingers itch to unlatch it. But not yet. That will come off later.

As she unzips her skirt, she shimmys her arse a little before it slips free of her hips to pool around her feet. And there's those fucking cheeky panties.

Fuck me.

"Bend over and pick your skirt up." Christ, my voice is husky. It's because I'm so fucking horny, something which seems to only happen when my Kitten is around.

Just as she did in class this afternoon, Rhys bends forward at the waist, pushing out her arse with the words *'Fuck Me'* written across it, and picks up her skirt.

"Shall I toss it over with my other clothes, *daddy*?"

Fuuuck. I want her to stop saying daddy like that, but at the same time, I want her to say it more. "Yes." I grit out, and she tosses the skirt in the corner, staying in the bent position, teasing me with her two perfect globes.

"Stay like that, Kitten. Brace your hands on your knees and spread your legs further apart." I glide my hands over the round of her arse as I speak, watching as she obeys once again. The new position gives me a better view of not just her pantie clad arse but the wet patch soaking her crotch. My dick jumps at the sight. "Here we go. Brace yourself."

Shifting on the chair to get in a better position, I slap my hand down on her arse and revel in the gasp that escapes her perfect mouth. It's not a hard slap, but enough to give her fair warning on what's to come.

Then I do it again, just a little harder this time, extracting a moan to escape her lips.

"Yes, Daddy. Punish me."

I growl as my control snaps, her words pushing me over, and I slap her firm cheeks harder. She cries out but pants, "More." So, I give her what she wants and spank her harder. I repeat this over and over until I've spanked her ten times, and when I look up, I see her hands clutching each side of the mirror. Her eager eyes are watching me in the reflection; her cheeks flushed crimson, her pink lips parted as she pants.

Rubbing gently over the red fabric, I reach up, hooking the band with my finger, and slowly drag it over her reddened skin and down her legs.

"Is it sore?" I ask as I gently graze my fingers over the visibly inflamed skin.

"Only in a good way."

I can't hold back my grin. "Good girl."

Then she moans again.

My little Kitten is definitely into a lot of different kinks, and it sounds like praise kink is one of them.

Leaning forward, I press my lips to her tender skin and feel the heat radiating from where I punished her. The need to care for her after inflicting that pain is overwhelming and fucking primal. I need to care for her as bad as I needed to spank her, so I glide my tongue over the area before licking a trail down between her cheeks. She stiffens a little under the press of my tongue, but she doesn't say no and doesn't pull away. If anything, she pushes back towards me even more. So I continue my exploration, gliding my wet tongue over her little puckered rosebud, then right down to her needy cunt.

My greedy Kitten rocks back into me as I dart my tongue inside her molten heat, and the moan she releases is animalistic. Fuck yes. I love how unapologetic she is about sex. There's nothing fake about the way she fucks; it is, after all, her most fluent language. In saying that, I hope she doesn't hate me for what I'm about to do.

Pulling back, I eye her in the mirror as my fingers glide through her slick folds, and I slowly sink two digits in.

"Look at me, Kitten," I growl as she moans, pushing back to match the thrusts of my fingers. "We are going to have a little chat."

"Oh?" She pants, "Are we now?"

"Yes. I'm going to ask you questions, and you're going to answer them. Truthfully." Reaching my free hand up, I graze the creamy skin of her back, coming to the red fabric of her bra, and I unlatch it.

"And what if I don't?" Her voice quivers a little as I sink my fingers in deeper, causing her eyes to roll back before her lids flutter shut.

"Eyes on me, Kitten," I demand, and she snaps them open again. "Good girl."

Instant moisture seeps from her pussy and fuck. Now I know for sure that she gets off from the praise.

"To answer your question. If you don't answer me truthfully, then I won't let you come."

"What?" She moves to stand upright, but I push her forward again with my free hand.

"Stay there, Kitten. Hold on to the mirror again."

I can see how much she wants to disobey me, so I remind her of how good I can make her feel by curling my fingers, and fuuuck, she's like putty in my hands. Her perk arse pushes back towards me as she chases the pleasure I'm delivering.

"Have you done edging before Kitten?"

She shakes her head.

"You know what it is?" I curl my fingers again and then give her a moment to respond.

"S-stimulation to the brink, and then backing off?" Her words are more of a question, but in a nutshell, she's right.

"That's right, Kitten. So, here's what's going to happen. I'm going to make you feel good. *So* good. And I'm going to ask you a question, of which I'll stop what I'm doing until you answer. *Truthfully*. Then. I'll make you feel good again. We will do this over and over until we are both satisfied."

"Why?" It's all she can get out as I drive my fingers in deeper.

"Because something is going on with you, and I want you to talk about it with me. I feel like this is the only way that will happen."

"You're being mean, daddy. I don't want to talk. I want to fuck."

"Well, this way, we both get what we want."

To prove my point, I sink a third finger into her tight pussy, and her moan is loud in the small cobweb ridden room. I shift on the chair to get in a better position and press my thumb to her needy clit, revelling in her pleasured gasp. My cock jerks, feeling left out, but it will be sinking into her heat in no time, so it can fucking wait until I have some answers.

"Does that feel good, Kitten?"

"Yes." She pants, her eyes falling shut as she gives in to the pleasure building inside her. I watch her face contort in the mirror as she lets herself fall into rhythm. I can feel her walls going tighter already, so I need to start my questioning before she explodes on my fingers.

"Here's my first question, Kitten." When her eyes crack open, I continue. "Why did you get so stoned this morning?"

Then I pull my fingers free.

"Ugh! This isn't fair." She bolts upright and huffs. "Fuck the questions, Tyler. Fuck me already. Give me your cock."

I chuckle at her outburst. I'm not surprised. There's no way she's going to make this easy.

"I will give you my cock when we finish our chat. Answer the question, Kitten." I push her forward again and remind her of how good I can make her feel by grazing my fingers over her clit.

"Put your fingers back in, and I'll answer you." My little sass queen shakes her arse in my face, so I bite my bottom lip, trying to suppress my smile and nudge her entrance with three fingers. I don't sink them in, though. I applying some pressure to remind her of who's boss right now.

"Answer me truthfully, and I'll give you four fingers."

I feel her entrance pulse with need at my words, and a moment later, she speaks.

"Usually, I smoke a little Mary Jane to keep my horny Kitty at bay."

"But not this morning? You must have smoked more than a little." I circle my fingers around her dripping entrance, teasing her, reminding her.

"Just put them in already." She whines, and I have to admit, I find it really fucking hard not to give in and sink them into her heat.

"Answer me, and I will. Four fingers, remember?"

"I had a crappy day yesterday. An even crappier night. I just wanted to make it go away." There's pain in her tone, but her eyes harden, and I know if I'm not careful, I'll lose this game.

"You gotta be more specific, Kitten. What did you want to go away? What made you feel like that?"

Since I've asked a couple of questions, I decide to ease her suffering a little, and I slowly sink four fingers in. She moans again, and man, I'm ready just to drive my cock in and finish this already.

"Answers, please, Kitten." I remind her as I stretch her. More wet heat slips past my fingers as her body accepts me.

"The pain wouldn't go away." She pants. "Garrett reminded me of something I can never have."

Now we are getting somewhere. I drive my fingers in and out, letting my thumb become acquainted with her clit again, pressing firm circles over the nerve ending.

"Good girl." I give her the praise that adds to her growing pleasure and let her feel it build before I ask more questions. "What can you never have, Kitten?"

When I go to move my fingers from her heat, her hand darts out, wrapping around my wrist, holding me in place.

"I'll answer your questions. Just don't stop." Her words are a demand that makes my cock ten times harder.

"That's not how edging works. I have to stop. Give your body time to settle down again before I restart the pleasure. The idea is *not* to come. Not until I say you can." I shake off her grip and pull out of her.

Angry, she stands upright and spins on me, her chest rising and falling in pure frustration. Then, in typical Rhys style, she surprises me.

"Fine, if you're going to torture me like this, *you* can get on *your* knees in front of me so I can at least sit down!" Her eyes are dark pools of fury as she points to the dirt floor at her feet, and fuck, my grin breaks free before I can stop it.

"Very well." Amusement laces my tone as I speak, and we trade places. I drop to my knees before the chair as Rhys sits down, completely naked with not an ounce of shyness, and she spreads her legs wide, hooking her knees over the arms of the chair, opening herself fully. Then the little devil quirks a brow.

I can't help myself. I dart forward and run my tongue up through her folds and flick over her clit. She reacts instantly, throwing her head back and thrusting her hips up, seeking more. Then, like the arsehole I am, I draw back.

"Answer the question. What can you never have?"

Her eyes flit between mine, looking so much more innocent now that no makeup adorns them.

"A normal relationship." She whispers, and fuck, her eyes turn glassy.

Gliding my fingers up her parted thighs, I maintain eye contact with her as I feel her heat and slowly sink my fingers back inside her. She looks like a goddess, splayed open on the chair like this, her creamy skin almost glowing with flushed arousal. Her long dark hair falls partially over her shoulders, tumbling over her chest with a deep pink nipple peeking through, tempting me to have a taste. There's a small dark patch of short hair that sits just above her swollen clit. It's a real fucking turn on. So many women wax themselves bare these days, but my Kitten is more woman than any of them, and I fucking love that small strip coaxing me to her heat.

I ease back inside her, giving her the pleasure she's seeking, and lean forward to take her nipple between my lips. My tongue lashes over it as it pebbles hard, and her hands sink into my hair, holding me to her. I let her take more pleasure this time as I replay her words in my head. She thinks she can't have a normal relationship. If I were to guess, it has everything to do with her need for sex. Hell, I'm all too familiar with it myself.

For me, I have never found anyone that matches my sex drive or my need to push the boundaries in the bedroom. I like to control who I fuck, and I like to fuck hard. I also like to try new things, and most women I have attempted a relationship with balked at my kinks. I can't do vanilla, that's for sure, and trying to find someone to have a relationship with just got too hard. Sex clubs allow me to explore my desires and not feel kink shamed for it. I've gotten used to having an empty house and empty bed over the years.

Would I like to grow old with someone one day? Sure, as long as they enjoy being bound and gagged and fucked every which way known to man, even when they are seventy years old. The likelihood of finding that person is slim fucking pickings!

"Kitten," I mumble around her hard nipple, flicking my eyes up to meet hers as she pries them open. "What do you class as a normal relationship?"

As I continue to work my fingers inside her, I pull my thumb away from her clit, slowly easing the climactic build, and regretfully draw my mouth from her breast.

She groans in frustration and pouts. "I don't like this game anymore, daddy."

"Answer me, Kitten."

Our eyes are level now, and I desperately want to kiss her again. But not until she gives me more answers.

"Monogamy between a couple." Her words are quiet, and for the first time, she lacks confidence as she speaks. I don't like hearing her that way. The thought of her being sad or in emotional pain is unfathomable. The only way to help her is to understand her, so I return my thumb to her clit and lean in, hovering my lips over hers, not making contact.

"Since when has Rhys George ever done normal?" I ask, feeling her panted breath on my lips.

"She doesn't. That's the problem." Her words are clipped before she closes her eyes to focus on how my fingers bring her closer to the edge.

"What if your normal looks different to everyone else's normal? Can't you have *your* version of normal?" I dart my tongue out this time and lick the seam of her deep pink lips. Fuck, I love her like this. Bare and natural.

"I'm pretty sure I'm not going to find a guy that is happy to share me, Tyler." Then she moans loud, so close to coming, so I release my thumb again and stop moving my fingers.

"Fucking hell, I'm going to finish the job myself in a minute!" She hisses.

My chuckle is low, and my grin is wide. I fucking love pushing her buttons.

"You want to come, Kitten?"

"Yes, damn it!" Her dark eyes go wide as she grits her teeth in frustration. Fuck, she's perfect.

"Have you looked for a guy that is happy to share? Perhaps a polyamorous relationship? They are becoming more popular. Maybe something like that is Rhys George normal."

"Would that be enough?" Her words are a whisper, as if she's asking herself the question, but I answer her anyway.

"You'll never know unless you try, Kitten. Nothing lasts forever, but you gotta take chances. Otherwise you'll only live a life of regrets."

Then, to my surprise, a single tear pops free from her eye. I reach up and catch the stray drop, and she watches as I bring it to my lips and taste the salt with my tongue.

"Why do you have to be practically one hundred years old?"

My brat is back. I can't hold in my laugh, and her pretty pink lips tug upward in the most stunning smile I've seen her wear.

"Why do you have to be basically five years old, Kitten?"

She pouts past her smirk before pushing her tits closer to me.

"Fuck me, please, Daddy."

She doesn't have to ask twice.

"You want to come on my hand or my cock, Kitten?"

"Cock." Her response is quick, and she shuffles her arse a little in anticipation.

"Fine, but just so you know, when we come together outside of the Feast, you will take me bare."

She grins wickedly. "Yes, daddy."

I pull my hand free of her heat and grip my cock, giving it a quick pump before I line it up at her entrance. In one smooth move, I drive myself into her molten heat, right to the hilt. She's so fucking tight. Her walls grip me like a vice, and fuck if I don't nearly spill my load there and then. By some miracle, I compose myself and revel in her moaning cries as I start my unforgiving assault on her cunt. She meets each of my thrusts with a crazed need that has my dick swelling even more, and fuck my nuts start their ascent.

"You feel so good, Kitten." I rasp out as I drive into her harder and harder.

She moans, loving the praise, before dragging her eyes open to focus on mine.

"I'm going to come, daddy." She cries, and something primal in me roars, making me slam into her harder before my lips latch onto her nipple, and I find her swollen clit with my thumb.

The moment she explodes, and her walls clamp around my dick, I lose all control and follow her over. My release is hard and long as she milks me, extracting ropes of cum into her greedy cunt.

I don't know what it is about Rhys George, but one thing is for sure, no one makes me feel as much pleasure as my Kitten does.

Chapter Seventeen

Kitten

There's one thing I know for sure, and that is that Tyler Foster will never feel like my teacher *ever* again. This may be just sex, and I might be feeling alone in the way I feel, but we have definitely gone past the point of no return.

I feel like I just had a therapy session that involved sex. Like, what the hell? If I knew that existed, I would have ditched my traditional therapy sessions years ago. And yes, Tyler may have only got to the bottom of one of my many worries, but shit, I'll spill all of my worries and secrets if he edge's me all day, every day.

Ok. That's a lie. There's one secret I won't reveal to him or anyone. He can edge me all he wants. He will never get *that* secret out of me.

To say we are late to the Feast is an understatement. I quickly paint my face—not my best sugar skull artwork, but good enough to still look good and hide my identity—and Tyler cleans me up while I get to work. I should probably feel embarrassed that he spends a good amount of time cleaning Kitty, but I don't. The little horn bag even starts to get aroused again, so I have to get him to stop. Otherwise, we will miss the entire night.

Once my face is complete, Tyler helps me dress into the purple corset number that Master Hill left for me. Master Hill likes me in purple, and it's beginning to piss me off because it's my favourite colour, and I'm starting to hate it.

By the time we walk through the entrance of Vixen's Lodge, the party is well underway. Brock meets us, taking our coats, and I can tell by the way his brows lift that he's surprised we are arriving together. Not once have I walked through the door with an escort, so I understand why it must seem odd.

We hurry through to the cocktail lounge and scoop up a glass of bubbles each. As I drink the bubbles down, I take one last look at Tyler, who is now Skipper with his face masked in red leather, hiding his identity. Only his lips and eyes are visible, and those eyes linger on mine a little too long, but I can't bring myself to break the connection first.

"Here we go, Kitten. Time to play."

His raspy voice takes my mind back to the barn only minutes earlier, and for some strange reason, I have the urge to grab his hand and head back out the way we came. I don't, though. Tyler Foster is my sponsor and nothing more. We fuck other people, and as of Sunday night, we fuck each other as well, but that's it.

Tyler Foster is also like... old.

You can't keep him, Rhys!

Making our way down the hall, the steady thrum of the music mingles with moaning, and my heart starts racing. I watch Tyler's naked back disappear ahead of me as he moves into the crowded room, and I deliberately walk in the opposite direction, trying not to think about him fucking someone else.

"Kitten!" Madam Vik's voice is unmistakable. Shit, it's like she watches the entrance, ready to pounce. After having Tyler only minutes ago, I really can't bring myself to lower my standards. Ugh. What if she wants me to eat her out? Ew. I just can't. Not tonight.

As I get closer to the pile of withering bodies surrounding the main couch, I can see Madam Vik sprawled out, legs spread wide as *my* Casanova fucks her hard.

Wait.

Not *my* Casanova.

Jesus, get a grip, Rhys!

Shaun's head turns to the side, and I see those familiar steel-grey eyes peer up at me, surrounded by the same black leather mask he had on Sunday night. His thrusts don't stop as he watches me but pick up speed, his eyes following me as I move closer.

"Kitten. I'm thirsty. Bring that sweet pussy over here so I can drink you." Madam Vik never shies away from what she wants, and just like on Sunday night, I know I'm going to have to give her what she wants before I can go off and have some real fun.

"Of course, Madam." I smile at her, stepping up beside her and Cass.

"Throw your leg over, honey. Piss in my mouth."

Ah… What?

I thought she meant…

She can't be serious?

Madam Vik must be able to read my expression. "Don't make me ask twice, Kitten. I'm thirsty, and I haven't drunk you before. Give me what you've got." Then the old bat licks her lips.

I fight the shiver that's desperate to escape, and luckily, I win. Madam Vik wouldn't take too kindly to me responding that way.

"Ah… I'm not really into *that*. Sorry, Madam. Is there something else I can do for you?" I shuffle on the spot, glancing up to see several eyes on me. Moxie is in the corner, her usual corner, getting fucked by a chick with a strap-on, but her focus is on me as I stand awkwardly.

Madam Vik's eyes darken in anger, and she darts her hands out, grabbing onto Shaun's hips to halt his thrusts.

"Do I have to remind you of *your* duty here, Kitten?" Madam Vik's words a quiet, but they carry an unspoken threat.

For fuck's sake. Is she really going to make me pee in her mouth?

Oh my god! What if she wants to pee in *my* mouth?

Uh-uh. No fucking way!

"N-no, Madam. I just haven't done *that* before. I'm…" I can't fucking speak. I've done a lot of stuff, but never this. It's never been on my radar before, and I'm pretty sure it never will be.

"How about I show Kitten how it's done, Madam?" Moxie's voice comes from behind me, and I glance over my shoulder to see her pink masked face. Oh, thank fuck.

"That's nice of you to offer, Moxie, but I've drunk you before. I want something new tonight, and that's Kitten." Madam Vik turns her furious glare to me.

"Kitten, I'll help you. It's ok. You'll be fine." Moxie's words are quiet next to my ear so only I can hear, so I nod, and Madam Vik's face relaxes into a smile.

She loosens her grip on Shaun's hips and waves her hand in the air for him to continue while Moxie runs her hands down my body until she gets to the purple lace G-string I'm wearing.

"Bend over a little Kitten," Moxie says as she drags the thin scrap of lace over my arse.

Doing as she asks, I tilt forward a little, which means I'm now leaning over Vik's writhing body, obstructing her view of Shaun.

"I'm not gonna lie, Kitten." Shaun's husky voice is low, so only I hear as he thrusts into Madam Vik's. "Thinking about you pissing in her mouth has me about ready to come."

Well shit. Now I actually want to do this.

Stepping out of my G-string, I look up to find Tyler standing behind the couch, his eyes assessing the situation.

"Hello, Skipper. Have you come to watch Kitten give her first Golden Shower?" Madam Vik's voice is full of excitement.

"I've come to make sure my liege is feeling comfortable." His voice is firm and unapologetic, while his eyes hold determination as he glares at Vik in challenge.

He's giving me a way out. If I say I'm not comfortable, he will support me. I'm unsure if I should do this, but Shaun's words egg me on.

"Would *you* like me to do this, Skipper?" I really want to say daddy, but I kind of want to keep that between us now, with everything that's happened.

Tyler's blue eyes flare at my question, and I drop my gaze to watch his dick harden before my eyes. I don't know when he took his boxers off, but I'm fucking happy he did. Leaning forward, Skipper braces his hands on the back of the couch, not caring about the growing audience.

"Yes." The rasp in his voice makes Kitty purr, "But only if you are comfortable with it."

Well, fuck, I'm going to make myself comfortable with it. If both my guys find this a turn on to watch, then I'm not going to deny them.

They aren't your guys, Rhys!

I nod and turn my eyes to Madam Vik, who's now rubbing her own clit with her fingers as Shaun picks up the pace. "Are you ready for a drink, Madam?"

Her smile is broad, and she nods eagerly. I can't fight the shudder this time, but Moxie grabs each of my shoulders from behind and leads the way, effectively hiding my reaction. I'll have to remember to thank her later.

With Moxie's help, I move into position. Still facing Shaun, I throw one leg over Madam Vik's head, resting my knee on the cushions, hovering over her mouth. I'm thankful that I'm facing away from her gaze. I don't want to look into her eyes while I pee in her mouth. This is way out of my comfort zone as it is, but if I have to see her while I do it, I'll probably vom!

I feel Madam Vik's tongue brush over my folds as she lifts her head a little before she rests it back on the couch again. "I'm ready, Kitten."

I brace one hand on the back of the couch, and warmth spreads through me when Tyler lays his strong hand over the top of mine. He is showing his support. Reminding me I'm not alone, and my chest fills with something more than butterflies. I'm not sure what this feeling is. It feels both wonderful and terrifying.

My hand is taken by someone else, and I look away from Tyler's hand to see that Moxie has it in her grip. She offers me a warm smile, giving her head a slight nod, showing me she, too, is here for me.

I take a quick glance around at the growing audience, and I don't miss the fact that Master Hill is lurking nearby, his eyes glued onto me as he rearranges the crotch of his black suit pants. His stare brings back memories of someone I don't want to think about. Not here. Not now in this situation. Or Ever.

The sinister eyes of predators are all the same. It's the heat in their stare. The way their nostrils flare. The way they lick their lips. They do these things at the most inappropriate times, not able to hide their reaction.

A chill runs up my spine as I mentally shake myself to ignore that the creep is there watching everything I'm doing to his wife, and I try to focus on something good.

My eyes land on Tyler, who is stroking his cock as he watches on, and then move to Shaun to see his eyes are directed between my legs to my parted folds, waiting to see the evidence of what I'm doing.

A flush travels up my chest as a wave of embarrassment hits me. I've never felt embarrassed with all the eyes on me before. It's a strange sensation, and I'm thankful no one can see the colour of my skin under the painted mask. I don't think I've ever peed in front of someone before.

"It's ok, Kitten. Close your eyes if it helps to concentrate." Moxie whispers in my ear, so I nod, letting my lids fall shut. After a few moments, I feel myself relax, and the warm fluid starts to slowly stream from me as I empty my bladder.

Loud moans dance through the air as I pee. Curious to see everyone's reactions, I pry my eyes open to see Tyler bending forward a little over the back of the couch to get a better view, while Shaun is slamming hard into Vik as she mashes her clit like crazy.

Crazy. That's a good fucking word for what's happening right now. I'm definitely not into this, but fuck, I love how turned-on Shaun and Tyler are. Others around us are too. Even Moxie is rubbing the heel of her palm over her clit.

The next moment, Vik's orgasm must hit her hard because she starts withering around like she's having a fucking seizure, and my pee starts going everywhere but in her mouth. That's when the moans of ecstasy sound around the room increase, and Shaun throws his head back as he reaches his climax.

"Kitten!" Tyler's voice is demanding, and I shoot my eyes to him immediately. "Bend forward. Open your mouth."

I don't hesitate, doing what my sponsor asks just in time to catch his cum as it pulses from his engorged cock. His load is too much for me to swallow in one, so by the time he's done, his white cum oozes from my lips and down my chin.

I may not have had an O myself just now, but fuck, if that wasn't fun watching everyone else get there. This is what I love about coming here. Yes, what I did wasn't *my* thing, but clearly, most around us fucking loved it. Where else can they do something like this? I bet if they have husbands or wives, they can't do this sort of stuff with them. And man, how sad is that?

As Moxie helps me move off Vik's face while someone hands Madam Vik a towel so she can dry my piss from her face and hair, Master Hill walks slowly past, keeping his eyes on me the whole time. He doesn't look at anyone else. Not Shaun, or Tyler, or Moxie, or even his wife. Just me, going so far as to turn his head back over his shoulder so he can maintain his view of me until he leaves the room.

I feel dirty. Not just because I pissed in someone's mouth just now, but because the lingering gaze of Master Hill is making my skin crawl.

Others move in around us, eager to get to Madam Vik. God knows why. I don't mind, though. It gives me, Shaun, Tyler and Moxie, whose real name is Agatha, a chance to flee. And flee, we do. We can't seem to dart through the crowd fast enough, eager to escape the crowd as we move out to the jacuzzi retreat, and I try to push all thoughts of Master Fuck Face to the back of my mind.

We are laughing by the time we stop in front of the self-serve bar, where Tyler hands me a coke, and I guzzle it down eagerly.

"I just gotta tell you right now," I gasp as the fizz works its way down, "if *you* ask to piss in *my* mouth, I will dick punch you!"

My words make them all laugh, and a lightness sweeps over me. It's nice having Tyler and Shaun here by my side. I'm used to being around Moxie at the Feast nights. We usually hook up for some girl-on-girl action, but aside from that, I tend to be on my own, fending for myself.

"Not your thing, Kitten?" Shaun asks teasingly, and I shoot him a glare.

"Absolutely not!"

"What if he wants *you* to piss in *his* mouth, Kitten? Would you?" Tyler's question throws me. As far as Moxie knows, we are all strangers. She has no idea that Skipper is my teacher and Casanova is my school friend. I don't want to give away that we know each other, but it's hard not to act familiar with each other.

I glance at Shaun and screw my nose up. "You wouldn't want that. Would you?"

He shrugs. "I dunno. I'm not ruling it out." Then he shoots me a wink.

"Ok. This conversation is fucked up! I'm taking a dip." I walk off on their laughter and climb down into the empty jacuzzi, the hot water feeling amazing on my skin as I step in. When the laughter dies down behind me, I turn to see three sets of eyes on me, watching my every move.

Still standing in the waist height of bubbling water, I reach back and unclasp my corset, tossing it over the edge of the spa once it's free.

"Who wants to join me?"

Moxie's grin stretches wide as she approaches me, her caramel eyes alight with mischief peering through the pink and white floral mask. It's a cute mask that leaves the bottom of her face free while it covers the top part and has a slit in the back for her light brown ponytail to hang free.

"May I join you, Kitten?" It's cute that she asks for permission even though we tend to hook up most Feast nights. But that's the rules, and Moxie always asks.

"Please," I respond to her, lowering myself a little more in the water.

Behind Moxie, I can see Shaun and Tyler watching on and quietly talking. What do those two have to chat about? Oooh! Maybe they want to hook up. A bit of guy-on-guy action. Fuck, why does the thought of seeing them together sound so hot?

"What is Kitten smirking at?" Moxie asks as she eases herself into the water before me.

"Well, if you must know. I was just imagining Skipper and Casanova fucking each other."

Moxie giggles while Shaun spits out his mouthful of drink, and Tyler's brows lift, disappearing under his red mask. I burst out laughing, and Tyler growls, approaching the jacuzzi.

"Have you ever seen me fucking a guy, Kitten?"

"No," I shrug, "It doesn't mean you haven't."

"Well, let me clear it up for you. The only dick I like is my own. And the only arse I fuck has a pussy in front of it. Not a set of balls!"

My insides clench in arousal at his admission of fucking arse. I don't know why. I've managed to keep that part of me a virgin. Surprisingly. To me, that region almost seems sacred—something not given over easily. Something shared with someone special.

Fucking hell that sounds so ridiculous. That's what I was meant to do with my *actual* virginity, or so I learned when I got a little older. Girls grow up thinking that they should keep their virginity until they find that one special person to give it to. When I lost mine, I didn't even know what the word virginity was. Maybe that's why I hold my anal v-card so close? Let's be honest, though. I'm never going to have that special person to give it to. When I do hand that bad boy over, I probably won't even see the person again.

"How about you, Casanova? Ever fucked another guy?" Moxie asks, and I shake my thoughts away, turning my eyes to Shaun as he comes to stand next to Tyler.

"Not yet." He grins. Not an ounce of shame in his tone, as if he's not ruling it out.

"I think I just came," I whisper yell playfully, causing Shaun's grin to broaden.

"You like the thought of me fucking a guy, Kitten?" He asks, his cockiness coming out in his tone.

"Fuck yes!" I dart my eyes to Tyler.

"Would you do that for me, *Daddy?* Would you bend over and let Cass fuck you so I can watch?"

"No!" He hisses, and we all laugh at his visible discomfort. Poor Tyler looks mortified.

Moxie shifts behind me as I calm my laughter, and she starts peppering kisses over my bare shoulder and up my neck as she weaves her hand around my front to cup my breast. It feels so fucking good to feel her delicate lips brush across my skin and the softness of her skin on mine. It's a clear contrast to having a guy do the same thing, which just adds to how excited it makes Kitty.

Tyler and Shaun are still standing outside the spa, but they are watching on with piqued interest, and my hungry eyes dance between both of their growing erections. Even though my Kitty is submerged in steamy hot water right now, I can still feel the wet heat between my legs.

"They like watching you." Moxie whispers in my ear before latching onto my lobe, sending a shiver up my spine. She tweaks my nipple, making it pebble hard, and her other hand snakes around to brush over my mound.

I release my moan, wanting the guys to hear it, as I push Kitty up out of the water, seeking some friction from Moxie's hand. She doesn't leave me hanging, cupping my Kitty and pressing the heel of her palm against my clit.

This time when I moan so do Moxie, Shaun and Tyler. Both the guys instantly grip their own cocks, and I desperately want to tell them to swap and take each other's, but I don't want to scare Tyler away.

He's not normally so involved in my playtime. Sometimes when I'm in the throes of sex, mingled and entwined in a mountain of bodies, he makes a brief appearance, like he's checking that I'm being treated right. And yes, I have often teased him, trying to get him to step over the line, mainly because I'm a brat, but I knew he wouldn't do it. Now, however, since Master Hill forced us to be together on Sunday night, here he is, not just checking on me but interacting. I kinda love it, just as much as I love the private punishment he dealt me earlier. It was unexpected, but fuck, it just makes me want to be a *very* naughty girl in Health class. He's going to regret making my punishment so fucking enticing!

"Shall we play with some toys, Kitten?" Moxie asks, and I nod. "Dildo or vibrator?"

"Dildo. Choose one that's nice and thick." My words are for Moxie, but I keep my eyes on the guys and revel in the way Shaun curses under his breath at the mention of the dildo.

"Can you help us out, Skipper?" Moxie gains Tyler's attention. "Can you grab a girthy dildo for Kitten?"

His smirk is almost sinister when he nods and turns to go to the toy bank. Just the thought of him standing there checking out the dildos and choosing one for me has me slick with need.

"Let's move you to the ledge in the corner." Moxie whispers before nipping my ear. Then she drops her hold on me, and I move to the corner where a small ledge sits just below the water level. It's the perfect height to prop your arse on, which is what I do, spreading my legs to give the room a good view.

Shaun situates himself across from me on the edge of the spa, dangling his legs in, still slowly pumping his hard dick, his gaze roaming over my body before meeting my eyes.

"You're fucking perfect, Kitten."

And now I'm burning up. The fucker knows I'm not good with compliments. So naturally, I shift the convo to a place I feel more comfortable.

"My Kitty is perfect, isn't it?" I lick my lips and watch his grin.

"It's as perfect as the rest of you."

Motherfucker! I bare my teeth and hiss at him, causing him to chuckle.

"I'm not going to stop reminding you of how beautiful you are, so get used to it."

"Well, Cass, I hope you like jerking yourself off because that's the only action you'll be getting!"

Moxie joins Shaun, laughing, even though I don't think it's funny.

"What's so funny?" Tyler asks, returning to the room carrying two dildos.

"You are if you think that monster will fit inside me!" My eyes are practically bulging out of my head as I cringe at the monstrosity in his hand.

"Come on, Kitten. We'll lube it up nice and good." Tyler tries to hide his smirk, but that just makes Moxie and Shaun laugh even harder.

"Oh, you're a bunch of funny fuckers tonight, aren't you!" I hiss as I watch Tyler sit the giant thing on the edge of the spa.

"It's ok, Kitten. I actually got the big one for Casanova. Thought he might like to take it up his arse."

That shuts Shaun up, but not Moxie, who is clutching her bare stomach.

"Keep that fucking thing away from me!" Shaun points at it like it's going to attack him any second.

Coming around the outside of the tub, Tyler ignores Shaun holding out a much more suitable sized dildo to me.

"This do, Kitten?"

I grin. "Perfect, daddy." I take the black rubber object from him as a low growl rumbles from his chest. He secretly likes me calling him daddy. I just know it.

The dildo has a suction cup at the bottom, so I hand it off to Moxie as I stand, and she holds it up as Tyler squeezes lube over it, rubbing his hand up and down the length of it to get good coverage.

Sweet baby Jesus, that sight gets my Kitty circling with her tail flitting from side to side. Tyler is a tall guy, built like a pro athlete with large hands. Watching him run them over the dildo makes me gush. My eyes dart over to Shaun, who grins knowingly at me, and

I bite my bottom lip. I bet he thought Tyler's hand running over the black rubber looked fucking hot as well.

When Moxie has the suction in place, I straddle the ledge, putting my feet on the jacuzzi seats under the water. Then I slowly lower myself down. Moxie and Tyler take each of my arms, supporting me, keeping me steady as I slowly stretch around the thick shaft. I take my time, so Kitty can adjust. Tyler really did choose a girthy toy for me. It burns a little as I sink down, but the desperate ache deep inside fuels me to keep going.

I moan as I finish taking the black object as far as my body will allow, and Tyler moves behind me to help hold me up. I let myself relax back against him a little and watch as Moxie stands before me. Then she leans in for a kiss.

Her lips are sweet, thin, and soft. There are no scratchy whiskers like you get from kissing a guy, just smooth skin that feels like silk. When her tongue darts into my mouth, my hips move on their own accord in a slow rhythmic rise and fall. Our kiss deepens, and Moxie clasps my head as my hands wander up her flawless skin to find the round swell of her tits. I feel her pebbled nipple under my touch. Firm. Straining. Needy.

The rougher surface of Tyler's hand makes itself known, sliding between my body and Moxie's, pinching my nipple. I gasp into Moxie's mouth, and she breaks the kiss, slowly shifting down to take my other nipple in her mouth.

As I continue rising and falling on the dildo, feeling the most addictive fullness, Shaun's black leather mask comes into view. His steel-grey eyes are wide with excitement, and the grip he has on his cock looks almost painful.

Stretching my hand toward him, he doesn't hesitate, sliding into the water, slowly walking to me. Once he reaches us, he grabs my chin and steals his own kiss, successfully rendering my mind a blank canvas of nothing but pleasure and sensation. The feel of Tyler's breath on my ear on one side, Shaun's breath on my cheek on the other side, and Moxie's tongue as it glides down to my aching clit is all too much, yet not enough. Having the three of them touching me, worshipping me, is mind-blowing.

There are so many sensations right now. So many hands and tongues. Pleasure shooting from my nipples, pulsing at my clit, throbbing in my core. It's fucking brilliant, and I know I'm not going to last much longer.

Thinking too soon, in a surge of pleasure that comes from nowhere, I erupt in a gripping wave of ecstasy that is so intense, I momentarily see stars. I scream, although I can hardly hear it with the blood coursing through my veins. Then, as I come down from my extreme high, which should have me sated and lethargic, something happens. It's like a switch is flicked in my brain, having the opposite reaction.

I quickly rise off the dildo, the movement pushing everyone back to stare at me in confusion. Then, like a possessed animal, I bare my teeth and leap on Shaun.

Chapter Eighteen

Casanova

S he's gone wild. Like a fucking animal! And fuck yeah, I'm down with it. Rhys George is a sex goddess. She has no shame. No restraints. Her only flaw is that she doesn't believe the compliments I give her, but we can work on that.

I catch her as she leaps at me after slipping that massive dildo from her pussy. Her legs and arms wrap around me as she claims my lips in the hottest fucking kiss I've ever had. We turn fevered, our teeth clashing together, and I can feel her heat grinding against my mate Thor as we sink lower into the water.

"Cass," she mumbles against my lips, "Call daddy over."

I can't help but chuckle. She's such a little brat, always causing trouble. Mr Foster—or should I say, Skipper, because it freaks me out to think that my fucking PE teacher is under that red mask—pretends he doesn't like her calling him daddy. But I've seen the way his eyes flare with heat and how his body reacts. He can pretend all he likes. He's not fooling anyone.

Breaking our kiss, she peppers her lips down my neck as I glance over her shoulder to Skipper watching on with his dick in his hand.

"Hey, daddy. Come here. Kitten wants you." I shoot him a toothy, shit-eating grin as he growls under his breath. Grabbing Moxie's hand, Skipper moves through the bubbling water, dragging her with him.

Pressing up against Kitten's back, Skipper leans close to her ear.

"I'm here, Kitten. So is Moxie."

Rhys moans, still pressing her heat against my dick, and fuck, I just want to sink into her right now. Lifting her head from my neck, she peers back towards Skipper and Moxie.

"I wanna fuck Cass while I watch you fuck Moxie's arse."

My dick fucking jerks like I'm about to explode like a fire hydrant right here, right now. I wasn't expecting her to say that, and I also wasn't expecting the filthy fucking grin that Skipper shoots my girl before turning to Moxie.

"You up for that, Mox?"

She nods, "Hell yes."

Skipper takes control before Moxie finishes speaking, moving to the edge of the spa, grabbing the lube and a couple of condoms before tossing one to me.

"Put that on, Fuck Boy!" He points at me sternly, and I try not to laugh. Motherfucker is protective of Kitten, that's for sure.

Rhys loosens her limbs, climbing off me, her eyes flitting between my hand, rolling the latex down my hard as fuck dick, to Skipper doing the same while smearing it with lube once it's on. One look in Kitten's eyes, and I can see how high she is. She's sailing on cloud nine right now, so high that I'm not sure she'll ever come down. It's a beautiful sight to see.

Rhys watches on in needy fascination as Moxie positions herself at the edge of the spa right next to us, bending forward to point her bare arse at Skipper, spreading her legs wide. Rivers of lube run over Moxie's tanned globes and between her cheeks as Skipper spreads it on, sinking a finger in and out of her back passage.

It's hot as hell to watch, and my Kitten must agree because she grabs my hips before palming my cock.

"Start slow and then go hard." Kitten orders looking up at me and then Skipper.

We both nod because fuck yes, that sounds like a good plan!

Besides the fact that my right arm is grazing my naked PE teacher's left arm, and I've seen way too much of his dick, this whole situation has me fucking salivating. I can't wait to feel Kitten wrapped around my cock again. Her pussy is paradise, and I know I'll never want to leave.

Bracing her arms back on the edge of the spa, Kitten prepares for me. Her creamy tits and those fucking ripe pink nipples are gleaming with droplets of water. The bubbles from the spa are pushing her arse up, giving me a glance at her needy pussy every now and then as it bobs up and down in the water.

"You ready, Kitten?" I ask, and she smiles wickedly.

"Get inside me, Casanova."

Grinning back, I grip her hips, keeping her still as I line my cock up and nudge her entrance. At the same time, I can see from the corner of my eye Skipper doing the same thing to Moxie's arse, and in unison, we sink into heaven.

Our four moans fill the room simultaneously, and when I pry my lids open, I notice we have a growing audience. The Feasters love their Kitten. And rightly so. She's not just stunning to watch, but her shameless bliss in her sexuality is something you can't take your eyes off.

Focusing my attention on my Kitten, I watch her perky tits bounce with each thrust I deliver and the way her lips part, releasing purring moans each time I slide back inside, filling her.

"Rub your clit, Kitten," I demand, and she obeys with a slight grin.

"You too, Mox." Skipper demands this time, and Moxie shifts her weight to one hand as she follows the order she was given.

With the motion of her black nailed fingers circling her clit, Rhys starts pumping her hips forward with more desperation, and I know she's close. Her chocolate eyes take everything we do in, and I can see she loves the visual. She loves seeing my cock disappear inside her tight cunt, and she revels in seeing Skipper fuck Moxie's arse. I have to agree with her. The whole thing is fucking hot and has me ready to blow my load.

"Is Cass fucking you good, Kitten?" Skipper grunts out as he thrusts, and it hasn't escaped my notice that while he is fucking Moxie, he barely pays her any attention. His eyes are all for my Kitten, and fuck if I don't feel like elbowing the motherfucker like some jealous prick trying to stake his claim.

"Yes." Rhys' voice is husky with desire. "Cass feels so fucking good, daddy."

"Good." He grumbles. Even though he said good, his tone doesn't sound all that happy. Yeah, he's definitely got a thing for *my* Kitten. If I were a better man, I'd let it go because he has no claim on her since he's her fucking teacher and all, but I'm *not* a better man. She's mine, and I'm claiming her *now*.

Leaning in, I hook my arm around Kitten's back and haul her up on the edge of the spa so I can lean in closer to her. Her silky legs wrap around me, and her heels dig into my arse cheeks as she meets me thrust for thrust. Our arms cling to each other, and I take her lips in mine, pushing my tongue in to meet hers. My grunts mingle with her moans as we kiss, and when I feel her tightening around Thor, nearly ready to explode, I release her lips and latch onto her neck. With a fevered desperation, I suck on her delicate skin as she replicates my move and latches onto my neck. Then we both detonate in unison.

My nuts fucking disappear as the ripples of ecstasy zap through me, my cum shoots into the barrier, keeping me from feeling her bare heat. I swear, I go blind for a moment. Either that or I've died, and I'm walking towards the light because that's all I can see—blinding hot white light.

Panting breaths and the feel of Kitten's tongue gliding up my neck is what brings my sight back, and with her in my arms, I cup her nape and guide her head back so I can taste her lips again. Our kiss is slow, and her limbs slacken as I ease us back down into the hot, bubbling water to submerge us until only our heads are visible.

"You're fucking perfect, Kitten," I whisper in her ear, suddenly wishing it was just the two of us. What I wouldn't give to take care of her right now. To clean her up, dry her off and lay her in my bed so I can wrap myself around her for the night. I'd love to hear her steady breathing as she sleeps. And I'd love to wake up with her next to me. It makes me wonder if there's ever a quieter side of Rhys George.

What would she be like to just lay beside and talk to about anything and everything?

"Cass," she whispers back. "I wish I could keep you."

I'm about to drawback so I can look into her dark eyes, but then Skipper moves in behind her, winding his arm around her waist and breaking the seal in our connection.

"Kitten." His voice is low before he nips her ear, extracting a sexy moan past her lips. "Are you ok?"

She nods at the same time I snap, "Of course she's ok!"

Those harsh blue eyes belonging to my PE teacher snap towards me in a clear scowl, but I don't care. I fucking scowl back. Fuck this arsehole! He deliberately came to interrupt our moment, for fuck's sake! I need to ask Rhys what she meant when she said she wishes she could keep me. Why does she think she can't? Does she think I wouldn't want more with her? Because hell yes, I do. I know I'm not meant to feel that way.

For one reason, we are in the throes of a Feast night, a fucking orgy club. It's strictly anonymous sex. No strings. I'm not meant to know the identity of who I'm fucking. It's set up that way to avoid feelings getting involved. But I do know *who* Kitten is. I've been craving her for a few months now, even when she was with Marcus. I knew those eyes the moment they met mine at Sunday's Feast when my lips were locked on her sweet pussy. Even what we shared in the Photo Lab at school was mind-blowing, and I'm not talking just about the sex. There's something more there. A connection I don't understand. Something I've never felt.

Skipper growls at me like he's a fucking grizzly bear or something, and the noise causes Kitten to moan.

"Jesus, daddy. Do it again." Rhys grins over her shoulder, and Skipper complies before stealing her lips in a kiss that has her grinding her pussy against me.

Fuck, she's insatiable.

The lights in the room start flickering, which means the Feast is wrapping up in about fifteen minutes. Even though there's time for another quick session, Rhys pouts, and her shoulders slump.

"I have to see everyone out."

Both Skipper and I frown. I don't know what he's frowning about, but my frown is because this situation seems more and more fucked up the more I think about it. Rhys is required to interact with Madam Vik when she first arrives. It's like an unspoken rule or something. No one else has to do that, just *my* Kitten. And I've learnt that Kitten is part of the farewell party as well. She gives farewell kisses that hold naughty promises if Feasters return next time. A little hug, maybe a gentle feel up as people exit.

By the way the light dims in her eyes, I have to think she really doesn't like this part of her time here at the Feast. Why does she put up with it?

"Let's get you dry and back in your outfit, Kitten." Skipper draws away, taking her with him to climb out of the spa.

Now that she's not in my arms anymore, I feel empty. Lost. It's a shit feeling, and I want it to go away, but that means having her in my arms again, and now isn't the time.

I watch Skipper help Rhys dry and get dressed while I dry off and wrap the towel around my waist before throwing the used condom in the bin. Once she's done, Rhys speaks quietly with Moxie before kissing her cheek, and then she turns her hypnotising chocolate eyes to me as she approaches.

"How's that pretty cock of yours, Cass?"

"Missing your tight pussy, Kitten." I grin at her, instantly feeling better now that her attention is on me.

Fuck, I think I'm Kitten whipped.

"Oh yeah? He's a greedy fella, isn't he? He's had more than most lately." Rhys presses her delectable body up against mine. The purple lingerie she's wearing is hot as fuck, and Thor starts to awaken again.

Down boy.

"I think he's addicted. When can he have another hit?" I snake my arm around Rhys' back, holding her to me. Something like uneasiness flits past her eyes. I think. It's hard to tell with the black, purple and white paint still unmarred on her face.

"He definitely is greedy. He will just have to be patient. After all, good things come to those who wait." Her grin is toothy and cheeky, and I can't help myself. I lean in and nip her bottom lip.

"That's a croc of shit. He'll have her when he wants." I growl, and her cheeky grin widens.

"He'll have her when I decide, Casanova."

With a quick peck to my lips, she drops her arms, and I reluctantly let her step back. I don't want to, but I can feel Skipper boring a hole into the back of my head, so I figure it's best not to cause a scene.

It's harder than I thought it would be to watch my girl walk away to give every other undeserving bastard her attention. It's an unfamiliar feeling. Possessive. Jealous. Needy. I should be scared. I should be bolting as fast as I can in the other direction. Shaun-Casanova-Bossier doesn't do possessive, jealous or needy. He's a giver and a taker. But not a keeper.

Well, he never used to be those things, but whether he likes it or not, he's exactly those things when it comes to Rhys George. I'm going to keep her, and even though she doesn't know it yet, she's going to keep me, too.

Chapter Nineteen

MARCUS

R hys has been avoiding me. I kind of thought she'd accepted my apology about being a prick the other day, but then she ghosted my FaceTime call on Tuesday night, and she dodged me all day yesterday at school. I wanted to call her or message her all fucking day, but I decided to back off a little. Smothering her will only push her away more.

"So, what's your plan, then?" Jared asks as we walk through the school gate on Thursday morning. He's been my best mate since we were kids. It had always been me, Jared, Lexi and Abbey, but now things have changed, and I feel like he's the only one left.

It's a ridiculous thought, and I know it's coming from a place of waning confidence. Lexi is still around. It's just different now, with her attention so glued to my cousin. It's almost sickening. I love them both, though, so I try my best to be happy for them. But Ayden's presence has changed the dynamics of our group. Of our bond.

Then there's Abbey Delany, Lexi's ex-best friend. She did some fucked up shit to Lexi when Lexi needed her the most, and now she's gotten herself into a twisted situation of her own. Abbey was a significant part of our foursome when we were younger. It's hard to believe how things have ended up.

So yeah, Jared Crowley is all that's left of our original group, and while Simon, Garrett and Shaun are all my good mates, for some reason, I feel like they are avoiding me lately. They seem alright when we're at school in a group, but every time I've tried to organise to hang out with them this week, they've been too fucking busy. I don't know what the fuck is so important that they can't give me an hour of their fucking time. Fuck, maybe they are sick of hearing me harp on and on about Rhys. Shit, is Jared sick of hearing it too?

"You really want me to repeat it, bro? Aren't you sick of me going on about how I'm gonna win Rhys over?"

Turning his frown to me, Jared shakes his head. "Dude! Why would you think that?"

I shrug, reaching forward to pull the door to the east block open where our lockers are.

"It feels like the others are avoiding me. I figured they must be sick of hearing my shit."

As we get to my locker, Jared leans on the one next to mine, eyeing me.

"I gotta be honest. The other guys *are* acting fucking weird this week, but I don't think it's because of you, man."

"You don't think?" Fuck, I sound like an insecure pussy right now.

"Nah, man. They understand that you're a lovesick fool." Jared grins, so I punch his arm.

"Fuck off, idiot."

He chuckles.

"Dude. Maybe you're overthinking it. Let's just focus on how you're going to win George over. What class do you have with her today?"

"Maths. Period four. Hastings is in that class, too. Maybe I can get him to help me. I need to make sure she has nowhere else to sit but next to me."

Grabbing my books, I close my locker before we head up the corridor to Jared's. This time I lean against the lockers as Jared gets his shit together, and when he slams it shut and turns, he immediately starts laughing as he looks past my shoulder.

"Fuck, Bossi! Looks like you got some action last night."

Turning, I see Shaun approaching us, his bag slung over his shoulder, and his dark hair still damp from a shower. All the chicks love this guy. They practically cream themselves just from glancing his way. Fucking Spanish genes make him look like a fucking underwear model, and the girls can't get enough of him. He was declared Fox Pines Catholic's Spanish Casanova a couple of years back. It's fucking fitting.

It takes me a moment to figure out what Jared is referring to, but as I take in the way Shaun has the collar of his school shirt sticking up, as well as his blazer collar, I notice the darkened skin on his neck. The fucker has a hickey!

I can't help myself. I start laughing.

"Looks like you got mauled, man." I chuckle, and he rolls his eyes.

"More like I got her so worked up that she lost control. They don't call me Casanova for nothing."

Cocky bastard. We all laugh at his expense.

"What's so funny?" Simon asks, bounding up like the ball of energy he is, with Garrett not far behind, looking as broody as ever.

"Bossi has a love bite." Jared chuckles before reaching forward and shoving Bossi's collars down to reveal the red and purple monstrosity.

"Hey! Hands off the goods, bro!" Shaun hisses as we all laugh. Well, all but Garrett. For some reason, he's frowning.

I mean, it's rare to get the big bugger to smile, but fuck, this is one of those times he would normally show us that smile that turns the beast into a fucking teddy bear. I wonder what's up his arse today?

We shoot the shit for a few more minutes before the bell goes. My first two classes are boring and repetitive, with the teachers focusing on finishing off any outstanding work and studying for upcoming exams. Term 4 is pretty cruisey. We only have two more weeks of school before exams, and then we're done for the year. I can't fucking wait. This year has been hard with all the shit that happened to Lexi, so I'm looking forward to a summer of carefree fun with my mates.

At recess, we congregate in the courtyard, piling our blazers into a mountain of fabric so we can enjoy the warm spring sun. Like me, most of the guys have their sleeves rolled up, while some of the girls are already wearing the summer uniform. Those who aren't have their sleeves rolled up too.

I'm half-listening to a conversation between Hastings and Ayden, which I'm fairly certain will end in Simon getting a dead arm. He's talking about Lexi, which usually results in him saying something to rile my cousin up.

I know the moment Rhys enters the courtyard. I wish I could say something like the air shifts, and I feel electricity in the air, but let's not get fucking carried away. Rhys George likes to make her presence known. Her laughter fills the air, and all eyes turn to see her walking with Lexi toward the table we all parked our arses on.

"Did you all get the invitation to Bonnie Mayer's Halloween party next Thursday night?" Rhys asks, and a round of *yeahs* answer her. Then she turns to Lexi, placing her hands on each of Lexi's shoulders. "It's going to be epic, Lex. What will we dress up as?"

"Ugh. Do I have to go?" Lexi whines, "I hate dress-up parties."

"OMG, Lexi West! Yes, you have to go!" Rhys declares, and Lexi rolls her eyes.

"Can I just dress up as Lexi West? I heard she's pretty badass." Lexi smirks at Rhys, which wins her a frown.

"Absolutely not!" Rhys sounds gob smacked. "Although, I think you should definitely go with the badass chick theme. What about Harley Quinn? You'd make the best Harley Quinn."

Lexi smiles and nods. "Yeah, ok. You win, Rhys."

Rhys beams, turning her proud smile to us.

"What are you going as Rhys?" Simon asks, and she shrugs. "What about a naughty nurse?"

At Simon's suggestion, all the colour drains from Rhys' face and her smile drops.

What the fuck?

"What's wrong?" Lexi asks Rhys, grabbing her hand, which seems to jolt Rhys out of the dark place her mind just went.

"What?" Rhys glances at Lexi and then at us, throwing us a smile, which is the fakest smile I've ever seen on her face.

Shit. Something really isn't right with my girl. What just happened?

"Rhys?" Lexi's voice is filled with concern, and her eyes dart to mine, but I shrug because I don't fucking have a clue what just happened.

Rhys turns her weird smile to Lexi and hugs her, jumping up and down excitedly.

"I can't wait to spend Halloween with you, Lexi."

As she stops jumping, Rhys pulls back from Lexi, and as if time slows, my heart stops dead in my chest.

No!

There, on the side of *my* girl's neck, is a dark purple hickey peaking through a thick layer of make-up that must have wiped off when she hugged Lexi. It's a big, dark, fucking love bite that is coincidently a new addition to her skin the same day that Bossi turns up to school with one.

Like fuck, that's a coincidence!

I don't even realise I've moved, but before I know what I'm doing, I grip Rhys' shoulder tight, holding her in place as I wipe my thumb over her neck to remove the rest of the makeup.

"Hey!" Rhys snaps, trying to push me away, but it's too fucking late. I can see what she's trying to hide, and by the curses behind me from the guys, so can they.

Shocked, I take a step back to look into her eyes. The same eyes I fell in love with. The same eyes that give her away when they dart over my shoulder to where I know Bossi is sitting at the table.

Blood pulses aggressively through my veins as I slowly release her and turn around to glare at a guy that I thought was my mate. Then, without a second thought, I fucking launch myself at Shaun.

My fist smacks loudly as it meets his nose, and he flies backwards off the table, with me following. When he hits the ground, I lose any sense of what's going on. I just swing my arms and let my fists speak for me as they pummel into his cheek, chin, eye, shoulder.

I'm fucking livid. I could kill right now!

It's not until I feel hands pulling me off Bossi that my hearing kicks in. I can hear Rhys screaming, begging me to stop. I can hear Lexi doing the same, while I'm almost certain the arms wrapped around me from behind are my cousins. Ayden.

As I'm pulled free and see the blood covering Shaun's face, Rhys falls to her knees next to my so-called mate with tears streaming down her face in concern. For him! And fuck if that doesn't just piss me off more. A feral growl rips from my chest as I escape Ayden's hold, and I dart forward, forcefully pushing Rhys away from Shaun as I lay into him again.

"Marcus! No! Please stop!" Rhys cries. But I don't stop.

Then, as someone pulls me off Shaun again, my fists keep swinging, hoping to land one more punch. The satisfaction only lasts a second when I feel my knuckles meet a face. The problem is, it's not Shaun's face. My fist connects with Rhys' face.

"Get back!" A roar shouts, shaking me out of my rage as I see Mr Foster, my PE teacher, skid over the grass on his knees as he comes to Rhys' aid.

What the fuck have I done?

There are multiple arms holding me back now, but I'm not fighting anymore as I realise that I just hit my girl.

No. Not *my* girl. Fucking Bossi's girl.

I can't help it. I scream, agony tearing at my insides. My knees give out, but I don't fall. Whoever has hold of me is keeping me in place. I wish they'd let go of me. I wish they'd let me fall to the ground so it could swallow me up and take away this pain forever.

Chapter Twenty

Rhys

It's not the first time a guy has hit me, but it's been a while since someone has struck me that hard. It's been long enough that I've forgotten how fucking bad it hurts. Marcus' punch was jam-packed full of rage. I know it wasn't meant for me, but it doesn't make it hurt any less. And I mean that in both the physical and emotional sense.

The thing is, I know how much he's going to beat himself up for this. And why? Because I'm a slut. Because I fucked his mate. Not just one of them, but two of them with the third mate definitely an accomplice in giving me an orgasm. *Fuck.* I hate this about me. It's toxic and always ruins a good thing. I tried to warn Marcus. I told him I wasn't good for him. Why the fuck wouldn't he believe me?

"Rhys, are you ok?" The concern in Tyler's voice is out of place for the role he's meant to be playing. My teacher, Mr Foster.

I nod, hating that I'm crying. Crying! Fucking hell, now everyone will have seen Rhys George cry. It'll be the talk of the school. Well, that and the fact that I'm fucking every guy. Yeah, Marcus only knows about Shaun, but the gossip mill will turn it into everyone who has a dick. No guy is safe. By the time tomorrow hits, the rumours will say that I've fucked every pimple-faced teenage boy in this school.

"Oh my god, Rhys." Lexi falls to her knees on my other side, ignoring Mr Foster as she looks at my face. I try to bite back my tears so I can lighten the mood. I fucking hate this sort of drama. Give me fun, scandalous drama that doesn't involve me, and we're good. But not this shit.

"Do you think the bruise will match my Purple Passion nail polish?" I try to smile, but I fail at making Lexi laugh.

Shit, I'm losing my touch.

"Can you stand?" Mr Foster asks, and I risk a glance at his concerned blue eyes.

"I'm fine." I snap. "Shouldn't you be helping Shaun?" I sit up and look over to see Shaun has his shirt off, holding it bunched to his nose, blood oozing everywhere. Garrett and Simon are talking to him quietly, which doesn't seem to lighten the dark expression furrowing his brow as he looks from me to Marcus.

"He's ok. The duty teachers are on their way. We need to get you up." Mr Foster tugs on my arm, and I let him pull me to stand.

My eyes catch Marcus' then. He's on the other side of the courtyard. Ayden has him pinned up against the wall while he talks in his ear. Even though he's a good distance away, I can see the hate in his eyes. He hates me, and shouldn't I be happy about that? Isn't that what I wanted? For him to get the message that we couldn't be a thing? He sure as shit knows it now, but fuck if I don't want to run over to him, hug him tight, pepper kisses over his face, and tell him I'm sorry.

Tears fall from my eyes again. And fuck me, I'm a mess. Cin is going to send me back to the Retreat for sure. I've fucked up so bad. Hell, she'll probably decide to wipe her hands of me once and for all and send me back to the group home. And shit, if that thought doesn't rip my heart wide open.

It's hard for me to pay much attention to anything as Lexi tries to comfort me while students stand around with their phones out, recording my demise. Fuckers.

When the other teachers arrive, we are led away in three different groups to the main office. I know what will happen from there. We'll receive medical attention and wait for the principal's wrath. Because I have an *in* with said principal, I know how things work. The teachers will keep us separated. That's so we can't get our stories straight and also to make sure the fight doesn't start up again.

Marcus is in the front group with Mr Thompson, Ayden, and Jared. Shaun is in the next group with Miss Dice, Garrett and Simon, and I'm in the last group with Lex and Mr Foster.

Most students worry about going to the principal, getting in trouble, having their parents called, and punishment handed out. For me, my principal and parent are one and the same, and I couldn't care less about the punishment.

It's the disappointment that I know Cynthia won't be able to hide that I'm terrified of. The moment she realises that her foster daughter is the reason behind the fight that has torn two friends apart and probably even divided a friendship group, is the moment she'll realise I'm not worth all the trouble I've already caused.

Ugh, I can't bear to see her disappointment.

Since Marcus is the least hurt, he gets put in the Vault, an all-glass room designed to provide no privacy and full supervision. Shaun, still bare-chested and covered in his own blood, gets taken straight into the school nurse while I'm put in a small interview room off to the side of the main office.

"Lexi, would you mind waiting outside for a moment, please?" Mr Foster asks, and she frowns, probably knowing what he's asking is unusual, but when I offer her a small smile and nod, she nods back and waits out in the hall while Tyler closes us in the small room.

Taking a seat at the table, I keep my eyes cast low. Does he hate me too? For what I am? For what I've caused?

"Rhys?" Tyler whispers, and I glance up through my wet lashes. "Please tell me you're ok."

Shit. I wasn't expecting the care in his tone. I know we have a thing. A sex thing. But we don't have a care thing. Do we?

My bottom lip wobbles as a few tears pop free again, and I shrug.

"Shit." He squats down so we are at eye level. "Baby, don't cry."

Baby?

"You're going to get busted," I whisper, reminding him of what's at stake.

As if on cue, the door flies open, and both our eyes dart up to see Cynthia barrel into the room. She glances briefly at Mr Foster, who is next to me, but her focus is fixed on me, emotion I wasn't prepared for swimming in her panicked eyes.

"Rhys. Are you ok?" She cups both sides of my face, her eyes boring into mine, making me feel even more vulnerable. Then my lip starts having a fucking seizure. I go to nod, but then, oddly, I let honesty fall free and shake my head, bursting into tears.

Cin's familiar, loving arms pull me to her, and I cry into her chest, accepting the safety she is offering. Her hands rub my back as she whispers over and over that everything will be ok, and I let myself believe her words, even if I know deep down that it's not true. I want to believe it. I really do. But how can things be ok after what I've done?

Eventually, I calm down and separate myself from my foster mum and notice that we're alone in the room. Tyler must have ducked out while I broke apart like a fragile child. I bet that little scene is a wake-up call to him. A reminder that I *am* a child and *he* isn't. I wouldn't be surprised if he asks Master Hill to be removed as my sponsor. I can't even let my mind go to that right now, though, not with Cin's dark eyes assessing me like she's trying to read my mind.

"I've been given a brief rundown of what happened, but I need you to tell me, Rhys. Not as your Principal. As your mum."

I can see that my principal isn't here right now—just a worried mum. So, I give her my honesty again.

"You know I was seeing Marcus for a while last term?" When she nods, I continue, "Well, obviously, I told him we weren't a thing. Just casual." She frowns at my words, not because she doesn't understand, but because she *does* understand. She knows what I mean, and she knows why. "He's had a hard time accepting that, and if I'm being honest, so have I. I really like him, but…"

"But you think you can't remain faithful to him." Cin finishes for me, knowing much more than any regular mum knows about their daughter's love or sex life. There's no point in hiding what I am from her. The only thing I hide is Vixen's Lodge. Oh, and that Julie has been contacting me.

"I knew the moment I started seeing his mates as possible… hook-ups, that I couldn't keep seeing him. And it turns out I was right. I didn't go looking for them, Cin." I plead, hoping she doesn't think I deliberately set out to ruin their friendships. "They came to me. Well, except for Simon."

Her brows shoot up. "They? Simon? I thought we were just talking about Shaun Bossier?"

My shoulders drop. "It was Shaun first, then Simon, then kind of Garrett. I don't know about him, but Marcus only just found out about Shaun."

"Does it have anything to do with that horrid thing on your neck?" She wrinkles her nose.

"Don't act like you've never had a hickey before, Cin." I tease, and she grins at me.

"Yes, well, you need to learn how to hide things like that, Rhys."

I grin back. "Any pointers?"

Cin shakes her head.

"Right so, Marcus has figured out you and Shaun have been together, and now here we are." She waves her hands around. "Is that right?"

I nod.

Right before my eyes, Cynthia transforms from my foster mum to the principal of Fox Pines Catholic College.

"Ok, so how did you end up getting injured?" She asks.

"I tried to help Shaun, but when Marcus swung a punch at Shaun, it got me instead because I got in the way." I clutch each side of my chair under my thighs, "Marcus didn't mean to hit me, mum. Please believe me. He's not like that. He'd never deliberately hit me. Ever."

Cynthia's face goes red. I'm not sure why and I watch in confusion as her eyes well with tears.

"You… called me mum." She whispers.

Did I?

I think back to my words. *Marcus didn't mean to hit me, mum.*

Oh wow. I did too. I don't know if that's a good thing or not. What if she doesn't want me to call her mum? Sure, I've been with her for a few years now, but that doesn't mean she wants me to call her mum.

"I-I'm sorry."

She frowns, "Why?"

"I don't know. I guess I'm not sure if you want me to call you that." My voice lacks any confidence as I stare up at my foster mum.

"Rhys, I've been waiting for three years for you to call me mum." A tear rolls down her cheek.

"Oh."

Oh? *Oh*, is all I can say? Seriously, did Shaun and Tyler fuck all my brain cells away last night?

Cynthia smiles and pulls me into a hug, wrapping her arms around me in one of those mum hugs that only a mum knows how to do. We stay like that for a long while, mother and daughter having a moment together before we eventually break apart. Cin leaves then, sending Lexi in, who sits with me for the next forty minutes as I quietly explain to her what I told Cin... my mum. I leave out Vixen's Lodge but admit to her about the photo lab with both Shaun and Simon. I tell her about Garrett confronting me, but I leave out that part where he called me out on my sex addiction. Then I tell her about the bathroom incident with Garrett.

By the time I'm done, Lexi's mouth is hanging open, and I'm sure she's about to dump me as her new best friend. Then she surprises me.

"Have you ever seen a therapist or someone like that about your sexual activity?"

She's starting to put two and two together. I could get defensive and deny it, but I did that last term, and we had an awful argument. It killed me that we weren't speaking for a while. I don't want to keep things from Lexi, so I know it's time to be honest with her as well. Shit, today has already been full of confessions. Why stop now?

"Yes. I see an addiction therapist for my sexual activities."

Lexi is quiet for a moment as she takes in my words, and then her shoulders drop as she relaxes.

"It makes so much sense now." She admits. "You told me you couldn't have just one partner. That you can't commit. It's because you have a sex addiction, isn't it?"

I nod, feeling a weight lift at having her know my truth.

"And Marcus doesn't know?"

I shake my head. "No. The only one that figured it out is Garrett. And you."

"Are you going to tell the others?" Lexi asks, but I shake my head.

"It's not their business. Although maybe, if Marcus ever talks to me again, I should probably tell him. It's just… hard. It's my ailment. It's private. I'd prefer people to just think I'm a slut."

"Rhys, no one thinks that." Lexi's words make me laugh.

"Oh, Lexi, stop. I am what I am. If people want to hate me for it, then I don't care. Well… except for those who matter."

"And who's that?"

"You. Marcus. Your pack, basically." I admit, referring to the guys as her pack, which I named them last term after they wouldn't leave Lexi's side.

"Wait! Do you have a thing with Jared, too?"

I could be a bitch and tease her and ask her why she cares if Jared and I have anything going, but now isn't the right time.

"No, Lex. Jared isn't on my radar."

"Why?" Lexi looks surprised.

"Well, because honey. He only has eyes for you."

She cringes at my words, and I giggle.

"He'll move on one day, right?" She whispers, and I can tell it's a real worry for her. She cares about Jared, just not in the way he cares about her. She only has eyes for Ayden, and Jared will have to accept that eventually. I hope, so I nod, trying to look reassuring.

When Cynthia sets me free, she asks Lexi to go back to class with Ayden, and I sneak into the nurse's office to see Shaun before I face the music, so to speak. The music being Marcus… if he'll talk to me.

When I enter the small medical room, Shaun is lying down with an icepack to his cheek while Simon and Garrett talk quietly, sitting next to the bed. Three sets of eyes land on me when I click the door shut, and I suddenly wonder if I'm even welcome in here. I caused all this chaos. I'm the reason there's a divide.

I don't have to worry for long because Simon stands and rushes to me, throwing his arms around my shoulders, dragging me to his chest.

"I was so worried." His words are quiet, but in this small space, there's no way Garrett and Shaun didn't hear them.

Because I'm weak and unable to stop myself, I hug him back, feeling my vulnerability come back to the surface. I feel safe here in Simon's arms, but I also feel like these three guys can see right into my soul.

"I'm ok," I say quietly, and he pulls back, his hazel eyes darting between mine. Then he reaches up to glide his thumb gently across the bruise forming on my cheek.

"I'm going to kick his arse for hurting you like this."

My eyes soften as I take in the rage on Simon's face. It's strange to see since he's usually playing the role of the class clown, and his features are normally full of mischief.

"No, Simon. It was an accident. I got in the way. Marcus would never hurt me on purpose."

"I'm not sure I care. Look what he did to Shaun." Simon's face contorts painfully as he glances back at his mate.

"You know why, though, right?" I glance from Simon to Shaun and then Garrett, trying to see if they have revealed the truth to each other.

Simon shakes his head. "It doesn't make it ok for him to do that to his mate." Simon points angrily at Shaun, and once again, I feel so God damn guilty.

"Doesn't it? He's just learned that his mate betrayed him." I shake my head, taking a moment to swallow down the lump in my throat. "This is my fault. Don't hate Marcus for reacting. He had no idea, and he feels deceived. Rightfully so. I'll tell him everything. And for that, I'm sorry, because I've probably ruined all of your friendships. I should never have sucked you into my world."

"No, this isn't just on you." Shaun groans as he sits up, mumbling past the icepack. "It takes two to tango, and I'm not going to apologise for the way I feel about you, Kitten."

My eyes widen at his use of my Feaster's name.

"Kitten?" Simon asks, and I panic.

Shit. What do I say?

"It's my pet name for her." Shaun shrugs. "She's *my* Kitten."

"Shit." Garrett curses, scrubbing a hand through his brown waves. He knows about Vixen's Lodge because Shaun told him about it, but Simon has no idea.

"*Your* Kitten?" Simon asks. "You gonna share her, Bossi, or do I have to swing fists too?"

"Oh my god, no!" I cry out, moving to block Simon's path to Shaun, holding up my hand.

"I'll share her if she wants you, Hastings," Shaun says from behind me, and I turn back to see the smirk on his battered face. Shit, Marcus really did damage. "Hey, come here." Shaun lifts his hand out to me, and I go to him, unable to stop myself from being near him.

"I'm ok, Rhys. I'll probably look even hotter with a few scars."

I roll my eyes. "I'm so sorry."

And here come the tears again. FML!

Shaun reaches up and sweeps them away as they fall and then tugs me closer as he swings his legs over the side of the bed, situating me between them, hugging me to him. His bare chest is smeared with dried blood, but I don't care. I need to feel him close and have his scent wrap around me.

"It's ok, Kitten. This was always going to happen." He strokes my head, and I wish more than anything that I could take these stupid fucking buns out and feel his hand in my hair. That hair is only for private moments and Feast nights, though, and right now, there are two other people in the room.

Eventually, I pull back to look into Shaun's steel-grey puffy eyes, hoping he can see the honesty of my apology there, too.

"Kitten." He whispers, "I know you're not a relationship girl. I get it. But I can't stay away from you. I'll share you if I have to."

"You'd be ok with that?" I glance back at Garrett, remembering the chat we had on Tuesday night. He told me that maybe I could find someone that would be happy to have an open relationship. Did he speak with Shaun about that? Is that what's happening here?

With a finger under my chin, Shaun directs my gaze back to his.

"I'm pretty sure I'd do just about anything to have you in my life, Kitten."

Well, fuck. I want that too.

Shaun leans in, hovering his split lips over mine, with our eyes locked. I feel like he owns me in this moment, and anticipation lights my heart on fire as he closes his eyes and presses his lips to mine. I'm conscious of his hurt lips, so I kiss him gently, brushing mine over his, using my tongue to glide against his.

When a throat clears, I reluctantly pull back to see Shaun grinning past the swelling on his face. Then his eyes dart over my shoulder as a warm body presses against my back.

"I hate to break up this little love fest you have going, but I'm pretty sure I just heard your old man's voice out in the hall." Simon's words are quiet next to my ear as he leans in close. Shaun nods and releases me, letting Simon wrap his arms around me from behind.

"Simon says it's time to go." He whispers in my ear, and I grin. Cheeky fucker.

"Call you later, man." Garrett fist bumps Shaun and follows Simon and me out the door just as a man, who I can only assume is Shaun's dad, rounds the corner with the school nurse.

My guilty eyes dart to the floor as we pass him, and he grunts an unhappy hello to Simon and Garrett. Then he disappears into the room we just left.

Is Shaun about to get into trouble with his dad? Surely his dad won't blame him for Marcus' actions. Right?

The Vault comes into view when we round the corner, and Marcus' eyes land on us. His nostrils flare, and I'm not sure if his anger is directed at me or Simon and Garrett. I know I need to come clean to him, so I stop and turn my back to him, not wanting to see his scrutiny while I talk to Simon.

"I need to tell him the truth, Simon."

He nods. "Yep. I know. It's ok. I'm not going anywhere without my bodyguard." Simon slaps Garrett on the back, and Garrett grunts unhappily.

"I'm sorry. I never meant for this to happen." I say the words again because I'm wracked with guilt.

"Stop apologising. It is what it is, Rhys. Bossi was right. It takes two to tango. You're not in this alone." Simon shoots me a wink before walking off, but Garrett holds back.

"You gonna say I told you so?" I ask, and he frowns.

"Nope. Not how I roll."

I nod. "Well, thanks for trying to stop things from happening."

He smiles. "Nothing was ever going to stop the three of you from coming together, Rhys."

I shrug. "Could have been four."

That gets me a grin. "Stop. You're in enough trouble."

Then I watch as my big brute walks off. I shouldn't call him mine. I know that. But if anything, he's my friend, so yeah. Mine.

I take a few seconds to steady my racing heart before spinning on my heel and facing a fuming Marcus Grady behind the glass walls of the Vault. After I approach the room with his eyes locked on me the whole time, I crack the door, only to flinch.

"Get out!" Marcus hisses, and I realise how unhinged he looks.

Shit. I don't like angry Marcus.

"I need to speak to you."

"No! Get the fuck out of my life!" He storms forward, his dark hair in disarray falling over his blazing eyes, making him look like a mad man.

My breath catches as I stumble back a few steps, and from my peripheral, I see the office lady stand from her desk, but I keep my eyes trained on Marcus.

"You need to hear the truth first, and then I'll leave you alone."

"Oh right, so you wanna tell the truth now that you've been caught? Is that it? Wanna make yourself feel better?" Marcus growls as he looms over me, but fuck him. He hasn't even given me a chance to say anything.

"You know what Marcus, you are going to hear what I have to say," I sneer, stalking forward and making him back up, "Firstly, I need to remind you that never once were we in a relationship. From the start, *the start* Marcus, I told you it was casual, and that I didn't *do* serious. *You* were the one who caught feelings. *You* were the one that wanted more. If I sleep with someone else, no matter if you know them or not, it doesn't make it ok for you to act like a thug who has a claim on me!"

When his face reddens with more anger, instead of stepping back like a sane person, I take a step forward.

"Yes, I have been sleeping with Shaun. And while I'm revealing my bed partners, you should know that Simon and I have hooked up once as well. Hate *ME* all the fuck you want, but don't you take it out on them like they have been having an affair with your girl. I have never been *yours,* Marcus. I am nobodies."

"And why is that Rhys? You going for the world record to be the biggest slut on earth?"

I can't help my reaction. I slap his face. Hard.

I rarely care if someone calls me a slut. But I fucking care if *he* does, which hurts because I know it means I care about him more than I should.

Marcus' head whips to the side, and he slowly turns it back to me, his chest heaving as he struggles to remain in control.

"I need you to know the truth about why I'm like this," I whisper, hoping to calm him so I can tell him everything. Marcus isn't calm, though. He's practically frothing at the mouth, ready to explode.

"GET OUT!" He screams barely a centimetre from my face, and it's so loud that my breath catches in my throat, choking me as I stumble back.

Hands grab at me from behind, dragging me out of the room right before Marcus lifts a chair and throws it through the glass wall.

Chapter Twenty-One

Rhys

U sually, when I hit a low, I seek dick. I hunt down someone willing to fuck me and take me to a high. Depending on why I've hit a low, I can usually fuck my way to happiness again. This time, I can't.

Yesterday was a clusterfuck in epic proportions. Shaun got hurt. The school witnessed my demise. And I pushed Marcus so far over the edge that the police had to be called when he started smashing up the office.

What's that saying?

It's fun until someone gets hurt.

Yeah, true that!

My foster dad, Will, picked me up from school after Marcus turned into the incredible hulk. I feel awful that my foster mum had to stay and fix the mess I caused. Even after Shaun expressed his feelings yesterday, I know now that I can't pursue him. Or Simon. Or Garrett. For fuck's sake, I knew before yesterday that I shouldn't, yet I did. And why? Because I need fuck buddies.

"Rhys, you say you were just looking for some fun sex, yet, over the last couple of years, you've had a rule to avoid sex with your school peers. What changed? Why did you seek out Marcus in the first place?"

Melia, my addiction therapist, cancelled a couple of appointments so she could Skype me for an emergency session. Not that I really wanted it, but Will stayed home from work today to keep an eye on me and insisted I have a session. I knew if I refused, the threat of being sent to the Retreat would come up. So here we are.

"I didn't really seek Marcus out. He sought me out." I mumble with my head in my hand as I look at Melia on the monitor.

"Ok, so he sought you out. Why did you start seeing him?" Melia's dark eyes look big under the glasses she wears. She's quite pretty in a Harry Potter kind of way.

"I didn't start seeing him. I started having sex with him."

"Fine, Rhys. Why did you start having sex with Marcus?"

I shrug. "He had a pretty cock."

"And how did you know it was pretty before you'd even had sex?" Melia knows my criteria. No foreskins allowed.

"He sent me a picture."

Melia sighs. "So you were obviously chatting before he sent you a picture of his penis, Rhys."

"Ew! Don't say that word. That sounds gross. Call it a cock, Melia."

"The correct term is penis, Rhys. And that's how I'll refer to it." She huffs and takes a sip of her water, "So why did you start chatting with him in the first place?"

"Well... my friend Lexi is friends with him, and with all the stuff that happened to her, we just kinda started talking. We were both worried about her."

"So, you came together during a tough time. It's natural to form close bonds with those who go through something emotional with you. I'm guessing somewhere along the way, your conversations moved from your mutual friend to more personal things. Like sex?"

"Yeah. I guess."

"And how was the sex?" Melia asks, and I shrug.

"Pretty good. I was surprised, actually. I thought being a high schooler that he wouldn't know what he was doing."

"Was he experienced then? Had he been with a few partners before you?"

I shake my head, "I asked him that once. He said it was just me. That his body just somehow knew what to do to please me."

Melia's brows shoot up. "How did you feel when you heard that?"

"I don't know," I shrug again, "Powerful. Beautiful... Loved."

"You felt loved?"

"Yes." I nod, hating to admit that.

"Was that when you decided to end what you had going?"

"No. That's when I stupidly let myself feel something I know I shouldn't have."

Realisation dawns on Melia's face, "So you did end up having feelings for him?"

I nod again.

"When did your feelings stop?"

I frown at Melia's question.

"My feelings didn't stop."

"Why did you end things then? If you have feelings for Marcus, why didn't you take things further?"

"We've been through this before, Mel. I don't do relationships, and I told him that before we even hooked up."

"Yes, but *why* Rhys? *Why* stop yourself from having happiness?"

"Why? Isn't it obvious with what's happened? I let myself have happiness, and he couldn't handle it. He can't share me, Melia, and I can't be with just one person."

"Did you ask him if he could share?"

"I asked him if we went to a sex party if he could handle seeing me fuck other people. Guess what his answer was!" I snap, wanting nothing more than to end this video conference. Maybe I can pull the plug out of the wall and call it a technical hitch?

Melia nods, not getting offended by my tone.

"Monogamy is a strong human instinct. Some people need a little time to come to terms with openly sharing. Some people will never come to terms with such an idea. Marcus may just need more time."

"I doubt that." I huff. "We are over. He hates me, Mel. Like pure hatred. He'll never forgive me, and even worse, he may never forgive his friends."

"If you two weren't a couple when things happened, then he has no claim on you to forgive Rhys. His mates may be a different situation, though. Bro Code and all. You didn't decide for them. You didn't force them."

I cringe. "I kinda lured Simon in, though. I presented him with something I knew he couldn't refuse."

"You're wrong, Rhys. You presented him with a scenario, and he had the choice of whether or not to follow through. I'm sure he remembered at the time that his mate had a thing for you. Still, he chose to be with you."

"Ugh," I huff, dropping my head back on the chair. "None of this is helping."

"Why? Because I can't make the situation disappear?"

"Yes!" I sit up again, looking at the screen. "Exactly. Can't you magically make this whole thing vanish?"

Melia laughs. "I would be a very rich woman if I could do that." When I stay quiet, Melia adds, "Rhys, you shouldn't ignore how you feel about these boys. Even though you don't believe in monogamy, it doesn't mean you shouldn't pursue relationships. The best thing for you to do is be open about your situation. Be honest about what you want. If you want an open relationship, tell them, but remember, it goes both ways. If your partner can be ok with you sleeping with other people, then you must be ok with him or her doing the same. I want you to think about that for a few days. Maybe Marcus isn't the person for that, but maybe Shaun or Simon are. And if they aren't, you will find someone one day. Just don't rule out having meaningful relationships. You deserve happiness."

"I don't feel like I deserve happiness," I whisper.

"It's been a hard twenty-four hours, I know. It may not feel like it now, but you *do* deserve happiness." Melia leans forward, closer to the screen as she studies me. "I want you to do something you enjoy. It will help your spirits."

"Well, I usually fuck to lift my spirits."

"Hmm, it's probably not the best time to have sex."

"When is then?" I snap, frustrated because sex is an any time and every time sort of thing to me.

"Tell me, Rhys. When you have sex when you're down like this, is it because you feel horny?"

My brows shoot up. "No. It's because I feel down, and I want to feel good."

"Right, well, sex should be more of a celebration. Usually, if you're horny, your spirits are already high. Having sex because you're frustrated or angry or sad can be a nasty trap to fall into. I'm not saying you shouldn't have sex at these times, especially if you have a close relationship with someone else. It can actually be quite therapeutic, but if you're just having sex to try and reach that high in order to lift your mood, then you can cause yourself or someone else more damage. While you're feeling low like this, you should try to do something non-sexual that you enjoy doing. It won't give you that quick high, but it will improve your mood. It might help to make things seem a little brighter."

"There's nothing non-sexual I enjoy doing." I sulk and pout. Melia giggles.

"Think again, Rhys." She reaches to get something on her desk, and then she holds up a frame with a black-and-white picture in it. It's of her. I took it earlier this year in one of our sessions while she was looking down at her notebook writing something. I sent it to her for her birthday. I didn't know she had it on her desk. "You love taking photos. You really have an eye for it. Maybe throwing yourself into that will help keep your mind busy."

Melia is right. I *do* love taking photos. I'm pretty good with video as well and editing clips. It's probably the one thing besides sex that I can effectively lose myself in.

"Ok. I'll try. But if I'm happy, I can have sex, right?"

She laughs. "Yes, Rhys. As long as it's safe."

When I finally end my session with my therapist, I feel slightly better. Not much, though. Not enough to make me want to shower and make myself presentable to see the world. Fuck that. I want to stay in bed.

At some point through the afternoon, Will comes in and makes me eat a sandwich before leaving me to wallow again. When I sink back down under my covers, my phone buzzes as a call comes in. Shaun's name flashes across the screen, and for a moment, I think about ignoring it. My racing heart wins out, though, and I hit accept and put the phone to my ear.

"Hey."

"Hey, Kitten. You doing alright?" His smooth voice instantly relaxes me, the centre of my chest feeling oddly warm.

"Yeah. I guess." Shit. I sound so weak right now.

"Are you at home?"

"Yep." I sigh. "In bed, being pathetic. I'm pretty sure I resemble a homeless person right now."

Shaun chuckles. "I doubt that."

"My bird's nest hair would disagree."

"Oh, that sounds so sexy. Send a pic of that hair." Shaun teases, and the lightness in his tone sends my lips north.

"Hell no. There's nothing sexy about it." I listen again as he chuckles, and I notice that the background is quiet. "Are you at home?"

"Yeah. Mamá has been fussing. I didn't want to worry her more by being a shit and insisting on going to school. I only wanted to see you, anyway. Garrett said you weren't there."

Mamá? Oh God, love his Spanish heart.

"School is the last place I want to be right now. Not that being home is much better. Will is hovering."

"Will is your foster dad?"

"Yep." I pop the p.

"So, where would you rather be? At the Feast?"

"Oddly enough, no. I don't feel right anywhere at the moment." Rolling on my back, I stare up at my white ceiling. Everything in this house is white. White walls, white floors, white furniture. Splashes of light grey décor is the only relief from all the white. I really fucking hate white.

"Damn, Kitten. You're worrying me." Shaun's voice is laced with concern, and I instantly feel guilty for causing it. I'm not used to people worrying about me. Well, except for my foster family.

"Sorry. I'm not good people to be around right now."

"It's ok, Kitten. Yesterday was fucked."

"It's not just yesterday," I whisper, and part of me hopes Shaun didn't hear. Yet, a part of me hopes he did.

"Talk to me, Kitten. What else is going on?"

I want to tell him the truth, I really do, but that will lead to questions I can't bear to answer. Maybe I can tell him a little bit. Talking about stuff is meant to help, right?

"One of my old foster mums has been messaging me."

"What about?" Shaun asks curiously.

"She's asked me to visit my old foster dad."

"Why? Were you close?"

"No. Not really." Liar! "It's actually kind of weird that she's asked me to visit him. I don't know why he'd want to see me."

"Oh. Well, I guess that is weird." Shaun agrees. "So what about that has got you upset?"

"When I told her I didn't think I could come and visit, she got a bit snarky. She's not a nice person. I'm not sure I want to see her again." Or my old foster dad, but I keep that to myself.

"Have you told your current foster parents?" Shaun sounds concerned again. I wish I could see his face. Smell his spicy scent. Feel his warm hands on me.

"Yeah-Nah, I haven't, and I'm not planning on telling them. It's all g. I'll get it sorted." I sigh. "Time to change the conversation."

"Oh really? What are we going to talk about now?" Shaun chuckles.

"How about your dad?"

"Nah, my dad is boring."

"Hang on a minute. When you spoke about your mum before, you referred to her as mamá. That's Spanish, right?"

Shaun chuckles. "You caught that, huh?"

"Sure did. It's pretty hard to miss. It's not just the word; it's the way you pronounce it. Got my knickers wet."

Shaun laughs, and I can just imagine him throwing his head back. "Mamá prefers I speak Spanish to her. My dad doesn't care."

"Well, if he did care, what would you call him instead of dad?"

"Padre."

Oh, good God, there's that accent again. Fucking hot as hell. Now I'm horny. I'll have to remember to tell Melia in our next session.

"Jesus Bossi. You could make a fortune from recording Spanish words. Chicks would pay top dollar."

Shaun laughs again. I wish I was there with him, wrapped in his arms.

"You want me to speak Spanish to you, Kitten?"

"Hell yes."

"Sabe a cielo." His voice drops low, seductively.

"What did you say?"

"You taste like heaven." With want in his tone, my Kitty awakens, and I feel the familiar ache deep inside.

"Fuck Cass. That's hot."

"Is your pussy wet, Kitten?"

"Is the sky blue? Hell yes, I'm wet." My admission makes my cheeks heat, but I don't care. He can't see my silly blush.

"You own a vibrator, Kitten?"

"Again... Is the sky blue?"

Shaun chuckles. "Grab it for me, baby."

I sit up quickly, ready to dive for my draw where I keep my toys, when the bedroom door opens. Freezing in place like I've just been sprung, even though all I'm holding is my phone, I wait for my foster dad to speak.

"Rhys, Cynthia has been trying to call you."

"Oh," I look down at my phone, "I'm on a call."

Will looks to my phone clutched in my hand and then back to my face. "Ok, well, Mrs West called her and asked if you're still coming to stay over with Lexi tonight. She said you two were going to have a girl's night or something."

"Oh shit. I forgot about that." I frown and look down at my phone to see the seconds ticking over on my call with Shaun. "Did mum say it's alright for me to go?"

Will's face softens then, a small smile tugging at his lips. "Yes, she said it was ok. Should I just refer to her as mum instead of Cynthia?"

Oh. I called Cynthia mum again. My eyes shoot to my phone, knowing Shaun can hear everything, and surprisingly, I like the idea of him knowing.

"Yes, please." I nod, and Will smiles, nodding back.

"Ok. Your mum will drop you at Lexi's around five o'clock."

When I nod, Will turns to walk out, and before I know it, I blurt out, "Can I call you dad? Or is that too weird for you?"

Will stops and slowly turns around. Even though he's taken the day off work, his dark hair is still slicked with gel, and his face is clean-shaven. He always looks way too clean to be a carpenter, but one look at the calluses on his hands and it tells a different story.

"You want to call me dad?"

I shrug, "Only if you're ok with it."

His lips tug wide in the biggest, goofiest smile I've ever seen him wear. "I'm more than ok with that, Rhys. As long as you're happy for me to refer to you as my daughter?"

I nod quickly, feeling warm tears of happiness prick the back of my eyes.

"Yes. I'd like that."

Then Will, I mean my dad, walks up to my bed, leans over, and presses a kiss to my forehead. It's nice, and I realise it's the first time I've really let him get this close to me. My past has screwed me up when it comes to dads. I'm not talking about the daddy kind of screwed up that I refer to Tyler as. No, there's no daddy kink going on here. But I've never had the kind of dad who nurtures, protects, and loves me unconditionally. I trust Will. I feel safe in his care, even when we're alone. I know he'd never hurt me. Never do things a dad should never do to his daughter. He's the first man in my life that truly deserves the title of my dad.

Pulling back, my dad wrinkles his nose.

"Kid, you need a shower before you go to your friend's house."

I laugh, throwing my head back as he chuckles and leaves the room. Smart arse.

I put the phone back to my ear, remembering that Shaun is still on the line.

"Shit, are you there?"

"Still here, Kitten." Shaun chuckles, and I relax.

"You heard all that, huh?"

"Yep. It was Hermosa." Shaun draws out the last word.

"What does that mean?"

"Beautiful. What I just heard between you and your dad was beautiful."

Tears well in my eyes.

"I feel safe with him. With Cynthia. They are my parents." I swipe at the stupid tears, glad Shaun can't see them.

"Are you smiling, Kitten?"

"Yes." It's the truth too. I may have tears, but I also have a big stupid smile.

"One day soon, you're going to let me in that house and show me where you keep your toys, Kitten. And then, I'm going to use them on you until you scream."

And now I'm burning up again.

"Is that a promise?"

"Fuck yeah, it is. For now, though, you should go shower and get ready to go to Lexi's. A girl's night is a great idea."

Chapter Twenty-Two

Rhys

This morning I felt like my world was falling apart, then this afternoon, it no longer felt so bleak. Chatting with Shaun on the phone lifted my spirits, as well as the whole mum and dad thing with Will. I'd always called them by their first name, yet Charlotte and the twins always referred to them as mum and dad. Well, except for when Char is being a bitch, she calls them by their first name then.

It's nice to know they like me calling them my parents instead of foster parents or by their first name. I'm not foolish enough to think they're going to adopt me, just like they did with Charlotte when she was sixteen. I'm well aware that I age out next year, and there's a big chance I'll be shown the door to go and make my own way in the world. Cin and Will are decent people, though. They'll probably let me finish year 12 before sending me packing.

I arrive at Lexi's a little after five. She shows me around her new house and is so excited about the possibility of her mum buying it from the landlord. Her mum, Ruth, never used to be much of a mum to Lexi. There's a dark fucked up story in their past that Lexi doesn't like to talk about, but somehow they both came out the other end better off. Now Ruth dotes on Lexi, so when I show up for a sleepover, she cooks us dinner and fusses over us until Lexi reminds her about the date she needs to get ready for. Ruth is seeing one of the police officers that helped them when Lexi's dad and brother were trying to kill them. It's so nice to see things finally looking up for the West women. They both deserve happiness after being through the nightmare they'd been living.

"So, Shaun, hey?" Lexi wags her brows. "I'm guessing he has a pretty cock."

I burst out laughing. Lexi had been so vanilla when we first got acquainted. She'd been shocked at my revelation that I only fuck guys with pretty cocks, which basically translates to guys that are circumcised. I remember wishing I could be her or *any* normal seventeen-year-old girl. To be vanilla at our age is to be inexperienced. I wonder what it would be like to not know so much about sex? Or what it'd be like to share my first time with someone I care about as much as Lexi and Ayden care about each other. I imagine having a guy see you naked for the first time must be a really big deal.

"You know it." I flash my teeth, pushing my thoughts down. "It's so fucking pretty, Lex. Like lickably pretty."

"Oh my God, I didn't need to know that!" Lexi's eyes widen as her face turns bright red.

"Yes, you did. Don't pretend you don't want to know. Bossi is a work of art. As if you haven't wondered what he looks like naked." I tease, and her blush deepens.

Shit, I'd forgotten how fun it is to stir Lexi up. She's like the classic girl next door, but with the incredible hulk hibernating inside her. She's a tough bitch, that's for sure, yet still has the most beautiful soul you have ever seen. Lexi has a purity about her that I'm envious of. Not like the virgin Mary kind of purity, but the purity of a saint. She's good people—the best.

"Fine, there's not a single girl at FPC that hasn't thought about that, Rhys. He's our Spanish Casanova, after all."

This time I blush. Like, what the actual fuck? Just the mention of Casanova and my cheeks are heating.

"Oh my God! You like him!" Lexi blurts. "Like… you like him, like him."

"Ok, calm down. Sure, I like him. Duh! He has a pretty cock, remember?"

"Uh-uh. It has nothing to do with sex, Rhys."

I duck my eyes away from her assessing blue gaze and stare at my fidgeting fingers in my lap. We're sitting on Lexi's bed, a bowl of Sour Patch Kids in between us and Paramore playing quietly in the background. I focus on that instead of my racing heart. I focus on the cosy feel of Lexi's attic bedroom. It's so different from her bedroom at her old house. There was no personality in that bedroom. It was as if she were just a guest in that house, not wanting to add her personal touch to anything.

Much like my own bedroom.

"Rhys?" Lexi gains my attention again, and I reluctantly lift my eyes to hers. She's such a beauty. Her natural golden blonde waves and blue eyes are hard to not stare at. She's such a contrast to me and my darkness.

"I really fucked up, Lex," I admit, letting my shame and guilt come to the surface. "I don't understand what's happening. Why do these guys have such an effect on me? I thought it was just sex, you know? Thought it was harmless fun." I sigh, my shoulders dropping as I start combing my fingers through my hair, loving that I've gone the whole day without wearing it up in the buns. "I didn't mean to feel something for them. It's ridiculous to care about so many guys at once."

"How many guys are we talking about exactly?" Lexi grins mischievously, and I roll my eyes.

"Definitely three, possibly four. Fuck, maybe five."

"Holy shit! Who?" Lexi's blue eyes dance in excitement. "Who are the definitely's?"

"Shaun, obviously. And Marcus, although I can probably rule him out because he hates me."

"I wouldn't be so sure about that. Marcus is just angry and confused."

"Angry? He smashed up the office yesterday, Lexi."

She cringes, "Ok, so more than angry then. But you know him, Rhys. You know how big his heart is. He's hurting. Bad. I know he knew you didn't want anything serious, but he obviously still believed he could win you."

"I know." I shake my head, looking back down at my fingers in my lap. "I may have spoken the words and said we couldn't be a thing and that I didn't want a relationship. But he could see the contradiction in my eyes. It has to be why he didn't give up trying. Right?"

"Maybe." Lexi shrugs. "But you admitting that you like him and Shaun, more than just a hook up means something, Rhys. Wait... Who's the third guy?"

"What?" I frown, and she giggles.

"You said that there were definitely three guys you feel something for. Who's the third? Is it Simon?"

Oh shit. Why didn't I think about her wanting details? I can't tell her about number three. Tyler. Or could I? She doesn't know him as anything but Mr Foster.

"Oh. It's this other guy. He's a bit older. Doesn't go to school. His name is Tyler."

"Tyler. Ooooh, tell me about Tyler." Lexi wags her brows, and I can't hold back my grin.

"He's one of those guys that come across as dark and mysterious. Maybe even a little scary, like he might have a bad temper, but when you get to know him, you realise he's not scary at all. Sure, he likes to be dominating, and I fucking love being a brat because it riles him up, but there's also this almost possessively caring side to him. Like he would hurt anyone that hurts me. I'm still trying to figure out if he's like that because he cares about me or if he's just like an overprotective big brother."

"That you fuck?" Lexi confirms.

"That I fuck."

Lexi grins at that.

"So, who is number four and five?"

I roll my eyes. "So nosey, Lexi."

She giggles, "Hell yes, I am. You're my best friend, aren't you?"

I flash my teeth, "Yes, my queen, I am your best friend."

At my tease, Lexi slaps my shoulder. "Stop trying to distract me. Who are the other two? Is it Simon and Garrett? You said something was happening with them when we spoke yesterday."

I nod. "Yep. Simon isn't backing off, and to be honest, I don't think I want him to. Garrett though… I'm not sure. We haven't crossed any lines. Kinda. Sorta. Well, maybe a little, but I've had some pretty deep and meaningfuls with him. There's more to that guy than the brooding hulk he looks like."

"Sure is. He's had a tough life and carries some dark secrets. His mum is lovely, and his younger sisters are adorable." Lexi smiles. "So even though you and Garrett haven't done… more, you still like him?"

"Yes," I whisper, feeling my face heat at the admission. I feel like I'm in third grade. This feelings stuff really isn't me.

"So, you have yourself a reverse harem. Just like those books you got me into." Lexi beams, bouncing on the spot with her legs crossed.

"Hardly. One guy hates me and will never be happy with sharing me. Another guy is too old to want to deal with these high school games, and another guy probably has no interest in me. Shaun and Simon hardly make a reverse harem."

"It's a start!" Lexi squeals doing some weird shimmy thing with her shoulders. I roll my eyes.

"I'm normally the hyped up one in this relationship, Lexi. What are you on?"

"I'm high on life, Rhys!"

"Bullshit. You're still high from riding Ayden's cock before I came over earlier, aren't you?"

"Maybe!" She laughs, and while she's distracted, I lift the pillow next to me and whack her shoulder with it.

"Oh! It's like that, is it?" Lexi grins, and her face turns mischievous. Then she picks up her pillow and slogs me over the head.

And… then it's on. With laughter filling the room, we pelt each other with the pillows, standing on the bed and spilling the bowl full of lollies. It's fun and light-hearted and exactly what I need.

We are both puffing in exhaustion when Lexi's phone rings, and she coughs a few times from laughing so much before answering it. I suck in air, trying to calm my racing heart and plonk my arse back down on the bed as I hear one side of Lexi's phone conversation.

"Hey… What?… Ayden, I told you we are having a girl's night… I know. I miss you too." That last part is whispered, but I still hear it. "He is?… Oh."

Lexi leaps off the bed, skipping to the attic window that looks out over the little courtyard at the back of the house.

"Ahhh, give me a sec." She turns to face me, lowering the phone from her ear.

"Marcus is here. He wants to talk to you."

My mouth drops open because I definitely wasn't expecting that. With how angry Marcus had been yesterday, I assumed it would take days, or maybe even weeks before he'd want to talk to me again. And frankly, I'm pissed at him too. He fucking hurt Shaun. He smashed up the school office, and I spent an hour trying to convince my mum not to press charges when the cops arrived. Even though all that happened, I know we need to talk properly, without all the screaming.

"Yeah, ok." My voice lacks any real confidence, and Lexi notices.

"Rhys, I can tell them to go away. You don't have to see him if you don't want to."

"I know. I need to speak with him, though. If he's calm and not going to smash up your house, then I'll talk to him."

"If he tries to damage anything on my property, I will kick his fucking arse!" Lexi hisses, and my grin returns. There's that fire I love about this girl.

"Agreed," I say, and she smiles, putting the phone back to her ear.

"She will talk to him, but you fuckers can stay outside. Light the fire pit. We'll be down soon." Lexi hangs up and strides over to me before pulling me into a hug. I sink into it, letting myself take the comfort she's offering. I'm not normally so fragile, and Lexi knows that. She knows what I need right now.

We take our sweet time before heading down to the courtyard. Even though Lexi begs me to leave my hair down and keep my face makeup-free, I paint black liner around my eyes and twist my hair into buns, although a little messier than usual. Then I glide on my black lipstick and instantly feel comfortable seeing Marcus.

He's never seen me without makeup or my hair down. Not even with all the sex we had, did he ever see me natural. I prefer it that way. I like people seeing me in my war paint. I feel too vulnerable without it. Even when Tyler walked into the barn on Wednesday night before the Feast, I almost screamed at him to leave because my face was naked. How screwed up is that? I'll open my legs for him, let him see everything there, yet showing my natural face makes me uneasy.

Yeah. I'm fucked up!

The small courtyard at the back of Lexi's house is paved with old bricks, and the fence is lined with some sort of green plant with white flowers. I don't know what they are. I'm no gardener!

In the centre of the courtyard is a small fire pit with four timber bench seats surrounding it, and overhead are pretty warm lights that dangle from a black cable. It feels so serene. Peaceful. That is, until I spot Marcus on the other side of the fire pit, shuffling nervously as he waits.

Ayden spots us coming first like Lexi is some kind of beacon to him, and a moment later, Marcus glances up from studying the flames in the pit to lock eyes with me. I don't know what I expected, but the sad regret isn't it. I guess I thought he'd still be angry, maybe even have steam shooting from his ears. But there's none of that now. *My* Marcus is hurting.

Ayden bypasses me, taking Lexi's hand to lead her over to the back veranda of the house while I keep my eyes on Marcus as he slowly walks around the fire pit. With a nervousness I'm not used to seeing,

Marcus gestures to one of the bench seats, so I sit down at the same time he does, only a few feet between us.

Marcus opens his mouth to speak, but then he snaps it shut. He does this two more times before he shakes his head, dropping his eyes to the fire, and rakes his hand through his dark hair.

"Marcus," I whisper, not able to speak louder with the lump forming in my throat. He glances back to me, his eyes two pools of dark pain.

"I'm so fucking sorry, Rhys." There is so much anguish laced in his words that it physically hurts, a sharp pain stabbing the centre of my chest.

"I'm sorry too." I choke out. "I wanted to tell you, which I know is strange, but it felt weird not sharing things with you." I try to keep my eyes on his, but he can't maintain eye contact. He looks away.

"Was I imagining it?" He asks, turning those brown pools back to me.

"Imagining what?"

"That you actually liked me? More than just someone to fuck?" His eyes swim with the agony I can hear in his tone. All I want to do is reach for him and pull him close.

"I did like you. I mean, I *do* like you, Marcus. More than I want."

His eyes flare at my words, darting over my face as he studies me.

"So, it wasn't just one-sided?"

Fuck. What have I done to this poor guy?

I shake my head. "No, Marcus. I care about you so much it hurts."

In a quick move, Marcus shuffles towards me, taking my hands in his.

"Then why did you push me away? Why don't you want a relationship with me?"

As guilt wracks me, my eyes drop from his, not wanting to see the hope in them because what I'm about to tell him will change all of that.

"I'm a sex addict, Marcus."

"What?" His tone forces me to look back into those dark pools swimming with confusion.

"I don't do relationships because I am addicted to sex. Usually with different people. Sometimes with multiple people at the same time."

And there it is written across his face—the disgust.

I look away. I can't bear to see him look at me like that.

"What?" He whispers.

I keep my eyes on our hands, still clasped together. "I can't be monogamous, Marcus. As much as I care about you, and as much as I love the way you make me feel in bed, there's always going to be a part of me that is seeking out my next fuck." Biting back tears, I glance up at him through my lashes. "I wish I wasn't like this, but I am. I'm into some pretty dirty stuff, and you…" I bite my bottom lip as my eyes well with tears, "You are just too kind. Too good to be dragged into my world."

"But… What about Bossi? He's good enough?"

I sigh. "Bossi and I aren't in a relationship, Marcus. I've already told you I can't do that."

"So, it's just fucking? You and him is just about the sex?"

"Yes… no. Fuck." I stand up abruptly, dropping his hands, knowing I'm making no sense.

"Well, what is it then? Yes or no?" Marcus stands too, balling his fists at his sides.

I tip my head back, looking up into the dark sky. There's still a hint of the sunset that pinked the rooftops earlier, but mostly, there are stars starting to twinkle. Sighing, I drop my gaze back to Marcus. He hasn't taken his eyes off me. He's studying me. Every move I make. Every expression that crosses my face.

"I don't know what it is. All I know is I have these feelings I haven't had before. For you. For him. For… someone else. I'm not normal, Marcus. I'm never going to be normal." I take a step closer, relieved when he doesn't back away. "And I don't think you can do anything but normal. Monogamous. It's not a bad thing. In fact, I wish I could be that way, so fucking much. But I can't."

He's quiet as his eyes stay locked on mine. It makes me uneasy the longer he doesn't say anything. I can see the wheels in his head working. Processing.

Then he speaks.

"So Bossi is ok with you not being monogamous?"

I shrug. "I don't know. He said he'd share me. I'm not sure what that means and how serious he is about what we have."

Sighing, Marcus drops his chin to his chest, his shoulders sagging as defeat washes over him.

I'm a bitch. A fucking good for nothing worthless piece of shit. I've never deserved Marcus. He's way too good for me.

"How did you two hook up in the first place?" Marcus asks, his eyes peering up at me through his dark lashes.

"A sex party," I whisper, and his eyes widen as he lifts his head.

"A sex party?"

I nod. "Yes. I've been going to sex parties for a couple of years now. I stopped when we were together, but I started going again. Shaun was there when I went back."

"A sex party?" Marcus asks again, and I nod again. "You go to sex parties?" The disbelief in his tone makes me wonder if he ever really knew me at all. "You asked me about going to a sex party once… you asked if I'd care if I saw you fucking someone else."

"Yeah, and you were pissed that I asked that question."

"I remember." He grunts, crossing his arms over his chest. "Why did you ask me that?"

"I was testing the waters. I wanted to see if there was ever a chance you'd be into it." Feeling a little cold, I move towards the fire, which is burning well now. A quick glance over my shoulder, and I see Lexi straddling Ayden's lap in the shadows of the veranda, their lips locked in a heavy make-out session.

"So, you were hoping I'd be into going to a sex party, where you would fuck other people in addition to me?" When I nod, he continues, "And what? I'd fuck other people too? And you'd be ok with that?"

I shrug. "Yeah. Those parties have nothing to do with personal feelings or attraction. Just sex. Doing things you may not normally do. It's a place of freedom without judgement to explore desires. Then afterwards, you go home and be more… normal, I guess."

"And you fuck multiple people at these sex parties? Like at once or…"

I bite back my grin because now isn't the time for my head to be conjuring up images of Marcus and orgies, but it's hard not to when I'm looking at him, and we are talking about this, and he sounds so adorable right now. Like a kid asking how a fire truck works.

"Yes. I fuck multiple people at the parties. Sometimes one on one with others in the room, sometimes others join in."

He frowns. "Both guys and chicks?"

I smile. "Marcus, you *do* remember me kissing Lexi at that party last term, right? You and the caveman over there dragged us out, throwing us over your shoulders like we were sacks of potatoes." I point my thumb over my shoulder in the general direction of Ayden.

"I remember," he grins, "That was the first night we slept together."

"It was." I smile too, but the moment his smile drops, so does mine.

"So, you're like… bisexual?"

I shrug, "I guess. I don't know exactly. I prefer dick, but sex is sex, and sometimes it's a real turn-on being with another girl."

"Shit." Marcus spins away from me, dragging his hand through his hair again.

I stay put next to the fire, giving him this moment he needs. When I realise he's not going to turn back to me anytime soon, I turn and face the fire, raising my hands out in front to warm them. Lexi and Ayden aren't lip locked anymore, but they are talking quietly. Those two are so into each other. I could say it's sickening, but it's not. It's fucking beautiful. I wish so much that I could have something like that.

"I wish you had told me all of this sooner. You know, about you and your… addiction."

Glancing up, Marcus' eyes pierce mine as he stands next to me, facing the fire.

"I know I should have. It's a secret I didn't want anyone to know about, but lately, things have gotten out of control. It kind of came out whether or not I wanted it to." I sigh, "I'm so sorry, Marcus. I never wanted to hurt you. I never wanted to come between you and your friends."

Marcus turns to face me then, the flicker of the fire dancing off his olive skin. Lifting his hand, he brushes the backs of his fingers over the bruise on my cheek.

"I never wanted to hurt you either, Rhee."

With one last intense gaze into my eyes, Marcus drops his hand from my face, turns his back on me and walks out the gate, leaving me standing alone by the fire.

CHAPTER TWENTY-THREE

RHYS

E ven though the air between Marcus and me has been cleared, after he left Lexi's on Friday night, I became a brain-dead zombie, incapable of conversation, so we went to bed. I can't remember the last time I went to bed before 11pm on a Friday night, but even when I woke after eight the next morning, I was still exhausted.

My Saturday is spent moping around at home. I told my mum—I don't know if I'll ever get used to saying that—about having a chat with Marcus, and she understood my low mood and declared that we were going to have a movie day. It's not often that Cynthia Rogan, the pristine principal of Fox Pines Catholic, doesn't bother getting dressed, so I was thankful for her small sacrifice.

A message from Julie on Saturday night reminds me that I have to lie to my parents and tell them I'll be with Tillie for all of Sunday and Sunday night. And like the shitty friend I am, I ask Tillie to cover for me. She typically does this anyway on Sunday nights so I can go to Vixen's Lodge, but that's not what's going on today, and I wish I could tell her the truth at least, but I can't.

The train ride into the city isn't too bad, and neither is the one out of the city on the west side, but the two town buses I have to catch just to get to Allansdale Prison is a pain in my arse. Mainly because they are jam-packed full of perverts who either ogle me or try to hit on me. It's safe to say I've entered a sketchy part of the outer suburbs of Melbourne.

It's around one in the afternoon when I reach the prison. The cliff height walls are surrounded by open fields, with section upon section of high-security fencing. I get a chill as I walk up the long path after I free myself from the bus, which has nothing to do with the black pleated skirt and baby pink sleeveless top I'm wearing. With each step towards the Allansdale entrance, I want to turn around and run in the opposite direction.

I'm nervous about seeing Brian, the man that groomed me. A shiver travels up my spine as I remember what he had me do when I was only eleven years old. I didn't know it at the time, but it was wrong, even though I clearly remember liking it. A chill runs up my spine, knowing that the dark, sick part of my mind has been embedded there by the man I'm going to visit today.

Before I reach the entrance, where other visitors are streaming in, I get a message on my phone from Tyler.

Skipper
?

Kitten
thumbs down emoji

That very brief conversation translates as Tyler asking me if I need to be added to the guest list for tonight's Feast at Vixen's Lodge, and my response is no. I can't go tonight. Not after what went down with Marcus at school. And especially not after I visit with my child molesting ex foster dad. My head isn't in the right place, and I'm trying hard not to give in to the need to seek out a high in order to make myself feel better.

Walking through the visitor's entrance of the prison is a strange experience. First, there are metal detectors, followed by some sort of x-ray screen, and then I have to empty my pockets and lock my backpack and belongings in a keypad locker. Separating myself from my phone makes me extremely anxious, even though I do it every time I go to the Feast nights. It's different today. I'm entering a prison to see someone I never wanted to see again. Ugh, I should turn around and go home now.

That would be the smart option. Am I smart, though? No. Nope. Not at all.

Julie's threat of consequences lingers in the back of my mind, which is the only reason I'm here, obeying her request.

I take a seat in the waiting area, nervously looking around at the other visitors who pay me little attention. By the time the corrections officers come in to announce that we can enter, I'm a jittering mess with trembling hands. Even when I stand to follow the flow of visitors, my legs feel like they'll give out from under me. I try to steady my breathing and focus on something else to calm my nerves. Tyler pops into my head. Then Shaun, Simon, Marcus and Garrett. Jesus, I'm a horn bag!

"Patrice George?"

The sound of my birth name sends all thoughts of my guys away, and I step out of the cue to see who called out for me.

"Is there a Patrice George here?" A corrections officer stands at a different entrance scanning the line of visitors.

"Uh-I'm Rhys George. I mean, Patrice George." I take a few steps closer as the tall man looks down his nose at me, even from where he's standing.

"This way. Your visit is private."

"W-what? Why?" I don't move, even when he turns to walk away.

"This way Miss George." His tone brokers no argument, so I follow, glancing back at the other people in line, going into the visitor's room. Why the hell is my visit private? Is that even a thing? Surely there will be people around… right?

A hot sweat breaks out over my nape, and my heart races as the sounds of the visitor's centre fades away. It's quieter the deeper we move down the passage, and when the officer stops in front of a door, he turns to me.

"No touching, and stay on your side of the line."

I have no fucking idea what he's talking about, but the next second he unlocks the door, swinging it open. I freeze as time slows, my eyes locking with the familiar dark eyes of Brian Bates. He's older than I remember. His dark hair has streaks of grey, and his brown eyes have lines framing them.

When I don't move, the officer urges me forward with a hand on my back before shutting the door and locking it. Frantic, I glare at the door, wanting to pull it open and bolt. It's too late now. I'm locked in this room with nowhere to go and no choice but to turn back to the man I once thought cared about me.

"Patrice. Thank you so much for coming to see me." His voice sounds the same. Maybe a little older than I remember, if that's even possible, and his smile opens up a thousand memories in my mind that I've worked so hard to keep buried. "Please, take a seat."

With his hands in cuffs resting in his lap, Brian gestures to the empty chair in front of him. It's sitting about two metres back from a thick yellow line that runs through the centre of the room, dividing us. On shaky legs, I move to the seat, gripping the back to steady myself before easing into it. I keep my eyes trained on Brian the whole time, not daring to risk losing sight of him. Not even for a moment.

"Wow. Look at my little girl. All grown up. Such a woman now."

"What do you want?" I snap. I'm not here for social chitchat, so it's best he knows that from the get-go.

My question makes his jaw tick, but when he speaks, his tone doesn't show the frustration he's clearly feeling.

"I'm dying, Patty. I have cancer, and I wanted to see you before I die."

"Well, you've seen me now. So I guess I'll be *going*." I stand as I snap the last word, and he frowns momentarily before a sinister grin tugs at his lips.

"Now, now, Patty. Julie won't be happy if you don't stay and chat for a while."

Translation… if you don't stay, Julie will still dish out the punishment.

Biting the inside of my cheek, I take a deep breath before lowering myself to the seat again. Julie never told me what the punishment would be for not coming to see Brian, but knowing her, it won't be good, and I'm not sure I'm willing to find out.

"I just want to spend a little time with you. That's all. I've missed you so much."

Bile rises in my throat, so I slowly suck in air, trying to find some calm. I don't want to vom in front of him. I don't want him to know how he affects me.

"How have you been, Patrice? Are you doing well in school?" Brian's smooth tone is friendly, instantly taking me back to the time we had together. His friendly nature was always calming to me. He made me feel safe. I didn't care that I had very few friends at school or that I never seemed to please Julie. None of it mattered when Brian was around. He cared for me in a way that even my own birth mother had never done.

"I've been fine. I'm doing ok at school." My tone is flat as I wearily eye him. His gaze shifts to my lips as I speak, something I remember him doing when I lived with him.

"That's wonderful. What's your favourite subject?"

I shrug, "Photography, I guess."

Brian beams. "You kept up with the photography? You have no idea how happy that makes me. We had so much fun taking photos together."

A shiver rolls up my spine at the reminder. When I was first removed from Brian's care, I kept taking photos, knowing it was something we did together, and I'd hoped we would be reunited and I could show him the pictures I took for him. Then, as time went by and I started to understand that what Brian did was wrong, I stopped taking photos for him and started taking them for myself.

It was something I was good at. Something I really enjoyed. Maybe I shouldn't have kept doing it, knowing he was the one to teach me in the beginning.

"Do you have some nice friends, Patrice?" Brian asks, sitting calmly in the plastic chair, not moving anything but his head.

"I do. They're great." I answer honestly.

"That's so wonderful. How about a boyfriend? Do you have a boyfriend?"

"Yes." I lie. I don't know why I do that, but my answer causes him to frown, his eyes darkening as he glares at me.

"Do you play *our* games with your boyfriend, Patrice?"

My heart starts racing, and I dart my eyes to the door. Surely, it's time to finish up?

"Uh-uh, Patty. You're not leaving yet. Julie won't like that."

I shoot him a glare as I drag my gaze from the door back to him.

"Answer my question. Do you play our games with your boyfriend?"

"No!" I snap, raising my voice as anger washes over me. Brian doesn't seem to mind, though.

"Have you spread those creamy thighs for anyone else, Patty?"

"No!" I spit again, and Brian bares his teeth and hisses.

"Don't lie to me! How dare you lie to me, Patrice, after the love and care I gave you!"

Then he does the unthinkable. With his face red in anger, he shifts on the seat, sliding his hands down the front of his pants.

"What are you doing?" I bolt up off the chair, moving to the door.

"Sit back down, Patrice, or Julie will make you regret it!"

My bottom lip wobbles as I stay rooted on the spot, not knowing what I should do.

"Stop. Please."

"No!" He growls, his hands moving at a slow pace in his pants. "I'm sick, Patrice. Dying. I need you to make me feel better, just the way you used to."

"Stop." I shake my head.

"If you don't sit back down now, Julie will make you pay."

My head swirls with images of when I was twelve years old, in his care. I feel like I'm back there—that little girl who only wanted someone to love her.

With great reluctance, I ease back down in the chair, trying not to look at what he's doing, yet unable to help myself. As he tugs on his dick, he manages to shift his pants down a little, the head of his cock straining out the top of the waistband. I should scream for help, but I can't. I'm frozen on the spot, only able to watch.

"Patrice, sweetheart. Make Brian feel better. Poke out your tongue for me." When I don't move to do as he asks, he adds, "Trust me, Patrice. Doing this for me is better than what Julie has planned for you if you disobey me."

Nausea sweeps through me as I do as he asks and slowly push my tongue out between my lips. Brian groans when he sees it, his hand picking up pace.

"That's it, Patty. Such a good tongue you have." He moans again. "I still remember how it felt gliding up my shaft. You always knew how to suck me, good Patty. Just like a lollipop."

Even though I know I shouldn't be giving him what he asks for, I can't help it. Something in me heats, and that familiar feeling of desperate need slams into me. I'm sick. Just as twisted as the man before me, because the next thing I know, I run my tongue over my bottom lip and then my top lip, repeating the action a few times.

"That's so good, Patty. Remember how good it felt to make me feel better? Remember how I made you feel things too?" Brian asks, his face going red as his fists pump in his pants. "Remember how you liked the way I touched you between your legs? You used to tell me you loved me every time I did that to you, and I took your ache away. Do you remember?"

"Stop." I whimper, my voice nothing more than the twelve-year-old that endured this. I hate the way my body is reacting to his words. To the memory of how it felt.

"Do you feel that ache now, Patrice? Do you need Brian to touch you there? To rub over that sensitive little mound and slide my fingers deep inside?"

I shift on the seat, feeling the betraying ache grow in intensity. This is so wrong. I know that, so why does my body want more? Why am I like this?

"Come closer, Patrice. If we are quick, I'll be able to touch you and take the ache away." Brian whispers across the small space, his hand moving faster as his hips start to rise and fall.

I shake my head. "No. You aren't allowed across the line."

Finally, my brain does something right.

"Then lift your skirt a little, so I can see. Help Brian feel better."

At his words, I'm suddenly no longer sitting in the prison but back in the house we lived in together. We are in his games room, where he would take me to protect me from Julie and make me feel better. It was our special place. Julie never came into that room. I was safe there, away from her and under the protection of Brian.

We would play games. His favourite was the hospital game, where I would dress up as a nurse, and he would be my patient. It was my job to help Brian feel better, to take his pain away.

I feel my legs part, and I lift my skirt, bunching it up around my waist so he can see my panties. He always liked me to start like this. Sometimes he would ask me to show him when we were out of the room, behind Julie's back when she was cooking dinner or cleaning the house around us. I liked that we had that secret from her. Sometimes, when we would watch movies at night on the couch and Julie would fall asleep next to me, Brian would play quiet games with me, and the rule was that we had to be so careful and quiet that we didn't wake up Julie.

A loud moan works like a bucket of ice, and I snap out of my past and into the present. The guttural noise comes from across the small space, and I realise Brian has just come.

What have I done?

"Let me out!" I scream.

Bolting from the chair, I slam my fists on the door. "Let me out!"

"Your behaviour isn't acceptable, Patrice," Brian growls, but I ignore him, slamming my fists over and over.

"Let me out!"

I hear a click, and the door starts to open, so I jump back in time to dodge it as the officer from before pushes it wide. I scramble from the room, ignoring the officer, and beeline to the reception area. I don't stop as I go to the locker to retrieve my things, my hands trembling, barely able to work. Once I have everything I walked in here with, I run like a bat out of hell from that God awful place that holds the perverted man that has ruined me forever.

Even though I'm crying, none of the prison officers stop to see if I'm ok. In fact, they fucking ignore me. Fuck them and fuck this place! I'm never coming back again! I should never have come here in the first place! Julie can threaten me all she wants. There's nothing she can do to me that will be as bad as having to go back to see that man.

By the time I reach the bus stop, I can't stop myself from hurling what little food I'd eaten today. My body is vibrating with repulsion, mainly for myself. Brian will always be a molesting bastard. But me? I thought I'd worked on this side of myself with the therapists. I thought I'd taught myself that what he did was wrong and that even though I enjoyed it at the time, I shouldn't have. Yet here I am, soaked with need after submitting to him and giving him sickening things.

I am a sick person. I will never be free of my vile need for sex. Ever!

Chapter Twenty-Four

RHYS

Rain pelts my face, and mud splatters my bare legs as I stumble along the dirt track at the back of Vixen's Lodge. I know I shouldn't be here, but I couldn't think of anywhere else I could go to get what I need. Not here in Fox Pines. Maybe if I were older, it would be easier. A dive bar on the edge of town, or even a quick taxi ride to Redfield to one of the strip clubs, would be easy if only I were eighteen already.

The barn is locked up tight, which is unfortunate because it means I don't have access to the face paint to cover my identity. Maybe they have spare masks inside I can borrow? I don't need clothes. I can walk in completely naked. What does it matter if I don't have an outfit to wear? I'll end up naked, anyway.

I try calling Skipper's phone again. He hasn't replied to my messages or answered my calls, which means he must be inside the Feast. Part of me had hoped that he didn't go tonight so I could go to him and get what I need, just the two of us. Sure, he would have questions about my current state of mind, but he won't judge me. Unfortunately, it looks like my only way to him is by going into the Feast.

Tracking through the slosh until I reach the main path, the sky ignites with white light, and a moment later, the loud crack of thunder sounds overhead. I squeal, feeling way too girly and weak as I run up the path towards the main house. Thunder rarely bothers me. I tend to love the unstable atmosphere that comes with a storm, but my nerves are shot, and I've just spent nearly six hours trying to get back to Fox Pines, all while working hard to hold myself together after seeing Brian.

I trip up the steps, my backpack weighing me down as I graze my knee, and suck in a breath at the bite as my skin rips open. Shit. Pulling myself up, I glance down to see blood trickling down my leg, the crimson flowing to mix with the mud.

I just need to get inside. I just need to get lost with someone, anyone, and forget all about what happened today. Hopefully, that someone is Tyler. Or Shaun. Or Moxie.

Hefting my backpack over my shoulder, I push forward, tapping on the door. I don't wait for it to be answered. Instead, pressing down on the handle to push the door open. Dashing in, I quickly shut it behind me before turning to see Brock frozen mid-step.

"Kitten?"

"Hey, Brock." I puff as I try to catch my breath.

"What are you doing?"

"I'm extremely late, I know. Sorry. Are there any spare masks?"

"What? No." He glances over his shoulder in concern before stepping closer to me. "You can't go in anyway. You're not on the list tonight." Brock moves to block my view as I stand on my toes, trying to look over his shoulder into the cloakroom. Surely there are spare masks in there?

"I know. I didn't think I could get here, but I made it after all. I just need a mask. Can you please grab me one?"

He shakes his head. "Spare mask or not, I can't let you in, Kitten. You know the rules better than anyone."

"Oh, come on, Brocky." I pout. "You know I'm a crowd-pleaser. Madam Vik will probably pay you a bonus for letting me in." I move to step around him, but I don't get far. His big hand wraps around my bicep, halting me.

"No, Kitten. You're not welcome here tonight."

"Get my sponsor. Skipper. He can vouch for me." I tug my arm free, looking at Brock hopefully.

"I can't." Brock releases my arm. "Skipper didn't book in tonight either."

"He didn't?" I frown. It's unusual for Tyler not to come to a Feast night. Especially after he messaged me earlier today to ask if I was coming. Plus, he hasn't answered my calls. Where else would he be?

Maybe with his girlfriend or lover! Or on a date!

Everything doesn't revolve around you, Rhys!

"Nope. Now leave." He growls, his burley tone a clear demand.

"Come on, Brock, *pleeease*. I *neeeed* to go in there. *Pleeease*. I'm fucking begging you." I slap my hands together in front of me to demonstrate my beg, but he shakes his head again.

"Please don't beg. It won't change my answer."

I hiss through my teeth at him, clenching my fists at my sides as the heat of humiliation sweeps over me.

"Let me in!" I practically yell, which doesn't sway him. He shakes his head again before taking his phone out and dialling a number. A moment after he puts it to his ear, he barks to whoever answered.

"Get Madam Vik for me, please." Brock glares at me with frustration, not taking his eyes off me once, not even when Madam Vik's voice comes on the line. "We have an unexpected guest not on tonight's list." He listens and then responds. "It's Kitten." I can hear Madam Vik's voice, although I can't make out what she's saying as Brock listens. "I don't know, Madam. Something's not right. Maybe she's on something?"

"What? I'm not on anything!" I hiss, but Brock ignores me and keeps listening on the phone. A moment later, he ends the call and crosses his arms over his chest, widening his stance.

"Can I go in?"

Brock doesn't answer, just keeps his glare on me. And here I thought we were friends. Shouldn't that get me some fucking brownie points?

The door opens down the hall, and a moment later, Madam Vik steps into the foyer wearing a silk wrap gown, her furious eyes landing on me. She runs her gaze over me, taking in my disarray.

"Kitten, you need to leave."

"But I want to join in. I just need a mask. Please, Madam Vik, I'll do whatever you want me to."

Her brows shoot up at my declaration.

"So, you'll spend the night downstairs with Master Hill, then?"

Straight for the fucking jugular. Bitch! Seriously, what the fuck?

I shake my head. "N-no. I mean with you."

Madam Vik steps up to me, lifting a pointy fingernail to rest under my chin, her green eyes piercing mine as she studies me.

"What's wrong with you? Your eyes look normal. Why would you come here like this?" She drops my chin and gestures her claws to my body.

"Nothing's wrong."

"Of course, there's something wrong. You're shaking." Vik screws her nose up in disgust.

"I'm cold. That's all. I got caught in the storm on my way here."

"No. You're not shivering, Kitten. You're shaking. Trembling. Coming here when you're obviously highly strung from who the hell knows what is just unacceptable. I should get Master Hill so he can deal with you."

"No!" I cry, and her eyes widen. "Please, I just need... I need..."

I try so fucking hard to fight back the stupid tears, but my emotions are shot. I'm fucking desperate, just not desperate enough to give myself over to Master Hill.

"You're a mess. You need to leave now before you make things worse for yourself." Vik turns to Brock. "Can you please take her home?"

"N-no, please. I can't go home. Not tonight. Not after..."

"I'll take her."

The voice comes from the hall as Shaun steps out, tugging off his black leather mask, his dark curls tumbling over his bruised eyes. Just the sight of him eases the panic racing through me.

"Oh, Cass. That would be fabulous, thank you, darling." Vik steps up to him, placing her hand over his bare peck, and I feel like mauling her. She needs to get her hand off my guy. Like right now!

"No problem, Madam. Happy to help." Leaning down, Shaun presses a kiss to Vik's cheek while keeping his steel-grey eyes on me.

My heart races as my chest heaves—the unfamiliar feeling of possessiveness rushing over me. When a quiet growl slips past my lips, Shaun pulls back, biting his lower lip as he tries to hide a smirk.

Fucker!

"Oh, and Kitten?" Vik gains my attention as she turns back to me. "I'll be raising this infraction with your sponsor. This sort of behaviour is unacceptable."

Great! Now I've gotten Tyler into trouble as well.

Seriously. All I want is a bit of dick, for fuck's sake!

Madam Vik speaks quietly with Brock while Shaun throws on his clothes, and she leaves Brock to watch over us so she can re-join the Feast. I don't say anything else to Brock while he glares daggers at me, and the moment Shaun steps out of the cloakroom, I turn my back on Brock and open the door, stepping back out into the storm.

The moment I hear the door close behind me, I feel warm fingers link with mine, and Shaun whirls me around, pulling me to his chest.

"What's going on, Kitten?"

I can't talk because the simple act of his arms around me, giving me the hug I've been craving all day, has me in tears. I wrap my arms around his torso, burying my head into the Shaun scented hoodie he's wearing, and let my tears fall. I feel him press kisses to my head as he holds me to him. His hands rub up and down my soaking top, trying to warm me up.

"Kitten." He whispers. "Let me take care of you."

I nod into his chest, and he relaxes like he thought I'd argue with him. Fair call since I probably would under normal circumstances. A moment later, he pulls back and takes my face in his hands, his eyes, still swollen from Marcus' fist, studying mine as salty drops continue to fall. Then, he steps back, re-linking his fingers with mine, and leads me along the covered veranda that wraps around Vixen's Lodge. When we reach the corner of the house, he points into the dark yard.

"We gotta make a run for that tree. My bike is there. You ever been on a dirt bike before?" I shake my head, and he grins. "Do you trust me, Kitten?" The slightest of grins tugs at my lips, and when he notices, his grin broadens. "Yeah, you do." Leaning down, he presses his lips to mine in a brief peck. "Time to go."

Tugging me along with him, we run out into the heavy rain towards a large tree behind the pool house. The wind has picked up now, and the sky lights up again, causing my heart to race even faster as adrenaline builds. When we reach the tree, we don't speak, just hurry so we can get out of the storm. Shaun slides the helmet over my head, doing it up as my body trembles, and once he's done, he holds up a finger, silently telling me to wait. Then he turns to the bike, kicks the stand up, and throws his leg over.

Fuck, that's hot.

With his hands wrapped around the handles, he looks down to one of his feet and rises before pushing back down. The bike roars to life.

"Climb on Kitten." He yells over the noise, and I move to where he gestures behind him, throwing my leg over and wrapping my arms around him.

"Now, hold on."

The bike lurches forward, and I let out a stupid girly squeal as we take off into the dark. I try to see where we are going over Shaun's shoulder, but we are moving too fast, and quite frankly, I'm about shitting myself with fear. Fun fear. It's exhilarating, and even though I know this is dangerous, I don't want it to end.

After a little time, we slow as we pass through a narrow opening in the fence, and then we take off quickly again. I can feel Shaun's heart thumping in his chest where one of my hand's rests, and I fucking love how much this excites him too.

The open fields we are flying through come to an end, and I notice the dark shadows of some sort of plants or shrubs on either side of us as we climb a bit of a hill. Once we reach the top, I can see light up ahead, and as we get closer, I realise the light is actually several lights coming from a house.

Reaching the back fence of the house, Shaun slows the bike, pulling it in under a large open shed before killing the engine.

"Where are we?" I ask through the confines of the helmet before pulling it off.

"My place," Shaun answers as he unravels my hands from around him and gestures for me to climb off. Once I'm no longer straddling the hunk of metal, Shaun climbs off too, taking the helmet from me and sitting it on the bike.

"You live next door to Vixen's Lodge?"

"Yep." He takes my hand, leading me out into the rain again.

We race across the yard, the grass logged with water, splashing up as we run before we reach the steps leading up to an old but adorable white farmhouse. We take a moment to shake some of the water off, and I take in the white weatherboard house. There's a verandah that wraps around the side of the house. I can't see where it goes, but I get the feeling it probably leads to the front. Off to the right, there's a large area with an outdoor setting and one of those cute porch swings you see in the movies.

"Kitten." Shaun gains my attention, and I turn to him. He's now just as wet through as I am, his dark curls dripping as they hang down over his eyes. "Let's get you inside. You can have a shower and warm up, and I'll get you something to eat."

I nod, speechless, as he uses his thumbs to wipe up the running mascara from my cheeks, being careful not to press too hard on my bruised skin. I can only imagine what I look like. A fucking mess, that's for sure, yet his eyes seem to warm as he looks at me, and then he leans in, hovering his lips over mine as he whispers.

"I'll take care of you, Rhys."

When his warm lips press against mine, I relax into him, letting him take control and loving the way he kisses me like I'm a delicacy. He spends a minute gently worshipping my mouth before pulling back with a grin and tugging me inside his house.

I'm not a take home to your parents kind of girl, so my nerves pick up tenfold as we enter. The first thing I notice, besides how warm and cosy it is, is the smell of freshly baked something. Pie maybe? Something sweet. Who knows? But it makes my mouth water.

The interior is a combination of whites, timbers, and blacks, with the large windows a real feature looking out to the yard beyond. It's too dark for me to see what the yard looks like, but given the house's charm, I'd have to say it's probably beautiful.

"Stay here a minute. I'll be right back." Shaun's voice is quiet, and I give him a nod before watching him retreat into a room off to the left. A moment later, I hear him talking in Spanish, and my Kitty stirs to life. Other voices join him in a quiet conversation, and because I'm a nosy bitch, I slowly creep forward and peer around the corner.

Shaun is standing in a small living room, his back to me as he talks to a man sitting in an old recliner that's seen better days. I can't see the man's face, but given the brief glimpse I caught of Shaun's dad on Thursday at school, I'd say the partially balding man is him.

Then Shaun turns his attention in the other direction, squatting down beside the couch. I didn't even realise there was someone on the couch, but now I can see a woman lying on it, a checkered blanket over her legs. She looks frail as she lifts a hand to cup Shaun's cheek, and even though I can only see the side of his face now, I can still see the love he has for this woman written across his expression. They chat quietly in the language I don't understand yet adore, and when he goes to stand, I move back into the little entrance he left me in.

When Shaun returns to me, he takes my hand and leads me quietly up the narrow staircase, across a landing to a door, which then leads to another set of stairs. Turning to me on the landing, he points up to them.

"My room is up there." Then he turns around and points to the doors behind us. "Toilet is the right door. Bathroom is on the left. Take a shower and then come up."

"Ok, thanks," I murmur, suddenly feeling nervous and self-conscious.

"Oh, wait. Do you need clothes?"

I shake my head. "Nah, I have a t-shirt in here I can wear." I hold my backpack up.

Shaun frowns. "Where are you meant to be staying tonight?"

"Oh, uh… My rents think I'm at Tillie's."

He nods. "Should I take you there? Is she expecting you?"

"No… I mean unless you want me to leave." Shit, maybe he doesn't even want me here in his house. In his space.

Shaking his head, he grips my hips with both hands and tugs me against him.

"I don't want you to leave, Kitten. Get that thought out of your head right now. I just don't want you to get into any trouble."

"Uh-ok. I'll let Tillie know I won't be coming. I don't always make it back to her house after a Feast night, anyway. She's used to it."

His dark brows shoot up, disappearing under his curls. "Where do you go if you don't go to her place?"

"Sometimes I go to Brocks or Moxie's. Sometimes I go home." I shrug, and his eyes darken.

"You go to Brocks? The arsehole bouncer that wouldn't let you in tonight?"

Nodding, I push back from him.

"Are you jealous, Bossi?" I tease, knowing I'm a hypocrite since I wasn't happy about Vik touching him earlier.

"Fuck yeah, I am. You're not going back to his place ever fucking again."

This time my brows lift. "I thought you said you would share me. Did you lie?"

"It was no lie, Kitten. I will share you with people *I* trust."

"Oh."

Jesus, why do I like the sound of that?

"What about Skipper? Or other people at the Feast?"

"Oddly enough, I trust Skipper. I can see he won't do anything to hurt you, but it does kinda irk me to see him touching you." Shaun's face is a mix of anger and a pout. It's adorable, and I can't hold back my smile. "I'm still trying to figure out if I'm happy about sharing you with him. There are so many things wrong with that whole situation."

"Because of who he is, or is it just an age thing?" I say quietly so no one else can hear. Not that I know if there's anyone else in this house, but I can't be too careful when it comes to Tyler.

"The age thing wouldn't be an issue if you weren't still classed as a minor, Kitten. And yeah, his job is a big fucking issue with me." As if he can't keep away from me, Shaun takes one of my hands in his, entwining our fingers again. It's a simple gesture. Innocent almost. Yet packs a punch I'm not used to. For me, hands linking together are done in the heat of passion as two bodies send each other spiralling into ecstasy. I'm not familiar with hand-holding that isn't linked to sex in some way, so sharing this is new and even more intimate than spreading my legs.

"Just remember Casanova, *I* was the one that manipulated *him*. He fought me until I blackmailed him. The fact he even shows an ounce of care for me after what I did speaks to the kind of person *he* is. He should hate me, but he doesn't."

Shaun nods, "Yeah, I know. I'm trying to wrap my head around it."

We fall quiet for a moment, our eyes locked with my hands in his as we linger on the landing. It's not an awkward silence. It's calm and comforting and another thing new to me.

"Go warm up in the shower, Kitten. Meet you up in my room afterwards."

Then Shaun drops my hands and leans forward, pressing his warm lips to my forehead before heading back downstairs.

His innocent kiss has my fucking heart flipping in my chest. Either I'm about to drop dead from an unknown heart condition, or those romance books I read are coming to life. If it's the latter, then I'm completely fucked because it means I'm falling hard for Shaun Bossier.

Chapter Twenty-Five

SHAUN

I can hear Rhys up in my room as I climb the narrow flight of stairs to the attic. There's music playing faintly, probably from her phone. It's a female singer, someone I haven't heard before, and it kind of sounds grungy. Edgy. It's a sound that suits the vibe my girl has going for herself—very Rhys George.

Yeah, yeah. I fucking said, *my* girl, because that's what she is. I never thought I'd lay claim to a chick, especially at my age, yet here I fucking am. Rhys George is mine, and yeah, I'll share her if that's what she wants and needs. I feel like I'd do just about anything for this crazy chick. She's got me by the balls, in a good way.

Reaching the top of the stairs, I step into my room and see Rhys standing at my bookshelf with her back to me. I thought it would be weird having her in my space. I've never brought a chick home before, yet as I watch her finger skim over the spine of one of my books, a warm feeling settles in my gut.

Her hair is down, its length brushing the top of her arse and fuck, I love that sight. It's still damp, but not the mess it was when she arrived at Vixen's Lodge earlier. My gaze travels down to see she's only wearing an oversized t-shirt. It's either grey or was once black and has been worn so much that it's now grey, and it ends right under her arse cheeks where her long legs begin. They look like silk, and I know if I run my hand up her legs, they will feel that way too. Everything about this chick calls to me.

"Hungry?" My voice comes out raspy, so I clear my throat as I watch her turn to me.

Like the fuckboy I am, my eyes enjoy a slow perusal travelling up the front of her legs, reaching that greyish t-shirt to see a faded picture on it with the word Flyleaf. Then I lift my eyes to her face. For a moment, I can't breathe. I'm not sure if my heart stops or my lungs forget how to fucking inhale oxygen, but I'm absolutely stunned and rooted on the spot as I take in her face.

Her soft creamy skin has a faint flush to it, especially over her cheeks. Her lips, which are usually painted black, dark purple, or a deep red, are now nothing but a blushed natural pink, looking plumper than I've ever seen them. Then there are her eyes. She usually has those dark pools covered in that black stuff chicks paint on their lashes and lids, so dark that it makes her eyes look nearly black. Now, however, there's nothing but her beautiful creamy skin encasing natural dark lashes that fan her rich chocolate eyes. Gone are the harsh standout features of the makeup she hides behind every day. Now, all there is, is the most stunning woman I've ever laid eyes on.

"Earth to Bossi." Rhys steps closer, waving a hand in front of my face. "You, ok?"

"You're stunning," I whisper, not able to contain my thoughts.

Instantly, her face drops, and she stops on the spot. She hates compliments. For some reason, they make her feel uncomfortable. I want more than anything for her to feel good about receiving them. To know, I mean them. If only she could see herself through my eyes.

I lift my hand as if to reach out to her, forgetting that I'm holding a plate of food, and I nearly drop the fucking thing. Darting forward, Rhys grabs hold of the plate in an attempt to save it, which leaves us both standing awkwardly, gripping the same piece of porcelain.

"Is this for me?" She asks quietly, so I nod and release the plate. "Thanks."

There's a faint grin lifting those kissable lips of hers. A sight I hope to see more often.

Moving over to my desk, Rhys sits down on my gaming chair and starts to eat the food I re-heated for her. Mama's carer cooks a roast dinner for us on Sundays, and there are always leftovers that we use for lunches for a day or two. Today, Jenny cooked roast pork. Not everyone is a fan of pork, but as I watch Rhys eat what I gave her, I get a sense of satisfaction. I realise I really do enjoy looking after her.

"Who's this singing?" Leaning against my bookshelf, I cross my arms over my chest and look down to those plump pink lips as they consume the food I served her.

Rhys leans back in the chair, sweeping her tongue over her lips before pointing to her t-shirt. "Flyleaf. Have you heard them before?"

I shake my head. "No, but I like what I'm hearing."

She smiles, "Lacey has the best voice, don't you think? She's the lead singer… well, was. She parted ways with the band, but their music lives on. I think she's pretty sick!"

I smile. It's nice to see my Kitten interested in something other than sex.

"Well, Kitten, I'm a fan. I'll look them up on Spotify."

Rhys beams, flashing her teeth before returning her focus to the veggies left on her plate. I watch her quietly, giving her this time to relax and feel safe. I want her to feel that here. I want her to feel that with me. She's been so off since coming back to school. I'm positive that whatever has her so rattled tonight has something to do with why she wasn't around at the start of term. I could be really fucking wrong, and I know the shit with Marcus on Thursday has made things worse for her. I guess she's got a lot going on right now. The problem is, she doesn't fucking talk about it. She just wants to fuck her problems away, which is only a temporary reprieve. But if that's what she needs tonight, I'll give it to her. If she thinks she's going to get away with not talking about shit, though, she's not gonna like me much by the time I'm done.

"Oh man, that was so good." Rhys moans, relaxing back in the chair again.

I grin. "I'll be sure to let Jenny know you approve."

"Jenny? Is that your mum's name?" She frowns, her eyes going distant like she's trying to remember if I've ever told her my mum's name. I chuckle.

"Jenny is my mama's carer. My mama's name is Gabriella."

Deep dark eyes lock with mine as Rhys' face softens, "Your mum has a carer... Is she sick?"

I nod. "Mama has MS. It's been getting worse lately."

A level of compassion I haven't seen Rhys express before sweeps across her face. Standing from the chair, she steps over to me, and I unravel my arms to tug her close when she presses herself against me.

"I'm sorry, Shaun. I didn't know your mum was sick."

"It's all g, Kitten." I offer her a small smile, but she shakes her head.

"No. It's not. *Shit*." She shakes her head again, her eyes darting down briefly before looking back to mine. "You don't need *my* crap on top of everything."

I can see she's about to pull away from me. Maybe even grab her bag and leave. Fuck that. I'm not letting her go, so I tighten my arms, holding her to me.

"My mama has been sick for years. Yeah, it sucks, and I hate seeing her getting frailer, but I've learned to live with it." I lift my hand, and using my fingers, I stroke her silky dark hair back and tuck it behind one ear. "As for *your* crap. I *do* need it. All of it. I can't explain it, Kitten. I just know I need you. I need to help you. Look after you." I lean closer. "Pleasure you." I wag my brows at that, hoping to get a smile out of her to replace the dead-serious expression on her face.

It works.

"Wanna tell me what happened today? Tonight?" I ask, hoping she won't turn and run.

Right before my eyes, I watch as her warm smile transforms into a cold, blank stare. Then she presses her palm against my chest, trying to push away. I don't give in, though. She's in my arms, and I'm not letting go.

"Kitten?"

"I don't want to talk about today. Can we just fuck, or if you'd prefer, I can leave and go to Tillie's?"

I shake my head. "Nope. Not happening. You're *my* prisoner tonight, Kitten."

I thought she'd gone cold on me a moment ago, but that's nothing to how her body stiffens, and her eyes widen now.

What did I say wrong?

"I'm joking, George. You're my guest, and I'd like you to stay the night with me." When her expression doesn't change, I whisper. "Please?"

"Sorry..." She shakes her head, her lids squeezing tight for a moment. "I'm a bit messed up right now," Rhys admits, and fuck if that doesn't slice my chest open.

My girl, who's normally full of life, laughter, and sexual innuendo, looks nothing but defeated.

"Let me take care of you, Kitten. Will you let me do that?" I keep my eyes on hers, even when she looks away to think. Then she nods, returning her chocolate gaze to me.

"Ok."

Her voice is so quiet and small, the opposite of who Rhys George is. She's a big personality. The life of the party. The bridge between a dull, boring world and one filled with colour and vibrance.

"You need the bathroom or anything before we head to bed?"

She shakes her head, "Nah. I'm ok." She steps back from me and picks up her drink bottle, taking a quick sip. "Oh, I forgot to tell you, I ran into your brother before, out in the hall."

"You met Derek?" Shit, I should've given him a heads up that we have a guest.

"Yep. He's a closet gay, isn't he?"

My brows shoot up at her observation.

"How'd you know? Did he say something?"

Rhys grins, "Nope. But he was so shocked to see me coming out of the bathroom that he didn't cover his phone. He was on Grindr."

"Oh." I chuckle. I'm going to give him so much shit for that. "So, how'd you know he's a closet gay, then?"

"Well, when I asked him if he's had any luck on Grindr and pointed to his phone, he fucking panicked and looked around like he just got sprung by the fun police."

"Fuuuck. I can just imagine his face." I laugh. "Our old man doesn't know, and Derek wants to keep it that way."

"Is your dad a homophobe?"

I nod. "Yep. He can't wrap his head around anything other than what the bible says."

Rhys pouts. "That sucks for your brother."

I nod, "Come on, Kitten, let's get you up to my bed."

She grins playfully, and given how upset she was earlier, I fucking love the sight of it.

"I have to say, Bossi, your room is epic. It's a good use of the small space."

I grin back, glancing around my small attic bedroom. There's a lot of wasted space in here because the walls are short, and we are basically standing in a converted roof space, but me and Derek built the small loft that sits above my desk area to make it more liveable. The small loft consists of my bed and a narrow wrap around ledge. One of the best parts is the skylight window in the gable ceiling above my mattress. It's a cosy squeeze up there, and I can't stand up or anything, but fuck, I love laying up there and falling asleep under the stars, or in tonight's case, a storm. It has to be one of my favourite places to be, other than between Kitten's thighs.

"Derek helped me build it when my mum's carer needed to start staying overnight. I gave up my bedroom, which is now used as a guest room. Jenny is the only one that uses it. She's been staying more often lately."

"You really gave up your bedroom for that?" Rhys asks, her eyes softening around the edges, and I nod. "Wow, Cass, you're such a good guy. Not many people would do that."

I shrug. "I'd do anything for my mama. I'd do anything for you too, Kitten."

There's that faint tinge to her cheeks again. So beautiful, especially with the way she is right now. Natural and makeup-free.

"So, is that thing going to support the both of us?" Changing the conversation, Rhys points up to my loft. "You know… because *you* built it."

The mischievous grin gives me a glimpse of the fun-loving version of Rhys George, so I dart forward to grab her, but the little minx darts away. She quickly realises she doesn't have anywhere to go because my room is like an oversized closet type of small, so I easily catch her wrapping my arms around her waist from behind and tugging her against my body. Instantly, Thor awakens, rising to meet his siren.

"You're not getting away from me," I growl against the hair falling over her ear, and she sinks back into me, causing friction with her fine arse that has Thor rock hard. With her pressed against my body, I run one hand up her front to cup one of her perfect handfuls, and I ease my other hand lower to cup the heat between her silky legs.

"Shaun." She breathes, pushing her hips forward, seeking more.

Still pressed up behind her, I steer her towards the step ladder that leads up to my loft bed.

"Up," I command, and Rhys moves forward out of my hold to climb up to the loft. As she takes each step, I get a devious view of her arse and the moist spot on her pink panties between her legs. Fuuuck. I can't help myself. I reach up and press my fingers against the damp patch.

"You're so wet, Kitten. Is that for me?"

Any other girl would probably squeal and go shy, darting the rest of the way up. Not Rhys George, though. Not my Kitten.

Stopping where she is on the step ladder, Rhys tilts her head down towards me, looking pleased as fuck. "Of course, Casanova. You make me gush."

Fucking Thor lurches forward, almost taking me with him like he's a fucking dog on a leash, dragging me along behind him.

In! In! I want in!

Calm the fuck down, you beast!

Drawing my fingers away from the heat that has me practically blowing a fuse, I slap her arse, which extracts a giggle before she moves quickly the rest of the way up.

Remembering that I don't have any protection up there because I never bring chicks home, I go to my bag and dig the new box out, tearing it open with my teeth before climbing up to heaven.

When I reach the top, Rhys has already positioned herself in the centre of the bed. Her face is peaceful as she stares up through the skylight, watching the faint flashes of lightning that still light up the sky from wherever the storm has moved to.

Reaching over to the switch next to the end of my bed, I flick on the LED lights that line the underside of the mattress and then turn off the main light in the room. A smile spreads across my face as Rhys notices the warm glow, giving my loft bed a different vibe. It probably looks romantic or something.

Grabbing out a dinger, I toss the box in the top corner of my bed and crawl up over Rhys, pressing my lips to the soft skin of her legs as I go. When I reach the hem of her shirt, I straddle her legs and ease her shirt up slowly, keeping my eyes locked on hers as she watches me.

For a few long moments, I'm able to keep her in my trance, her eyes held to mine by an invisible bond. With our eyes connected like this, a new level of vulnerability opens up between us. The thought has me excited because I'd do anything to see past her walls, but it's short-lived.

Our connection is severed when she darts her eyes away, and I realise the intimate connection we shared has made her uncomfortable. I want to ask her why, yet I hold my words in, too chicken shit that I'll make her bolt. We've exchanged intimate looks before, maybe not quite as intense, so hopefully, her discomfort is related to reeling from whatever happened today that sent her over the edge, and not because she feels awkward from some sort of unrequited love thing.

Get your head back in the game, Casanova. Show her what things could be like.

After I help her out of her Flyleaf t-shirt, tossing it in the corner on top of the condom box, I take a moment to run my gaze over her stunning body. Her nipples are pebbled into hard peaks, and goosebumps feather across her skin as she lies on my bed, her long dark hair fanning out under her head on my pillow. Fuck, she looks like a goddess. A goddess just for me.

A small whimper falls from those plump pink lips, her hips lifting a little at the same time.

"What's wrong, Kitten? You hungry?"

"Famished." She whispers.

"You haven't eaten today?" And no. I'm not talking about actual food. Rhys George is a sex-machine. I doubt she'd go a day without an orgasm or two.

She shakes her head. "Not really. Just an appetiser or two."

I know what she's talking about. My little minx has done the job herself and got herself off today.

"When?" I ask, and her brows lift in question. "When did you touch yourself?"

"Earlier." She's giving me nothing, but I need to know more.

Leaning forward, I softly roll and pinch her nipple, causing her back to arch, pushing those two mounds up until she's straining.

I chuckle.

"Be more specific. When did you *touch* yourself, Kitten?"

"This morning. And this afternoon." She bites her lower lip as I use both hands to tweak those fucking lickable nipples.

"Where were you this morning?"

"At home." She whimpers.

"Where at home?" Leaning down, I flick my tongue over one nipple and then the other.

"Bedroom." She pants.

"How did you do it?" I urge, and she shakes her head as another whimper falls past her lips. "Tell me, Kitten. How did you get yourself off this morning in your bedroom? Did you use your fingers?"

She shakes her head, keeping her eyes shut as her desire builds.

"A toy?" I ask, and again, she shakes her head, so I pull back, and her eyes fly open. "Tell me how you made yourself come this morning."

"On my bed." She growls, shooting me daggers.

"Not where. I asked how."

"That is how. My bed." Her face reddens in frustration, making those cheeks glow like beacons.

Her bed? "I'm confused. You used your bed to get yourself off?"

"Yes." She nods. "Enough with the questions. Fuck me, Cass."

This time, I shake my head.

"Yeah-Nah. I'm not fucking you until you answer my questions. Tell me *how* your bed made you come."

"Cass, please." She begs, but I shake my head, not backing down. "Fine! I rubbed myself on the corner of my mattress until I came. Now fuck me already!"

I tilt my head to the side. "You rubbed yourself against the mattress. The corner?" I point to the corner of my mattress to make sure I understand correctly. When she nods, I try to picture it. "Fuck, that's hot, Kitten. One day, I'm going to ask you to show me. Would you do that?"

Again, if she were any other girl, she'd be embarrassed and shy, but not my girl. She nods.

"Of course. As long as you come all over my naked arse the moment I come."

And there's Thor. Pre-cum oozing out as the fucker drools.

"Deal." I dart down and claim her lips, not wanting to waste any more time. Our tongues clash in desperation, and I ignore the sting from my cut lip as she winds her arms around my neck, trapping me against her. With our bodies pressed tight, a frenzy takes over as our hips meet with feverish friction.

As much as I want to bury myself between her silky thighs, I don't want this to be over too soon, so I can't let Thor sink inside her just yet. I want to make her explode. I want to watch her come undone.

Pulling back, I kiss a trail down her neck and chest as she writhes under me. Then, sitting up, I drag those pink panties off her and spread her legs wide. My mouth waters at the glistening sight of her bare pussy, the small patch of dark hair like an arrow directing me to heaven just in case I somehow forget where her on-switch is.

"Rhys." I keep my voice quiet so she knows I'm being serious. When her dark eyes lock on mine, I tell her the truth, even though I know she doesn't want to hear it. "You really are the most stunning woman alive. Every time it's just you and me together, I want you to be like this for me." I gesture to my face as an example. "No makeup. Just all you. It's the most beautiful thing I've ever seen."

Her withering stills under me, and my normally confident minx is gone, leaving behind a seventeen-year-old girl with a world of worry in her eyes.

Remembering what Mr Foster said to me the other day, I speak the language she knows and understands so well. I use the currency she's comfortable with.

Sex.

"I'm going my make you come, Kitten. And then, I'm going to fuck you until you realise how fucking serious I am about how beautiful you are, so that next time we are together like this, you will feel just as beautiful as the way I see you."

Those perfect pink lips part as a small breath escapes her, and then I slide my fingers down through the centre of her folds before slipping two digits home.

We both moan as my fingers fill and stretch her. She's so wet. So ready. So needy. I'm desperate to dive in and lick her clean. I hold back, though, because I need more answers.

"Kitten, tell me where you were this afternoon when you got yourself off."

Her eyes dart open, and she goes to speak a refusal, but I hook my fingers up, pressing on her upper wall as my thumb reacquaints itself with her needy clit, and her words are lost. The only sound her pretty pink lips reveal is a pleasured moan and some gasping pants.

"Answer me, Kitten. Where were you?"

"I-I-I, oh fuck, I can't think when you're doing that." She moans out, and my lips tug north.

"Ok. I'll stop then." I still my fingers, and she whimpers, her hand flying to mine, pressing it hard against her wet heat so I can't withdraw my fingers.

"Don't stop."

"Answer me then," I growl.

"I don't want to talk about this afternoon."

Now I know that whatever bad thing happened to her today, happened this afternoon.

"You give me the answers, Kitten, and I'll reward you."

"For fuck's sake, have you been talking with Tyler? Comparing fuck stories?"

"What?" I frown. "No! What does that even mean?"

Grabbing my hand, she starts moving it with her own, seeking the pleasure I stopped giving her. "Never mind, just make me come, Cass."

"I will. Give me answers, though. Where were you?"

"I'll answer if you *don't* stop."

"Deal." I grin, and I start moving my fingers inside her again, my thumb pressing gently to her clit.

"I was… on the train." She pants out, and I frown.

"Train?"

"Yes." She moans.

"Why were you on a train?"

"That has nothing… to do with me getting… myself off." She pants again.

"True," I say reluctantly, knowing that the destination of that train ride *is* important, but maybe not for the current situation. "So, you made yourself come on a train. Where were you on the train?"

"Toilet cabin." She licks her lips, and her hand flies to her nipple as she rolls it between her fingers. Fuck, she's perfect.

"Please tell me you used your fingers this time and not a surface in that room?"

Laughter bursts free as her eyes fly open, her white teeth bright in the dark space. "No, I didn't rub myself up against the train toilet."

"So, you used your fingers?" When she nods, I add, "Rubbing on the inside or outside?"

"Both." She whimpers as I work my thumb faster.

"How many fingers?"

"Three." She declares, so naturally and unabashed, that I reward her by adding another digit to the party, sinking it in and stretching her. Her moan is loud and the most beautiful sound. I want to record it so I can listen to it every time I jack myself off.

"Were you sitting on the toilet?"

She nods.

"Another thing I'm going to get you to show me one day, Kitten."

She nods again, her inner walls swelling as she gets closer to the climax she's seeking.

"And when you show me that, I'm going to cum in your mouth."

She explodes. Her cries are loud, and I slap my hand over her mouth, hoping my brother didn't hear. Then her teeth sink into my palm, and she rides out her orgasm until her body falls lax.

Watching Rhys George's face as she comes has to be the most exquisite thing I've ever seen. Her expression is almost pained, yet her body tells me how epic it feels. If there was any pain, it was the good kind.

As Rhys livens up again, her body igniting to life, desperate for more, she reaches for me, and I quickly sheath my cock in latex before slamming home.

I've fucked Rhys before. I've fucked many chicks before, but nothing was like this. Not tonight. Not right here with me and her alone in my bed, her vulnerability on display, her naked face nothing but the natural beauty of an angel.

All I can think as Thor pistons inside her is that this right here is my ultimate. Nothing will ever compare to Rhys George and the way I feel about her. I know here and now that even if she thinks she can't have a relationship with me or anyone else, I'm going to make it my mission to prove her wrong. I'll show her it doesn't matter if she leads a different lifestyle and has different needs than the average girl. She can have everything she's ever dreamed of and more. Rhys George is mine, and I'm never letting her go.

CHAPTER TWENTY-SIX

RHYS

A noise jolts me from sleep, and the first thing I see is the night sky with twinkling stars. As my memory kicks in, reminding me of where I am, a smile spreads across my face as Shaun's scent wraps around me like a safety blanket. I'm in his bed, and I never want to leave.

A noise sounds again, and I realise it's coming from somewhere else in the house. Rolling over, I expect to find Shaun, but the bed is empty. Sitting up, I lean forward a little to see if he's in his room below, but I'm met with an empty space. Reluctantly, I climb down from his heavenly bed and scan the small room again, confirming that he's definitely not in here with me.

Maybe he's gone to the toilet?

When I hear the noise again, like a chair scraping across the floor, I climb back up to the bed, tug on my panties and t-shirt, and go in search of Shaun. I find the bedroom door wide open, but there are no lights on beyond it.

What is he doing in the dark?

Hearing more noise, I follow it downstairs and freeze in place when I enter the open plan kitchen living area. Shaun is sitting in the dark at the kitchen table, with the moonlight filtering in from the window behind him. And he's completely naked.

What the?

Taking a step forward, my heart nearly leaps out of my throat, and I almost scream when I hear someone whisper from the other entrance of the room.

"Don't wake him."

Squinting in the dark, I see the silhouette of a man that morphs into Derek, Shaun's older brother, as my eyes adjust. He's leaning against the door frame with his arms crossed over his chest, his eyes moving between me and Shaun, who hasn't acknowledged our presence. I'm so confused.

"What?" I whisper.

Derek pushes off the door frame and pads over to me, leaning around the door jamb next to me to flick on the light in the hall. He's about the same height as Shaun, maybe a little taller. His appearance is uncanny to Shaun's, yet his jaw is a little squarer, and his eyes are brown and not the steel-grey that Shaun's are. Like all the yummiest of guys, he's wearing grey sweatpants and a navy tight fitting t-shirt. I don't know why his dad doesn't know he's gay; he is exceptionally well-groomed.

"Shaun's sleepwalking. It's not a good idea to wake someone when they're sleepwalking."

I flick my gaze back to Shaun.

"He sleepwalks?"

"Yep. Hasn't done it for years until recently. I think it has to do with our mama getting worse. He pretends he's not worried, but I know he is. The old man doesn't help with the pressure he puts on Shaun to leave school."

"Leave school? Why?" It really isn't my business, but I can't help it. I have this need to know everything about Shaun.

"Running this farm is hard work. We need more help, and since business isn't great and with mama's extra medical needs, we had to lay off most of our staff. Shaun has a deal going with the old bat next door. She has weird fucking parties all the time and made a deal to buy a shit tonne of our wine in exchange for Shaun's time to do some work over there a couple of nights a week. Even with that deal, the money isn't enough. So, padre puts extra pressure on him to drop out and work on the farm full time."

Madam Vik is a bitch, yet now her arrangement with Shaun makes total sense.

Shaun mumbles something, regaining my attention.

"So, if I shouldn't wake him, how do I get him back to bed?"

Derek smiles. "You in a hurry to end this already?" He gestures to his naked brother sitting at the table, moving his hands about as if he's busy doing something invisible. "It's the perfect time to fuck with him."

Getting his meaning, I grin, "Be right back."

As quietly as I can, I rush back up to Shaun's room, grab my phone off the charger and return to the kitchen. Shaun is still in the same place, mumbling something about Pelicans.

I flash Derek my phone, and he grins before I tiptoe over to Shaun and take a few selfies with him in the background. Then Derek joins me, and we take a couple more before Shaun's voice rises.

"Don't you know that carrots are wine?"

I giggle, but he speaks again.

"The rabbits will fuck the pelicans."

I slap my hand over my mouth, trying to silence my laughter, and Derek does the same.

"She's the most beautiful girl I've ever seen," Shaun says then, and my laughter dies. Who is he dreaming about?

"Who is?" Derek asks, and I freeze. He's going to wake him up.

"Rhys. She's mine." Shaun answers, and my eyes widen.

When Derek grins over at me, I mouth, "What the fuck?"

Still grinning, Derek comes to my side and whispers, "I can have full-on conversations with him while he's like this. I usually get his honesty, although sometimes his responses make no sense."

"Oh," I whisper.

Derek nudges my shoulder with his. "Ask him something."

I think about this for a moment, desperate to know if he will speak the truth.

"Who is Skipper?" I ask, testing to see if he will speak honestly while asleep.

Shaun's head angles towards me.

"Tyler. He's ok. Loves my girl, though."

Holy shit.

"Who's your girl?" Derek asks, and I could punch him. The cheeky fucker just grins.

"Kitten," Shaun answers dazily.

"Who's Kitten?" Derek asks, clearly confused.

Shaun's relaxed face morphs into an adorable sleepy smile.

"Rhys."

My heart does a flip, which is stupid, right? He's sleeping. None of what he is saying is true. Well, except for knowing who Skipper and Kitten are, but that doesn't mean he's speaking the truth about me being his girl. Or me being Tyler's girl, my fucking teacher and sponsor for Vixen's Lodge. He doesn't love me. He's like... old, and I'm like a kid to him. A brat that needs a guardian watching over her because I'll just get myself into trouble without it.

Shit.

"Let's go to bed, Shauno," Derek says then, his eyes on me as I have an internal freakout.

Shaun nods lazily, "Yeah, I'm pretty tired. Gonna hit the sack."

Slowly Shaun stands, the chair scraping, while Derek darts his wide eyes towards a passage at the other side of the room. That must be where his parents sleep. I bite back a giggle as Shaun shuffles away. And I say shuffle because that's how he is walking. It's like a shuffle where his feet hardly lift off the ground. I could record it on my phone, but that's too mean. Derek said he sleepwalks when he's worried, and there's a fair chance I'm adding to that worry. Worry he doesn't need.

Following behind slowly, it takes a little while to get back up to Shaun's bedroom. Derek even comes all the way up to the attic to make sure his brother climbs up the step ladder without hurting himself, and then he whispers good night to me before closing me in with Shaun.

Climbing back up, I find Shaun already snoring quietly, taking up most of the mattress, so I carefully squeeze in next to him, closest to the skylight in the gable ceiling. The moment I get comfy, he rolls over and hugs me, tugging me back against his chest so I'm nestled as the little spoon.

I know I should be freaking out more at Shaun's declarations tonight, but for some reason, I'm not. It feels right in his arms, just like it felt right in Marcus' arms. So why was I so freaked out about it with Marcus and not with Shaun? It's definitely something I need to figure out because even though things with Marcus are bad right now, I still care for him and miss him terribly.

I eventually fall asleep in Shaun's arms, and when I wake next, the sun is beaming through the skylight, and Shaun is cursing. Rolling over, I see Shaun lying awake next to me, looking at something on his phone.

"What's wrong?"

Steel-grey eyes find mine, and Shaun turns to me, holding up his phone. I giggle at the picture of Derek's selfie with me in the background, taking a selfie with Shaun. I didn't even realise Shaun's brother had taken that photo.

"I sleepwalked? And you witnessed it?" He sounds mortified, and I slide my arm over his chest as I snuggle up against him.

"Yes, and yes. We had a good chat."

"Ugh!" Shaun groans, slapping his hand over his face. "What the fuck did I say?"

"There was something about penguins, carrots, and wine." I giggle again, and he sighs before removing his hand to look at me.

"What else?" He holds his phone up again. "Derek said we had a good chat about *you*."

Fucking Derek. A shit-stirrer, it seems.

We are going to be great buddies!

"It doesn't matter, but if you want to know, you can ask him. I'm happy with not being involved in that conversation."

"Jesus, what the fuck did I say?"

I giggle, "Nothing bad. Don't worry."

"Ugh." He groans again, throwing his arm over his eyes.

It feels so nice to wake up with Shaun next to me. Not to mention how fucking sexy he looks with his lazy sleep eyes and tousled hair. A girl could get used to this… which is exactly why I should be running. Yet here I fucking am, snuggling against him even closer.

Shaun takes that moment to move, and he rolls over to face me, his hand snaking through the blankets to glide over my hip before cupping my arse and dragging me against him. I immediately feel his hard dick pressed between us, and Kitty stirs to life, purring with interest.

"Wanna fix my morning wood?" He grins, arching his hip forward as I hitch my leg over his waist, pressing my heel to his arse in answer.

That's when Shaun's bedroom door flies open, and Derek rushes in.

"Get up! The barrel room flooded last night, and the old man is going off. I need to go into town and pick up some stuff to help dry the room out, so you two need to get ready fast."

Shaun sits up abruptly. "Any damage to the stock?"

"Nah, not as far as we can tell. But there will be if I can't get it dried soon." Derek looks frantic.

"Yeah. Ok. Do you need me to stay home today and help?" Shaun asks as he slips a t-shirt over that fine chest of his.

"Nope. You're going to school. Hurry up." Derek turns and rushes down the stairs, before the door closes behind him.

"Shit." Shaun rakes his hand through his messy curls, and I sit up to join him.

"You alright?"

Turning to me, his eyes find mine, and he grins.

"I fucking love having you in my bed, Kitten."

I smile, and *shit,* I can feel the heat rising to my cheeks. Jesus, what is this guy doing to me?

"I'll fix your morning wood next time."

Shaun throws his head back, laughing, and I shuffle across the bed to the end, readying myself to climb down. Shaun's hand comes down hard on my pantie clad arse, and I squeak as his teeth nip at my other arse cheek.

"I'm gonna hold you to that Kitten."

With grins on our faces, Shaun and I rush through our morning routines, and I get ready in record time, having a quick shower to wash off the sex smell, which is fucking devastating to do. I throw my hair into my regular middle part with a twisted bun on each side and then apply my mask: black eyeliner, mascara and shadow, and black lips. My uniform is creased from being squashed in my backpack since yesterday, and I'm sure I'd care if I wasn't in this happy little bubble with Shaun right now.

We get a few sideways glances as we walk into school together, and even though Shaun and I are holding hands, Simon still bounds up and slaps a kiss on my lips in front of everyone. I'm not usually freaked out by PDA, but for some reason, I'm struggling with everyone at school seeing me receive a kiss from one guy while holding another guy's hand. Is it because I'm sober? Maybe I need to absorb some Mary Jane before classes start? That idea gets quickly doused when Shaun doesn't let me go until I step into my first class of the day. Pastoral Care.

As Shaun and I part ways, Simon sends him a teasing wave, dragging me into the classroom to a table in the back corner and claiming me as his study partner. Bell and Allister shoot me a weird look that I can't decipher, but they take their usual table—the one I usually sit at with them—and they turn their backs on me.

Simon keeps me busy through the first class, questioning me about what I'm dressing up as for Bonnie Mayer's Halloween party on Thursday night, and then before the bell goes, he invites me to come to his house for dinner tonight. Obviously, I say yes because I like food, and I like him, and I like the way I feel around him. So yeah, I agree, and he Yee-haws in front of the whole class. Adorable clown.

In English, Shaun looks pleased to steal me back, taking my hand this time and leading me to the back row of tables. Garrett is already there in the seat he occupied last time we had this class together, and Shaun deposits me in the middle seat again, between him and Garrett.

Bell is in this class too, and when she walks in with Dale, her black eyes land on me before she glares at me and rolls her eyes. My brows furrow as I watch my friends turn their backs on me again and take their seats, not paying me any more attention.

What the fuck is her problem?

I think about sending her a message to ask but decide I'm better off waiting to talk to her at recess, so I put my phone on the desk above my books and try to focus on the analysis task I need to finish in preparation for the upcoming exams.

I didn't think it was possible, but I manage to forget about my surroundings and the two guys on either side of me. I become absorbed in my work, having better focus than I've had in weeks, so when Garrett's hand lands on my thigh and squeezes, I'm in a bit of a daze when I look up.

"What?" I whisper, taking in his confusing expression.

"Who's Julie?"

I freeze. "What?"

"Who's Julie?" Garrett repeats, and my eyes go wide before I look away from those icy blues and search for my phone.

A moment later, Shaun waves my phone in my face.

"Who's Julie?" He asks the same question Garrett did, and my heart rate picks up as I reach for the phone. With a determined look on his face, Shaun holds it away from me. "Uh-uh. Who's Julie, Rhys?"

"No one. Give me my phone." I whisper yell, and his dark brows disappear under his curls. Then his eyes narrow.

"It doesn't seem like no one. She's messaged three times." Shaun speaks quietly before Garrett gains my attention again.

"Why have you saved her as *Fuck You Julie* in your phone?"

My heart races as Garrett studies me, but I turn back to Shaun and try to get the phone out of his hand. My efforts cause Shaun's chair to scrape back, and Miss Fletcher's voice comes from the front of the room.

"What's going on back there?"

All eyes turn to us as Shaun freezes with his arm arched back as I practically climb on top of him to get my phone. I don't want to get Shaun in trouble, but I need my phone.

"He has my phone, Miss," I complain, and she rolls her eyes.

"Shaun, put her phone back down on the table, please." When we both don't move, she stands and bellows. "Now!"

Quickly, I shuffle back off Shaun and sit in my seat as Shaun lays my phone face-up on the table above my books. When I move to reach for it, Miss Fletcher yells.

"Do not pick that phone up, Miss George!"

I halt in place, my hand mid-air, just itching to pick up my phone. Nodding at my English teacher, I shift back in my chair and pretend to do my work as blood rushes loudly past my ears. I'm worked up big time, and I can't concentrate anymore. Not now that I know Julie has sent me a message.

"Unlock your phone, Kitten," Shaun whispers in my ear, and I look down at my phone and back up towards the front of the room where Miss Fletcher is occupied on her computer. "Technically, if you leave it on the table and don't pick it up, you're not breaking her rules."

He's right, but that would mean he and Garrett will be able to read my messages.

"Open it," Shaun whispers again, so I lean forward and key in my passcode before opening my messages.

Fuck You Julie
Brian isn't happy!

Fuck You Julie
How can you be so cruel to a dying man?

Fuck You Julie
Go back and see him by Wednesday!
And do exactly as he asks of you.

"Who's Brian? And who's *Fuck You Julie*?" Garrett asks quietly.

I can't find the words to answer him as I read over Julie's messages. Of course, Brian wouldn't be happy. I already knew that, so these messages aren't news to me. I've been expecting them, although I wasn't expecting Julie to tell me to go back to the prison to see Brian again.

Ignoring both the boys as they crowd me in, I type out a response and hit send.

Rhys George
I can't go back, Julie. Not just because I can't make it there by Wednesday, but also because you and he can go fuck yourselves!

I hear Garrett and Shaun suck in a breath, which tells me they are reading over my shoulder. Then Julie replies.

Fuck You Julie
Visit him by dinner time on Wednesday or pay the price.
This is my last warning!!

"What the fuck?" Garrett hisses in my left ear, and I turn my phone face down so I don't have to see the messages anymore.

"What's going on?" Shaun asks in my right ear, and I suddenly feel like I'm suffocating.

"None of your business." I snap, and I see Shaun flinch out of the corner of my eye. I shouldn't be a bitch to him. I knew they would see the messages when I opened the phone, so why did I do that in front of them if I didn't want them to see?

Because you want to tell someone, Rhys.

Oh, shut up, annoying inner voice!

Do I *really* want to tell *them,* though? They will most definitely look at me with disgust and run in the other direction when they learn about my depraved past. Learn what I did yesterday at the prison. I'm a sick person. Vile. They won't want anything to do with me. No one will.

Tears well in my eyes, and I turn to Shaun to see the hurt on his face.

"I'm sorry. You didn't deserve that."

His eyes, usually so calm that they soothe my soul, are nothing but a festering storm. Leaning towards me, he takes my hands in his as he speaks softly, so only I can hear. "I'm not prying to be nosey. I care about you, Rhys. I care what happens to you."

"I can't tell you," I whisper as a tear pops free, and he reaches up to wipe it away.

"Does it have anything to do with yesterday afternoon? Why you were in such a state last night?"

Swallowing the lump in my throat, I nod slowly.

"Are you in some sort of trouble?" He asks, and I nod but then shake my head, only to shrug. "Why won't you tell me?"

"I can't," I whisper.

"But why? Don't you trust me?"

Do I trust him? I realise it's not something I need to consider for long because I *do* trust him, so that's not the problem.

"I do trust you."

"Then why can't you tell me?"

I shrug.

"Please, Kitten." He whispers, ignoring Miss Fletcher when she calls to him to focus on his work. "Why can't you tell me?"

It takes three swallows to get the lump away this time. "Because it will change things."

"Change things how?" He asks just as Miss Fletcher approaches the table. Even though I know Shaun can see her, he still pays her no attention.

"It will change the way you look at me. The way you think about me."

He frowns right as Miss Fletcher slams her hand down on the desk, this time gaining our attention.

"This is not the time for a heart-to-heart!"

I jump so high that I knock my books off the table and fall back into Garrett, who catches me half on his lap, half on my chair.

"For fuck's sake, woman! There's no need to scare the living shit out of me!" My words fly free before I can stop them and Miss Fletcher, who I usually get along with, goes red in the face as she stares me down.

"Rhys George, get your things and leave this class right now!" She points a strong finger towards the door. "You can go to the principal's office and explain to your *guardian* why I've kicked you out of class today!"

Garrett's hands loosen on me as I stand, glaring Miss Fletcher down as I bend and pick my books up, taking the ones Shaun helps me to retrieve as well.

"No problem, Miss. I'll go visit my *mum*. Better than this shitty class, anyway." As if my behaviour isn't already immature and bratty enough, I flip her the bird and blow her a fucking kiss with it! Oh yeah. I'm on a roll, one that's only going to get me into more trouble, but the thing is, right now, I don't care.

Chapter Twenty-Seven

Rhys

The school office is bustling with building tradies as they work to put the office back together in the aftermath of Marcus' tantrum last week. Meanwhile, the office ladies try to do their work on the other side of the room, and upon seeing me, one rises from her chair, calling out to stop me from entering the principal's office. But yeah... I still don't care, so I ignore her.

I push the door open with force, and it ricochets off the wall in a bang, causing my mum to jump where she sits in her chair at her desk, the phone clutched in her hand as she frowns furiously at me.

Ignoring her, I close the door, drop my books on her coffee table and toss myself on the couch, laying down and putting my feet up on the arm at the end. It's not a very long couch. It's also not very fucking comfy.

"Donald, is there any way we can change the board's mind? Expulsion is extreme."

My ears prick up at my mum's words.

"I've spoken with him and his parents. He's so upset about what he did. It was totally out of character for him, so much so that his parents are taking him to a therapist." Cynthia's eyes dart to me then, and I know she's talking about Marcus. "He's a good kid. I plead with you to call the board for another meeting to discuss this. There has to be a way we can keep him here instead of punishing him for a situation that was clearly too much for him to handle. Isn't it our job to nurture these kids? To help them through these hard times instead of washing our hands of them?" She listens while Donald speaks, sighing every now and then but finally nodding. "Yes, thank you, Donald. I appreciate that."

When she ends the call, I sit up.

"You can't expel Marcus. It was my fault, not his."

Cynthia sighs, standing from her chair and coming around her desk to sit on the coffee table in front of me.

"Actually, Rhys, it isn't your fault, and how he responded to the situation is *not* ok, no matter who is at fault."

"I know, but he was so shocked and hurt. I did that to him, and he didn't deserve that. He's such a good person, mum. He deserves a second chance."

Cynthia smiles softly. "I know Marcus is a good person, Rhys. That's why I am fighting the board on their decision to expel him. Donald is going to see what he can do. But technically, you know nothing, ok? No telling anyone what you heard in here."

When I nod, she adds, "I mean it, Rhys. I'm trying so hard to keep you out of trouble, but divulging confidential information will not only get *you* into trouble, but it could also mean *I* lose my job."

I don't want that. Not for Cynthia. Unfortunately, the whole *me* getting into trouble ship has already sailed.

"Why are you here, anyway?" She frowns, and I shrug.

"Miss Fletcher sent me."

"Why?" She narrows her brown eyes accusingly.

"I think she knows how much I missed you after spending the day with Tillie yesterday."

Now she really squints, and I flutter my lashes innocently.

"What did you do?" She growls in that funny *I'm trying to be serious but failing* parent voice.

When I shrug again, she stands from the coffee table and rounds her desk again, taking a seat and using her mouse to do something on her computer. Then her eyes go wide, and she darts them back at me.

"Really, Rhys?"

"What?" I ask innocently.

"Did you say, and I quote," She makes air quotes, *"For fuck's sake, woman! There's no need to scare the living shit out of me!"*

"In my defence, she really did scare the shit out of me with the way she slammed her hand on my table. I knocked my books flying and everything."

"Why did she slam her hand on the table, Rhys?"

I shrug again. "I guess she wanted my attention."

"Why didn't you have your attention in the first place?"

"I was busy having a conversation." I roll my eyes like as if that was obvious.

"With who?" She asks, crossing her hands over her chest.

"Don't you mean, with whom?" I correct.

"Rhys!"

"Mum!"

"Using mum isn't going to soften me up, you know?"

"Are you sure?" I flutter my lashes, and after a moment of silence, Cynthia grins, causing me to laugh.

"Stop it. You're in trouble, young lady!"

"Am I, though?" I shoot her a toothy smile.

"Yes! Because apparently, you also flipped her the bird!"

"I mean... I blew her a kiss, too. Maybe she was confused and didn't realise that I was blowing her a kiss?"

"Rhys!" Cynthia growls.

"Want me to show you?" I offer, and her face turns red in anger.

"No! What has gotten into you lately?"

"Don't you mean who has gotten into me lately?"

"That's enough!" Her raised voice bounces off the walls, making me still, and I realise I've taken it too far. *Whoops!* It's not often that Cynthia yells like this. "I'm trying so hard not to push you too much, Rhys. To give you the freedom to explore your needs, even though it goes against everything I believe. I know if I tighten the reins, it will make you worse, but Rhys Mave, you are walking a very fine line lately, and I'm starting to double guess all the decisions I've made when it comes to caring for you."

My heart stutters and then stops altogether.

"You don't want to care for me anymore?"

"What?" Her brows furrow, and then she squats down in front of me, taking my hands. "Of course, I do. Don't get my words twisted in that head of yours. I mean that I'm not sure I'm doing the right thing giving you so much freedom. Perhaps it isn't good for you. You're still so young to be doing the things you're doing."

She's referring to allowing me to freely explore my sexual needs, something she decided a couple of years ago when she realised I was going to sneak around on her and probably do worse things in order to seek what I need. Yeah, I'm still not completely honest with her, but for the most part, she knows how I roll.

"I was too young when it first happened," I whisper, and her hands tighten around mine.

"Yes, you were, and it's steered your path ever since. I just worry about you. This world is so dangerous, and I know you've experienced so much more than the normal seventeen-year-old, but that doesn't mean you should be doing things that people many years older than you are doing." She sighs again, dipping her head. "I just worry. So much. If I change the rules, you will end up in a situation like you got yourself into when we were on our trip a few weeks back. Then you'd have to go back to the retreat or somewhere worse. I don't want that for you, Rhys. I don't want them to take you away from me."

I cry then. Like a little girl who's just watched her barbie get run over by a truck. I cry hard. So hard that I actually fear my chest is going to crack open. Here's my chance, right now, to tell her about Julie and Brian. To fess up to what I've done. But the words don't come. They stay locked away in the place I bury all of my shame.

Say the words, Rhys.

They never come.

Cynthia pulls me into her arms, hugging me tight, and when a knock sounds on the door a few minutes later, I hear Tyler's voice, which stops my tears but not my pain.

"Oh, sorry. You wanted to see me?" He asks, and I burrow my head against Cynthia's chest, needing to hide.

"Yes, come in and close the door." At Cynthia's words, I still. Why is she inviting him in while I'm still here?

The door clicks shut, and I hear Tyler sit in one of the chairs by my mum's desk.

"I hope you don't mind having this conversation with my daughter here? She's aware of the situation anyway, and right now, she needs a hug."

"Of course, I don't mind. Is everything ok?" His voice is so soothing to me, and I can sense his eyes on me even as I keep mine squeezed tight, a lousy attempt at blocking out the world.

"I figure you have a little knowledge of the situation since you came across the fight that broke out on Thursday. Rhys is still having a tough time." Cynthia explains.

"Yes. I can imagine. What can I do to help?" Genuine concern laces his voice, and I wonder if that's because of the *thing* we have going or just because he's a decent human and a dedicated teacher.

"I was hoping you could help me sway the board to reconsider their decision to expel Marcus Grady. Perhaps you can meet with Stephen Matthews. He has some great counselling strategies that might compliment the new boxing program you set up."

"I'm not sure, Cynthia. Marcus was out of control. He hurt Rhys." At Tyler's words, my eyes snap open, and I push away from Cynthia.

"He didn't mean that! I got in the way!" I snap, my eyes connecting with his deep blue gaze.

"Rhys!" Cynthia scolds as I keep my focus on the teacher that, only last week, was buried deep inside me. "Please don't speak to Mr Foster like that. Your attitude towards your teachers has been questionable lately."

I roll my eyes before shooting Tyler a dagger that Cynthia can't see. Then the smug fuck bites his lip as he tries to hide a smirk.

"It's fine, Cynthia. Miss George has been through a lot lately." Tyler turns his eyes to my mum, but I know he can still feel my glare. That's ok. I'll make him pay for his smuggery later. "Look, I can certainly try to help Marcus. He's always been a well-behaved student. The fight was definitely out of character for him."

Cynthia nods, "Yes, it was. Your help would be greatly appreciated, Tyler. You are a well-respected member of this school. I know the board will listen to what you have to say."

Tyler nods while I cringe on the inside. Fuck, if only Cynthia knew the truth about Tyler. It would destroy his life if anyone found out about him and me. Cynthia sure as fuck wouldn't respect me, let alone want to care for me anymore. It might be time for me to find a new sponsor so I can stay away from him.

The thought hurts. It shouldn't, because what we have is just sex, right? Fuck. What am I doing? Do I really have feelings for my fucking teacher? He's like, old. Not that age has been much of an issue to me where sex is concerned, so why is his age an issue now?

FML, I'm so exhausted from my fucking brain. I want to switch it off, but the only way I can do that is the very thing that has gotten me into all of this shit in the first place. Typical of a sex addiction, I guess. Like any addiction, it manages to fuck up your life. I'm only seventeen, and I've already sent my life down the path of royal fuckery.

"Consider it done." Tyler smiles warmly at my mum, standing from the chair, his towering height capturing my attention. As usual, he's wearing sports shorts, and his long muscle defined legs are sprinkled with light hair that I distinctly remember the feel of as they pressed against mine while we fucked on Wednesday night in the barn.

My body heats as I remember how he made me feel, and I know by the pinched expression he shoots me that he can see the flush on my cheeks.

"Thanks, Tyler." Cynthia smiles while I try to look at every spot other than where Tyler is standing.

"No problem." He says before turning his attention to me. "Miss George, I expect to see you in Health class after recess." He uses his teacher's voice, and I shrug, acting bratty.

The funny part is, he can't call me out on it because his boss is also my mum. That and what we have going is against the law, in more ways than one.

After Tyler leaves, I spend a bit of time in Cynthia's office while she works, and then at recess, I leave in search of my friends. Tillie and Bell aren't in the courtyard, so I shoot them a message asking where they are before lobbing up to Lexi's side.

"Oh, hey." Lexi stands back, her blue eyes assessing as they roam over my face. "You ok? Garrett said you got kicked out of English class."

I shrug. "It's all good, Lex. Don't worry your pretty head about it." I throw my arm over her shoulder, "Now, please tell me you have your costume ready for Thursday nights party?"

She rolls her eyes. "Kinda." Her reply sounds more like a question than an answer.

"Oh, come on, Lexi. Please don't bail out on me. We need a night of fun. It's been too long."

"I know," she smiles, "I'm going to the party. I'm just a lazy costume organiser."

"Don't stress, George," Ayden butts in, coming to stand in front of us. "I've already got Lexi's costume sorted."

"You do?" She asks, and he shoots her a wink. And just like that, the poor girl swoons. Jesus, he knows how to use those winks.

"I do." Ayden leans down, pressing his lips to Lexi's, kissing her like I'm not standing shoulder to shoulder with her.

"Unless you want me to join in, you should probably step away. Lexi's *my* girl." Even though it's a tease, it doesn't sound like one falling from my lips, and Ayden slowly pulls back and glares at me, causing Lexi to giggle and slap his shoulder. As soon as he returns his gaze to her, she melts into him like I'm not even here.

Oh, for fuck's sake.

Firm hands snake around my waist then, pulling me back into a familiar firm chest as warm breath flutters across my ear.

"Are you alright, Kitten?"

Shaun.

I shouldn't let him claim me like we are a couple in front of everyone, especially after the whole Marcus incident last week, but do I pull away? No. No, I don't. It feels too nice to have his arms around me.

I nod, "Yeah. Bad morning, I guess."

"Hmmm." He hums, clearly aware that it's more than just a bad day. "Come with me."

He doesn't give me a chance to respond before he hauls me away from the busy courtyard. At first, I think he's leading me to the toilets for a bit of fuck time, but then he steers us into the stadium and takes me into the new gym, which is just about empty, all except for Garrett and Simon.

I stop on the spot, digging my heels in when Shaun tries to lead me in deeper. When he turns a questioning look at me, I tug my hand free of his and cross my arms over my chest.

"What is this?"

"I just want to talk to you. Away from everyone." Shaun explains, but my eyes dart across the small space to where Garrett and Simon are sitting on some gym equipment, their eyes on me.

"Then why are *they* here?" I gesture my head to the other guys, but Shaun doesn't look at who I mean. He already knows they are there.

"We just want to talk," Shaun states, and I roll my eyes before throwing my arms up and slapping them back down again.

"Is this like some sort of intervention? You gonna tell me what a fuck up I am?" I hiss, crossing my arms back over my chest. "I'll save you the effort. I already fucking know."

Shaun frowns. "Stop it. We don't think that, but something isn't right, Rhys, and we fucking care about you, ok! We want to help you."

I laugh. "You can't help me. No one can help me. Do yourself a favour and forget about me and my drama. I'm not worth it."

"Bullshit!" The booming voice comes from Garrett as he hauls himself up and storms over to me. "You don't get to decide how *we* feel about you, Rhys! And we wouldn't be here asking you to talk to us if we didn't think you are worth it!"

For a moment, I can't speak. Garrett has been dancing around me, warning me off his mates, yet here he is admitting to something more. Of course, I could be totally misreading it, and he could be just a caring friend.

"He's right. I get that talking about feelings and stuff isn't your thing, but it helps, especially when you talk to people who actually care. Not just a therapist who is being paid to listen." Simon's words shock me, mainly because he's goofing around more often than not, and it's strange to have him be so serious.

"What's so bad that you think I will change the way I look and think about you, Kitten?" Shaun asks next, and man, this conversation is tough. How did I ever think I could have a reverse harem? It's hard trying to take in what one guy is saying, let alone three.

My eyes dance from Shaun's grey gaze to Garrett's blue stare, and Simon's hazel focus. They're all so intent on helping me. I just have to find a way to open up and speak my truth. Can I do this?

"Rhys, who's Julie?" Garrett asks this time, and my shoulders sag.

"She's one of my old foster mums," I whisper, not sure if they hear.

"And who is Brian?" Shaun asks this time, taking a step closer to me, taking my arm and prying it from my chest.

"My old foster dad." Am I really answering their questions right now? Can I really handle divulging this information?

"And he's dying?" Shaun asks again, and I nod and shrug at the same time.

"So they say. He didn't look that great when I saw him yesterday."

"Yesterday afternoon?" Shaun asks, and I nod.

He knows from our previous conversations last night that something happened yesterday. He just doesn't know what. There's no way his brain would ever imagine what I did. He's not that depraved.

"What happened when you saw him yesterday, Kitten?" Shaun asks, and I shake my head, unwilling to answer that particular question.

"Where did you see him?" Garrett asks, and I take a breath before I spill this truth.

"Allansdale prison."

"What?" the three guys say in unison, and I shrug like it's no big deal.

"That's where you were coming from last night? Allansdale Prison?" Shaun asks, taking my hands in his again, tugging me to his chest as I nod, sinking into his warmth.

"Why did you go there and see him?" Simon asks, appearing to my right next to Shaun.

"Julie… she reached out to me a couple of weeks back. Asked me to go and see him." I pull back to see Garrett step up to Shaun's left.

Garrett frowns. "But why? Are you two close or something?"

I shake my head, knowing they'll misinterpret my response as Brian and I not being close. When in fact, we were too close. Sickeningly so.

"I don't understand." Garrett's brows furrow. "Why would she ask you to go and see him then? And why did she ask you to go back and see him by Wednesday?"

"Wow, you remember everything those messages said, hey?" I ask in surprise, and he nods.

"Yeah, I do. I also remember her telling you to do exactly what he asks of you. What does that mean? What would he ask you to do?"

I shrug, playing dumb.

"Kitten." Shaun breathes. His hand coming up to brush his fingers over my cheek. "You told this Julie lady that you can't go back and told them to go fuck themselves. Then she warned you if you don't go back by Wednesday night that you will pay the price. What price will you pay?"

I shake my head again, not wanting to reveal anything else.

"Rhys," Garrett growls, "What will happen if you don't go?"

"I don't know, ok!" I jerk out of Shaun's hold, feeling suffocated again, and I start pacing. "I don't know what she'll do. For all I know, it's an empty threat." I stop pacing and face the three guys who I've somehow snagged the attention of. "I don't care, though. Empty threat or real threat. Nothing will be worse than me going back to *that* place and sitting in *that* chair in front of *that* man to… to…" I gag.

"Hey." Simon rushes forward, taking my shoulders in his hands, and he sucks in a deep breath. "Deep breaths Rhys. Simon says, slow deep breaths."

I do as he says, locking my eyes with his and copy his breathing pattern because I don't want to hurl the breakfast Shaun made me this morning. As I suck in the much needed oxygen, my eyes dart over Simon's shoulders to see Garrett and Shaun looking at each other. They aren't talking, but I get the feeling they know what each other are thinking.

"That's it." Simon smiles, gaining my attention again as my breathing returns to normal, the need to vom no longer there.

The blare of the bell indicating the end of recess has us all frowning, and even though I don't want to talk about this bullshit anymore, I know I'd rather stay here with the three of them instead of going to class. I know I can't ditch, though, so I turn and walk out of the gym with the three boys on my heels.

Chapter Twenty-Eight

Tyler

The little brat is late for class, which seems to be her MO lately. Making sure to maintain our cover, I'm about to call Rhys out on her tardiness when she strolls in, but one of Rhys' weird friends, Bell Bishop, blocks Rhys from sitting with their weird group. She snaps something at Rhys, and a look of hurt crosses Kitten's face before she slams that bratty wall back up, saying something in response. Her words fall on deaf ears as her so-called friends give her their back, noticeably shunning her.

What the fuck is that about?

Fucking teenagers! Why the *fuck* do I teach them? They are a bunch of ungrateful little entitled fucktards who wouldn't know the first thing about hard work.

Lucky for me, Bell's little exclusion game works in my favour because the only seat left is at the table right in front of my desk. The same spot she sat last week when she gave me a little peep show of her panties when she bent down.

Pretending like she doesn't have a care in the world, Rhys moves to the free seat, placing her books down before taking her phone out and blatantly ignoring any class work she needs to do. If she's trying to get sent to the office for the second time today, she can think again. Yeah, I heard all about her getting kicked out of her English class earlier, but the bad news for Rhys is that I *want* her in my class. She can rebel all she fucking wants, but by the end of this class, my Kitten will fucking submit. I'll make sure of that.

Since she's on her phone, I take mine out and place it on my tabletop so the students can't see it past the low petition surrounding my desk. Then I send her a message.

Skipper
You're late.

Kitten
Am I? Oh, sorry, I didn't notice.

Skipper
Open your books, Kitten.

Kitten
Yeah-Nah. I'm all g, thanks :)

Skipper
I wasn't asking. Open your damn books!

The little minx raises those deep chocolate eyes to glare at me past her dark lashes, and then she smirks before returning her gaze to her phone.

Kitten
Make me.

And just like that, the little brat has me hard. I can't fucking stand up now. Not without showing my boner to everyone. I should remove her from the class, take her to my office, and punish her right fucking now.

I wish.

Skipper
If I could, I would.
Why were you upset earlier?

As she reads my message, I watch the mischief fall from her face as sadness replaces it.

Kitten
I've got a lot going on.
And before I forget, Master will probably contact you before Wednesday night.

Skipper
Why?

She looks up at me again, this time with a look of regret written across her face.

Skipper
Kitten! What did you do?

Kitten

I may have turned up at last night's Feast.

Skipper

What!
You weren't on the list!
You said no!

Kitten

I may also have turned up with no mask.

Skipper

What!

Kitten

And I may have begged them to let me in.

She has to be fucking kidding me!

My eyes flare wide as I read her messages, over and over, while trying to rein in my anger. It's no fucking use. I'm set to explode, and not from fucking pleasure.

Standing abruptly, I walk out of the room and into the quiet hall, my fists balled tight as I start pacing. She's lying. She has to be! She can't be that fucking stupid. She knows Master Hill will punish both of us for breaking the rules.

Fucking hell.

Sucking in a breath, I try like fuck to compose myself before returning to the classroom. Luckily, most of the students couldn't give a shit if I'm there or not, so they pay me little attention. Not Rhys George, though. Not those big brown eyes that I swear can see into my fucking cold soul.

Situating myself back at my desk again, I type out another text.

Skipper
Tell me you're kidding!!!

Kitten
I can if you want, but it would be a lie.

Skipper
Fucking hell! What were you thinking?

Kitten
I wasn't!

Skipper
Why? Why would you do that?

Kitten

I fucked up, ok! I already know that.
No need to make me feel worse than I already do!
And why are you getting so mad? I tried to call you and
message you, but you wouldn't respond! I thought you
must have been inside at the feast.
Arsehole!!!!

What? She tried to call? Message? I scroll back up through our messages but find nothing like what she is talking about. Then I look at the call log, only to find there are no missed calls from Kitten either.

Skipper

I'm sorry, Kitten. I didn't get any calls or messages. And
I'm not trying to make you feel worse. I'm just trying to
understand why you would do that.

Kitten

Because I needed to fuck.

I internally flinch at her comment. She uses the term so matter of fact, which is just sad. I know there's more to her story that makes her like this, and I know I shouldn't want to know about it. Yet I do. I find myself wanting to know way too much about this sex kitten who's fifteen years younger than me.

Skipper

Why?

Kitten

Because I just needed to, ok!
I had a day, and I needed release.
Don't fucking judge me!

Skipper

I'm not judging you, Kitten.
If you feel like that again, come to me. I'll help you.

She glances up at me then, and I raise a brow.

Kitten

Firstly, I thought I was coming to you, but you weren't
there, and you wouldn't take my calls!
Secondly, I can't come to your house, remember?
I'm me, and you're you.

Skipper

I'm sorry, Kitten. I didn't feel like going to the Feast last
night. I should have let you know, but I really didn't get
any calls from you. Or messages.
And yeah, we can't take that to my house, but I would
have found a way to see you.

I watch those white teeth of hers bite down on her black lips as
she mulls over something.

Kitten

You would have done that?

Skipper

Yes.

Kitten

Why?

Skipper

Because you are mine, and I take care of what's mine.

Her brows lift, and those dark eyes glance up to meet mine. Even though we are in a room with twenty other year eleven students, I feel like it's only her and me in here. I wish it were only the two of us. Maybe then I could get more information from her about what the fuck drove her to break the rules at Vixen's Lodge last night.

Kitten

I seem to belong to a few people these days.

Skipper

What do you mean?

Kitten

Cass says I'm his too.

Skipper

And are you?

Kitten

What would you say if I said I am?

Skipper

I'd say that Cass better be ok with sharing you, or we will have a fucking problem.

Kitten

He said he'd share me with someone he trusts.

Skipper

I'm not asking here, Kitten. If he can't get on board with me, then he can fuck the hell off.

Kitten

So what does all this mean?
He says I'm his.
You say I'm yours.
What does the word 'mine' mean?

Skipper

It means unity. Protection. Family.

Her teeth go to her bottom lip again. Is she trying not to smile?

Skipper

What are you trying to hide by biting your lip?

Rhys flicks her gaze to me as she releases her mouth, and a small smile pulls at those soft black lips.

Skipper

So, what do you think about the word 'mine' now?
Do you like it?

Kitten

I'm pretty sure I'm going to regret admitting this, but yeah, I really do.

Corey Michaels takes that moment to put his hand up and demand I be a fucking teacher again, so I reluctantly put my phone away and do the job I'm being paid to do.

The double lesson of Health drags, mainly because most of the students are up to date with their work and are just revising for upcoming exams. So when the lunch bell rings, it's a fucking relief.

"Ok, class, keep up with your revision. See you next lesson." I yell above the noise of chatting teenagers that pay me no attention once again.

"Rhys George, since you were late, you can stay behind and make up the time."

Just like I knew she would, Rhys whines to cover up whatever we are to each other.

"But I have boys to flirt with, Mr Foster!"

Laughter filters out of the room as the students leave, and I notice Rhys' friendship group pay her no attention.

Once the room is empty, I go to the door and lock it before turning back to Rhys.

"Why aren't your friends talking to you?"

She shrugs. "Apparently, I'm spending too much time with Lexi's pack, and I just use them for places to stay, and they are sick of it."

That must have been what Bell said to Rhys when she came into class that had hurt her feelings.

"What did you say to that?" I ask, and she grins.

"I told her that when she wants to stop acting like she's in grade four, I'd be happy to have a discussion about it."

I smirk. "I guess she didn't like that?"

"Nope." Rhys pops the p and stands from her chair, coming around to lean back against her table. "So, how bad do you think my surprise visit to the Feast is?"

I mimic Rhys, propping my arse on the top of the partition at my desk.

"I'm not gonna lie, Kitten. It's probably not good."

"Do you think they'll boot me out?"

"Nah. They need you. Madam Vik will probably make you eat her out for the entire night on Wednesday, though."

She fakes a gag, and I grin.

"Will it make you feel better if I'm eating you out at the same time?"

The seductive smirk that lifts her black lips is enticing, and fuck it; I wish we weren't on school grounds right now!

"I think I could handle that." Her eyes darken as she stares at me, and I know she's thinking about my head between her legs.

"Kitten," my voice is raspy as I change from joking to serious, "Why did you end up at the Feast? What happened yesterday?"

She sighs, "I went to see someone I didn't want to see, and then I did something I didn't want to do, and I kinda spiralled and needed to replace the memory and consume myself in something I wanted." She shakes her head. "I can't fucking believe I just told you that. What's going on with me? I told Shaun, Garrett and Simon some stuff before, too. I'm losing my fucking mind."

I smile, "No, you're not. You're learning that you can trust us because you know we care. You probably feel like you're losing your mind because you're not used to being so honest about things. Even though what you just told me is still vague."

"I could have said nothing." She raises a brow, crossing her arms over her chest.

"Yes, you could have. So I'll take the vague for now, but I'm here, Kitten, when you want to tell me more."

She shakes her head. "I told the guys this, and I'll tell you this too. You won't want to know me once you know the truth about me. My past is... depraved." She looks down at her feet, rubbing the toe of her black school shoes over the linoleum floor. "*I'm* depraved. The things I've done are fucked up. The things I enjoy doing are fucked up." She whispers the last two sentences.

I want to pull her into my arms so badly.

"Kitten, have you forgotten who you're talking to?" I jab my thumb into my chest. "You've seen how I fuck at the Feast, and honestly, that place doesn't even begin to let me have the freedom I want. I have some fucked up desires, so don't you let those self-destructive thoughts in your head tell you that how you like to fuck is bad. It's not Kitten."

With glassy eyes, she stares at me for the longest time. I feel like she wants to tell me something. Part of her does. I can see it. The other part is screaming at her to keep her mouth shut.

"What is it, Kitten?"

She licks her lips and looks down at her feet again before looking back up at me through the fan of her dark lashes.

"Do you ever do things you don't really want to do, but you do them because your body is screaming at you with desperate need to do it? Like you know you don't want to do it, but you just can't win the fight between your brain and body, and you lose the battle, and your body wins, doing things you know repulses you, but it still gets you off?"

Fucking hell. I understand what she's saying because, yeah, I've fucking been there before, which leads me to wonder what the fuck my Kitten has done.

"I wish I could say no, but there have been times when I have… done things I'm disgusted about, even though my dick enjoyed it."

Her bottom lip wobbles, and fuck, she's going to cry. I don't want her to cry. I hate seeing that sort of pain in her eyes.

"I did that yesterday." She whispers, and a single tear pops free.

A buzzing noise sounds, and she brings her phone out to read a message as she bats away the salty drop. Then she holds it up to me.

Shaun Bossier
Kitten, I'm on my way to your health classroom, where I assume you are talking to your teacher about your overdue work. The guys are with me.

"Well, shit. It looks like I can trust fuckboy after all."

"Don't call him that." She smiles, and I shoot her a wink before rising from my desk and unlocking the door.

A moment later, Shaun and his mates reach the door, pulling faces through the glass at Rhys. My little brat gathers up her things and saunters past me, brushing her hand over mine as she does in such a way that no one can see, and before she opens the door to leave, she glances over her shoulder at me.

"Daddy, I still need to be punished for turning up late to class."

Then she kisses the air and turns to leave with three boys who look at her like she is their queen.

Chapter Twenty-Nine

Simon

Keeping my hands off Rhys George is getting more and more futile. What makes it worse is that Bossi has already staked his claim on her. As soon as he realised I'd had some Simon Says fun time with her, he'd let me know that he'd already been with her. Then he said he'd share her with me.

How fucking generous of him! The idea was fucking weird until Garrett pointed out that Rhys isn't going to commit to one guy, which is why her and Marcus didn't work out. I mean, share her. Really? That's fucking absurd, right?

My head has been a mess because, for some fucking reason, I didn't think Marcus would take it as bad as he did. Clearly, I was thinking with Big Simon and not my fucking brain. Of course, Grady has feelings for Rhys. Whatever they had together went from zero to one hundred in like a day, so yeah, he fell hard, and after having a sample of the girl in question myself, I fucking understand why.

She's like a sex goddess or something. The royalty of fornication. Queen of copulation. Just fucking epic. A siren sent to lead us into her trap, and fuck yeah, I intend on diving headfirst.

Am I a little obsessed? Absa-fucking-lutely. The Hastenator has an addiction that just so happens to match my type of crazy. So, will I share her like Bossi suggested? Fuck yeah, I'll take her however she'll have me.

The thing is, this thing with Rhys isn't just about getting my dick wet. It's more than that. I've never really felt like I've connected with a girl before. I'm the class clown. The goof. Too playful to be serious. I give everyone the fun version of Simon Hastings, yet most of the time, I'd rather just disappear.

My parents have no interest in me. It began when I was about six years old. They paid for nannies to raise me while they travelled the world. If it weren't for my mates, I would have checked out a long time ago. It's knowing this about myself that helps me understand Rhys so well. We are the same in a lot of ways. We hide behind humour and take the piss so no one can see the real pain we are in. It's also why I feel so comfortable with her. Why our time together is actually fun. Like the real kind. It comes so easy like it's meant to be.

That's why I can't ignore the pull she has on me. Why I just couldn't deny myself the need to be closer to her even when I knew I'd be hurting my mate. Does that make me a fucking prick? Probably. But I'll try to explain it to Marcus one day. If he ever speaks to me again, that is.

At lunchtime, Lexi stole my girl's attention, declaring they were having girl time, so all of us horny fuckers sat on the table with our eyes trained on them as they lay in the sun, chatting quietly. During Maths this arvo, Rhys was unusually quiet, and when I asked her what was wrong, she told me that things didn't feel right without Marcus here.

Yeah, she can pretend all she likes, but she does care about him more than she's willing to admit. I could have a chat with Marcus and see if he's willing to share her too, but there's a fair fucking chance that when he sees me, I'll be eating his fist. Rhys told him about her and me after he punched the fuck out of Bossi's pretty face last week, so it's fair to say I'm next on the list.

That's a problem for me to worry about another time because right now, I'm expecting Rhys to arrive at my front door any minute, and I need to calm the fuck down so I don't bowl her over like a Labrador hyped up on energy drink.

I don't know why I'm so nervous. I've been alone with Rhys before. I've been naked and deep inside her before—just the two of us hiding away and getting wrapped up in each other in the photo lab. I guess now it's different because she'll be in *my* house. Just the two of us. No worries about getting busted by anyone else. For some reason, it feels more intimate.

The doorbell rings, and my heart races like I'm on crack or something. Not that I know what that's like, but I feel like it would be pretty similar. I straighten my black shirt, and blow into my palm, hoping my breath isn't rank, and then the doorbell rings again and again, over and over and over. All signs of my nerves fly out the window as a grin spreads across my face—this chick. Always clowning around, just like me.

I swing the door open and grin at the cheeky smirk on Rhys George's face.

"Please tell me your parents aren't here." She peers over my shoulder, and I shrug.

"What if they are?"

"Then I just royally fucked up by my impatient bell ringing." Her eyes go wide as the idea of my parents being here and witnessing her being a brat sinks in.

I chuckle. "Relax, George. My olds are never here. Come on in." Stepping back, I gesture to the foyer of my house and watch her relax, stepping over the threshold.

Rarely does Rhys George wear pants, and tonight is no different. She has on a short black skirt with some fold things on it. Pleats? Whatever, it looks good on her. It shows off those long legs that disappear under it, and fuuuck. I want to slide my hand up that skirt.

Not yet, man!

She has on dark red Dr Martin boots with a black frilly sock, and her t-shirt is a deep red colour, similar to her shoes. It's a fitted t-shirt if that's even a thing? I don't know what chicks call them, but it accentuates those heavy tits of hers, and the black lacy choker thing that wraps around her long slender neck disappears between her cleavage and under the shirt.

Her hair is in those bun things she wears all the time. I wonder if she'll let me take them out? I'd love to run my hands through her hair. I bet it's like silk.

"I forgot how big your house is, Simon." Rhys spins on the spot in the middle of the foyer, and as she twirls, her skirt flies up enough that I can see the bare globes of her arse. The G-string she has on does nothing to hide those tempting mounds. Fuuuck now I'm hard.

Big Simon is awake and ready to copulate.

Yeah, I just made a fucking rhyme.

Kinda.

I'm on fire tonight!

"Nah, my house isn't that big."

"What?" She stops spinning and raises her dark brows at me. "You have a fucking foyer in your house! It's bigger than my bedroom, Simon. Dude, your house is massive."

My smile is broad as I chuckle at her, and I step up, pulling her against my body.

"My house isn't the only thing that's massive."

She bursts out laughing, "You're very confident about that, aren't you, Hastings?" She reaches up, winding her arms around my neck. "With good reason, I suppose. I can feel your massiveness, and it's making me very hungry."

I can't stop fucking smiling like a goof, but then again, neither can she. Tonight her lips aren't black. They are a deep dark red colour to match her top. She's so fucking enticing. I can already imagine what those lips will look like wrapped around my dick.

Not able to hold back any longer, I lean in and press my lips to hers, and just like that, the fire ignites. Her lips part for me, and her tongue meets mine in the middle as we grip onto each other, tugging our bodies closer as need surges through my veins and straight to my dick.

"Simon." Her voice is husky as she speaks between kisses. It's like her arousal has affected her voice. "What's for dinner?"

"You." Locking my lips back onto hers, I slide my hands down over the curve of her hips and grip the round globes of her arse before hoisting her up. Her legs wrap around me, and the moment I feel the heat of her pussy against my dick, I moan and grind against her.

"You should eat now," Rhys suggests, and I chuckle against her neck as my lips pepper kisses there. I start walking, carrying my girl, and take her into the kitchen to the breakfast bar that runs along the front of the bifold glass doors overlooking the pool. Propping her arse on the granite bench-top, I step back and gesture to the side where I have our meal laid out.

"Oh. When I said you should eat now, I meant me, but hey, I'm down for food first." Smiling, she leans to her side and dips her finger in the gravy jug before bringing it to her lips. When the tip of her gravy finger disappears between those deep red lips, my dick jerks.

I've already jacked off three times since getting home from school, so I don't arrive at the party prematurely, but I don't think it's going to matter. This little minx has super sex powers. I'm already close to blowing my load.

"Why do we have to wait? Why can't we eat and fuck at the same time?" I ask.

Having just inserted that finger of hers covered in gravy for the second time, Rhys freezes, her finger rooted between her lips.

"What? Haven't you ever done food play before?" I grin, and Rhys' finger pops from her lips, her expression unreadable. Shit, is food play like some sort of trigger for her?

"I've done a lot of different things, but the closest thing to food play I've done is licking whipped cream and body chocolate off someone. Even whiskey a couple of times. But this," she turns to the array of food on the bench, "never anything like this."

"Oh. We don't have to." Shit. Have I fucked up already?

When I see the mischievous grin spread across her face, my body relaxes, and I watch as her eyes darken with heat that wasn't there before.

"Oh yes, we do have to. Now I'm imagining so many fucking scenarios that involve mash potato, gravy, carrots, and peas. Jesus, how did I not know how fucking hot the thought of peas is?"

Throwing my head back, I laugh. Her tone and expression are like a kid walking through Disneyland. "Let's dig in then, shall we?"

Her nod is exaggerated as she starts stripping off her clothes. Her top comes off first, and then she sets to work on her boots while I drop my pants and jocks and tug my shirt over my head. Once she's kicked off her boots and socks, instead of hopping down off the bench to tackle her skirt, Rhys stands on the counter and looks down at me as she slowly unzips it. When it falls to her feet, she kicks it away, and I take a moment to look up and soak in her beauty. Her body is perfect. Slender curves in all the right places and a nice swell to those perky tits. The thin black lace G-string she's wearing plays peekaboo with her pussy, and the lace bra she has on is what the choker thing is attached to. Fuck, that's hot.

Grinning wickedly, she goes to sit down, but I stop her, holding my hand up as I take the two steps to the counter to come face to face with her pussy. Gliding my hands up the backs of her silky legs, I peer up at her as she watches me from above, and the moment my palms find her arse, I grip her and bury my head between her legs.

Rhys gasps as I moan, wetness meeting my lips, showing me just how soaked she already is. Nails scrape my scalp as her fingers grip my hair, and she grinds her cunt against my face. This is fucking heaven, right here between her thighs. The day I take my last breath, this is the place I want to be. I graze my tongue over the lace and kiss it like it's her mouth, and fuck, she's so responsive. Her hips push forward, seeking more, and I love that she's not scared to show exactly how she feels and what she wants.

I may have been a virgin at the start of last week, but I still had experience with girls, and none of them are like this. They were shy. Too scared to make a noise or move their hips too much. Rhys George is no girl, though. At seventeen years old, she is nothing but a woman.

Pulling back, I reach for her hands and tug, silently telling her to sit on the bench.

"Exactly how long is that tongue of yours?" She pants, and I feel the shit-eating grin that morphs my face.

"You like my tongue?"

"God, yes. I'm gonna need you to fuck me with it at some stage." Her serious expression shows me she's not kidding. And hell yes, I love the way she speaks. It's dirty and honest and free of any shame.

"Deal. But first. It's time for food." Pressing my hand to her chest, I slowly push her back until she's lying on the counter, and then I reposition her, placing her legs wide on each side of the counter with her arse mere inches from a cherry pie. "I'm going to take these sexy fucking things off," I glide my fingers over her bra and panties, "because I don't want them to get dirty."

"Ok." She grins, working on her bra while I peel her G-string off. Once she's bare, I take a moment to study her straining nipples and glistening cunt. Last time I saw them was in the red hue of the photography darkroom. Now, she is on full display for me under the bright downlights that line the ceiling. Fucking beautiful.

Climbing up on the counter with her, I pour the gravy over the mashed potato and, using a spoon, I scoop up a decent pile before smearing it under her navel. She moans even though I'm not touching her erogenous zones, and my eyes flick from the spoon to her eyes as I drag it down to smear the rich gravy and potato over the epicentre of her clit.

Rhys' back arches off the bench as her hands slap down on the cold granite, latching onto the edges. Rolling the spoon around to get good coverage, I drag it through her folds, filling them with the delicious side dish.

"Holy fucking-hell." She gasps.

"Is it ok?" I place the spoon down, leaving her slit filled with the thick mash, and then use my fingers to pick up a glistening honey carrot.

"Yes. It's kinda weird," she pants, rolling her hips a little, "yet it feels like I'm being teased there. A warm pressure that has me wanting more."

Oh yeah. Rhys George is my soul mate. I've always loved food, and I have so many fantasies that involve food and a woman's orifices that I've been craving to try. Never thought I'd find a willing participant, though, especially at my age.

I've won the fucking lottery, that's for sure.

Hovering over her body, I bring the carrot to her right nipple and circle it before moving to the left. She moans each time I do it, and once I see her dark pink nipples glistening in the honey juice, I bring the carrot up to her parted lips.

"Simon says, open."

A grin tugs at her lips before she opens them and lets me slide the tender cooked carrot into her mouth. She moans again, tasting the rich sweetness, and then she bites it in half. As she chews, I eat the other half and then repeat it with another carrot. The next time she bites down on the carrot, I press two fingers to her clit and slowly start moving through the mash. Her back arches again, and I lean down and swipe my tongue over her honey covered nipples, over and over, until she's withering and panting.

"Do you want to come, Rhys?" I ask against her nipple, and she whimpers while nodding.

"Yes. Fuck yes."

"Ok, but first, I need more food."

Her eyes fly open, the dark pools of desire meeting mine as I push some of the plates out of the way. I climb up on the bench with her and swiftly mauver myself between her legs. My fingers move to her filled pussy, mash potato and gravy oozing everywhere, and I drag a finger from her puckered arse, up through her filled folds, to the tip of her swollen clit. She's already close to losing her composure, her frustrated whimpers giving her away, so after I lick my finger clean of the mash I collected from her folds, I dive down and eat her pussy.

I swipe my tongue through the mash, loving the texture of the food and her satin skin, and I swallow down the food, making sure I clean away most of it from her opening before sinking two fingers in. One of her hands delves into my hair, and I glance up, making eye contact with Rhys as she watches me devour her. Her other hand is busy at work, her fingers pinching her nipple as she thrusts her hips to meet each swirl of my tongue and thrust of my fingers.

"Fuck Hastings. You look perfect between my legs."

I grin around my working tongue, now focusing on her needy nerve ending as I clean away the mash.

I can feel her walls squeezing as she seeks her orgasm, so I hook my fingers up as I finger fuck her, and that's when she starts screaming as she clenches over and over around my digits.

Even after she stops pulsing, I keep licking her slowly as I clean off the last traces of food.

"That… that was… unexpected," Rhys whispers before lifting her head off the granite to look at me.

Yeah, I'm a smug fucker right now.

"In a good way, I hope?"

"Hell yes!" Rhys props herself up on her elbows. "I want more."

I can't hide my smile. It's so big it fucking hurts.

"You want my dick now?"

"Yes. In my mouth first. Then in Kitty."

"Kitty?" I sit up, a little confused.

"Guys aren't the only ones that name their sex organs, Simon."

I chuckle. "I guess not. Your pussy is called Kitty?"

"Yep." She reaches out a hand, and I pull her up to sit. "Now, it's my turn to eat something." Looking over my shoulder, Rhys studies the array of food. "Mmm, cherry pie. Yes, please."

I chuckle as she moves excitedly, reaching for the pie, and when she sits back, she's balancing it on one hand.

"Do you like cherry pie, Simon?"

"Yes. It's my favourite."

"Mmm, mine too." Then she slaps it on my bare chest and drags it down until my torso is covered in chunks of cherry pie.

We both laugh, and I brace my hands on the counter behind me as she drops the foil pie tray and uses both hands to rub the pie in as if she were smearing sunscreen on me. Lowering her head, she licks over my nipple before biting her teeth down, and fuck, my dick jerks, pre-cum beading at the top.

"You taste delicious, Simon." She moans out as she brings her hands up to slap sticky cherry pie on my face as she palms my jaw.

"Oh, you really want to get messy, don't you?" I growl, and she grins like a little brat.

"Yes. Messy and dirty as fuck." She agrees before leaning in to kiss me.

Our tongues clash as she holds my chin still, then her finger slides in past our joined lips, and the sweet taste of cherry explodes on my taste buds.

In unison, our moans fill the room, and she pulls back, gliding her tongue from my mouth, over my jaw and down my neck. Making a trail, she weaves through the cherry pie, taking short breathers so she can eat down some of the mangled pie smeared over my skin. As Rhys licks her way down my body, I lean back further, giving her better access, and she gathers up more pie before smearing it over my straining cock.

"Oh, fuck, baby. That feels so good."

Rhys grins. "You like how juicy that feels?" She asks, her eyes wide with excitement as she watches my expression.

"Yes. So fucking good."

"Tell me what you want, Simon?"

"Simon says suck my dick."

The smile she shoots me is utterly evil, right before she drops her head and the hot heat of her mouth sucks Big Simon in.

"Oh fuck." I hiss, my mouth dropping open as I pant, worried I'm about to spill into her mouth already.

She starts working her hand up and down my shaft, her mouth moving in sync and her tongue gliding over my throbbing cock. Every now and then, she pops me free, gathering up more pie and smearing it over my dick.

"Rhys," I pant, and she takes me so deep she gags. "I need to fuck you now."

The pop in the room is loud as she releases my cock, and I reach back on the counter where I placed a condom earlier, tearing the top off the packet.

"You want me to lick the pie off first?" Rhys glides her finger up my shaft, bringing the gathered pie to her lips and licking it off.

"No. I wanna feel the pie as I fuck you."

Her lips part, and her cheeks flush pink.

"That's so fucking hot. Get that condom on now. I need to ride you."

I chuckle as she stands on the bench, moving carefully, so she doesn't slip on the mess we've made. I roll the rubber down my shaft, looking up at her standing over me, covered in cherry pie, looking like a fucking queen.

"Saddle up, baby." Gripping the base of my shaft, I hold him up, and she moves to straddle me, hovering over my dick. The moment my tip sinks in her heat, we both become frenzied, and I tug her down hard, impaling myself inside her.

Our gasps are loud as we start moving together. With Rhys pressed up against me, her tits smear in the red cherry pie, and fuck, it looks like the same shade as her lipstick. Fucking cherry pie. My cherry pie.

Rhys shifts, wrapping her legs around me, and I feel like there's no way possible for us to get any closer to each other than in this moment. I circle my arms around her, claiming her lips in a sticky, sweet, hungry kiss as we grind together frantically. Keeping one hand on her upper back, I shift my other hand to her arse and grip her hard, helping her rise and fall, revelling in the way she rubs her clit against my pubic bone as she seeks another orgasm.

I'm so deep inside her that I feel like I'm going to hurt her, but she demands my deep thrusts, and there's no way I'm going to deny her. My balls tighten, and I know I'm close. I don't want to ruin it by coming too soon, but even as I think it, Rhys is contracting around me, throwing her head back and screaming her release. I'm gone at that point; white light fills my vision as I explode, filling the latex barrier with my cum, mixing in with the cherry pie.

Our panting breaths are loud in the room, and as we both start to come down from our high and relax, I pull back to look at my girl.

Her face is smeared in red cherry pie, her cherry red lips are full, puffy from being kissed, her deep brown eyes look lighter than usual, like little flickers of light dance behind them, and her hair, usually so slick, is messy with some flyaways, her buns looser than when she arrived.

"You are the most beautiful thing I've ever seen, Cherry Pie."

Her dark brows lift. "Cherry Pie?"

"Yep. That's what I'm going to call you from now on. Just like the song, you're my Cherry Pie." I dot a cherry blob on her nose with my finger, and she scrunches it up.

"Is that so?"

Then, her hand slaps a big chuck of cherry pie into the side of my head. She laughs at my expression, and before she sees it coming, I repay the favour. Then it's on. Still buried inside her, as she straddles my lap, we have a fucking food fight. I smear gravy on her back, and she repays me with carrots, squashing them against my spine as I nip at her ear.

We are laughing so hard that I don't hear the front door close or the approaching footsteps.

I *do* hear my mum's shriek, though, and the sound of her suitcases crashing to the floor when she steps into the room. With Rhys straddling me as we sit naked on the granite breakfast bar, food smeared not just all over us but on the bench-top and floor too. My mum's mouth drops open as she imitates a fish.

"Uh… Hi mum."

Chapter Thirty

Rhys

Even though I've had three showers, I can still smell the cherry pie that Simon and I lathered over each other last night. Even now, as I think about what we did, I can't fight the grin or the flutters of those fucking butterflies in my stomach. I love doing new things, and that was fun. So fitting, really, since Simon is nothing but a party. Well, usually he is, but by the time I'd showered in the guest room and met Simon back downstairs in his mansion, his mood was flat. Like really flat. And it had nothing to do with the fact that his mum found us in the throes of a pornographic food fight.

I'd heard Simon asking why she was home unexpectedly. Why his dad wasn't with her. While they are great questions, all I wanted to ask her was why she is never home in the first place, always going off on trips and leaving her son behind. Not my business, I know, but I can't help it. He's such a kind-hearted guy, and I know he acts like a clown to cover up the pain he really feels. I know it too well because I do it too.

After I called my mum to come and pick me up early—because, let's be honest, with the arrival of Simon's mum and being sprung fucking on the bench-top, the party was over—Simon led me out his front door, where he cuddled me to his chest and kissed me with such gentleness that I wanted to cry. Then, as I pulled away reluctantly to go to the car when Cynthia arrived, he said the sweetest thing.

"You are my everything, Cherry Pie."

"What's that face?"

Garrett's question pulls me out of my thoughts, and I play dumb.

"What face?"

"I don't know. But stop pulling it, will you? It's freaking me out."

I glance at Garrett lounging opposite me on the bus' back-row seat, and I grin.

"It's fun freaking you out."

He rolls his eyes and glances back at his phone.

We are on our way to the city with our history class for an excursion to the Melbourne Museum. I considered ditching today, but since I've dug myself into a hole of trouble lately, I decided to give Cynthia a break from my drama. So here I am, at the back of the bus with Garrett as we take up the whole seat with our legs propped up so no one else can sit with us.

The vibration of a text message draws my focus back to my phone, and for a minute, I think it might be Garrett being annoying, but I'm wrong. It's a group chat for a new group.

Cherry's Merry Men
Simon Hastings created a group.
Simon Hastings added Rhys George to the group.
Simon Hastings added Shaun Bossier to the group.

Shaun Bossier
Who the fuck is Cherry?

Simon Hastings
Our girl is Cherry.

Shaun Bossier
Uh- no! She is Kitten!

Simon Hastings
Nah, man. She's my Cherry Pie.

Shaun Bossier
Why Cherry Pie?

Simon Hastings
Because she's a…

Shaun Bossier
She's a what?

Simon Hastings
Oh, come on, man! You know the song?

I giggle at Shaun's lack of knowledge of the song and decide to jump in.

Rhys George
Cool drink of water.

Simon Hastings
Such a sweet surprise.

Shaun Bossier
What?

Rhys George
Tastes so good.

Simon Hastings
Makes a grown man cry.

Shaun Bossier
FFS! I can't keep up with the two of you.

Rhys George
Sweet cherry pie!

Simon Hastings changed Rhys George's name to Cherry Pie.

Simon Hastings
How's the history trip with grumpy?

Cherry Pie
It's fine so far. Nice and quiet. We bagsed the back seat.

Cherry Pie changed Simon Hastings' name to Simon Says.
Cherry Pie changed Shaun Bossier's name to Casanova.

Simon Says
Nice! Miss me?

Casanova

How do I change your name, Kitten?
Cherry Pie just won't cut it!!

Simon Says

Hey, don't you dare change her name!

Casanova

What are you gonna do about it, Hastings?

Cherry Pie

As much as I love a good cockfight, I'm not in a position
to be fully invested since I'm stuck on a bus.
And yes, Simon, I miss you :)

Casanova

Sorry Kitten. How's my girl today? Simon tells me you
two got caught last night.

Cherry Pie

Is that so? Maybe Simon should keep his adorable
mouth shut!

Simon Says
Naw, you think I'm adorable?

Casanova
I don't think it was a compliment, man!

Cherry Pie
It is a compliment! You in a bad mood today, Cass?

Casanova
Sorry. Yeah, I'm a bit cranky today.

Simon Says
A bit! That's an understatement!!

Casanova
I'm about ready to rescind my offer to share Rhys with you, arsehole!

Cherry Pie
Hey guys, let's calm down a bit. Take a breather.
And imagine my mouth wrapped around your cock.

Simon Says
Oh yeah, I like that mental image!

Casanova
Kitten! You don't play fair!
Now I'm hard, and you're not here to fix me.

Cherry Pie
Go to the bathroom and jack off for me, Cass.
Film it so I can have something to look at when I'm alone in my bed with Big Jim.

Casanova
Who the fuck is Big Jim?

The bus slows, and I glance up to see the museum come into view.

Cherry Pie
Big Jim is my biggest vibrator. I'll introduce him to your arse one day, Cass :)

Simon Says
Shit, yes, please do that! I wanna take a picture of his face when Big Jim slides home!

Casanova
Hastings, you do know that sounds creepy, right?

Cherry Pie
Gotta go, guys. Bus is pulling up at the museum now.

Simon Says
Ok, Cherry. Talk later xx.

Casanova
Stay safe, Kitten xoxo

"Fuck me. Are you in love or something?" Garrett's voice disturbs my foolish grinning, so I slip my phone into my blazer pocket and glare at him.

"Jealous?"

His brows shoot up. "Why would I be jealous?"

"Because you're feeling left out." I shrug, and he bites back a smirk. "What's wrong, Gaz. You want a taste too?"

The bus pulls to a stop, and the teacher gets up to talk with the driver while the students start shuffling around in their seats like they have ants in their pants.

"You know what, George; you wouldn't be able to handle me even if I did want a taste."

Oh, that's a challenge if I ever heard one.

"I think I'd be able to handle you, but hey, feel free to prove me wrong."

I'm a smug bitch for dangling that before him, and I watch his eyes widen the slightest bit at my reverse challenge. He's lucky I'm feeling more like myself today, otherwise, I would probably pounce on him and grind over his cock until he gives in.

"Ok, class. Please stand and exit the bus in an orderly fashion. Leave your bags on board, but bring your phones and money." Mr Elliot, my Ed Sheeran lookalike with a long beard History teacher, bellows down the bus, and students stand before he even finishes, ignoring him completely.

I slide across the seat and stand, taking a few steps to fall into line at the back. Garrett does the same, standing a little too close for someone that wants to stay away from me, and I bite my lip, trying to hide my grin.

"You're my partner today, George." Garrett's deep voice rumbles next to my ear, startling me, and my heart races. Not because I'm scared, but because I'm excited. He's making an effort to hang around me more. That has to mean something, right?

"I guess we can partner up, but you'd better pay attention. I want a good mark on the test."

"The test doesn't even matter. It doesn't go to our final grade. This is just a bullshit excursion to give us something to do."

He's right. We are studying for exams now, so this excursion is just a filler day.

I shrug. "Whatever. I like to do well no matter what."

"Fine." His breath flutters over my ear again, and I turn my head to the side a little to see that he's leaning down, so much closer than he needs to. He's so close that if I move back an inch, I'll be pressed up against him. And oh, how tempting is that? To be pressed up against big, bad, broody Garrett Cole.

Too fucking tempting!

Following the other students in our class, we walk across the open area at the front of the building and gather under a partially shaded space where Mr Elliot stands on one of the concrete bench seats to address us.

"You have two hours to find all the things on these lists." He holds up a stack of papers. "Make sure you answer the questions relating to each item. Do not, under any circumstances, leave the building, and make sure you use the maps to navigate your way around the building." Mr Elliott's face turns serious as his eyes roam over the group, glaring, "Stay with your partner! Do not get lost! Do not do anything that will bring shame to our school! And finally, meet back here at 1pm. No later."

As the other students move into line to get their map and list off Mr Elliot, I turn to Garrett.

"Ugh, too many rules. This sounds boring already."

He rolls his icy blue eyes, shooting me a smirk. "Come on, George, let's get this over and done with." He tugs on the sleeve of my blazer and pulls me along with him.

I over-exaggerate heavy feet like I just can't walk, but he keeps dragging me, anyway.

"You really aren't selling this whole museum thing, you know." I pout.

"Not that it's up to me to sell, but how exactly am I going to make it sound more interesting?" With impatience, Garrett reaches over everyone's heads, holding his hand out for the papers, and Mr Elliott, too busy being bombarded, doesn't even notice that Garrett pushed in. When he turns back to me with the papers in his hand, I smirk.

"Do they have sex stuff in there?"

Garrett drops his shoulders and gives me a *'really'* look. "Not everything is about sex, Rhys."

"Umm, of course, it is. What planet are you living on?" I frown up at Garrett as he grins and shakes his head.

"Come on, George. Let's go."

He walks off, and I stay rooted on the spot for no other reason than I'm a brat. Ohhh, if only Tyler were here now.

Realising that I'm not walking beside him, Garrett stops and darts his head around, not taking long to locate me standing alone with my brows raised and a face full of attitude. He mutters something to himself, which looks a lot like, *for fuck's sake*, and I bite my bottom lip to stop my smirk from showing. Marching back towards me, I expect him to whine at me or scold me, but all he does is snatch up my hand in his and leads me in through the museum doors.

I'm a little shocked that he's actually holding my hand, breaking his unspoken rule about touching me. He tries to avoid it as much as possible, yet here he is, holding my hand in front of people. I'm almost certain the moment we navigate through the entrance gates, he's going to drop my hand, so when he doesn't, I duck my head and grin as he leads us through the crowd to the side of the room. That, however, is when he drops my hand.

I instantly miss the contact, and I fight the urge to reach out and retake his hand, but he's busy holding the map and list with both hands, scanning over them.

"Let's go backwards." He looks up from the map.

"What? Why?"

"Well, because everyone else will start on this floor. Let's ditch them." The grin that lights up his face is sinful and fucking gorgeous. I love that he shares his smiles with me when he keeps them from most people.

"Now you're talking, Cole." I grin, and he tucks the map away in his blazer pocket before taking my hand again.

"Let's go."

Oh… he's holding my hand again, except this time, his fingers weave through mine, linking us together. My stupid heart does that flutter thing again. Like, what the actual fuck is wrong with me lately? Should I go to a doctor? Maybe I really do have a heart condition that I never knew about?

I stay quiet as he leads me in the opposite direction of the masses travelling up the escalators, and we make our way through the expansive hall to enter the Aboriginal Cultural Centre. There are only a few groups walking through this section, so Garrett leads me through the exhibits before stopping at the First Peoples area.

"There are some questions about this part." Garrett moves to drop my hand, but I clasp my fingers tight halting his effort. Angling his head towards me, a single dark brow shoots up. "I thought you wanted to pass the test?"

"I lied. I don't care." I admit, and the corner of his mouth quirks.

"So we aren't going to bother with the questions?"

I shake my head and look forward at the display cabinet, not paying any attention to the exhibit but rather watching Garrett's reflection in the glass. His eyes are still on me as I pretend to be preoccupied, and then I see him smile and lean down towards my ear.

"Let's explore then."

I dart my head back to face him. He is so close. His lips near enough that I could kiss them.

"Let's explore," I whisper, grinning back at him.

So that's what we do. We explore the ground level, weaving through the Forest Gallery before entering the Science and Life Gallery. I'm not that into science, but I find myself enjoying the experience as we examine each display, talking together while still hand in hand. Even when I skip through the Dinosaur Walk, all excited to see the skeletons of the giant creatures, Garrett matches my pace, keeping our fingers locked together. He even laughs at how ridiculous I am when I struggle to try to get a selfie with the towering bones behind us, not willing to release his hand.

As we travel to the upper floor, we pass kids from school travelling down. I see a few eyes fall to our linked hands, but most don't even notice us as they talk amongst themselves.

Next, we venture into the Melbourne Gallery, where we see the Phar Lap exhibit and then find somewhere to sit for the next thirty minutes until it's time to meet up with the class.

"You ever going to let go of my hand?" Garrett holds up our joined hands as we sit back on the bench seat, leaning against the wall.

"Nope." I flash him my teeth and flutter my eyes in a playful smile.

"You're gonna have to at some point."

"Nope." I shake my head.

"I need to take a piss. You gonna come with me into the men's toilets?"

"Yep." I smile again, and he shakes his head.

"You gonna hold my dick for me while I piss?"

"You know I will."

"You're right. I do know you will." He sighs. "Just so you know, I'm not coming into the girl's toilet with you."

"Why not? You did the other day."

"That was… a mistake." Garrett looks away from me then, and my heart sinks. Why is he even holding my hand if he thinks that was a mistake? Did I force him into that situation? I think it over, trying to remember how he came to be in the girl's bathroom with me. I'd gone in there to masturbate like the weird fucker I am, and he'd followed me. So no, I hadn't forced him into it at all.

Loosening my grip on his hand, I slip mine free. His attention snaps back to me, and I turn my focus to my phone, opening it up to check my messages. There's one from Simon. A selfie of him pulling a face with the caption, *I'm going crazy without you.* Shaun sent a selfie too, but it's the complete opposite to Simon's, with his selfie more of a sexy smoulder and the caption, *I can't stop thinking about you, and Thor won't go to sleep!*

Ha! Thor! He calls his cock Thor! He's so fucking adorable.

"You not talking to me now?" Garrett nudges my shoulder, trying to gain my attention, and I sigh, slipping my phone back into my blazer pocket.

"All g, Cole," I answer, looking around at the people walking by.

"It's obviously not. Why won't you look at me?"

Sighing, I make it a point to angle myself towards him, looking into his icy blue eyes as he studies my face.

"I'm looking at you. See? All g."

His eyes narrow. "Rhys."

"What?" I snap, wishing I'd ditched school instead of coming on this excursion. I'm generally not so fucking easy to rattle. My lows have really kicked my arse lately.

"You didn't like what I said about it being a mistake." He states and moves to take my hand, but I pull mine away.

Everyone knows I'm easy, but I'm not that fucking easy. I still have a fucking heart, and for some reason, this guy and his fucking mates have gotten under my skin.

"It's not exactly what a girl wants to hear after she shares something like that with someone."

He sighs. "I only meant that I shouldn't have stepped over the line like that. Marcus is my mate, and I knew he still cared about you. It's why I was trying to help you with your... issue. I didn't want Marcus to get hurt by his mates as well as you."

"So why did you step over the line, then?"

His lips thin at my question, and he looks away from me, pretending to watch people walk by. I wait a minute, thinking he'll answer me soon, but it never comes.

All of a sudden, I feel like crying. It's a ridiculous reaction since I don't fucking care about Garrett. Right? I only care about fucking. It's not like I've never been rejected before. So why is this towering wall of sex appeal fucking with my emotions so much?

I stand quickly, needing to get away from him.

Dashing through a group of people, I head down the oversized passage towards the elevator bank. Garrett's voice sounds somewhere behind me, calling my name, so I quicken my pace and slam my finger into the elevator button, pressing it repeatedly until the doors slide open. I nearly clean up a man exiting the lift, and I ignore his glare as I move inside and push the door closed button over and over until the doors start to slide shut.

I relax a little then, thinking stupidly that I'm in the clear, but a large hand grips the doors before they close, sending them wide again, allowing Garrett to step into the lift with me.

"Fucking hell! Can't a girl get a moment to herself?"

Ignoring my harsh words, Garrett presses the button for the basement, and the doors ease shut. "Don't run from me."

His words are a gentle contradiction to his hulking form, and when those icy blues lock with my eyes, I can see the storm brewing in them.

"What does it matter if I run from you? Am I just a puzzle for you to solve? Will it make you feel better about yourself if you fix my addiction, Garrett? Are you trying to play the hero here?"

"You can be a real bitch when you want to, George."

"No shit." The elevator dings and the doors slide open, so I bolt out, needing to get away from Garrett... again.

"I stepped over the line because despite everything I do, I'm still drawn to you."

My steps halt, freezing me in place at Garrett's words, and I slowly turn to watch him approach. He keeps his eyes locked on mine, sending stupid butterflies dancing through my chest.

"At the time, it felt wrong to step over the line when Marcus was so recently involved with you. I knew he still cared."

My eyes drop to the floor as guilt oozes its way into my heart. I shouldn't be angry at Garrett. He's a good friend to Marcus. And hell, he's stronger than I am. Stronger than Shaun and Simon are. We all thought about Marcus, yet we still went over the line when we should've been standing back, just like Garrett.

Garrett's strong hand grips my jaw, forcing me to look at him. I want to pull away, tell him not to touch me, yet I can't because I'm weak. I fucking yearn for his touch.

"I wanted to be there anyway, Rhys. Actually, I wanted to be in that stall with my hands on you. I wanted to be the one sinking my finger inside you." He shakes his head, his face contorting into a frown. "But Marcus…"

He wanted to touch me?

So, I'm not imagining his attraction to me?

"I couldn't do that to Marcus." He whispers, his eyes darting to my lips briefly.

"You wanted to touch me?"

He nods, "Yes."

"So, touch me now." I practically beg, and his face softens as he shakes his head.

"Nope. I can't do it, George. I'll never betray Marcus, no matter how much I want you."

I can't speak. I feel like a treat is being dangled in front of me, and I can't get to it because there's a big mother-fucking glass wall in the way. He wants me. He just fucking said it, and the knowledge hurts. It burns in the centre of my chest. Not at all the sort of reaction I typically have to rejection. Normally it's Kitty hissing at me, reminding me of her hunger. In fact, right now, I'd give just about anything to have her bitching at me instead of this ache squeezing my heart.

"Ok," I whisper, biting the inside of my cheek as I fight my emotions.

"Ok?" Garrett frowns.

I shrug. "Ok. I'll leave you alone from now on. Marcus is a lucky guy to have you as his friend." I turn and walk down another passage leading me somewhere I don't recognise.

Shit. Where the fuck am I right now?

"George." Garrett halts me, his hand gripping my upper arm as he spins me back to him. "We can be friends too."

My brows shoot up. "Friends?"

"Yeah. You know, a relationship that doesn't involve sex."

"That's absurd." I narrow my eyes at him, and he gifts me with that rare smile of his. Fucking hell. Why do I want to kiss those lips so bad?

"Oh, come on, George. You can leave sex out of the equation. Look at you and Jared. There's no hint of sex between the two of you."

"Duh. He's in love with someone else."

"So, if he didn't have it bad for Lexi, you would totally be sizing him up?" Even though Garrett tries to hide it, I can still see how much it annoys him to think of me being with Jared.

"I'd tap that. He's as hot as the rest of you. I'm only human, Gaz." I shimmy out of Garrett's grip and move back towards the elevators.

"Would you really?" He asks, coming to stand next to me when I press the button for the lift.

"Sure. If he has a pretty cock, I'd be all over that."

Garrett frowns down at me. "I disagree. I don't think you would."

"You do remember I have a fucking addiction to sex, right?"

"Yes!" He growls.

"And even though you know that, you still think I can leave sex out of the equation? You think I'd be able to control my desire to sink onto a willing dick?"

"Yes." He nods.

"You've lost your fucking mind!" I snap.

"Have you ever tried to have a relationship with a guy that didn't involve sex?" He reaches for my hands again, but I seize the opportunity of the lift doors opening and step inside.

"Yeah. They're called friends. That thing *you* only want to be with me."

Garrett rolls his eyes as he steps onto the lift, and he pushes the button for the second floor. "I'm not talking about friends. I'm talking about a boyfriend. Haven't you ever just had a guy that you held hands with and spent time with, maybe kissed every now and then, but never went any further?"

"No!" My brows draw together.

"Never?"

"No!"

"Not even when you were like thirteen years old?"

"No!"

"How old were you when you lost your virginity, Rhys?"

I still.

Shit. I'm not having this conversation with him.

Hurry up, you stupid elevator!

The ding sounds and the doors slide open, so I take my chance and rush out into the crowd, hoping to get lost amongst them.

"Rhys!" Garrett catches up to me, grabbing my arm and hurling me around. "Stop running from me."

"Then stop asking me questions that are none of your business!" I hiss in his face.

"How old were you, Rhys?"

"Why? What does it matter?" I hiss.

"It matters a hell of a lot. Tell me." He growls back in my face this time, and I just want to slap him. Or kiss him. I don't fucking know! "How old were you when you lost your virginity?"

My chest heaves as emotions I typically keep hidden swirl to the surface.

I open my mouth to speak but then shut it again as a lump forms in my throat.

"Rhys?"

"I was young enough not to know what losing my virginity was."

My words are quiet so only he can hear, and he grips my shoulders, steering me backwards until we are in a small alcove doorway.

"What age was that?" He whispers, and heat pricks the back of my eyes.

"Eleven," I whisper.

Garrett's eyes grow wide, shock evident as my words sink in. He obviously knew I was young, but he hadn't considered I was still a little girl when it happened.

"Rhys." He whispers, emotion laced in his eyes.

I shake my head. "Don't." I try to step away from him, but he cages me in. "Don't you dare say sorry. It wasn't your fault, and if you knew all the circumstances surrounding it, you wouldn't be looking at me with so much fucking pity."

I duck under his arm and beeline for the escalators, moving quickly to travel down so we can meet the rest of the class. Even though Garrett doesn't say anything, I can feel his presence right behind me. He sticks close, and even though I'm feeling out of sorts from admitting that truth to him, I'm glad he's still there.

Mr Elliot does a roll call before asking the group questions. We hover at the back of the crowd, not at all interested. In fact, all I'm interested in doing is going home and shutting myself away in my room.

Fingers brush mine as my hand dangles by my side, and then those same fingers link with mine from behind, clasping my hand tight. A strong warm body that I know without a doubt belongs to Garrett presses against my back, letting me know he's there, as my friend.

"I'm not going anywhere." His whisper in my ear nearly causes a sob to escape my throat. I manage to keep it in by clamping my lips shut.

It feels so fucking perfect to have him so close. I want to cry. A bubble of uncontrollable emotion sits like a choking gobstopper in my throat, but the gentle brush of Garrett's thumb on my hand at our sides captures my focus, and slowly, the feeling of pending doom slips away.

Chapter Thirty-One

Garrett

H er face. Fuck, when she said that word. The age she was when she lost her virginity. I should have backed off when she said she was young enough not to know what losing her virginity was. But I just couldn't comprehend what that age would be. Stupidly, I thought maybe thirteen or fourteen. Sure, that's young, but not unheard of, especially when hormones are involved. Teenagers are nothing but horny all the time. But eleven? There's no fucking way that was consensual.

Rhys must have been raped.

My stomach churns at the thought of the little girl version of Rhys being violated. It's fucking sickening. The thing is, her behaviour towards sex makes so much more sense now. Not everyone who suffers trauma fears it. Some people run towards it, wanting to re-experience it in a way they have more control over. It's a twisted way of thinking, but it's a real fucking thing.

I hurt her feelings when I told her my involvement in the bathroom incident last week was a mistake. I was a little surprised that she cared so much. Normally, she'd brush it off like it doesn't bother her either way. Things have been different lately, though. *She's* been different. Something is going on with her, and the more I learn about Rhys, the more I realise I know nothing.

"Aren't you like, fucking Shaun Bossier?" Allison, one of Lexi's old friends, is in line in front of us as we wait to go into the IMAX theatre. I feel Rhys stiffen a little next to me, but I tighten my grip on her hand, not willing to let her go. Ever fucking again.

Wait. I mean that in a platonic way.

Yeah, sure you do!

"Aren't you meant to be Lexi's friend?" Rhys bites back, and Allison flinches.

"What? Breaking Marcus' heart wasn't enough? You had to move on to all of his friends?" The bitch snarls at Rhys, and I feel my girl's chest rise and fall as anger washes over her.

"Why don't you mind your own fucking business!" I snap, and Allison's eyes flare in shock as she looks up at me. Then I growl at her, baring my teeth.

Allison's eyes dart back and forth between my face and Rhys' before she spins on her heel and gives us her back.

Leaning down, I hover my lips next to Rhys' ear.

"Ignore the bitch."

In answer, Rhys leans into me, trusting me to make her feel safe.

When the cinema opens, we hang back a little and let everyone find their seat before we veer off to sit a little away from the FP Catholic herd. Taking our seats, I get comfy before sweeping up Rhys' hand again and bringing our joined hands to rest on my thigh. I sneak a glance at her and see her brows dipped in a frown.

"Hey. What's wrong?"

Her confused gaze peers up at me, her brown eyes studying my face. "I'm confused."

"About?"

She frowns again. "This." She holds up our joined hands. "Why are you holding my hand?"

I don't fucking know why I'm holding her hand. It's one of those lines that are a little blurry, yet I can't fucking help myself. I just need to touch her. To show her she's not alone.

"I'm just trying to be a supportive friend. I can see that things are tough for you at the moment, and I want you to know you're not alone."

Sounds blare through the speakers as the movie trailers start, turning the chattering patrons to focus on the screen. Rhys doesn't turn her eyes away from me, though. She studies me with a slight crease between her dark brows.

"So you're holding my hand as a friend?"

I nod, even though deep down, I know I'm lying. Rhys tilts her head to the side as she takes in my expression. It's like she is trying to read my mind. Trying to see the truth I'm hiding from her.

"I'm calling bullshit."

Her words make me flinch, and a sinful black-lipped smile sweeps over her face. She has an infectious smile, especially when it's full, showing her white teeth. I wonder if she realises how beautiful she is?

The movie starts up, and Rhys sits back in her seat, squeezing my hand tighter as she turns her focus to the screen. The feature is something called Alita. This cinema isn't a normal one. They say it has the world's largest cinema screen. I'm not sure how true that is, but there's one thing I know. It's fucking big.

I try to concentrate on the movie, but it's not really my thing, and I can't stop my mind from drifting to all the things I wish I could do to this siren sitting next to me. Rhys is all about sex, and I'm practically frothing at the mouth to dive into that world with her. But something is holding me back, and it's not just my loyalty to Marcus, although that has a hell of a lot to do with it.

I could man the fuck up and talk to Marcus about how I feel. He'd probably hate me, but going behind his back is worse. Even now, as I hold Rhys' hand, I feel like I'm a betraying prick. It's never going to be an ideal situation, but I need to decide what I want. Can I ignore these feelings that have been brewing for a couple of months now? Can I ignore the magnetic pull she has on me? Her black soul is akin to mine. She has a level of darkness that I find hard to ignore. Like her addiction and her past. She has a tortured soul that calls to me, that matches my own, and fuck if I don't find it hard to *not* be near that every fucking minute.

"Can I give you a hand job while the movie is on?" Rhys whispers in my ear, and my cock jerks to life, desperate for her touch.

"No." I keep my eyes on the screen, not really seeing anything as my thoughts turn devious.

"Why not? It will feel sooo good." She nips at my ear, and my cock jerks again.

Fucking hell. This is going to be harder than I thought.

"No," I grunt, and the little sinner reaches her free hand over towards my crotch. I slap it away quickly and glare at her as she pouts with those dark lips. Fuck, I want to kiss her until there's no black left on them. I bet she looks just as hot without the bold black smile.

"Oh, come on. How about you rub my Kitty then?"

"No."

"Not even over my clothes?" She asks, her expression totally serious.

"No."

She huffs, throwing herself back in her seat in frustration. "Fine, I'll do it myself."

Not scared to admit to getting herself off, Rhys slides her free hand down the front of her uniform, and I twist in my seat to grab her hand before she makes contact.

"No," I growl in her ear, and she glares at me.

"Is that all you know how to say?" She whisper-yells, and I nod.

Then she rolls her eyes.

We sit back, both of us frustrated as we pretend to watch the movie for a bit longer before she can no longer help herself.

"Garrett." She whispers, and I dart my eyes to glance at her out of the corner of my eye. "I'm horny."

Turning to her, it takes everything in me not to kiss her.

"You're always horny."

"Exactly. It's worse than needing to eat food to function. Help me come. Pleeease?" She practically begs, and even though I know it's a ploy to make me cave, I stay strong.

"No, Rhys. If that's all you're after, then you won't find it from me. You have two other boyfriends for that anyway, don't you?"

"Three." She says, and then her eyes widen. "I mean two."

I frown. "You said three."

"See, this is what happens to my brain if I don't come regularly. It turns to mush." She flutters those dark lashes at me innocently, but I see straight through her little act.

Does she have a third guy? Is it Marcus? Did he decide to share her after all?

I narrow my eyes at her, and she clamps her mouth shut. Shit, she *does* have a third guy.

"Why can't I have that from you, too? We would be good together. Fucking great together." She's trying hard to sell the idea to me, but it won't work. I'm not going to give her what she wants.

"I want to show you that there's more to a relationship or spending time with someone other than sex."

She frowns, and it's fucking adorable the way her dark brows tug together.

"*Is* there more, though? Isn't sex like the endgame?"

That question is why I need to show her there's a difference. Sure, sex can just be sex, but it can also be so much more. The only way I know how to show her is to help her see the other side of what a relationship can look like... just without the sex. Bossi and Hastings are happy to keep her *Kitty*—as she calls it—occupied, but it's just a bandaid. It's not helping her because something else is happening with Rhys, and I'm determined to find out what it is.

I manage to keep Rhys at bay for the rest of the movie, and once we pile on the bus to head back to Fox Pines, we take the same seats as earlier. The back seat of the bus is a long bench seat to fit five people, so it gives us room to kick back and stretch out our legs.

I watch Rhys squirming around where she sits as she does something on her phone. She can't sit still, and either she's still horny from before, or she's chatting with Bossi or Hastings, and they are riling her up. I swear if she starts touching herself, I'm going to fucking cave, and I don't want to cave. I don't want to think with my dick and ruin things.

"Hey." I wait for her to look up from her phone, her big brown eyes softening as they take me in. "I wanna show you something."

I need to distract her. It's only about half an hour before we get back home, so I open my photo app on my phone and drop my legs off the seat, gesturing for her to meet me in the middle. She takes a moment, looking back down at her phone and then back to me as if deciding which option to choose—boring Garrett or phone sex with someone else.

The moment she slips her phone into her pocket, I relax and watch her slide across to park her arse next to me. I'll call that a small win.

"Are you going to show me your dick pic?"

I roll my eyes and hold up my phone. "This is my little sister Britney."

Rhys' face falls neutral, no longer holding the mischief it did a moment ago.

"Oh, she has your eyes. How old is she?"

"She's nine, and even though she's the youngest in the house, she fucking rules the roost." I grin when Rhys laughs.

"I can tell. She has fierceness in her eyes. A true warrior." Rhys grabs my wrist and tugs it closer so she can get a better look. "She's really pretty, too. You'll have your hands full fighting off boys soon."

"They won't dare to come near her," I growl, and Rhys giggles.

Angling my phone back towards me, I swipe across a few pictures and then hold it towards Rhys again.

"This is Polly. She's …" The words get stuck in my throat, and I try to cover my stumble by clearing my throat. "She's eleven."

Rhys' brows hitch, and I know she's thinking the same thing I just did. Polly is the same age Rhys was when her virginity was taken away from her. Anger builds inside me like a simmering volcano getting ready to combust. If anyone ever touched my Polly like that, I'd fucking kill them.

"She's really pretty, too. Same eyes but different hair colour to you. Who has the blonde hair in your family?" Rhys looks up to me then, her eyes curious and no longer filled with the need that has been plaguing her all afternoon.

I shift a little on the seat, leaning in towards her, and she sinks in to meet me in the middle.

"My old man has blonde hair," I grumble, not really wanting to talk about that prick.

"Oh. Do you have a picture of your parents?"

Maybe this was a bad idea. I don't want to show her my dad. He's a fucking psycho prick sitting in prison where he belongs. Although, if he gets his way, he'll be out on good behaviour soon. Way too fucking soon.

I scroll through my pictures and find one of my mum. She's standing in the kitchen, cooking. I hold it up, and Rhys smiles.

"Your mum looks nice. Sweet."

I nod. "She is sweet. Too sweet for her own good sometimes."

"You get your brown curls from her." Rhys beams, turning her eyes to mine before lifting her hand and ruffling my hair.

"Hey! Watch it." I hiss playfully, and she giggles.

"Oh no. I think one of your curls is out of place now." She teases, and I narrow my eyes.

"Maybe I should mess your hair up?"

"Oh no, not my stylish hair." She mocks, laughing, and reaches up to mess my hair again.

I grab her wrist just in time, tugging down and pinning it behind her back. The move brings us close together. So close that I'm in the perfect position to kiss her. My heart suddenly flips in my chest, and my eyes dart to her lips, right as her pink tongue pops out to wet them. When I look back up to her eyes, they're focused on my lips, so I copy what she did and lick them. I don't know why I do that. I know I'm playing with fire here, but I can't fucking help myself. Her breathing increases as she watches my tongue, and when her eyes finally lift to meet mine, I purposefully refrain, reminding myself that

I can't cross that line. Aside from the fact that I can't betray Marcus, Rhys doesn't need another dick in her life. She needs a friend.

Reluctantly, I pull back from the most tempting lips I've ever come across.

Glancing down at Rhys, I immediately see the hurt in her eyes.

"Sorry." It's a useless apology, but it's all I've got.

"No need to be sorry." She shifts back further from me, breaking the invisible chain between us.

When her lips tug up in a weak smile, mine matches, and I steer us back into conversation about our families. I manage to dodge talking about my dad, and I focus on asking about her family. She fills me in about her twin foster brothers and her older foster sister, and then how she only just started calling her foster parents, mum and dad. Her eyes glass over a little when she talks about that, and I realise what's been missing out of Rhys' life.

It's unconditional love.

Chapter Thirty-Two

RHYS

My Wednesday at school is surprisingly uneventful. Garrett and Shaun sit on either side of me in English with one hand on each of my thighs, and even though Garrett's interactions with me are confusing the fuck out of me, I'm not strong enough to tell him to leave me alone altogether.

In Maths class, Simon tells me he overheard Ayden telling Lexi that Marcus has been suspended for two weeks and will do community service around the school for the rest of the year and pay a fine to cover the damages. I smile at that. My mum and Tyler must have been able to sway the school board not to expel Marcus.

Recess is spent with Lexi, kicking back in the spring sun in the courtyard, followed by a double History class with Garrett, where we thoroughly fail the test about yesterday's museum excursion.

Whoops!

I don't care, though, because even though my pride was hurt by Garrett's rejection, I kinda enjoyed getting to know more about the brooding beast.

Lunchtime is spent trying to track down Tillie and Bell, who are doing a stellar fucking job at avoiding me, and during Viscom, I receive the usual text message from Skipper with the question mark. Today I answered with a thumbs up.

After my royal fuck up on Sunday night, I know there will be some sort of punishment for me tonight. There's a big fucking chance that Master Hill will deal with my punishment down in his dungeon since

Skipper was my punishment the time before. The smart thing to do would be not to go, but then I risk getting kicked out, and I need that place. For the first time, however, I hate that I need that place. I wish I didn't have to go there. I wish I could get what I need from people I trust.

Even though I have something going with Shaun and Simon, who knows how long it will last, and if it will even be enough for me? There's kinda something going on with Tyler too, but I can't include him in whatever I have with the other two. Not when Tyler is their PE teacher.

No. The only way I can have him with one of my guys is to have him and Shaun together at the Feast. Which is exactly what I am hoping for tonight. Surely that's worth enduring a punishment for?

Vixen's Lodge has a private room that can be hired out for more intimate experiences. I have some cash. Maybe I can hire it for the three of us? Just the thought of having Shaun and Tyler alone together has my anticipation skyrocketing, so much so that I arrive early at the barn to get ready.

I know I'll have to spend some time when I go inside the Lodge grovelling to Madam Vik. At least if I get it over and done with early and take my punishment without complaint, it will be over with quickly and I'll still have the whole night to play.

After I've painted on my sugar skull—white, black and red tonight to match the red number Master Hill left for me—I slip on the red stilettos and finger comb my long hair before I eagerly exit the barn. Just as I round the corner of the Lodge, Tyler comes into view as he heads in my direction.

"Kitten, I was just on my way to see you. You're ready early tonight."

"We can go back to the barn if you like?" I point my thumb over my shoulder, and his lips pull into a grin under his red leather mask.

"Unfortunately, I was coming to get you. Our presence has been requested." Tyler's lips turn down, and I frown.

"Madam Vik?" I ask.

"No. Master Hill."

"Shit," I whisper, darting my eyes to the ground. I was hoping to have a little time to warm up before I face him.

"Hey, we can leave now, Kitten. We don't have to go in there." Tyler's tone is gentle. Caring. Not at all matching the kinky red leather mask hiding his identity.

Staring into his deep blue eyes, I see the concern swimming in them.

"No." I shake my head. "I need to get it over and done with. Leaving now will just make it worse."

Tyler sighs. "I'll follow your lead. If you want to leave, then we leave. Ok?"

I nod. "Ok."

Reaching up, Tyler pinches my hair between his fingers before letting it fall back over my breast. "You look stunning, Kitten." He whispers, and I'm glad I'm wearing face paint so he can't see my stupid girly blush.

We sigh in unison before turning and walking into Vixen's Lodge. Brock tries to make eye contact with me, but I avoid it. I'm not sure if it's because I'm so embarrassed about Sunday night when I showed up unannounced and without a mask, or if I'm pissed at him for being such a drill sergeant about the whole thing. I know he has a job to do, but we've fooled around numerous times before, so I stupidly assumed it counted for something.

Sex is sex, Rhys. Don't forget that!

As soon as Tyler and I step into the cocktail lounge, one of the waiters approaches us to let us know that Master Hill wants to see us straight away.

Fucking hell. Can't a girl have a drink first?

The shirtless waiter, who is the same one that typically brings me my tray of shots, leads us through the house and down some narrow creaky stairs. My heart practically explodes as realisation sets in.

Master Hill wants to see us in his dungeon.

It's not exactly a dungeon. It's a room behind their wine cellar, which I expect resembles a torture dungeon, hence why I call it that.

As I follow behind the waiter, I don't notice my trembling hands until Tyler's strong hand links with mine before he leans in to whisper near my ear.

"It's ok, Kitten. I've got you."

His words work like a safety harness, tethering me to him with a promise of not letting me fall. It's a brief reprieve because a few moments later, we approach a large, heavy door being held open by another shirtless waiter. I've seen this guy here before, too. He's bigger than the other waiter we're following, ripped with so many muscles I can only imagine he lifts weights at the gym while blowing himself kisses.

My heart rate spikes as we step over the threshold, leaving the wine cellar behind to enter the Lion's Den. I dart my eyes around frantically, taking in what I can of the room to discover that it is, in fact, a fucking BDSM dungeon.

There's a huge four-poster bed in the centre, with various chains and bars hanging off the back. The wall to the left is lined with shelves and drawers that hold a vast selection of whips, paddles, blindfolds, chokers, collars and leashes, ball gags, mouth spreaders, dildos... you get the gist.

Fucking hell!

The wall on the right has some sort of contraption coming off it, plus restraints chained to the wall. Just what you would expect from A FUCKING DUNGEON!

"Sit down, please." The deep, very pissed off voice of Master Hill makes me jump. I turn around to see him sitting in the corner of the room, shadowed like a fucking creeper.

There are no chairs for me and Tyler to sit on, just two small cushions side by side on the floor. I glance nervously at Tyler as the waiter exits the room, clicking the door shut behind him. The urge to flee is almost suffocating, and it takes everything in me to fight it. This place is fucking creepy. *This* man is fucking creepy. This situation is fucking creepy.

Tyler gestures his head toward Master Hill so slightly that I nearly miss it. I frown, watching as he moves in the general direction of the perve in the corner. It takes me a moment to realise that I should be following, so I move to catch up, watching as Tyler falls to his knees on one of the cushions at the feet of Master Fucking Hill.

Is this really happening?

I have to kneel to the fucking Master?

Of course, I do.

Following Tyler's lead, I fall to my knees on the other cushion and mimic him by linking my hands together behind my back. Then I wait, avoiding Master Hills' glare, and instead, I study his shiny black shoes.

"Eyes up, Kitten." Master Hill demands, and like a fucking puppet, I do as he says.

"I was going to ask what on earth you were thinking by showing up here uninvited and without your identity hidden on Sunday night, Kitten, but there *really* is no excuse."

"But you said I had to keep up my attendance."

"Keep your mouth shut, and do not speak until I ask you to!" Master Hill booms, and I jump, my breath catching in my throat as an embarrassing whimper escapes me.

Then Tyler growls.

"Do you have something to say, Skipper?" Master Hill spits and Tyler hisses.

"As Kitten is my liege, I ask that you do not scare her, please. She is well aware of the mistake she has made."

"Is that so?" Master Hill asks, his eyes returning to me. "You understand that you did something bad, Kitten?"

I nod.

"You may speak to answer me when I ask you a question." Master Hill growls, and I just want to flip the arsehole the bird.

"Yes. I understand." I mutter.

"Do you also understand that when someone breaks the rules, they must be punished?" Master asks in a sinister tone. The arsehole is fucking loving this right now, his green eyes wild with excitement behind his glasses. Sick fucker.

"Yes. I understand."

"Good. Now I need to decide what your punishment will be. The risk you took on Sunday night was quite serious, so I can't just deal out a simple punishment like last weekend. It needs to be a firm hand. Firm enough that you will know to never *ever* break the rules again." Master Hill leans forward in his chair, resting his elbows on his thighs. "Normally, an infraction of that nature is dealt with in public so that other members understand not to disobey the rules. But since you are so young, Kitten, I will give you the choice of a public punishment, or a private punishment, in here, with just me."

Fucking hell. Once again, that sick perve is trying to get me alone in this fucking dungeon. My heart races as my mind creates scenarios of what he will do to me once he finally has me alone. Scenarios I know I'll never recover from. Mentally.

"I will take her punishment for her." Tyler hisses, and I turn to look at him. Even though I can only see one of his eyes and part of his mouth, I can tell he's furious right now.

"Actually, Skipper, since she is your responsibility, you too will be punished, so no, you won't be taking her punishment for her. She will never learn her lesson if you coddle her."

Tyler hisses and Master tuts.

"Be careful, Skipper. You don't want to make things worse for yourself." He lets the words hang there for a moment before he adds. "Or for Kitten."

That fucking fucker of a fuck!

This is all my fault. If I hadn't gone off the rails and turned up here looking for a hit of sex the other night, Tyler wouldn't be in this position right now.

"Now, so you don't intervene, you will be restrained while Kitten receives her punishment. If she chooses to do her punishment with me, you will be restrained outside the door." Master Hill points at the door we came through only minutes ago. "And if she chooses public, then you will be restrained at the back of the room where you can watch."

"No!" Tyler shoots to his feet, his fists in tight balls by his sides.

"Back to your knees, Skipper!" Master Hill bellows, and Tyler puffs out his bare chest. "Are you defying me, Skipper? Because you *know*, Tiger has been requesting to take over Kitten's sponsorship. Maybe he's a more suitable Sponsor for her. He might be able to control her, which you seem to be failing at."

"No," I whisper, and just like that, Tyler falls to his knees.

"Smart decision." Master smirks.

I'm gonna punch this fucker in the nuts!

Tiger is an overweight fifty-year-old never been married man that dresses in a skin-tight tiger suit. Some people might be able to pull such an outfit off, but this guy can't. It clings to him like a glove, showing his too round belly, and the stupid suit is made to expose his bare arse, his little wiener, his hairy nipples, his hands, and the lower part of his flabby face.

"So, Kitten. What will it be?"

"Public," I say fast, and I fucking love the way Master Hill's face drops. I will never give him the satisfaction of having me alone in this room.

"Right, well, let's get on with it. It will make a fabulous opening to the evening, don't you think?" Master Hill stands and opens the door to talk to the waiter standing outside, keeping guard like I was going to flee or something.

WTF!

"Kitten?" Tyler stands, hauling me up with him. "Let's just go. We'll leave now. We don't need this place."

I frown. "What? Don't be stupid. Of course, we need this place. I'll be ok. The crowd loves me. They won't let anything bad happen to me."

"You don't understand. A public punishment is a public humiliation, Kitten."

"What?" I frown. A public humiliation?

"Even if he lets you get a drop of pleasure from this punishment, it will be nothing compared to the level of humiliation he will dish out. I don't want that for you. We need to leave. Now."

Humiliation? No, surely not? I'm into many kinks, but humiliation definitely isn't one of them. I don't know anyone that would willingly let themselves be humiliated.

My eyes widen as the situation sinks in, and before I can change my mind, the door flies open, and the room fills with men. The shirtless waiters charge in with Brock on their heels, his expression murderous as he glares at me and then Skipper.

What the fuck is going on?

Tyler seems to read the situation better than me, and he steps back, bracing himself with his fist raised, ready to swing a punch. I gasp as fear slithers through my veins, watching five men leap at Ty in unison, tackling him to the ground.

A scream rips from my lungs, and I jump backwards in an attempt to avoid being collateral damage. Strong, familiar arms wrap around me from behind, and I go to scream again as Brock holds me tight against his chest and slaps a hand over my mouth.

"Quiet, or you'll make it worse for yourself." He hisses in my ear, but I pay him little attention as I thrash in his arms, my eyes frantically trying to find Tyler underneath all the bodies.

Master Hill ignores the struggle on the floor and approaches me with something in his hand.

"Don't worry, Kitten. They aren't hurting him, just restraining him as we agreed."

"We didn't agree to that." I try to say, but it comes out muffled from behind Brock's hand, causing Master Hill to chuckle.

"Of course, you did, Kitten. Now, let's get you prepared."

As Master Hill steps away, panic seizes me, and I hear Tyler grunting and growling as he tries to fight off the men piled on top of him in an unfair fight.

No!

This can't be happening!

I'm so busy letting panic grip me that I don't realise Master Hill is reaching for me. With rough hands, a ball gag is shoved in my mouth and secured around my head. I try to struggle away, but Brock has me held to him like a vice, and before I know it, Master Hill is attaching leather cuffs to my wrists and ankles.

I shake my head and try to speak. I try to say stop. I try to scream no!

I want to demand that I be let go so I can leave, but all that comes out is muffled gibberish and a decent amount of drool.

Fear like I've never known courses through me.

No!

I don't want this!

I try to scream that safe word, Cactus, but I can't get it out. I thrash my head from side to side, trying to say no over and over. I know everyone in this fucking room knows what I'm saying, but they ignore me, like what I want doesn't matter.

STOP! I don't want this!

Tears streak down my face, and I'm shaking all over as I watch the mountain of men lift a now restrained Tyler up from the floor. Our eyes meet with frantic fear, and I see that he, too, has been fitted with a ball gag. He tries to thrash in the fierce hold of the other men, but it's no use, even given his height and strong build. His arms are restrained behind his back, fastened over some sort of bar, and his legs are held apart with a fucking spreader bar.

No. No. No. This can't be happening. This is too extreme to force us like this. This is illegal. Right?

I can't make sense of anything as I watch in disbelief as the men lift Tyler. His eyes are screaming at me to run, but I can't. I can't get free. I try to thrash in Brock's firm hold, but it's useless. I'm not strong enough to fight him off.

Tears burn my eyes, falling violently as if they, too, are screaming for these men to stop! Then my heart seizes as the men manoeuvre Tyler, carrying him as they disappear through the door.

No!

A guttural scream rips through me, but it doesn't make its way out of my mouth because Brock cuts it off when he turns me around and throws me over his shoulder, my world turning upside down.

HOLY SHITBALLS!
What just happened?

Find out in Tainted Kitten
Insatiable Series Book 2 !!

https://geni.us/Taintedkitten

Sarah JDs Books

READING ORDER

SERIES ONE

THE HEAVY HEARTS SERIES

A DARK NEW ADULT ROMANCE

TROPES: MF – Tortured Souls – Kidnapping – Trauma – Violence & Bullying (not between FMC & MMC) – Blackmail – Found Family – SERIOUS CONTENT WARNING!

HEAVY (Book 1):
https://geni.us/heavyhearts1
DEEP (Book 2):
https://geni.us/heavyhearts2
BURIED (Book 3):
https://geni.us/heavyhearts3

SERIES TWO

THE INSATIABLE SERIES

A DARK REVERSE HAREM NEW ADULT ROMANCE

TROPES: RH – Some MM - Age Gap – Forbidden – Tortured Souls – Kidnapping – Past Trauma – Violence (not between FMC & MMCs) – Blackmail – Found Family – SERIOUS CONTENT WARNING!

INSATIABLE KITTEN (Book 1):
https://geni.us/Insatiablekitten
TAINTED KITTEN (Book 2):
https://geni.us/Taintedkitten
VICIOUS KITTEN (Book 3):
https://geni.us/Viciouskitten

SERIES THREE

BREAKING THE SILENCE

A DARK NEW ADULT ROMANCE

TROPES: MF – Tortured Souls – Secret Identity – Organised Crime – Assassin – Kidnapping – Violence & Gore (not between FMC & MMC) – Blackmail & Coercion – Non-con – Found Family – SERIOUS CONTENT WARNING!

SILENT HUSH (Book 1):
https://geni.us/silenthush1
SAVAGE SCREAM (Book 2):
https://geni.us/savagescream2

STANDALONE

SUBBING FOR SANTA

A DARK CHRISTMAS ROMANCE WITH STALKER VIBES

TROPES: MF – Stalker – Secret Identity – Mafia/Organised Crime – Violence (not between FMC & MMC) – Found Family – SERIOUS CONTENT WARNING!

SUBBING FOR SANTA:
https://geni.us/subbingforsanta

SERIES FOUR

THE CRUZ KINGS MC SERIES

A DARK ENEMIES-TO-LOVERS MC ROMANCE
by B. Lybaek & Sarah JD

TROPES: MF – Motorcycle Club – Tortured Souls – Organised Crime – Kidnapping – Violence – Blackmail & Coercion – Dub-con – Non-con – SOMNOPHILIA – Found Family – Bets – SERIOUS CONTENT WARNING!

TEMPTED BY A KING (Book 1):
https://geni.us/cruzkings1
WANTED BY A KING (Book 2):
https://geni.us/cruzkings2
CLAIMED BY A KING (Book 3):
https://geni.us/cruzkings3

CHECK OUT ALL OF SARAH JD'S BOOKS HERE:
https://sarahjaneduncan.com/book-links/

Sarah JD's Books

Stay Connected

Want to find out all the Tea before everyone else?
Join my VIP readers list to hear more about Lexi and the gang, plus the other characters that join them along the way.

SIGN UP HERE!
https://sarahjaneduncan.com/newsletter/

Want to join the conversation about your fav characters?
Join my Facebook Readers Group
SARAH'S VICIOUS KITTENS

JOIN HERE!
https://www.facebook.com/groups/
sarahjaneduncanreadersgroup

For more information on books & book signing events
please visit:
sarahjaneduncan.com

STALK SARAH HERE:

SARAH JD

Sarah JD, also known as Sarah Jane Duncan, is a dark romance author living in Australia with Mr Duncan who stole her off the market back in high school.

Sarah can be found in her writing room plotting out her next smut filled romance filled with angst, violence, and themes so dark you should probably question why you love it so much.

Sarah writes about strong females who have to fight against the odds to find their power, their voice, and their truth. Her heroines possess the strength that only comes from being a survivor, and through their trauma, battles and struggles, they learn to trust again, and find love.

There's nothing easy about their stories. They are hard, gritty, and painfully heartbreaking at times. But what doesn't kill us makes us stronger, right? And when you throw in a swoon worthy guy, or an alphahole that you just want to slap, but also fall to your knees and obey, it's the recipe for a rollercoaster ride.

So buckle up. Read the warnings. And let yourself get lost in the dark stories Sarah creates.